LIGHT AMIDST THE SHADOWS

The Chronicle of the Keepers

Syreeta Benjamin

JOURNEY2ALTRUISM STUDIOS

www.journey2altruism.com

Light Amidst The Shadows

Copyright © 2024 by Syreeta Benjamin

Book Cover & Illustrations by Syreeta Benjamin & Naomi Lundy

First Edition 2024

Digital Edition ISBN: 979-8-9909022-0-6

Paperback Edition ISBN: 979-8-9909022-1-3; 979-8-9909022-3-7

Hardback Edition ISBN: 979-8-9909022-2-0

To my children,

Aim high, further than the Cosmo of stars,

to a dimension unexplored.

This is for you.

THE SEVEN

Ancient of Grace (Zuri)

Ancient of Justice (Justice)

Ancient of Ambition (Desire)

Ancient of Wisdom (Sage)

Ancient of Chaos (Raven)

Ancient of Strength (Osmond)

Ancient of Tranquility (Miro)

"When the moon sits full,
basked in an orangish glow,
the hidden one will reveal herself.
Enemies will bring the Age of Fury,
and the downfall of two kingdoms
shall be its outcome."

PROLOGUE

Penumbra

THE MOON, IN ALL its glory, lit up Dragon's Cove as the *Penumbra* made way. The gathering waves grew like peaks of the tallest mountains. On the bow, clad in bitterness, the General stood with his boots planted on the wooden deck while his shadow cloak whipped behind him. An orbit of lively wind and shadow swirled around him while his hands danced like a skilled conductor.

His *Essence* resonated deep within him, bending the wind to his will as he navigated through the waves as if mere ripples. Inferior tillers and oars that fascinated humans had no purpose on the *Penumbra*. Within a moon cycle, he would arrive in Osmondia and his plans would finally fall into place.

Suddenly, a tingle of energy brushed against his shadows. So faint, only a feather of a touch, yet powerful enough to almost make the general's heart stop completely. Pushing his bitter thoughts away, he looked up to find a flying creature gracefully soaring in the sky above. A golden eagle gliding just under the clouds.

Impossible, he thought. Yet the brush of magic was unmistakable—a slight charge of energy that heaved open the chained doors of his recollection.

The General pondered the creature's distinct Essence—both pure and familiar—evoking memories of a distant past. A past he locked and buried away long ago. It had been over two centuries since he felt any inkling of magic that was not his own. However, as he stared at the flying creature, trying to evade onlookers, a spark of hope kindled deep within his icy heart.

The familiar gait of the king's advisor reached his ears. Any slither of optimism immediately shut down. The rhythmic tap echoing against the deck made his muscles tense, reminding him of the figurative chains the king of Sagia wrapped around him and his Essence.

"General, we are hitting speeds never done before! It looks like we will arrive in Osmondia by the Harvest Moon as planned."

We?

Cane's pompous tone grated on him like sandpaper, and he wanted nothing more than to wrap him in his shadows and throw him overboard. To the General's dismay, Cane came just near enough not to be swept away by his orbit of swirling shadows and wind. The greedy man was like a prickly thorn in his side, always there for no good reason other than to spy for his pathetic king.

Cane's red wizard robes with a gold cincture rippled in the wind as he said, "General?"

He loathed the name "General" or any other human term. Master would have been more fitting. The human wizards in his company only breathed because he willed it. Humans were useless beings with limited understanding. They marveled at their creations of triremes, toll bells, and structures reaching towards the heavens. Meanwhile, they bickered like children, as if the cosmos revolved around them alone. Their finite minds would never understand or fathom the power of a Celestial.

So he continued the ruse, masquerading as a filthy human, buying his time for his greater purpose.

"Are the wizards ready?" He growled, finally acknowledging the disingenuous man.

"Yes, they are waiting for your command." Cane said.

"It is time!"

King Dargan, the Sagian king, sent the General with a few of his strongest wizards on this long journey to squash Osmondia's fleets. A spy on the inside confirmed the hiding place of the fleets off the coast of the island kingdom.

He couldn't care less about human warfare. It had no baring on the greater scheme of things. However, the mission played into his own plans of liberating his sister from the clutches of the self-serving king of Osmondia.

"General?"

He looked over his shoulder to find his shadows shooting out across the deck, wrapping around Cane's boots, ready to devour him at last. Lost in his thoughts, he forgot himself. A grin crept across the General's face. There was nothing quite like the sweet smell of human fear to lighten the mood.

His unruly nature and power made them cower. Even his eyes, darker than the hush of night, reflected the cosmos. So different from the rigid human wizards with cunning, green stares that always turned away in his presence. *Chaos,* they whispered.

"General!"

His shadowy tendrils now wrapped around Cane's neck. Realizing his brooding would destroy everyone on the ship, the General pulled his shadows back. Cane scrambled below deck faster than a human had the right to be.

The General returned his focus to the majestic golden eagle soaring above. A wild turn of events was about to unfold, and he welcomed it.

1

FIRE HEART

THE CRISP AIR IN the clearing danced around Kissa, awakening every fiber of her being. Her lungs filled as she pulled her bowstring taut. The subtle vibrations coursed through her fingertips as it seemed the world around her held its breath. Then she loosed her arrow, letting it soar like a wisp of determination finding its mark.

Thunk.

As she let the last of her arrows fly, a smile crossed Kissa's lips before she even opened her peculiar eyes. Her gaze brightened as she scanned across the clearing, shrouded in the shadows. She catalogued each of her arrows protruding from their makeshift targets. The saffron tinged feather fletchings sparkled like shimmery golden stars in the dark forest.

She lifted her eyes to see rustic streaks in the twilight sky. Her favorite time of the morning. The sun's upper rim emerged from the horizon, casting a warm glow on her lands. Gradually, it dispelled the darkness, unveiling the ancient Za trees that stretched as far as the eye could see, standing like silent watchers.

Kissa took her time as she retrieved her embedded arrows. She noticed the light rays revealed an inkling of rust with hints of ginger and amber adorning the tips of the green leaves. The morning air blew across her skin and she rubbed the gooseflesh rising on her arms. Autumn was here.

As she trudged over to the last tree, a familiar burning sensation made her pause. She rubbed her chest above her heart, beneath her keepsake. Archery usually tamed the ever-growing embers in her heart that seemed to have a mind of its own. Growing up, it only flared when she felt indignant or wronged. Now, the flames ignited at odd times, even with no instigation.

Deciding to call it done for the day, Kissa put her last arrow in her quiver and walked toward the sea cliffs. She placed them and her bow near her hammock, swaying against the wind. She claimed this area of her land long ago and named the eroding slope of rock her *Oasis*. A fitting name since it was her quiet space to work out her mind and heart.

Her breath caught as the rising sun revealed the twinkling sapphire sea and woke up the world. It didn't matter that she watched this scene play out each morning. Ever since she could remember, Kissa felt an unexplainable connection to the blazing star.

Closing her eyes, she embraced the rays across her face. The feeling felt indescribable, but enveloped her and wrapped her in enkindling warmth like a sentient being. It vitalized her spirit most days and even eased the fire in her heart.

Kissa's shoulders fell. It seemed not even the sun's embrace could calm her this day.

A great breeze swept in, carrying the salty sea air. Dressed in only a white short-sleeved tunic, brown leggings, and no shoes, a shiver went through her. She unraveled her sand-colored scarf from her head and wrapped it around her exposed shoulders. Then closed her eyes against the wind whipping through her Jata locs and cooling her scalp.

Walking over to the very edge of the cliffs, she sat down, allowing her feet to dangle. A sharp drop-down of at least a league to the sea lay underneath her. She rubbed her chest as she took in deep breaths, but it did nothing to assuage the burning sensation.

When she woke up, Kissa brushed the feeling away as just anticipation of her birthnight, only a handful of hours away. At the hush of night, she would finally turn 18, the legal adult age in Osmondia. Then she thought maybe it was her father's long-awaited promise to permit her enrollment at Serenity, the kingdom's school of healing. It was a lifelong dream of Kissa's, one she thought of since she could remember. A dream so close to her heart she felt like she could reach out and grab it with her hands now that it was before her.

However, even though both events excited her most positively, deep down she knew they were not what caused the restlessness within her. The feeling felt... more.

Kissa fiddled with her keepsake, a subconscious habit since small. The necklace was a peculiar piece, for she had it all her life and not once added leather to lengthen it. The sundial hanging from the leather replicated the round sun, carved of wood and gold. A gold gnomon and glass dial plate comprised hour and minute lines. Underneath, a compass sat unused and engraved on the back was a mountain with a tree atop it.

Kissa did not care for trinkets and jewelry, but this one felt like a part of her. She couldn't remember a time without it, only taking it off to bathe. The sundial rested right at her heart and proved an invaluable tool for time.

Abandoning her restless thoughts, Kissa stood up and spread her arms like wings. Her scarf fluttered to the grass behind her as another sharp wind whipped her locs through the air. She closed her eyes against the ascending sun's light and the brisk breeze, imagining flying above the waves as she heard them crash against the rocks far below. She smiled, imagining that for once she was free.

"Kissa, come! The morning meal is almost ready." A familiar voice lilted.

Kissa opened her eyes, and her smile widened. She turned and observed her mother's no-nonsense face, framed by obsidian Jata locs that hung down to her lithe waist. Though slender and petite, her mother had curvy hips, which she set her hands upon. Her deep gold eyes always smiled at Kissa, even when her full lips turned stern, such as at that moment.

"Please, put on your scarf!" She said with concern and a bit of annoyance.

Holding back her slight irritation at the command, Kissa eyed the scarf on the grass. Then looked up at her mother and poked her bottom lip out. "Mama, I'm careful. Nobody is out here. Our nearest neighbors are leagues away."

Her mother raised a brow in answer, not moved at all by the reply. That firm look would never budge. Onya Ashtar was a free spirit of most things, but quite adamant, like a stubborn clam, with Kissa's safety.

With a quiet huff, she dragged herself from the cliffs, picked up her scarf off the grass, and tied it around her head with practiced ease.

"If you want your father to trust you to go to Serenity, you must mind the rules that keep you safe!" her mother said.

Always wear a head covering...

Always remain on the family lands...

The rules, though simple, felt like the stifling bane of Kissa's life. Other women wore hats and scarves—though she'd never met said women—and she knew they wore them by choice. Lately, the Za trees she regarded felt like bars of a gilded cage, and her head coverings felt akin to bindings. She didn't dare express her irritation enough for her mother to notice. Instead, Kissa tucked her annoyance into the ever-growing box inside her, then ran over and put her arms around the stern woman. She kissed her cheek and her mother's lips lifted, inducing Kissa's smile to return.

"Is it my favorite?" she asked.

"Come and find out!" A hand shorter than her daughter, her mother had to reach up as she caressed the side of Kissa's golden-brown face with her knuckle. Then, the bossy woman started her way back toward their cottage.

"I'll be there soon, Mama. I want to wait for Aya a little longer."

She returned to the cliffs as worry tugged at her at the thought of her sister. Aya left for an important mission over a cycle ago and promised to return well before Kissa's birthnight. Though their bond transcended time and space, she could not help feeling the emptiness that crowded inside her. With Aya gone, she felt lonelier than she ever remembered, and the restlessness in her spirit felt tied to it somehow. She rechecked both the sea and sky, but like every day since her sister left, Kissa saw nothing. Not wanting to keep her mother waiting, she swiped up her quiver and bow and headed toward the house.

Joy replaced some of Kissa's concern as she saw a familiar warhorse tied to the hitching post in front of her house. As it drank water from the trough, the percheron stood proud and tall with its all-black coat, tail, and mane. Her head raised as Kissa approached, making circles towards the sky.

"Hello, Dream. I missed you too," she cooed as she rubbed the eager horse's neck.

Walking through the gardens she and her mother cultivated, Kissa eyed her rows of arnica and tea tree herbs with pride. Staying clear of the herbal patch, she reached the front deck, but slowed to a stop before the door. Whispers filtered from the open window.

"It's time... she needs."

Kissa moved closer, pushing her back up to the house's wood frame, and craned her neck to hear better.

"I have confirmed the rumors are true, Onya. This is not the time. I have guaranteed their silence for now. We should wait another summer, after the threats are gone."

Her father. She tried to piece their conversation together in her mind. Was he speaking about Serenity? The thought caused her chest to tighten, and her fire rose in agitation. Her father denied her requests to attend every season prior. He'd said it was not safe—his answer for everything. Her father would keep her home until she was gray and withered away, and Kissa refused to let that happen. She was about to bust in the door and tell him her mind, but then she heard her mother's voice sharp as a whip.

"Guaranteed? You know as well as I do there are snakes in every grass! We should tell her, then she can make up her own mind. Keeping silent gives me a bad feeling, Omani!"

"What would you have me do? I will protect her as long as I draw breath. There are too many unknowns. We can't make moves without knowing the consequence!"

"I know, my love, but we can't keep her stifled and in the dark. That is no life to live. Let her go, or she will resent you and leave, anyway. Is that what you want?"

Her father's silence felt louder than anything else as Kissa waited for his reply, but it never came. Hearing her mother passionately advocating for her smothered some of her ire. Now, she hesitated to go inside. Her parents rarely argued. Their whispered tone indicated they didn't want her to hear them, and the emotion behind the words conveyed something of great importance. Why did attending Serenity cause their quarrel?

Kissa pushed past her reluctance and walked into the cottage. She observed her parents standing close together near the fireplace. As a commander of the Scorpion military, her father wore his leather armor and dark brown locs twisted up into a bun, the custom way of Osmondian warriors. His dark beard extended to his chest, braided with wooden beads. His choice of weapon, a one-and-a-half-hand long sword, rested in its scabbard at his hip. Though her father appeared regal, his deep brown eyes always held a soft tenderness for her.

He smiled as he saw her walk in and it tugged at her heart, a reminder of how much she missed him. Despite their differences, her heart sang for him to be home.

Pushing her anger and what she heard aside, Kissa returned the smile. "Father, you're home!" She said as she put her bow and quiver by the door.

"I told you I would be. Come!" He gestured towards himself with his arms open. When Kissa fell into them, he hugged her tightly, smoothing away her anger and concern.

"Aya has not returned?" Her father asked as they broke apart.

Kissa gave a solemn shake of her head. His throat rumbled in response. Though he said nothing, Kissa saw the spark of worry behind his eyes, compounding her own.

"Come. Let us eat this good food your mother prepared." He said with a clap.

The entire house smelled of well-thought-out spices. After they all washed their hands, her mother spread a warm flatbread on a platter in the center of their wooden, three seated table. Then she delicately placed rich chickpea shiro, blueberry, and apricot jam, on the outer part with a ladle. Finally, she sat a pita bowl steaming with spicy chicken stew in the middle. Kissa's stomach growled in agreement. Her favorite, indeed.

They set wooden bowls and spoons before them, and once the three of them settled, her father turned his hands over on the table, offering them to Kissa and her mother. She hesitated briefly, her only show of defiance on the matter.

Her parents believed strongly in *The Seven*—Ancients worshipped as gods and goddesses throughout their world. Osmond, the Ancient of Strength, was the god of her father's people. Zuri, the Ancient of Grace, was her mother's.

The kingdoms normally worshipped only one Ancient, but her parents' forbidden intercultural marriage allowed their household to worship two. Her father always included the Goddess of Grace in his prayers. Their home displayed equal symbols and representations of both Ancients.

Kissa respected this, of course, but she had her own unsayable feelings about the fickle deities. She decided long ago not to worship any of them.

Her father stared at her for an extra moment with a brow raised. Kissa placed her hand on his and stared at her lap as he prayed. After they served each other, content silence filled the space.

Kissa sipped her stew. The spice and flavor burst around her mouth, delighting her taste buds, and she closed her eyes and grinned in pleasure. "Mmm, delicious, Mama."

Her mother gave her a knowing wink. Zuranians did not eat meat, but she always cooked it for Kissa and her father. She always wondered how the woman made it so perfect without tasting it.

Kissa's eyes settled on the commander, still in his armor. "Are you leaving soon?"

"Yes, I promised you, so I took a temporary leave," he said.

Her father practically lived in the barracks at the capital, sometimes only visiting home once or twice a season. He oversaw the new recruits, training, and even the patrol of the capital and Za Forest. But even knowing all his responsibilities, it still hurt that he was leaving so soon.

It must have shown on her face, because he said, "Kissa, the Harvest Festival is soon upon us. You know it is my duty to ensure the safety of our people. I am here now. Let us make the most of it."

The world held the Harvest Festival every fifth season in each of the seven kingdoms. It lasted for seven days and ended on the Harvest Moon. Osmondians traveled to the summit of Aarusha to Horus Citadel for the celebrations.

Not that Kissa knew personally, though. She had never partaken in such activities, or any festivities, for that matter.

"Can Mama and I come this season?" Maybe if she added her mother, he would be more reluctant to say no.

Her father finished a bite of his flatbread, ending in a grunt, and slowly shook his head. "News of the Queen's illness has brought down morale within our kingdom, especially among the warriors. We know next to nothing about the sickness. I can't risk you and your mother succumbing to it. Next season, Kissa."

A solemn silence surrounded their meal. Just two days ago, King Lan publicly announced the grave news that Queen Safiyah caught the Sleeping sickness. The silent disease continued to spread faster than those working on a cure or investigating its source. It spared no victim's life, which meant, eventually, the Queen would perish and leave their kingdom mourning. The thought saddened her and snuffed out her feelings on the matter.

As she continued to sip her stew, she looked at her father's cool gaze. It was like playing a strategic game with him, and she needed to choose her battles wisely. She knew not to push the issue.

Besides, something more important pressed on her heart. "Will I be able to attend Serenity, Father?"

She subconsciously held her breath for his answer. Her heart quickened in anticipation. She spent the last few days planning this request and a rebuttal if he refused.

He sipped his ale in thought. A look reached his eyes that told Kissa he was not ready to talk about it. "Can I sit down and enjoy my meal before you interrogate me?" He asked. "Is it too much to ask to enjoy the eve of your birthnight, daughter?"

Her mother covered her mouth, smothering a chuckle. Kissa pressed her lips together. She didn't always say or ask things at the right moment. Her tongue seemed to have a mind of its own.

Pushy, her father called her. Kissa liked to think she was just determined.

The commander glanced at her mother and they stared at one another in some silent communication. His eyes tore away reluctantly as he turned to Kissa. "Yes, your mother and I agreed to allow you. Ultimately, though, it is up to the Shadora Council to accept you. I wanted to deliver their letter to you personally."

He slid a folded parchment across the table. "It's not that I don't want you to attend, Kissa." His brow raised as he said, "Your mother and I know the wolves that sit on that council."

His voice dripped with warning, but Kissa heard none of it. Everything else fell away as her eyes stared at the letter before her with her name written across the front. The Zuranian seal of a dove mid-flight was still intact. The Shadora Council were Seven High Healers carefully selected from their best that governed the school.

Kissa's heart thumped in her chest. She had waited for this moment since she could remember. Her hands trembled as she read her name frontward, backward, and in between. All she ever wanted in life was to become a healer. She thought of nothing else, an ambitious student of her mother's rigorous teaching. Graduating Serenity, traveling the world, and becoming a High Healer felt set in stone.

Yet, she felt the weight of the letter in her grasp now, as her dream hinged on the written words inside.

Finally, Kissa sucked in a breath, cracked the seal, and slowly unfolded the letter.

Greetings Kissa Ashtar,

We reviewed your submission for this upcoming season's Healer Apprenticeship Program, and have decided that proof of your natural ability to heal, cure, and post-treat shall need to be submitted for further consideration.

Furthermore, the council discovered that there is no record of your birth and this requires further clarification. Due to the timeframe needed for the above specifications, we regret to inform you we are denying your application for this season's program.

Once you have completed all the above requested and we have reviewed and accepted it, then you will be considered for next season's program.

Kind Regards,

The Shadora Council

Kissa's body trembled as confusion washed over her. It made little sense. No record of her birth? She pushed the letter back to her father—most likely the real reason they did not want her at Serenity. Her mother stood swiftly, coming around the table and wrapping her arms around Kissa without a word.

Her father handed the letter to her mother in silent anger. Her mother glossed over the words and her eyes widened.

"What does it mean, Mama? Why would there be no record of my birth? You specialize in midwifery. Did you forget?" Kissa implored.

Her parents stared at one another with severe looks. Another one of their intense silent communications. A debate, it seemed, because her mother looked away with a resigned look that told Kissa she was not happy in the least.

What were they keeping from her? "Mama?"

After a few more moments of charged silence, her father was the one to speak. "Kissa, it was an error. We will fix this."

The heated unspoken words between her parents felt a hell of a lot more than just an error. Her mother was the most meticulous person she knew. Everything needed to be in its proper place. Normally, she would let them have their secrets, but this was her dream, her life. Kissa wasn't backing down.

"What are you keeping from me?" She asked as she stared between the two of them.

She clenched the fabric of her tunic, hands still trembling. Her father looked away, as if wrestling with his thoughts, uncertain. Clearly, something the Shadora Council wrote made him uneasy.

She tightened her grip on her tunic, if only to keep her tethered. "If it is a matter of my life, do I not deserve to know?"

Her own voice surprised her. She had no qualms with speaking her mind, but she never spoke in that tone to either of her parents, especially her father. However, the growing blaze in her heart encouraged her to demand answers. "What is it? For all the stars! You act as if...."

The truth smacked her in the face hard, like a windstorm, unmistakable. The only reason a seasoned midwife would not record her own child's birth. Every question Kissa asked growing up that was explained away by fanciful statements appeared in her mind. Things she never allowed herself to look too closely at, if she were being honest.

The words fell from her lips like poison. "You're not my blood parents."

The statement sat heavily in the air like an anvil. Her mother and father's stricken countenance made her knees weak—an answer in itself. Guilt riddled her mother's next words.

"We wanted to tell you, Kissa, but we could not."

"Tell me what? That everything I know is a lie?" Her own voice felt far away.

Inside, Kissa felt a hairsbreadth away from imploding. This was no rejection letter. This was her life. The loving home she grew up in suddenly felt oppressive, and she found breathing hard. Her chest burned too fiercely, hotter than ever before, swallowing her mother's next words. Her lips moved, but Kissa heard nothing over her roaring heart.

She rose from the table and said nothing as she threw on her cloak and satchel. Snatching up her bow and quiver, she left the house.

Once the cool air hit her face, Kissa ran.

2

Heavy Heart

Taji

From the top of the Scorpion Tower of Horus Citadel, Taji watched the first threads of vermillion light breach the dark sky above Zuberi. Soon, smoke from a thousand set hearths filled the air with the hope of a new day. But it was beyond the city that always captured him. The lush canopy of trees as far as the eye could see took on a golden hue at first light. Flaxen tinted mist blanketed the ancient crowns of Za Forest and for a moment, everything felt warm and good in the world.

All too soon, the toll bell swung from the top of the adjacent keep. Before him, the facade of grotto homes and shops that layered the entire mountainside came to life. Just as the last toll finished, hammers and hacksaws clamored through the air, masons working hard to prepare for the kingdom's upcoming Harvest Festival.

Taji watched for many moon cycles as the masons created the recent addition to the Horus Citadel, a new age amphitheater. The grand structure was nearly as wide as the citadel, and almost as tall as the keep Taji stood on. Its immense size aimed to welcome citizens from all corners of Osmondia who flocked to witness the renowned King's Tournament this season.

Hope was in the air. Yet, every stone carved, or joyful song that was sung in their midst, served only as a reminder of the precious time that was slipping through Taji's fingers like fine sand.

A set of boots pounded on stone, his relief. He nodded at Corwin, who looked at him with hopeful eyes, searching for something in Taji's own. Before the young warrior could utter a word, he lifted his cloak hood over his head and silently descended the ladder that led back down through the keep. He weaved through the citadel corridors with a single mind to escape it. As he entered the kitchens, he heard the baker, Tora, and her assistants shuffling around as they prepared meals for the day. The smell of something fresh baking made his stomach growl. He ignored it. Anything Taji ate lately tasted like ash.

Unnoticed, he slipped through the back doors. When he finally left the confines of his duty, he inhaled a lungful of air. The usual royal guards, Erin and Law, stood quietly on patrol by the kitchen door, only nodding as Taji moved past them.

Lately, he felt grateful for the many escape routes from the citadel. He couldn't stomach people's frowns laced with pity or, even worse, for them to tell him how sorry they felt. Pity and sympathy would not change his Fate.

Taji nodded to the Scorpions that guarded the southern wall. Then he slipped through the gate, a hidden exit along the outer ward, and spilled into the uninhabited land of the capital. When he reached the wooden bridge that spanned across the ravine, separating the city from Za forest, he paused.

The stream below transformed into a waterfall, cascading down Aarusha's back into the vast Sapphire Sea. Cirrus clouds and mist from the water encased him on the bridge, but Taji still caught the breathtaking view of the sea in the break of clouds. Among creation's grand landscape, he felt like a tiny speck. Majestic mountains emerged from the depths of the sea from Osmond's hand.

His people firmly believed that their city, made from the pliable limestone of Aarusha, would last forever. They were born to be formidable warriors, and, once upon a time, they embraced their divine duty as protectors above all else. However, after the war of the Great Divide two centuries ago, Osmondia stopped safeguarding the other nations, deeming them no longer part of the kingdom.

Now, it seemed his people only protected their own interests.

Slowly making his way across the bridge to breach the forest, he unsheathed his sword at his hip. No human inhabitants lived in these parts, so it grew thick and wild, but various predators called it home. So Taji moved cautiously along the thicket.

Eventually, a wide clearing covered in rubble and remnants of stone lay before him, the *First Temple*. Or at least, what remained of the ancient sanctuary. The war of the Great Divide, two centuries ago, destroyed the temple. Now it was just a purposefully forgotten reminder of his people's loss in the war against Sagia—a perfect place for Taji's secret training.

Away from people, devoid of distractions, he felt the burden of expectation on his chest. It seemed larger than him and heavier than any armor. He let out a lengthy breath as he discerned what weighed on him most.

This season, Taji was chosen as the new Challenger in the King's Tournament. It was a great honor, really. Yet he couldn't shake the restlessness inside him. He had worked hard and won every local challenge in recent seasons, but uncertainty wrapped him in its thralls. Taji was young and untested.

Currently, Maru Laux, held the Champion title, a revered Leviathan Commander over two naval fleets. He was also a ruthless fighter that Taji watched earn his title twice in a row. But it didn't matter how he felt. Not really. The Scorpion leaders decided he was their best chance at reclaiming the Champion title from the Leviathans. Taji felt like a mere pebble being thrown at a megalith and now, with it set in motion, he couldn't let his father and fellow Scorpions down. It didn't matter that grief shrouded his every waking moment.

Courage, Focus, Strength...

Among the whirlwind of his thoughts, a deep, resonant whisper echoed in his mind. It brought with it a sense of calm, like a refreshing drink on a hot summer's day. A wave of tranquility washed over his body, releasing the tension that had settled in his chest and shoulders. The weight lifted, allowing his mind to clear and dispel the fog that liked to accompany his heavy heart.

This mysterious voice had been a constant presence, a guardian guiding him since before he took his first steps. He initially believed it was his conscience, but that term felt insufficient. Though it protected him from foolish choices more often than Taji cared to admit. As he grew older, he recognized that the voice was not a figment of his imagination, but rather sentient. He eventually referred to it as his Keeper.

Conversations did not exist. It felt more like a one-sided exchange of emotions mingled with a few cryptic words, whether or not Taji welcomed them. He developed the ability to understand the mysterious signals of his keeper by being patient and persistent, despite the challenges. Then, one day, like a master delighted in his pupil's progress, the sentient voice gifted him its true name—*Osiris.*

Taji took off his armor and tunic and sat it on a nearby slab of stone, along with his boots. Conditioned under his commander, he learned to block out the frigid cold near the summit. He moved into his stance and lifted his sword. Ignoring the frozen grass underneath his feet, he inhaled the crisp air, allowing it to fill his lungs. Then as he let it out, he swept his leg back and began his various poses of the *Maa-kyia.*

He swung his sword in precise, controlled movements time and again. As his heart sped up, the sound of drums echoed alongside it—another recent 'gift' from Osiris. Though Taji did not quite understand its purpose yet, it felt right within him, as if the war cadence always existed.

Taji closed his eyes and continued his ancient regimen poses, now in tune with Osiris' drums. It increased its vigor as he increased his speed. Soon he danced to the lost song only he found as he moved through his sets.

A little more than half-way through, a slight rustle of fabric and light bootsteps reached his ears, and a smile crossed his lips. "A mountain goat is far more stealthy than that."

A chuckle followed as Taji's oldest friend leaned against a broken pillar in front of him with a smirk. Mischief danced in his amber eyes. A dark cloak covered him from head to toe, though Taji knew a healer's robe lay hidden underneath. A flicker of surprise washed over him as he recognized the long sword in his friend's hand.

Benji pushed off the stone and moved into his stance, swinging his sword, beckoning him. "Do you want to put on your armor? It wouldn't be fitting for you to appear all bruised and battered for your battle with Maru."

Another flicker of surprise. It was tradition to keep the Challenger's identity a close secret until the battle. Only the Challenger, the King and the High Commanders knew. Then again, his friend's penchant to see the unseen was exactly why he was his secret scout at Serenity.

"Come now, I thought I taught you better jokes than that." The corner of Taji's lip curled in amusement. He couldn't very well confirm or deny the secret. "Armor is reserved for true opponents."

In reply, Benji moved forward swiftly. Taji lifted his sword and deflected the thrust just in time. They broke apart, assessing each other. Benji was faster than he remembered. He followed up with a swipe at Taji's midsection. He jumped clear of the attack, then brought down his short sword and eased it against the healer's shoulder.

"Point. You seem a bit rusty under those healer's robes," Taji taunted, though he knew his friend still practiced in secret. Since the last time he remembered, Benji's footwork had improved, and the sharpness of his blade told him that the healer took excellent care of it.

Ignoring the jibe, Benji shot forward as he said, "I have some new information for you."

Taji parried the stab to his chest with his sword and countered with a swipe to the healer's ribs that landed. "Point." He said as he backed away. "Go on."

"Last night, I overheard the snake talking with a strange visitor. Something about making a trip to the Fathomless Pit in seven nights' time."

As intended, his words caused Taji to falter. Merely a breath, but ample enough for an opening. With lightning speed, Benji aimed at Taji's left ribcage. It was intended as a friendly swipe that he normally would have blocked, but his slow reaction caused it to slice through his skin. He ignored the stinging sensation, aware that it would cost him. His eyes narrowed as he backed away.

Benji smirked. "Point."

Taji blew out a harsh curse. The Fathomless Pit, a secret place deep in the bowels of the citadel, kept prisoners of war. A place so deep, it lay under the common jail, and then *underneath* the dungeons. Only high-ranking officials—The Elite, High Commanders, and the King himself—had access to it, and they kept it closely guarded.

Taking full advantage of the distraction, Benji closed the gap, aiming his sword at his throat. Taji ducked and pivoted right, coming up underneath, narrowly avoiding the underhanded move. Countering swiftly, he punched Benji square in the mouth with his sword hand, resulting in a sharp crack echoing through the clearing. His friend stumbled, losing his balance, but braced himself at the last moment before hitting the ground.

"Point!" Taji heaved with a victorious smile as he rested the tip of his sword on Benji's neck. Then he sheathed it and offered his hand.

With narrowed eyes, Benji clasped it and pulled himself up. He wiped the blood dribbling from his mouth. "Still a cheater, I see."

"Nothing one of your salves can't handle."

Taji briefly checked the cut on his side. His fingers came away with blood on them. He grabbed his tunic and wiped it away, then wiped the sweat off his face and chest.

After a few moments, Benji's face became uncharacteristically serious. "He was speaking to someone in the night's hush. A cloaked figure I couldn't make out. When I tried to trail them, it was like they simply vanished."

Alarm curdled in Taji's chest. Benji never exaggerated, and his observations were always accurate. "Shit!"

Benji tilted his head and looked towards the forest, casually swinging his sword. "There are rumors the witch is alive."

Taji heard the same whispers. The Queendom of Ravenia proved to be enemies to the kingdom because of their position in the war and their unwavering support of Sagia. Over a decade ago, his commander captured a Ravenian witch scouting near his lands. He always found it odd how she breached Za forest unnoticed. It was even stranger that this specific commander caught her near his lands.

The King's Elite claimed to not know how she did it, despite interrogations and a "thorough" investigation. Taji always wondered what she crossed enemy territory in search of.

However, a few days later, the King issued a command for her public execution. At the tender age of nine, his father forced him to witness the horrifying spectacle. A woman with dark hair and piercing black eyes dangled in the air, her life suspended by a rope around her neck.

He shook off the shudder that always accompanied the memory. "Seven nights?"

Taji needed to get into the Fathomless Pit somehow. This scheme needed meticulous planning, or it may be his life's forfeit in the end. Seven nights wasn't enough time.

"I'll figure it out. There's nothing quite like the danger of losing your head to get the adrenaline pumping," Taji said.

Benji chuckled, then shrugged his shoulders. "We knew what we were up against when we started this." Then his look turned thoughtful. "How are you holding up?"

Taji knew that question was the main reason his old friend tracked him down. Though he hated to talk about it, he knew Benji didn't look at him with pity, nor did he spit out empty condolences.

"I feel like my sanity is being held together by tethers. Any day now could be her last," He finally said.

Benji nodded in solemn understanding. "Well, I am here, old friend, whether you need to duel or talk."

Taji appreciated the statement. He knew that beneath Benji's mischievous jesting, there was passion and sincerity. It had been almost many summers since they dueled together, and Taji found he had missed it. However, now they were investigating the cause of the Sleeping sickness, which was a dangerous task. Being seen together was risky.

"I'll visit Serenity in a day or two." Taji said. "Thanks for checking up on me."

With a farewell nod, his friend headed south towards the trail that led to the coast. Taji went back to his practice stance to continue his sets, but he couldn't ignore the sensation that time was slipping away. Without a cure for the Sleeping Sickness, their only hope hinged on Osmond's willingness to listen to his servant's prayers and take action for the sake of his people.

So, Taji prayed.

3

STRANGERS

Kissa

The fire fueled her legs, and Kissa sprinted faster than she ever had in her life. The sturdy trees whipped past her peripheral, nothing but a blur. She gazed ahead at the ancient Za trees that stood taller than the rest, like wardens signifying the edge of her land. For a breath, her mind warred with itself.

She never ventured beyond her lands until now. Her father's voice burned in her mind, but the outer forest beckoned her, called to her. The fire in her heart answered for her as it roared its defiance, encouraging her legs to move faster.

As she passed the ancient trees, she almost thought their long gnarled branches would snatch her back. Instead, a strange buzzing sensation slowed her momentum just a touch. If Kissa was not expecting something, she may have never felt the faint tug of resistance. The feeling quickly passed before she registered it fully, but she made a mental note.

Now past her lands perimeter, Kissa continued running, and the sense of exhilaration washed over her. Slowly, her raging fire became smoldering embers, bringing a calming effect to her heart and mind. Kissa was unsure how much time passed, but she finally slowed when an old garden bridge caught her eye.

She paused and pressed her back against the rough bark of a tree, gasping for air. The forest, to those unacquainted, appeared like a maze. To Kissa, the subtle impressions of the well-worn path beneath the tangled undergrowth were evident. She was on a trail.

The dense canopy of leaves obscured most of the sky, rendering her sundial useless. As she leaned there, she noticed rays of sunlight brushing against the farther end of the bridge, illuminating a small clearing up ahead. But before she made it one step, hooves stomping in quick concession had Kissa's heart seize up.

She ducked behind the tree, hiding amidst the underbrush. Then she raised her head to glimpse the passing rider cross the bridge toward her. Her heart threatened to stop altogether when the horse halted only a few paces from her.

As if searching for something, the rider turned from one side to the other. The light was dim, but the few rays that breached the forest shined on their dark cloak and the tip of the long sword that peaked from underneath.

"Who is there?" The deep voice of the male rider echoed across the forest.

Turning fully in the saddle, his hood shifted, revealing half his dark face and unmistakable amber eyes. Kissa's breath caught, and her mind rapid fired. He was *Zuranian*. Her mother's people did not carry weapons of any kind and they clung to that law like their afterlife depended on it. So, what was a healer doing in Za Forest with a sword, no less?

The rider sparked her curiosity, though fear kept her from revealing herself. She did not know who he was, or his reasons for traveling through the forest. She stayed quiet and waited. Two breaths, three...

Finally, the rider turned forward and continued on the trail. Still, she waited, and when she no longer heard hooves, Kissa stood. She imagined the bridge used to be beautiful as it arched over a small stream that ran underneath, but its wood weathered away from the elements and the lack of upkeep. She crossed it, and before her, a meadow filled with blue alpine greeted her.

Closer to the summit, the trees became scarce. Kissa smiled, taking in the sun's warmth that hit her face. For a moment, she stood there soaking it in, then she ventured deeper and came across a layout of stone rubble.

Various sized stones, some taller than her, lay broken and scattered like pebbles. Vines snaked through the grave of limestones sprouting purple morning glory flowers—the flowers of the dead. The scene left her uneasy, wondering what could have possibly caused such destruction.

Looking up, she took in her position. She strained her eyes to see one of the towering stone spires of Horus Citadel emerging over the scarce treetops to the east. She was near the summit, far from home.

Her attention went back to the ruins, pondering its past. She grew closer and made out shapes and partial letters that remained of greater passages on some stones. Her eyes drew to a towering broken pillar, its intricate engravings telling stories of a forgotten time. Something about them moved her, and she approached.

Tilting her head, she read the inscription out loud. "Cultivate Oneness."

Those two words stood out to Kissa. She recalled a lesson about the Ancients from the Archaic Scripture. A text explaining the beginning of life and the world's origins.

Grace, Strength, Tranquility, Ambition, Justice, Chaos, and Wisdom—the core attributes of each of *The Seven*. Despite their differences, they came together to create Haava. Humans, made in their likeness, received the attributes of the Ancients. Over time, seven different nations of people emerged, and their own unique abilities according to their god. She recalled reading that the Ancients commanded the First Parents to populate Haava and to teach their decedents to cultivate oneness in worship and in life. According to the passage, *The Seven's* intentions were never for the world to divide. They needed each other for their civilization to thrive.

She pushed the thought away as she surveyed the broken stone and pillars, the age of it, and the holy words. *The First Temple*, she thought as she took in the ruins in a new light.

A profound feeling wrapped around her chest. It seemed almost unbelievable to stand where human life began. Despite Kissa's indifference towards the Ancients, she valued the deep history that surrounded her. She questioned why no one ever rebuilt the once revered structure. Most likely, the Osmondians no longer wanted to visit the stark reminder of their defeat long ago to the Sagians.

Kissa could almost feel the stones call to her, painting a solemn picture of the war of the Great Divide—broken and scattered. One magnificent kingdom shattered into seven fragments, dispersed across the world.

Underneath the heartache of the remains, she imagined the beauty of the temple in its former glory, all people gathering as one. The pillars suggested a once grand structure. Kissa could almost see the men and women with their heads bowed in prayer, while the laughter of children echoed through the meadow. No seeds of dissension bloomed in their little hearts just yet.

Suddenly, a strange sensation came over her. A hum that sounded and felt like drums slowly vibrated a rhythm inside her. Kissa tilted her head. As if responding to her inquiry, it flowed into a beautiful cadence, and she swayed in place.

Was the sensation coming from the ruins? But just then, a growing tug in the center of her chest urged her to move, like the fire in her heart beckoned her to find out. She closed her eyes and internally wrestled with the force, but it would not ease, only intensifying its thrum. Ignoring the unsettling feeling in her stomach, she surrendered to its guiding force, curious to discover where it would take her.

As she moved around a large stone, she paused mid-step. Only a few paces away, the ruins opened up to a small clearing. In the center, a sword-wielding man dressed in only pants twirled and spun as if dancing to a melody.

Kissa *felt* that song pulsating through her entire being.

The stranger had a lean physique, unlike her father, the only man she could compare him to. Despite the chill in the air, his dark sepia skin glistened with sweat, showcasing his well-defined muscles. His tied-up dark locs gave her a clear view of his back, flexing with every swing of his sword. A warrior.

Though she stood near the summit, Kissa's cheeks warmed with each intake of breath. She had never seen a man half dressed before. Other than her father, she never seen a man at all. She wondered why he practiced so far from the barracks alone.

Kissa crept behind the stone, though the pull beckoned her closer. The man skillfully swung his short sword from side to side. His body moved with grace, bending and turning, matching the rhythmic thumping of the drums within. Eyes closed, he didn't miss a step as he moved along the broken stone.

Now facing her, Kissa took in the light stubble on his face that framed his jaw perfectly, giving him a sort of roughness that made her heart flutter.

At last, he came to a halt, and the captivating cadence that drew her towards him faded away. Now, without the urgent beckoning inside her, every sound returned, and Kissa felt very much like a lurker.

Go now, she thought.

Just when she was ready to turn away, the man opened his eyes and the intense gaze of vivid blue eyes startled her. His eyes reminded her of the serene, crystal-clear waters of a sun-kissed sea. For a moment, Kissa felt entranced. It was rare for someone to have blue eyes. Almost as rare as her own. Something about them niggled at her mind, but she couldn't quite place it.

With a smug look on his face, the warrior examined her. He tilted his head. "Do you like what you see?"

Those simple words sent a shiver through her. She blinked twice, shaking herself free of his hold.

Yes.

"No!" Kissa scowled. "I mean..." she shook her head. "*What?*"

His eyes sparkled with mirth as he watched her bumbling. She desperately tried to find words that wouldn't make her seem like a prowler, but her heart pounded in her chest and her mind raced with countless outcomes for this exchange, and none of them seemed favorable.

"I-I'm sorry to disturb you." Kissa felt sheepish. She knew her entire face was flushed red. "I should be on my way."

She didn't think he would decapitate her, but she remained uncertain. Her hands flexed near her bow.

He lifted his free hand up slowly, like she was a startled deer. He sheathed his sword with the other. "I mean you no harm. I am merely curious."

Kissa shifted, uncomfortable, but didn't move her hand from near her bow. "About what?"

A smile graced his lips, and she gazed at their perfect fullness. Then he asked, "What is your name?"

Kissa hesitated, her brows furrowing at the unexpected request. Giving her name to a stranger didn't seem like a wise idea. She blurted out the first response that came to mind. "To give someone your name is to give them power over you."

His smile widened even more, and Kissa did not like how her heart sped up at the sight of it. "Fair enough. Where do you hale from?"

She lifted her chin. "I am from Osmondia. Born and raised."

The strange warrior nodded, though his assessing eyes continued. "Your eyes. I never seen ones quite like that before."

Kissa stiffened. His curiosity made her uneasy. Her father's voice echoed in her mind, reminding her she shouldn't be there.

"I think it is best that I go now. My father will come looking for me." She meant it as a parting and warning. Without waiting for his reply, Kissa turned and fled from the ruins and the strange warrior that entranced her.

"Wait!"

She dared not look back as she ran across the meadow, crossed the bridge, and then retraced her path. After making sure that he was not following her, Kissa paused amidst a cluster of trees to collect herself.

She placed her hand on her chest, right above her heart, where the rhythm had led her to the mysterious man. Kissa realized she had experienced nothing like it before, nor had she come across any mention of it in her books. She wondered what kind of sorcery was at play? It was a joke to calm her panic, of course. Magic did not exist in the world.

Yet, she could not explain the sensation. With no immediate answers and her need to return to her lands before the sunset, Kissa continued forward.

Eventually, retracing her steps, she found her way back just in time. Not yet ready to face her mother and father, she walked to her Oasis. Her legs felt like jelly, and sweat clung to her every part as she leaned her bow and arrow against the tree. Kissa slumped into her hammock and pulled out her waterskin from her satchel, and drank deeply.

Finally catching her breath, Kissa reclined, her body sinking into the comfort of the hammock's embrace. With one leg dangling off the side, she gazed up at the sky. The fiery red orb slowly descended and the gentle breeze whispered through the trees, carrying with it the scent of the salty sea.

Overwhelmed by exhaustion, Kissa surrendered to the hammock's rhythmic sway, her mind drifting away, longing for the solace of a new day's dawn.

"Kissa…"

She heard the melodic voice somewhere in the recesses of her mind, but her exhausted body refused to comply. Ignoring it, Kissa pulled an arm over her head, preparing to return to her dreamless sleep.

Suddenly, a shimmery white door materialized in her mind, its surface glinting like freshly fallen snow. The glistening crimson knob turned, and the door opened, revealing a brilliant light casting dazzling reflections of emerald green and gold. The intensity of the light overwhelmed her senses, blinding her.

"Kissa!"

The commanding voice seized her attention completely, but she couldn't determine if the scene was real or just a dream. Apart from the door and the radiant light, the surroundings resembled a night sky devoid of stars, with murky gray clouds beneath. Kissa glanced down and found herself still lying in her hammock, suspended by nothing.

"I am in your mind's eye." The feminine voice emerged from the dazzling green and gold light, but she had no mouth or eyes that Kissa could see.

Uncertain, she gave a slow blink and found herself still in the scene. Deciding to play along and see where it led, she asked, "What are you? What do you want?"

"I am a star. This is my pure form," the light said. "For now, I am here to unbind you."

"Unbind me?" Kissa wondered what her mind stumbled into.

"It is not a natural occurrence to bind one's gifts, but it was necessary for me to bind you when you were a baby to keep you hidden. However, these gifts come with significant risks, and before unbinding you, I must make you aware of the danger."

Kissa's mouth opened, but nothing came out. What was she to say?

"Inside you is energy. It is called Essence. You may have felt it already, like a suppressed fire inside you," the light said.

Kissa eyes widened and her hand clutched her chest above her heart. To have a name to the burning fire inside her felt vital somehow.

The star continued. "Once unlocked, your powers will draw from a well deep inside you. We call it the core. You must not drain your Essence entirely, for you will lose your gifts permanently. Consider the consequences before casting any magic."

Her snort turned into a full on laugh. One of those exhausted, delusional laughs that she had no control over. She concluded that her mind must have fractured. Now, it had run away from her.

Magic? Power? Only the selfish gods had those things. She was just a simple insignificant human and this...this wasn't real.

The shimmery star's head, if it could be called that, tilted sideways. "You think I speak false? The Divine cannot lie." This only made Kissa laugh harder.

Then the star said, "I see. Onya and Omani neglected to tell you that you're gifted."

Hearing her parent's names sobered her. She sat up straighter in her hammock. "Yes, they said I was special, like normal parents tell their child."

"Your parents are good and pure. If they withheld information, they had their reasons. I imagine even they struggle to comprehend that you are a gifted child. Essence flows freely, but the devout remain unaware."

Kissa's eyebrows raised as questions bubbled up inside her, but she couldn't trust herself not to burst into another fit of laughter. So, she stayed quiet as the star continued.

"Not everyone is ignorant. Unfortunately, some desire to wield Essence for themselves, and there are those who have accomplished it. In order to establish balance, the gifted had to be born. Seven humans imbued with gifts from the Ancients. It is called Divine Magic."

"What?" Now calm enough to be taken seriously, Kissa couldn't even gather her thoughts.

The light's countenance—what Kissa could only describe it as—conveyed a deep sadness as she warned, *"The enemy draws closer. We must act without delay, regardless of your readiness to see the truth. Unfortunately, Kissa Ashtar, a hard journey awaits you."*

She scoffed. "I am stuck at home in my gilded cage, where I have been all my life. There will be no journey for me." She shocked herself with the bitterness of her words.

"A little time can move the sun itself, young one." The star's melodic tone carried the scent of possibility.

Unfortunately, it was being shrouded by Kissa's resentment and pain. Her wounds were still fresh and she couldn't see past it just yet. Even more, she didn't believe any of the star's melodic words for one moment.

"Our time is running out. Some gifts, like empathy, will come effortlessly to you. You must hone and understand it. Practice each day, or it will overwhelm you. Other gifts, like visions, come without warning. You will need to learn the difference between these and dreams. More complex gifts will develop when you are stronger."

"Empathy?" Kissa snorted again. Clearly, this was a dream. Shimmery talking lights, gifts of magic, abilities she never even heard of. She was ready to wake up now.

The light tilted her head again. "You will understand everything in its appointed chapter. Find the seven gifted, and together you will defeat what comes."

Before Kissa could open her mouth, the star suddenly reached out and touched her sundial with her sparkling light. Then, like the sands of the beach picked up by the wind, she disappeared and the door with her.

⸺◈⸺

KISSA AWAKENED WITH A start. Her sundial felt hot against her skin, like a blazing hot coal. Crying out, she fell out of her hammock onto the soft green grass. Her keepsake now dangled from her neck, no longer touching her skin. Gripping the blades of life under her, she hastily breathed in the salty air, trying to make sense of everything.

Suddenly, a blinding flash of light erupted from her sundial, and she squeezed her eyes shut. Yet, the brilliance pierced through her eyelids and she curled into herself, shielding her eyes with trembling hands.

From deep within her chest, her fire surged to the surface, causing her body to arch with momentum. Kissa screamed as the inferno climbed through her entire being. Energy flooded her from the top of her head to the tip of her toes. Her skin tightened, and with it, a strange humming sound emerged.

The moments felt like they stretched into eternity, then, just like that, the pain vanished. A flood of release she had not expected washed over her, leaving Kissa sprawled on the grass.

Then everything plunged into darkness.

4

BIRTHNIGHT

KISSA

KISSA'S EYES SNAPPED OPEN. Frantically, she looked around, only to realize that she was in her own bed. Her old finger paintings adorned the walls, and in the corner, her bow and arrow leaned against the wall. Right above her bed, her small window framed a night sky that blanketed the dark forest.

A dream, she thought as she reached up and gripped her sundial.

Kissa's hope shattered as she felt the warmth of the amulet against her skin. A reminder of the searing burns she had endured. Surprisingly, her skin remained unblemished, even though she was certain that an inferno had engulfed her.

She swung her legs off the bed, but her body shuttered. Kissa tried to stand up, but paused as her mother's voice filtered in from her cracked door.

"She will be confused. We should have told her..."

Her parents were arguing again. With a grunt, she rose on shaky legs. Eyeing the door, she gave into a defeated sigh.

When had the damn thing moved so far?

Slowly and painfully, she made it to the door, one foot after the other. Upon opening it, she found her parents engaged in a heated discussion right outside her door. Her mother was the first to see her and wasted no time admonishing her.

"Kissa!"

Her mother's eyes were slightly puffy, as if crying recently. Her brows furrowed with concern as she placed her arm gently around her shoulders and guided her back to the bed. As she settled back down, Kissa couldn't help but feel the piercing gaze of their worried eyes, like tiny pinpricks on her skin.

"We found you by the sea cliffs unconscious," her father said.

Kissa didn't know how to tell them what occurred, since she was unsure what actually happened. Instead, she looked at her father's brooding face and then back at her mother's puffy eyes. She found she was no longer angry at them. She just needed answers.

"I'm ready to listen."

Her father nodded, then walked over and pulled a chair to the bed and sat in it heavily as if something weighed on him. Kissa had an uneasy feeling that whatever they were keeping from her would change her life significantly. But the hard part was already out. Now she needed to know everything else.

"She needs to hear it from us, Omani. It is her 18th birthnight. She will know soon enough." Her mother said next to her.

"Know what?" She was tired of all the whispering and unspoken feelings between them.

"Your mother and I took Oaths before your birth that bound our tongues from speaking of this. Therefore, it was physically impossible to tell you before this night," her father started.

Kissa nodded for them to continue, though confusion settled upon her. An Oath bound two parties by the honor of an agreement, but she had never heard of one that physically bound a person. She thought of the star from her dream that allegedly unbound her gifts.

"What we are about to tell you will answer some questions, but most likely add to your burdens." Her father looked at her mother with a sad smile. "But your mother is right. You need to have all the knowledge you can to make informed decisions."

Just tell me, Kissa wanted to scream. The suspense was killing her.

Her mother spoke up beside her. "Your father and I tried having children for many years. The elders said that, because of our different bloods, it wasn't physically possible to fall pregnant. So, I prayed earnestly for a little girl." She looked at Kissa, tears gathering in her eyes. "I prayed for you."

Her mother stood and paced the room as she gathered her thoughts. "One night, my goddess finally answered me during a dream. Zuri said that she heard my prayers, that a little girl needed my love and protection, and she chose me. Of course, I immediately said yes."

Her mother's face turned solemn. "I told your father of my dream, but many summers passed, and we had heard nothing further. We thought maybe it was just a dream I evoked from the deepest desires of my heart. Then, one autumn morning, a woman appeared at our home with a basket. I peered inside to find a newborn baby girl laying there. I knew in my heart she was the child spoken of from my dream."

"So it is true. You are not my birthmother." Kissa's heartbreak erupted like a massive crater, the weight of confirmation engulfing her entirely. The bitter taste of betrayal tainted her mother's beautiful tale. They concealed the truth from her all her life, leaving her wondering what other secrets they kept.

Her father's voice broke through her turmoil. "Before the woman left, she explained you were very special. That you would develop unusual gifts as you grew older, and you were to live a normal life, but closely protected. Nobody could know of your existence."

Now it all made sense why she could never leave her lands. Nobody ever bothered to visit their home, and she always wondered why her father was so overprotective.

Her mother said, "We don't know who your blood mother and father are, and we were never privy to that information. But we made an oath not to speak of what little we knew. Your father and I speculated for a time. We thought about many possibilities—"

"Eventually," her father cut in with a raised eyebrow directed at her mother, "we let the thoughts go. *We* are your parents. Kissa, we have always loved you as our own."

The walls seemed to close in on her once more, igniting a familiar fire within her that seemed to spread through her entire being now. Her *Essence*, if the star from her dream could be believed. Her eyes burned from tears she held back.

"I need some time to process all of this," she said.

"I am sorry, my love," her mother said. Before leaving, she kissed the top of her head.

Her father stared at her for a moment. "I know this is surreal to you and will take time for you to fully grasp it. But do not hate us too long. Your mother's heart can't handle it." Then he walked out and closed the door behind him.

Kissa drudged over to her dresser and lit a candle, then shrugged off her clothes. The tears she held back flowed down her face like a river as she threw on a nightgown and tucked herself into her small bed. She let out a harsh breath as she stared out of the small window above her. A hollowness she had never felt before emerged inside her as she finally let the hurt and discoveries of the day envelop her.

She had nothing now. No future, no blood mother and father, no true origins, and no friends. They may have told her the truth to help her make informed decisions, but Kissa felt lost now. She wished she never knew at all. They didn't even know her true parentage, and Kissa didn't know where to start to even find them. Or if she even wanted to.

Those angry thoughts slowly turned into erratic dreams filled with shadows, and darkness, as eventually, Kissa's exhausted body succumbed to sleep.

⸺⬦⸺

A SOFT KNOCK STARTLED her out of her deep slumber. Her eyes fluttered open to see it was not yet morning. Her eyes felt gritty, and she wanted nothing else but to sleep her pain away.

Only her mother knocked that way. Kissa knew she would never let her lock herself away in her room forever, though she wanted to desperately.

With a deep breath, she said, "Come in."

Onya walked in with puffier eyes than before, now rimmed in red. Her golden eyes wore a sadness Kissa had never seen before. Taking her in, she realized she looked nothing like her.

Compared to her mother's lithe, petite stature, Kissa was at least a hand taller than her, with broader shoulders, and more curves. Her deep golden brown skin had a reddish tone, darker than her mother's fawn complexion. Her parents always told her that being half-blood accounted for all of that.

However, Kissa's hair set her apart from all Osmondians and Zuranians. A memory surfaced unbidden.

Three summers old, Kissa shuffles across the floor in her mother's gold slippers and an oversized yellow sun hat on her head. She stops and spins around in front of her mother's standing mirror. Bouncy, curly hair showing underneath the hat.

She studies herself curiously, then asks, "Mama, why is my hair red? Your hair is not red."

Kissa looks up to see her mother walk over and sit on the floor beside her. Then she softly pulls one of her titian curls loose with a warm smile.

"Because you were born special, little Firebird. The goddesses wished for your hair to be the color of fall, the season you were born."

Kissa thought about how simple those words truly were. She remembered feeling content with that answer, proud of her unique hair. Now, her locs felt more like a death sentence. Though her mother encouraged her to love her hair, it was a trait unique to Sagians—Osmondia's sworn enemy that stole their independence through blood and death.

How can I love such a thing?

For the first time, Kissa truly understood the rules that bound her. She was the enemy. Previously, she avoided scrutinizing that fact, but now she felt openly declared. Perhaps her father was right in keeping her hidden. It was a simple, effective solution.

Yet, Kissa didn't want to spend her entire life hidden in the forest.

Her mother sat beside her on the bed, waiting patiently with a gift in her hand. Feeling exhausted, Kissa couldn't find it in her to keep up the appearance of being angry. Deeply sad? *Yes.* Broken? *Definitely.* She felt like her sorrow could fill the entire world at the moment.

Though tears threatened to undo her, she forced a smile on her face and said, "Is that for me?"

"Happy Birthnight, Firebird." Her mother whispered.

Those three words. The dam barely holding her emotions at bay broke instantly, and sadness gripped her tightly. Onya said nothing as she wrapped her arms around Kissa and held her tighter. Tighter than the sobs that racked her body uncontrollably. Tighter than the hollowness that seemed to want to pull her deeper in the abyss. They stayed that way for a moment, an hour, forever, it seemed. Kissa allowed her mother's scent, love, and warmth to soothe some of her conflicted feelings.

Finally, her mother said, "I am so sorry, Kissa. I did not wish for you to find out this way. Many times I wanted to say something, but the oath forbid me." Her mother's sadness, deep and regretful, seemed to spill into her own. "I do not understand everything you are feeling, but I know a bit of what it feels like to not have your blood parents." She then took Kissa by the shoulders. "The love I received from two people who raised me as their own was instrumental."

Marquis and Mira Harmon raised her mother when hers passed away suddenly when she was 11. Kissa did not lose her blood parents to such travesties. She never knew them at all. It seemed more likely that she mourned the idea of her mother and father not being her blood. She mourned her old life. Her father was right. They loved her deeply, but the hurt of not knowing remained.

Onya handed her the gift, and Kissa forced another smile as she unwrapped the red silk and found a beautifully crafted black granite mortar and pestle.

"It's beautiful, Mama."

Just a day ago, she would have been so excited about this gift. However, now, it brought up a broken feeling of rejection. Kissa didn't need healing tools now. There was no record of her birth, because she did not exist. A numb feeling arouse from the thought.

Clueless of Kissa's turmoil, her mother said, "It will be one of the most important tools you will have for all the wonderful things you will accomplish."

Kissa seemed to feel the sincerity that radiated from her eyes. Her mother believed that wholeheartedly. "Thank you."

After she placed her gift in her old leather satchel with her other healing tools, she returned to bed. Not missing a beat, Onya crawled in behind her and held her tight. Feeling her mother's gentle fingers rub her scalp felt like a familiar comfort, making it hard to keep her eyes open.

Eventually, Kissa said, "What will I do now?"

"Despite how you feel now, your father and I are proud of who you are. He is right about one thing. You have many strengths. Though the world will tell you it's not possible, you can be whatever you want to be, Kissa, and no school can tell you differently."

The passion in which her mother said it surprised Kissa. To attend Serenity, or any other healer's school across Haava, was of the highest honor for Zuranians. Her mother attended Calendula, the academy in Zurania. Then, when Queen Safiyah and King Tor enacted treaties between their kingdoms, her mother came with her adopted family to help establish Serenity and the House of Life.

It was the future Kissa wanted so much she couldn't breathe, but only Zuranians attended the schools. According to their laws, only those with the capability passed down from generation to generation, blessed by the Ancient of Grace, could attend. They never, not once in all of history, allowed "others" to attend.

She should have seen this coming, even if they had found her birth records. Her father's Osmondian blood ruffled their feathers. Now that she knew why there were no birth records, she couldn't see a way forward.

As if knowing her thoughts, her mother said, "This is only a setback. One that I am confident you will blaze your way through."

Kissa wished she felt as confident. From the moment she could speak a word, her mother taught her everything she needed to know. A healer was a person of compassion who served others in need. The schools were a stamp of approval, so the world accepted her training as a healer. Even more, it would make her more recognizable if she donned the white healer robe with references backing her from the Shadora Council or even the Overseer himself.

But did she really need that?

Seeing her in thought, her mother added, "You will figure it all out in due time. For now, celebrate your night. You are now officially an adult."

Kissa gazed out her window and rechecked the moonless sky. With everything going on, she forgot about her birthnight. It was indeed the hush of night, and she was officially 18. The new moon felt significant somehow. She tried to tell herself that she felt no different. A symbol of a girl's journey into womanhood. Except now, she felt very different.

Her plans faltered, her origins awaited discovery, and an weird hum resonated within Kissa now. She reached for her necklace and noticed the sundial still felt warm. The shimmery light from her dream didn't feel like just a dream. She desperately wanted to tell her mother, but say what?

She inhaled, blew a long breath, and instead said, "I don't even feel like an adult."

Onya chuckled. A tinkling sound that broke the severity of the moment. "Of course you need to give it a day or two," she said, eliciting a hint of a grin from Kissa. "However, this moment is bittersweet for me. It seems just yesterday, you were just a little girl hiding within my skirts, and now you have grown into this beautiful, fierce woman."

Kissa sighed. She would give anything to be that little girl again. Life was far more simpler then. "Thank you, Mama."

"I remember growing up, girls could not wait until their 18th summer. It meant they were old enough to accept marriage offerings."

Kissa heard the smile in her mother's voice, so she turned towards her with a scrunched face. "Ewe, Mama. You make it sound like a sacrifice." Onya burst out laughing, causing Kissa to smile—a genuine smile. "Besides, I would have to meet a breathing, living boy first."

Thoughts of the strange warrior she stumbled upon earlier came to mind. Werid feelings swam through her stomach. He probably thought she was some weird stalker and she doubted he wanted to see her again.

"Ah, I don't know. The Fates made sure your father and I met. A Zuranian healer and an Osmondian warrior. Think about that!" Then her mother chuckled again and said, "I remember only a day after my birthnight, a boy named Rubin asked for my hand."

All thoughts vanished in an instant. Kissa's brows raised in intrigue. She had never heard of this *Rubin* before. "What happened to him?"

"Well, a few of us at Calendula became close, our circle of friends. I grew up with Rubin. He was very handsome and charismatic. Naturally, all the young men flocked to him, and all the girls wanted to be his love interest, including me. In our fourth year, the end of one class cycle, we planned to meet at his family's house to go horse riding. A new girl named Orel from a small village had just enrolled a week prior. As my new roommate, I wanted her to feel welcome, so I invited her to come."

Kissa sat up as her mother's smile fell. "When we arrived, Rubin looked right at Orel with contempt I had never seen in him. He embarrassed her in front of all of us by stating that she was not permitted in his home. I felt so ashamed."

"Why did he do that?" Kissa asked, upset for the girl herself.

"I think because Orel's family didn't have prestige. Now, looking back, Rubin was always snooty. And you know what? I think he was jealous I had a new friend."

"So what happened to her? To Orel." Kissa asked.

"I wouldn't let her go back to school by herself, humiliated. So, I left with her. I apologized for his actions, but it seemed everyone knew I was Rubin's intended. So, even though I tried to make amends, she went her own way."

"Wow. So, that's why you didn't marry him?" Kissa wondered.

"Yes, I refused. I told him I needed to focus on my duties. Honestly, I couldn't see myself marrying someone so callous." Her mother said with a sigh. "But I knew the ramifications of slighting him. His family had the power to ruin my future. Though now, when I look back, I see it didn't matter."

"How so?"

Her mother paused and smiled. "I did not lie. I dreamed of traveling to different kingdoms. When I graduated, I volunteered here in Osmondia. I jumped at the opportunity. We helped establish the school, working with Osmondian warriors side by side. Then, one stormy day, running back to Serenity, I bumped into your father. Literally, too." Her mother chuckled. "His warm brown eyes stole my breath as he picked up my falling parchments and books. He was so compassionate and strong, honorably so. I had no regrets when I married your father because I knew."

Kissa thought she could actually feel her mother's love. It felt like a cold winter in front of the fire, bundled in each other's arms under a blanket, stealing kisses. The old memory of her parents made her grin.

"Knew what, Mama?"

"That your father was my other half to my token of life." She stroked Kissa's cheek as she said, "I could have waited and traveled the world, but my heart knew. After we married, we traveled together and I haven't looked back since."

Kissa's heart felt full to bursting hearing her mother's declarations for her father. It seemed strange, not entirely her own feelings—almost like her mother's nostalgic love leaked over into her own heart. She was unsure what to make of it.

More importantly, Kissa was relieved that her mother didn't marry someone heartless, like Rubin. He would have never raised Kissa with unconditional love like her father did. She wondered if the callous man was part of their hardships later on. She couldn't imagine him being happy about being discarded for an Osmondian warrior.

Her mother interrupted her thoughts. "Kissa, when we are young, adults encourage us to plan our lives meticulously. Taking control of our destiny is worthwhile, but occasionally...Fate has other plans."

Her words fell over Kissa's shoulders like a comforting quilt. It stirred something in the depths of her. She knew little about destiny and Fate, but her parent's marriage weathered many storms. The leaders and lawmakers frowned upon anyone marrying 'outside the blood.' They felt it weakened the abilities passed down from the Ancients. Despite that, though, her parents proved true love withstood the tests of time.

Kissa looked back at the moonless sky. She wondered if it was Fate that brought her to them that day. Her mood felt lighter now. A healer's touch, or perhaps a mother's.

She opened her mouth to ask more about Fate, but another knock sounded at her door. Her father popped his head in. Another time then.

"Happy Birthnight, Kissa!"

His deep coffee-brown eyes searched hers for something. Forgiveness, she realized. Her father had never been good at speaking of matters of the heart. They've agreed to disagree before, and most likely will again.

"Thank you, Father," she said as she gestured for him to come in. He carried in a familiar cake on a dish. She smelled cardamom and cinnamon—another favorite.

"Did you tell her, yet?" Her father asked with a warm smile.

Kissa reached for a slice of cake, but paused at her father's words. "Tell me what?" She reached her limit of heartbreak and wanted no more surprises.

"I have extended my visit for a couple of more days and..." He looked toward her mother.

Her mother appeared anxious, as if her words might sever the fragile bond between them. Kissa forced a smile. She didn't want her mother feeling like she was walking on eggshells.

"What is it, Mama?"

"I-I have decided to return to the House of Life. My duty calls to me more now than ever." Her words flowed with passion now. "I want to help Elder Harmon find a cure. So many in our kingdom are suffering and dying, and they need me."

Kissa heard the unspoken words. *Now that you don't.*

Or at least, she was not supposed to. Right now, Kissa should have been packing for Serenity. The House of Life sat in Sapphire City, on the coast. Her heart ached at the thought of her mother so far away. However, she pushed the selfish thought away because her mother was the most selfless person she knew.

"I am so proud of you, Mama."

"Oh?" Her mother looked earnest. "That benmeans a lot to me, but if you need me to stay longer—"

"No, Mama." Kissa shook her head. "The stars know I will miss you, but I can't be upset with you for helping our people," Kissa said. "Besides, I am an adult now. I will care for our land while you are both away." She looked at her father now. "You both have important work to do. I will be fine."

Her mother sighed in relief, then hugged her tight. "Thank you, Kissa."

"Yes, well, you and I have the pleasure of accompanying your mother there." Her father said. He wrapped his enormous arms around them both.

Kissa gasped as she looked between the two of them. "I'm going to Sapphire City?"

With a glint in her eyes, her mother said, "Indeed. Now let us go pack."

5

SAPPHIRE CITY

Kissa

As usual, Kissa practiced her archery before the dawn light. Her father accompanied her, much to her surprise. Kissa couldn't remember the last time they practiced together. She felt a sense of nostalgia, as if she were twelve years old again, yearning to make a good impression on him.

After a couple of rounds, her anxiousness eased, and she fell into her routine. Her father made small suggestions here and there, but when she hit the targets with her eyes closed, his face lit up.

With an approving smile, he said, "Amazing!"

A warm feeling enveloped her from her father's praise. He didn't give them often, but when he did, she treasured them.

His face turned contemplative. "I wonder if you can hit a moving target that way or how you would do in an uncontrolled environment? Have you been practicing on horseback as I showed you?"

"Yes, I take Sky out often."

"I know that the idea of training in the military goes against everything your mother taught you, but my archers could learn a thing or two from your skills."

Kissa's eyes widened at his words. The possibility stirred something deep inside her. She long knew that her aptitude with a bow surpassed even her father's, but the weight of her healing responsibilities prevented her from fully embracing it. Maybe because she always knew she'd have to choose one. For reasons she still didn't quite understand, it was forbidden to have more that one ability.

As the first light approached, her father led them out, and his firm commands echoed in her mind.

Keep close to me...

Stay alert...

Kissa allowed the exhilaration of the new journey to wash away the day before's burdens, even if for only for a time. She decided that as her first venture to the coast, she damn sure would enjoy it. Sky, her gray and cream spotted filly, must have felt the same because her gait hastened through their lands in anticipation.

As they exited, the strange sensation from the day before wrapped around Kissa again. Expecting it, she gripped Sky's reins tighter as the buzzing sensation made their movements feel like wading through marmalade. With the horse's momentum, it only lasted a breath or two.

Strange. She wanted to ask her father about it, but her he was too far ahead.

The trail paved by centuries of travelers was swift and uneventful. The air grew warmer closer to the foot of the mountain. No longer cool wisps of air, but a tropical feel. Though she tried not to, her thoughts kept returning to her origins. More specifically, her blood parents. Who were they? What did they look like? She gathered that at least one of them was of Sagian descent. Her fiery locs left no room for doubt about that. A question lingered in her mind: Why in the stars did they leave her in enemy territory?

"We are close to Black Pearl. We are making good time," her father said as he pulled beside her.

Kissa smelled the brine, signaling they were closer to the sea. As the dark canopy of trees broke, the view ahead took her breath away. It was a picturesque day with a cerulean blue sky. The sun gleamed on the sea like peppered diamonds. Kissa found it difficult to tell where the sea began, and the pinkish-white puffy clouds ended.

She flicked her attention closer to the crystal clear waters that leisurely lapped the black sand. Her father told her of the onyx sand on the coast growing up, but to actually see it felt dreamlike, and Kissa felt giddiness bubble up within her. Without a second thought, she led Sky to the edge of the beach. She swiftly dismounted, pulled off her riding boots, and ran to the shore.

The black sand coated the bottom of her feet as she let it fill between her toes. A joyous giggle left her lips at the prickly sensation. Then, Kissa rolled up her pant legs, held up the bottom of her cloak, and jogged through the sea foam and small waves rolling on the beach. The water's warmth surprised her as it caressed her ankles.

She bent over, scooped the crystal clear water in her free hand, and watched it drip back to the sea. The briny deep called to Kissa, beckoning her to swim in its current. Literally, too, because as she stared into its never-ending distance, a chime like a faint hum of a woman's voice sang to her. She tilted her head to the side and closed her eyes, listening to the sea serenade her. She did not know how long she stayed that way, moments, perhaps minutes, as she concentrated on the faint melodic calling.

"Kissa, we must get going." Her father's voice broke through her trance.

Startled, she turned to see her father atop Dream, holding the reins of Sky, huffing behind him. An amused but stern look draped his face. Her mother, behind him, held Kissa's boots with a curious look. Their distance surprised her. She looked down and found herself waist-deep in the water, the bottom of her cloak drenched as it floated behind her.

Kissa didn't remember moving this deep into it.

She nodded to her father and waded back to the shore. Once her boots were on, still wet, she mounted her horse, and they followed the coast going east. It was here that she finally saw boats out at sea.

From her sea cliffs at home, they always appeared like tiny dots on the water. Now that she saw them up close, they fascinated her. One boat, at least four men long and seven hands wide, rode the light current. Two men held long wooden poles with woven nets at the end, and another had oars.

"Those are fishing boats," her mother explained, pulling beside her.

Kissa nodded in reply as her gaze drew beyond the boats to a tower that stood at least two hundred spans tall on a small island further out. Osmond's Light. The bottom form was square, and the octagonal middle part held a tolling bell. Made of stones, it stacked up and slanted inward toward the top. A roaring fire on top of it. Kissa found that odd, since it was daylight. However, there was something so masterful about it.

She wondered who made it and what inspired them to build such a structure. As they rode a little closer, she saw the island connected to a solid platform above the water. She surmised that this was how the people traveled to the tall tower. The platform reached past the shores all the way to cave-like dwellings flushed against the foot of the mountain.

"That is Osmond's light. The watchers light the very top, so anyone out at sea can find their way," her father said as he stared into the distance with her.

Kissa smiled, contemplating what they used to light it, but her attention snagged on the peculiar platform again and the cave-like dwellings. "Father, what is that?"

His mouth turned into a broad smile as he said, *"That* is Sapphire City."

As they rounded the base of Aarusha mountain, the naked beauty of the coast changed, and Kissa realized the solid platform extending from Osmond's Light was a pier. Her father explained that it also connected to the Sapphire Boardwalk, where travelers from all over the world come to purchase goods from the merchants.

Once they reached the boardwalk, they had to travel by foot and took their three horses to a stable at an inn near the city's edge. As her father spoke to the stable boy and gave him the reins of their horses, Kissa eyed a fish-shaped canopy sign above the establishment that said "Fisher's Cove." From the commotion inside, the inn was pretty busy.

The noise only grew louder as they strode through the market and rows of canopy booths lined the boardwalk. Merchants yelled out aggressively, catching the attention of those who passed to look at their wares or haggle prices. Despite the noise, Kissa felt excitement as she strode past stands filled with jewelry, produce, fish, and clothing. On her other side were rows of weaved rugs, spices, and trinkets she had never seen before.

There were so many people. Not just Osmondians, but others with different shades of hair, eyes, and clothing. As she pushed her way around them, a man caught her attention. His cunning silver eyes and matching hair that flowed loose and long stood out. His skin was dark, like smooth chocolate. An Eashitan. His tunic was cream, with matching loose flowing pants and sandals on his feet. Jewelry adored his ears, fingers, and around his neck.

"Stop gawking." Her father said.

Kissa clamped her mouth shut. The beautiful man winked at her and her cheeks turned warm as she twisted away. She knew it was rude to stare, but everything around her was so...new.

Despite trying, Kissa's eyes did not stay focused, and it was hard to stay close to her parents when maneuvering around the fast-moving people. She almost lost them for a second time, staring at a chinchilla with big glassy eyes sitting on a woman's shoulder. Exotic Animals from Around the World, her sign said.

She caught her father's head above the crowd and hurried to catch up when a lyrical voice made her pause.

"She is found..."

The voice seemed to be everywhere and nowhere. It sounded collective, an echo of many voices at once. Kissa looked around the busy market, but nobody seemed to pay her any attention. Everything was as it should be.

"We have found her..."

Kissa's shoulders stiffened. Where were the voices coming from? She looked to her right. A gap between the exotic animal lady's tent and a rug merchant revealed a stand that sat secluded from everything else. Her eyes traveled to a small table with a neat display of gawk worthy jewelry, but that was not what moved her closer.

A glass orb reflecting the light stood next to the stand. Inside, something silver and dark swirled within like smoke. Sitting casually, an older woman with jet-black hair and not a hint of gray stared back at her with deep black eyes. Her skin was fair, lighter than Kissa's, and crow's feet creased the edges of her onyx eyes. Eyes that felt ageless as they seemed to see her past, future, and present. She knew right away that this woman was from the Queendom of Ravenia.

Their eyes and hair were dark, like the cosmos they studied—an ability from their goddess, the Ancient of Chaos.

Prior to the war, they created medicinal potions for the Zuranian healers, but rumors that they delve into darker, more poisonous treachery earned them the name of witches. Oddly, nobody ever seen a man hale from that region. According to some periodicals, they claimed to use men for procreation before sacrificing them in gruesome rituals.

Kissa's curiosity quickly turned to alarm. This woman was not supposed to be here. She scrambled for something to say as she looked down at the woman's smooth hands—no wrinkle in sight—holding a black ring with some golden signet. Despite her alarm bells rapidly firing inside her, Kissa drew closer, inspecting the ring. She stiffened the moment she saw a mountain with a tree engraved—just like her...

"Where did you get that?" She asked brusquely, scrutinizing the older woman.

The woman smiled, seemingly amused at her discomfort, then pointed to Kissa's chest. Or rather, her sundial necklace concealed under her tunic.

"This is your house signet, is it not?" The older woman drawled.

Her eyes widened at her words. "House Signet?" she mouthed. "I am from Osmondia."

Only royalty claimed house signets. Yet, Kissa could not explain the draw toward the ring somehow, like it called to her. Like it belonged to her.

The crone chuckled. "You have no idea what runs through your veins." She looked at Kissa like a lost artifact she wanted to examine closer. "Your mother hid you well, but He sees all things." She said with an otherness to her voice.

Kissa saw something swirl in the woman's onyx eyes that reminded her of another time, many summers ago. When she blinked, it was no longer there.

She shook her head. "My mother?" she repeated. Suddenly, she felt unsure of herself. Kissa knew the woman wasn't speaking of Onya.

"Soon you will see your life is nothing but a lie." The woman crooned, as if reading her thoughts.

The joke was on her. Kissa already knew her life was a lie. Her attention stayed on the ring. "What do you want for it?" Kissa asked, pushing a confidence she didn't truly have behind it.

"It is not about what I want, is it?" The witch cooed. She tilted her head to the side, and her eyes narrowed. "You have always felt different. Too scared to question why that fire burns through your veins, accepting it as you do everything else. You have experienced a sense of being too immense for the chains of this tiny world that bind you."

The flicker in the crone's eyes made Kissa stiffen. It was unsettling, really. How did this woman know her deepest thoughts? Suddenly, the tropical humidity she came to appreciate when she reached the coast felt stuffy. She took a few steps back from the stand.

Kissa didn't know what to make of the woman's words or how she knew so much about her. Growing up, she never allowed herself to look too deeply at her questions. If Kissa was being honest with herself, it was fear that had kept her from asking. Fear of the unknown, fear of losing all that made her world. But Kissa always knew she was different. Even at three summers old, staring at herself in her mother's mirror.

The witch smirked as she watched her with keen eyes, as if she knew all the things that floated through Kissa's mind. "This is a Chonda ring. There are only three in existence. Your father created them to give its user their deepest desires." Then she shrugged indifferently. "With limitations, of course."

Her father...

The casual comment shook her to her core. The witch watched her like a fish on a hook, and at that moment, Kissa had a strange feeling that the witch had everything to gain in telling her the truth. She straightened her face and looked back at the trinket like it was just an ordinary ring.

Ignoring the rest of what the woman said, Kissa asked, "It grants wishes?"

"It can change anatomy such as eyes and hair." She said as she stared at Kissa with her own raised brow. Reeling in the hook line, she added, "It can even help you get into that little school you so desperately want to attend. If that is what you desire, of course."

Kissa shivered at the woman's knowledge of her. "How do you know these things? Who are you?" She snapped.

The woman only chuckled in reply. "The real question is, who are you?"

Kissa was tired of these games. She felt trapped in a spider's web, spinning around uselessly only to be devoured. Every word seemed to only trap her deeper. Yet, her eyes never left the ring. It called to her, beckoned her.

If—and that was a strong if—the ring could truly give desires, Kissa could have everything she ever wanted. But that would mean magic existed, and Kissa wasn't sure she believed that. However, the humming inside her since the dream with the shimmery light pierced holes in her certainty in that fact.

"What do you want in return?" Kissa asked suspiciously, hoping to uncover the crone's scheme.

"Hmmm," she feigned contemplation. "A favor that I will come to collect at a later time."

There it was. Kissa didn't think she wanted to give the favor to such a woman. Everything about her felt wrong. A tingling up her spine since she encountered the woman felt all too much like a warning. But what else did Kissa have to lose that she hadn't already lost? With no prospects of being a healer, and her parents away on their duties, Kissa couldn't think of one reason not to test it out. If it didn't work, nobody would be the wiser.

"Okay," Kissa said, although she still had some doubts.

The woman cackled with delight as a scroll and quill suddenly appeared out of thin air. Kissa stopped breathing.

"Sign here." The woman purred as she pointed to an X, marking a spot at the bottom of the parchment for a signature.

The parchment itself appeared ancient, like it would crumble to dust at the slightest touch. She read the legal words that filled the long paper just fine, but it was hard to grasp them. The words Oath, Ring and Payment stood out to her, but the others seemed to slip through her mind like the elusive newts she tried to catch near the springs when she was young.

"What does it say?"

"That you accept the ring. For payment, you will give a future favor that I will collect at an appointed time."

Kissa eyed the paper. There were a lot of words for something so simple. Again, warning bells and the prominent tingling told her to run away and never look back. However, the thought of her dreams right at her fingertips led her on. Her desperation seemed to grow of its own volition.

"And what are the consequences if the oath is not fulfilled?" she asked.

"You forfeit the ring...and your life," the witch said pointedly.

Kissa blinked in shock. "M-my life?" Warnings flared erratically within her.

"Yes, such a meaningless one, wouldn't you say? Of course, you can go back to your empty little cottage, wishing you took charge of your life until you are nothing but a shell of what you could have been." She shrugged in that nonchalant way. "It's definitely the safest option."

Yes, safest. But was it what Kissa wanted? Nobody even knew who she was...except this woman, it seemed. Why or how, Kissa didn't know. Nothing was adding up in her mind. She had no reason to help her. Or did she?

"What favor could you possibly want from me?" Kissa asked suspiciously.

The woman stared at her with those ancient eyes for a moment, as if seeing something beyond them. "Let's just say, when you are living the destiny you are meant to, I will come to collect your gratitude."

Though the woman's words were obscure, she heard what she didn't say. Kissa thought of her future as a healer, traveling the world. Was that it?

"And then what?" she pressed.

"I never answer that question until I come upon it," the witch said, with a glint in the depth of her onyx eyes.

Of course she didn't. Kissa's eyes trailed to the ring. She wanted to know her origins. If her blood father made that ring, she wanted to know more about it. Deep down, she had already decided.

Kissa let out a heavy sigh. Then, against all logic, she signed next to the marked X.

The parchment rolled itself up and disappeared right in front of her eyes. Her heart hammered as the witch opened her hand and the ring magically floated in the air and stopped in front of Kissa. So many alarms went off inside her. What would happen if she even touched the ring?

She carefully plucked it from the air. It felt strange in Kissa's hand, humming like the sensation buzzing through her since last night. She expected something extraordinary to happen, but sighed in relief when, after a few moments, nothing did. She decided not to put the 'Chonda' ring on her finger. Her parents would ask questions she didn't want or know how to answer. Instead, she placed it in her satchel.

"What are its limitations?" She asked, now realizing she forgot to ask.

However, before she received an answer, a stern voice broke the silence. "There you are. Kissa, come. We can't be late."

She whipped her head back to see her father. His brows furrowed in obvious frustration, his eyes severe as he studied her. Kissa realized she was breathing hard, and her heart was beating much too fast.

Her mother, beside him, walked forward. "Kissa, why are you back here?"

"I was just," She turned back to the old woman she possibly bargained her soul with, and an empty stall greeted her. She disappeared, just like the scroll, along with any more answers she needed.

"Kissa," her father said impatiently.

"Sorry, father," she said as she shook her head.

Then she dutifully followed her parents back through the sea of people on the boardwalk. Wondering all the while what craziness she just entangled herself in.

6

HOUSE OF LIFE

KISSA

HER FATHER SEEMED WOUND tight and flanked her for the rest of their travel. She *felt* the worry from him in waves, though his face revealed stoic calm. Eventually, they left the loud and busy boardwalk, and the beach became more of a landform of rocks, stone, and a few sparse trees. Steps carved into the stones led to a gate with trees around it for privacy. Behind it was a dome-like structure that sat secluded on a hill—the House of Life.

Kissa took in the Zuranian symbol of a dove in mid-flight engraved on the dome part of the building. Its massive size made it easily seen, though its location set it apart from the bustle of the city. Directly behind the building, Za forest sat as its backdrop. Kissa realized that her mother and father took her through the city to experience it.

They climbed the stone steps and went through the gate, spilling out into a courtyard. It was here that dozens of people gathered as if waiting to get inside. A handful of soldiers patrolled the area silently, keeping watch. The emblems on their chest plates displayed a sea serpent—*Leviathan warriors*. They nodded respect to her father from across the way.

Some people lay stretched across the grass while others sat with contorted faces that revealed their pain. Flitting tirelessly, healers identified by white robes checked those waiting, assessing and giving out water and other necessities.

Kissa's attention snagged on the white cloth tied around the healer's faces. Her chest tightened. The Sleeping sickness.

"There are so many," Kissa said, barely above a whisper to her mother beside her.

"They have reached capacity, so they are being attended out here. The healers are doing what they can." Her mother whispered back.

The tightening in Kissa's chest became an ache as her people's suffering became clear. Now she understood her mother's urgency. She was glad she supported her and didn't give into her selfish, childish inclinations. The kingdom needed all the healers willing to come to their aid, and even that was not enough.

She followed her parents along a path to the back of the hospital to another smaller courtyard. Kissa saw healers and staff sitting at little tables, eating and chatting. They went through the back entrance, and no sooner that they entered, a warm, deep voice greeted them.

"Ah, Commander, Onya, welcome!"

"Ba, it is so good to see you!" Her mother said as she hugged the willowy, tall man with deep gold eyes that reminded her of honey. His goatee connected to his sideburns, and his dark brown hair, full and curly, showed peaks of white at the edges. He wore a pristine white robe with gold cinctures. Kissa decided his booming voice didn't quite match his tall, lithe frame.

Beside him stood a young man with the exact willowy figure. However, his robes were gray. His gaze immediately settled on Kissa when she entered. If she had to guess, he was just as curious about her as she him. Something about him felt familiar.

"Benji!" her mother gasped, startling her.

The young man's eyes widened as Onya hugged him, almost tackling him. "I didn't know you would be here!" she said excitedly as she pulled back.

So this is Benji, Kissa thought as she tried and failed to figure out why he looked so familiar.

She knew her mother delivered him herself when his mother, Mira, birthed him. Mira and Onya exchanged letters often, so Kissa knew Benji was a fourth-year student at Serenity, and his father was currently grooming him to be his successor as overseer.

"You are a man now. How old are you, 20 summers?" Her mother said with a wink.

"19," Benji replied with a sheepish smile.

Onya grabbed Kissa's hand. "This is my daughter, Kissa. She will be a healer, too." She said proudly. Kissa's cheeks burned, and she did not know why her mother said such a thing.

Benji's eyes widened a fraction, the only sign of shock, before saying. "It is a pleasure."

Kissa stood awkwardly. "It is nice to meet you." She said.

"Let me look at you," Elder Harmon said loudly across the space, grabbing her attention. He walked over and took Kissa's hand with warm, smooth ones of his own. She shifted on her feet, unsure of herself, as he assessed her.

"Hazel green with gold and silver. I've never seen eyes so beautiful," Elder Harmon said.

Kissa's cheeks burned further. While she knew her eyes were rare, she wasn't used to someone calling attention to them. She forced a smile and said, "Thank you, Elder Harmon."

"Marquis, when we are among family." He said warmly. "I am sure my dear Onya taught you everything she knows. It is good that you are here to see the importance of the work you will do."

While this was precisely what she wanted to do with her life, the letter from Serenity niggled at her mind, and she glanced down at her shoes. Surely the Overseer knew about her rejection letter.

Saving her from responding, her father clasped Elder Harmon in greeting. "Thank you, Marquis, for having us. It is always good to see you."

Harmon clasped her father's arm but looked into the Commander's eyes sternly. "Yes, it has been *far* too long."

Her father returned the stare, then conceded with a nod of his head. Kissa watched on curiously, wondering what the exchange was about. Whatever it was, they did not speak to it.

It was Kissa's mother who broke the tension. "I'm honored by your trust in me to continue your work here, Ba. You have always been a face of change. It is my honor to serve with you."

His stern look softened as he flicked his attention to Onya. "The honor is mine. You are one of the best High Healers that ever lived, and I am overjoyed at your return," Harmon said with a wide smile.

Kissa felt like an observer looking in—never really allowed to partake, no matter how much she wished to. A foreign feeling bloomed within her. She could not decide if it was yearning to be a part of them, a family that clearly loved one another, or jealousy that her mother had a life before her.

For a fleeting moment, she imagined visiting them and having dinner as a normal family would. She and Benji playing with one another, telling secrets and growing up together as they should have. Kissa decided then and there that she loathed the woman that delivered her and bound her parents to an oath, shattering any chance of Kissa having a genuine family. A normal life.

The inner door opened, interrupting her dark thoughts. A few young women walked in, and Elder Harmon introduced them as newly graduated healers. Kissa barely paid attention as Benji passed the white fabric to everyone. As she grabbed it, he held on to it a moment longer with his amber eyes trained on her. He did not seem angry or happy, and she was unsure what to make of it. Possibly curiosity. Then he let go, and she nodded her thanks.

At the front of the room, Benji showed them how to wear the masks and explained their necessity. Kissa found the fabric stifling, but understood why. Despite Elder Harmon's continued work, they still weren't close to finding a cure. They did not fully understand sickness, it could bore some type of contagious pathogens and it was better to be safe.

Thereafter, the group began touring the hospital, and Kissa sensed a feeling similar to a heaviness of heart within the House of Life. As if the very walls mourned and grieved, dampening Kissa's spirit even further.

They started from the lobby, a meeting point for multiple corridors circling it. In the center, various people sat in white uniformed chairs waiting to meet with a woman at a wooden desk taking down notes while another took vitals and assessed them. Elderly, children, and ages in-between filled the crowded lobby. Despite the long windows letting in sunlight all around them, a sense of desperateness dimmed the air. The people spoke in inaudible whispers or not at all.

Above them, various levels reached the dome ceiling, and Kissa counted four. Stairs on both sides of the space led to the upper floors. She looked down the hall closest to her. It was long and ended with a tall stained glass window that opened slightly, allowing the salty sea air through.

The hospital was exceptionally clean, the tiles that covered the entire floor area were meticulously white. Kissa smelled a hint of peppermint and lavender underneath the salty air. Though the walls were a bland eggshell color, the seascapes and painted landscapes gave the depressed ward some small sense of serenity.

The group started down a corridor to the right, and Elder Harmon introduced them to other healers and staff. Multiple doors lined both sides of the halls, most of them critical care rooms holding at least four patients each. These doors were closed to give privacy and to protect the staff.

Benji allowed the others to move ahead and walked beside Kissa. "So, why am I only finding out about you *today*?" He said with a raised brow.

He looked at her as if she were a puzzle he needed to figure out, and Kissa didn't know how to answer him. She didn't know what she *could* say. Truthfully, she didn't understand the oath that bound her parents.

"I'm not completely sure," she replied honestly.

She was unaware of the reason her family kept her separated. Surely, the Harmons would have said nothing. Though they knew absolutely nothing about her, between letters and stories of her mother's time with them, she felt like she knew them already. Like smeeting characters she read about in one of her books for the first time.

A few moments of silence passed between them, and their walk grew awkward. "How is Mira?" she asked, changing the subject.

His other eyebrow raised. "You know my mother?"

"Well, I know of all of you from Mama. She told me stories of growing up, Serenity, and the House of Life. Your mother is the Royal Healer for the Osmondian Kingdom. I would think everyone knows of her." Kissa said, trying a smile, but knew it fell flat.

Benji nodded his head. "I'm glad to know Onya spoke of us. Please forgive me, but this is all...new to me. Even though I rarely saw your mother, I grew up seeing your father every day at the Citadel, and he never once told us he had a daughter."

Kissa paused her steps. His words stung like a slap in the face. The silence of her existence felt deafening. She did not live a normal life, free to be who she was outside her family's lands, but Kissa didn't understand the why of the matter.

Why could she not see the Harmons? Why did her father never even mention *having* a daughter? As if outside the shelter of her home...she didn't exist. *Nobody could know of your existence.* Her father's words burrowed a hole in her heart.

As if sensing her sorrow, Benji said, "I am sure he had good reason. If it is any consolation, you are a pleasant surprise. My father is overjoyed and, I, for one, look forward to getting to know you."

His words were kind and Kissa felt the genuineness of them. They softened the sharp ache, a touch.

"Me too." She said.

"As of my mother, she and the Queen are very close. Her illness is taking a toll on her, as you can imagine. But she refuses to leave her side. I visit her from time to time and check on her."

Though she didn't know Mira personally, her heart hurt for her. All the Royal Healer could do for the Queen now was make her comfortable. Kissa didn't think she could watch her friend waste away before her.

"I would like to come with you next time if that is okay," she said without thinking. "I want to meet your mother, I mean." Kissa was not even sure if she could visit the capital and do so. This visit seemed to be an exception to her father's usual stance.

"She would love that," Benji said with a smile.

His words felt warm and true, and Kissa felt an immediate connection to him she didn't quite understand. Like the seasons apart seemed to melt away under his smile.

"How is Serenity? You're a fourth-year student, right?"

"That is correct." His face darkened. "It's alright, I guess." He said with indifference.

"How do you mean?" Kissa asked, surprised he would speak of Serenity that way. *Wasn't he like royalty there?*

"I mean, the classes are fine. It's the atmosphere I find stuffy." He looked at Kissa's confused face. "The people there find it difficult to serve with their heads stuck up their asses."

Kissa gasped, and a chuckle slipped. Benji flashed her a sly wink in return. His crass bluntness felt like a breath of fresh air.

"I am surprised to hear that. You and your father seem anything but *stuffy*." She said with a grin.

Benji nodded. "My mother and father have been trying to change the policies for decades. It is a tedious process to change the deep-rooted anger among some of our people. Don't take my word for it, though. You should develop your own thoughts on the matter. Hopefully, your presence at Serenity will speed things along."

Kissa's brows raised at that. She didn't want to embarrass herself by contradicting him and speaking plainly of her rejection. She had every intention of *one day* getting accepted to Serenity.

"Benji!" His father's deep voice snapped their attention to the front of their group.

"Duty calls," He drawled. "We will speak more of it later."

"I would like that," Kissa replied.

The tour continued, and Elder Harmon took them through two other corridors similar to the last. Though she wanted to grasp it all eagerly, Kissa felt a heaviness to her eyelids. A person could only see the same walls and doors before it became just plain boring.

However, her interest peaked as she noticed a room with a door ajar to her left. She moved closer to get a better look as the rest of the group continued down the hall. At first, Kissa thought it was another utility room, but it was dim, not lit up like the corridor, and she could make out the bed nearest the door.

A man lay with his eyes closed with a sea of dark Jata locs haloed around his head. Dark veins mottled the skin on his face and hand—a frail hand resting in a woman's who sat at his bedside. He didn't respond to the woman's tears, but Kissa keenly *felt* her grief, just as she felt the hospital's aura. She wondered if the woman was a wife, a sister, or a friend.

The wife, she decided, faced the door on the man's other side, looking straight through Kissa with troubled, stormy brown eyes. Her breath caught and everything else blurred out as Kissa's eyes lingered on the man's chest for a breath, two breaths... three. It did not rise.

A few moments later, an older healer, a woman with a severe bun and sad eyes, whispered in the woman's ear. The logical part of Kissa knew she should look away and not invade their privacy, but she stood transfixed as she stared into the desolate, dark room. She didn't hear what the healer said, but the grieving woman nodded in reply. Then she stood up, looked at the man, and kissed his brow. Finally, she left the room.

Kissa tried to look away as the woman walked past, but her eyes stayed glued to the man. Another precious life, snuffed out by the sickness. How many others shared the same fate? It was one thing to hear about the toll on the kingdom from her father, but another to witness it herself, all around her.

As she gaped, a woman older than the first strode over to the bed and placed a white fabric over the man. She closed her eyes and whispered a few words Kissa could not hear. She clenched her chest and the necklace underneath her tunic, barely registering her quickening heart rate. The white fabric was a preparation ritual for the dead to pass to the *After*.

It seemed so...final. *Absolute*.

A tingle crept along her skin. Not a warning this time, as beads of sweat collected on her forehead. Still, she did not move as if glued to the very tile she stood on. Kissa had never seen death before, and while she knew it was a part of life's cycle, nothing she had ever studied could have prepared her.

How presumptuous was she for thinking she would heal people and not even think of the possibility that some may die? No, *all* of them died. The ominous sickness wiped out her people every single day.

She didn't know how long she stood there, and she did not feel when her father touched her arm and led her away from the room. Kissa's heart sank with shame as she registered her movements, realizing in that world crashing moment, she could not watch people die.

Suddenly, the vibrant colors of her dreams faded into the dullness of reality. The deafening thrumming of her cowardice heart drowned out the echoing sounds of her hopes and aspirations. Feelings of warmth and purpose slipped through her fingers, leaving behind an emptiness she never expected.

It seemed becoming a healer wasn't in her future, after all.

7

A DUTY EARNED

KISSA

Kissa said very little while the men spoke in hushed voices. Benji and his father accompanied them back to their home, since it was on their way to Serenity. She felt far away, wrapped in her uncertain thoughts. She supposed witnessing death for the first time would do that to a person.

Even more, leaving her mother seemed like one of the hardest things in her life. She never spent more than a day apart from her. They cooked and ate together, gardened and studied. Though she wanted independence, Kissa didn't want to be alone.

They stopped halfway to give the horses water and eat rations, but Kissa was not hungry. So, she sat on a rock awaiting the others and drank deeply from her waterskin. Her ever-watchful father kept his eye on her, but she couldn't help her souring mood. Everything she ever wanted felt far away now, and Kissa felt crestfallen about returning to an empty home.

Yes, such a meaningless one, wouldn't you say? Of course, you can go back to your empty little cottage, wishing you took charge of your life until you are nothing but a shell of what you could have been.

The old woman's words crawled beneath Kissa's skin.

Sky's ears twitched before she sensed the strong tingle on the back of her neck—like being watched from the shadows of the slowly darkening forest. It kept her on edge, and her eyes swept the brush as she cursed herself for leaving her bow and arrow in her saddlebag. Family or not, the Overseer of Serenity accompanied them, and she didn't want to lose her chances of one day attending the school altogether.

Sky shifted her hooves. Kissa looked behind her and saw something move amongst the trees. It appeared like shadows drifting through the brush, and she couldn't make sense of it. Whatever it was, used the settling night and darkness as cover. Kissa stood up swiftly, and the surrounding chatter ceased.

"Kissa, what is it?" Her father asked. His hand gripped the hilt of his sword.

The warning flared within her, igniting her fire and urging her to run. Unlike the witch in the market, this warning felt like a direct threat. "We need to go now, Father! Something is out there."

As she grabbed Sky's reins, Kissa heard the scrape of metal as her father unsheathed his sword. "Mount up!"

That was all the warning they needed as Benji and Marquis immediately repacked their bags and mounted their horses as Kissa swung atop Sky. Her father led them out toward their land. Her instincts kicked into overdrive, and Kissa grabbed her hidden bow and quiver of arrows from her satchel, chiding herself for not having them ready.

Then, they suddenly heard it: a chilling howl that carried the promise of death, echoing through the stillness of the night. Its otherworldly sound sent shivers down Kissa's spine, as if it were a sound that didn't belong in the realm of humans.

Sky leaned her head back, sensing the danger, but Kissa controlled her with the reins and rubbed her side as she whispered to her. Though they all tried to calm their startled horses, they immediately picked up their paces as one. With the uneven terrain, she knew their horses would not outrun it.

Something moved in her peripheral, snapping her attention to it. To the right of their flank, a wolf as black as ebony and half the size of her father's warhorse formed from the shadows just as it...

"Watch out!" Kissa cried out as it launched from the thicket.

As it moved, the creature appeared to grow. It now stood almost as large as a black bear. With relentless aggression, the wolf lunged towards Elder Harmon's horse from behind, viciously snapping at the steed's legs. Panicked, the horse desperately tried to escape, rearing up on its hind legs. Kissa watched in horror as Harmon was thrown off the saddle, landing on the ground with a sickening crunch. As the horse regained its footing, it bolted away, racing for its life, abandoning its fallen rider.

As the wolf chased after it, Kissa tried to rein in Sky, but only managed to slow her down. Her father had already halted and turned Dream around to go get Elder Harmon.

"Father!" Benji struggled to get his horse to stop so he could help his father.

"No, Benji!"

As if he didn't hear the commander, Benji half slid, half fell off his horse, and scrambled to his father. This action grabbed the wolf's attention. With a deadly growl, the creature prowled toward father and son and Kissa swore the beast grew wider and taller all at once—as if it were solid and shadow.

She didn't have time to reason with what she saw. Kissa felt time slow. She nocked an arrow, releasing it in the next breath, and hit the wolf in the leg. A sharp growl emanated from the animal, but it didn't stop its pursuit. She nocked another arrow, but the darkness of the forest and the frantic movements of the horses did not give her a clear shot.

She spotted her father approaching them, then heard another growl, followed by a shout from Benji. Her heart hammered in her chest as she flitted through her options. Kissa jumped off of Sky, arrow nocked, and ran towards them. As she stepped around Benji's flailing horse, fear for the worst filled her.

The Commander sliced the neck off the wolf, toppling its head in the dirt right next to Elder Harmon's terrified face. A shuttered sigh left Kissa. A black substance dripped from its head and the Commander's sword. Then, all at once, the wolf formed into a mist of shadows and disintegrated with the wind.

Kissa and her father stared at one another with the same expression, eyes filled with shock. Then she flicked her attention to father and son. Black specks of the substance got on Benji's face, but he wiped it off quickly with the sleeve of his robe. Kissa's focus zeroed in on Elder Harmon, who lay conscious on the ground. His leg looked wrong, and he didn't dare move.

"By the Stars, what was that?" Benji said. His eyes just about fell out of his head.

There was no need to answer. None of them knew what had just happened. Kissa slung her bow over her shoulder and kneeled next to Harmon, whose face contorted with pain.

"Can you speak? Tell me what ails you." She said.

"My leg," he croaked.

She looked him over and saw blood soaking his pant leg and robe near his ankle. "May I?"

Elder Harmon gave a nod of consent. Kissa wasted no time shifting his robe and gently lifting his pant leg. A broken bone protruded from his skin right above his foot, causing the bleeding. She looked up to see Sky—exactly where she left her.

"Benji, please go to my horse and grab my satchel," she said, pointing toward her filly. "Father, get me an extra cloth and a filled water skin." Then she turned to Marquise. "You have a broken tibia. I need to stop the bleeding and set it. This will hurt."

Harmon nodded once in understanding. As she gave him a stick to bite down on, she realized he didn't ask for Benji to do this or question her abilities. Being a High Healer himself, he would know if Kissa failed to heal him right. A stroke of nerves settled on her shoulders, but they didn't have time for that. Once the men returned with the requested items, instinct kicked in.

Kissa immediately rinsed her hands and pulled her new mortar and pestle out. She poured water, the arnica herbs, and the tea tree leaf she regularly stashed in her satchel, grinding them together to make a paste. She set it aside and rinsed Elder Harmon's wounded area with the water gathered, and he hissed in pain.

"Hold him down for me. I need to set his bone." Kissa ordered.

Benji held his father's legs without question, while the Commander held his shoulders down. Elder Harmon bit down on the stick and closed his eyes. She set the tibia back in place as fast and carefully as she dared. She heard Harmon's growl in the background, but she focused on setting it right. If they waited until Serenity, he might lose his foot, maybe worse, part of his leg.

Kissa only fixed a broken wing of a raven once, but she wasn't letting that thought deter her. She studied anatomy thoroughly with her mother and knew with confidence where each bone in the human body aligned. It was pure adrenaline and intuition that drove her now.

Suddenly, Kissa's eyes blurred, and when they refocused, she saw the broken ends lined just right inside the Overseer's leg. A faint glow surrounded the tibia, and little tingles of light heated her fingertips. Kissa shook her head, and when she blinked, her vision returned to normal. No time to think more of it. She quickly applied the salve to prevent infection and faster healing.

Finally, Kissa wrapped Elder Harmon's leg with one of Benji's tunics and a makeshift splint from wood from the forest. Feeling sated that she did what she could for now, Kissa released a breath. Then she rinsed her hands again with water.

"Thank you, Kissa." Elder Harmon said. The exhaustion from the pain encased his eyes.

Kissa, tired too, still gave an encouraging smile. "I'm sorry I can do nothing for the pain, but I set it correctly to heal."

Benji gave his father water, and then, with a group effort, they sat him on Dream. Without their horses, her father's warhorse was the only one suitable to carry two. Though the stomp of Dream's hooves and the huff she gave said she didn't like it one bit.

Benji rode with Kissa on Sky. Then the group continued in the night. The Commander eventually rode up next to Kissa. His face was stern, watching the forest keenly, but he didn't say a word. None of them did.

As they entered Kissa's land, her cottage grew larger in the distance, and so did her anxiousness, though they left the danger behind. It was what awaited her that caused her nerves to tighten like a taut bowstring. She told herself that being alone wasn't the worst thing in the world. She knew how to keep up the land on her own. Better yet, the land seemed to care for itself, an unusual fact she never looked too close at until that moment.

"We will rest when we return and leave at first light," her father said. Then he looked at Kissa with a pensive look. "You did well back there. Your mother will be very proud."

"Thank you." She felt the warmth of his simple words.

Her father was not an outwardly emotional man, so she knew his praise was from the heart. Kissa looked over and saw Harmon sleeping against his chest. She had checked on him occasionally to ensure he did not chafe his ankle on the journey. When she looked back at her father, his eyes were now on her. Worry gathered like a storm cloud behind his stoic look.

He didn't have to say anything. Unease rolled through the Commander's eyes and it seemed to gather with Kissa's own concern. Not much ruffled him, but the shadows and black blood were unnatural. She also couldn't shake the distinct feeling that someone was targeting them. Who? Kissa did not think she wanted to know.

———◇———

When they reached her home, the three of them helped Elder Harmon down, and then Benji and her father took him inside the cottage. Kissa tied up the horses, watered and fed them, then started brushing them down. The motion of it calmed her nerves and helped her put off going in and saying goodbye to her father a little longer.

However, it didn't matter. Her father's unmistakable silhouette exited the cottage, no doubt coming to check on her. When he approached, he said nothing as he picked up a brush and stroked down Dream. They tended to the horses in contemplative silence.

"Have you thought about what I said this morning?" The Commander asked, breaking the hush over the night.

Kissa forced a smile. "I have. I appreciate your confidence in me."

"But?" her father asked with a brow raised.

Her smile turned sad. "I am considered different no matter where I go, Father. My hair and eyes will never change, but that is something I have learned to conceal my whole life. But the barracks...I cannot change being a woman."

Her father nodded. She knew he understood. There were no women in the ranks of Scorpions.

She touched his shoulder. "When I aided Elder Harmon... I cannot explain it. It was a euphoria I never experienced before. There is no greater feeling than helping others." A genuine smile crossed her lips as she thought of what she did. "I know where my heart lies...I want to be a healer, Father."

His mouth twitched, the make of a smile. Pride flickered in his eyes as he said, "I know, without a doubt, that you will be amazing in everything you do."

Hearing her father's approval smoothed over the ache of facing life alone. It made her feel confident in her decision. Her smile widened, and she realized something in that moment: Being a healer was her self paved destiny, as her mother put it. If the Fates had something else in store for her, she would cross that bridge when she came upon it.

They walked back to the cottage together. When they entered, there was an intense exchange between Benji and his father. A fire warmed the space, and Kissa smelled heated-up leftover stew from the morning.

"It looked similar to those with the sickness," Elder Harmon said. He looked much better as he sat on Kissa's favorite cushioned chair, resting his injured foot on the pouf.

This perked her ears. "What do you mean?"

"Their blood. It turns black as they're infected with the sickness." Benji said. "We are trying to figure out the connection."

She thought about the dead man's skin. From a distance it looked mottled, something that occurs when someone is near death. In all her studies, Kissa never read of any disease causing one's blood to turn black.

"Do you think it has something to do with the witches?" Benji asked the Commander who was now stoking the fire.

The malevolent name made her immediately think of the old woman who sold her the Chonda ring. In her gut, she sensed a connection between these two events. Something urged her to tell her father, but tell him what?

His face was unreadable as he said, "I have never seen a wolf like that. There is a possibility that there is a connection to the sickness. That it was a lone wolf is unusual. I have a strong feeling there are more of them. I'll need to alert the High Commander and the Elite when I return."

Kissa agreed with her father's assessment. The beast that attacked them was not a natural creature of the forest. The way it grew in size and evaporated like smoke, it felt otherworldly. As she tried to figure out the connection between the crone, the sickness, and the wolf, she grabbed a clean towel, thread, and needle, then sat beside Elder Harmon to inspect his injury.

She knew he needed stitches, but wanted to see if it could hold off until he returned to Serenity. Kissa unwrapped the tunic fabric and makeshift wood from around his leg and her eyes widened in disbelief. The skin had already mended around the injury—only a dark, jagged scar showed.

Kissa felt around, and her fingertips glowed underneath like before. Again, she saw through his skin and flesh right down to the bone—the bone that was aligned properly and already showed on the mend as if the injury occurred weeks ago. Kissa had no words.

How? she thought.

Elder Harmon looked at her worriedly. "Is everything alright?" He asked, now trying to look closer at his injury.

Kissa forced a smile as she said, "Yes! You don't need any stitches."

"Well, that is good news indeed!" He said, smiling warmly.

She noticed him look upon her thoughtfully as she re-wrapped his ankle. He winced slightly as she tightened it. Then, she grabbed him a bowl of strew from the table and passed it to him. He nodded his thanks and held the bowl for a moment.

"Kissa, are you ready to fight for your right to attend Serenity?" He asked.

The question caught her off guard. She didn't know what she expected him to say, but that was not it. She looked around and noticed they were alone. The crackling fire was the only movement around them.

"The Shadora Council has already rejected my submission."

Harmon scooted up in the chair in a fluid motion and pointedly looked at her. "That is not what I asked you." His eyes softened. "It will not be easy. Serenity is rigid and set in its ways. Laying down the seeds of inclusion takes time. But Kissa, we need healers like you. The kingdom needs you."

Kissa's mind drifted to earlier in the forest. She knew exactly what to do, as if by instinct—a natural urge fueled by adrenaline. The fear of seeing death didn't stop her from nocking her arrow, jumping to Benji's aid, or assisting Harmon's injury. Kissa knew now that she could push her fears aside when it mattered.

A feeling of resolve fell over her, already kindled from the conversation she had with her father. The deepest part of her that wanted to save her people had not changed, but she needed to wrap her mind around the reality of it all. Becoming a healer would not be easy or quick, and Kissa had to accept that narrow-mindedness and death were two enemies she would cross swords with often.

"Yes!" she said. "I am ready to fight."

Harmon grinned with a hint of pride in his eyes. "Very good. You have proved that you are a fighter. The way you attended to me despite the dangers—calm and focused. That, my dear, tells me you have the makings of a High Healer. Just like your mother."

Kissa's eyes widened at the compliment. A High Healer was one of the highest titles for a Zuranian. They oversaw healers all over the world, running hospitals and small clinics.

Her brows furrowed. "What about the Shadora Council?"

"While I normally agree with the majority votes in the Council's decisions, I feel I must overrule them this time. I am Overseer and a vital part of that council. You have proved your natural ability. I have seen it with my own eyes." His eyes filled with pride.

Kissa felt nothing but gratitude for his advocacy for her. To think she started this day feeling like her dreams were no longer fruitful. Now she had the chance she always wanted.

"I am ready." She said with even more conviction.

"Then let us get to Serenity with haste." Elder Harmon said with enthusiasm.

Amused at his anticipation, Kissa stifled her chuckle and settled for a smile. "I think you should eat your stew and rest for a while."

"Yes, slow down, Father. You won't be going anywhere with haste anytime soon." Benji said. He and the Commander walked in holding wood for the fire. The Overseer scowled at his son. Kissa couldn't hold back her smile. She knew Harmon would be on his feet before they knew it.

Benji winked at Kissa knowingly. She'd proven her abilities in a natural setting—well, as natural as a wolf of shadows that bled black blood could be. But she earned her acceptance, and that felt greater than any ring that gave her any wishes.

A thought came to her. She turned to the Overseer. "What about my birth records?"

"I have already handled that, Kissa," her father said. "That will not be an issue. We will leave at first light. Everyone, get some rest."

Harmon looked at her with a smirk. "Tomorrow then?"

Kissa's heart warmed with satisfaction as she grinned from ear to ear. "Tomorrow."

8

SERENITY

KISSA

THE WHITEWASHED STONE OF Serenity reminded Kissa of the ruins of the First Temple, and she wondered if the same builders made them. Two towers flanked the main building, lending a touch of enchantment to Serenity, as if it were a realm unto itself. In a way, it was.

As per her mother, Queen Safiyah bestowed the abandoned small castle upon the Zuranians as a gesture of peace twenty-five summers ago. The small castle had originally belonged to them before the war, and as a gesture of gratitude, King Tor, the ruler of Zurania, transformed it into a school for healing.

The land around Serenity displayed a natural fence of shrubs and white orchids, with violet harebells that grew between. Benji led them through the manicured property and around a serene pond with vibrant yellow lilies on top of the water. The water surrounding the school was calm, resembling a peaceful moat that added a touch of charm to the campus. Their path led them across a beautifully constructed, white-painted wooden bridge. They dismounted, and Kissa's eyes drew to the intricate details of the lovely sculpted fountains that lined the pathway to the entrance.

Benji helped his father off his mount and all of three of them stared in awe as he walked on his own with a makeshift cane her father made him. She knew they thought what she did—that he shouldn't be able to stand, let alone walk. They saw the broken tibia just as she did, but Kissa didn't want to think too much about the light on her fingertips or his speedy recovery and what that might mean.

A young page, wearing brown robes, ran toward the group quickly. Benji nodded with a smile and handed their reins to him. Brown robes signaled staff and not students or teachers.

The young man peered at Harmon's foot with concern. "My Lord, you are injured!"

Marquis smiled before saying, "I am fine. Nothing some rest won't mend." He turned to Kissa and her father. "Atsu is our loyal page. He will take good care of your horses while here."

As the others walked toward the entrance, Kissa subconsciously gripped her keepsake hidden underneath her tunic as she stood in the school's grandness. Its natural exquisiteness made it all feel like a dream. The long towers with lancet windows built into the stone seemed to stare right into the heart of her. The confidence she built on her way there felt unsteady, making her question her resolve.

Am I ready for this?

As if sensing her anxiousness, her father walked up next to her as Benji and his father went in. "This is where your mother and I first met nearly 30 summers ago," he said. "Even then, I remember feeling a bit intimidated."

Kissa felt amused by that. Her father was the most formidable man she knew, leading legions and commanding respect in everything and from everyone. But as she entered the school's foyer, she understood exactly what he meant.

Despite not being a sacred temple like the House of Life, Serenity still held a loftiness to its air. Kissa stared at an alabaster sculpture of her mother's goddess, taking up most of the space from floor to ceiling. Wearing a regal crown, the Ancient of Grace kneeled down and tenderly touched the head of a small human child at her feet.

Though the work was fine craftsmanship, Kissa held back the eye roll she wanted to give. She knew the reverence Zuranians held for their goddess ran deep, so she held her tongue. However, the proud, massive sculpture didn't soften her inimical feelings toward the deities.

The door to their left opened, and a slightly built man taller than Kissa stiffly approached the group. He was no older than her father, with dark, short curly hair and a long goatee that reached his upper chest. Kissa would have thought him handsome if the blades he shot from his citrine eyes and the disdain on his face weren't present.

He seemed to struggle to mask it or, more likely, he didn't care. His robe was a pristine white with gold edging and cincture, just like Elder Harmon. An Elder, then. He held books, Kissa couldn't see the title of, in his arm.

"Ah, Fadel, we finally made it. How are things here?" Elder Harmon asked.

The man's face morphed into concern as his attention rested on the Elder's wrapped foot and cane in his hand. "Harmon, what has happened to you?"

The Overseer waved his hand dismissively. "I am quite fine. All I need is some rest."

"If you are sure," Fadel said. He nodded to Benji as an afterthought. Then, with a haughty air, not even acknowledging Kissa or her father, he added, "You will find that Serenity is in the perfect condition you left her in."

Kissa glanced at Benji, who rolled his eyes and murmured something under his breath. She noticed Marquis did not mention the wolf attack or the extent of his injuries. She wondered about the relationship between the two elders underneath all the pleasantries.

"Of course, I left it in the best of hands. Councilor Fadel, you know Commander Ashtar, Onya's husband." Then Harmon touched Kissa's shoulder. "Let me introduce their daughter, Kissa. She will be our newest student. I am hoping to enroll her this cycle." Then he squeezed her shoulder lightly. "Kissa, this is Councilor Fadel. He leads the school in my absence and oversees all the student's progress."

If the Councilor's eyes were truly blades, she knew that she and her father would be dead on the spot. Maybe it was the commander's presence that gave her courage, but she kept her composure and refused to look away under the man's glare of indifference.

Fadel cleared his throat. "I regret to remind you we rejected her submission some time ago."

"Yes, I am aware. I have overruled that rejection. Kissa has more than proven her capabilities. If it weren't for her quick actions, I might have lost my foot." Harmon countered.

Kissa swore she saw the vein in Fadel's temple pulse as he looked at Harmon's foot again. Clearly, he did not take kindly to being overruled. "And her birth records?"

"They should be on my desk as we speak. Onya sent them right away."

Kissa's heart pounded with anxiousness. Though she already knew all of this, it didn't stop the slither of doubt creeping into her mind—that it was too good to be true for Elder Harmon to bypass the council's decision.

However, Fadel finally conceded with a curt nod. "As you wish. I will get her schedule and assignments ready this afternoon."

"Well, then that's settled." Harmon concluded with a smile.

Fadel looked at Kissa as if it hurt him to address her and his words came out clipped. "I will allow you to settle in. Tomorrow, before the first meal, come to my office. I will review the schedule, guidelines, and rules with you."

Kissa nodded in respect. Though she couldn't help the satisfaction that coursed through her with Harmon's words, she didn't want to count her berries too early. The Councilor strode to his office and closed the door without giving them another glance.

Elder Harmon chuckled softly. "Don't mind him. He is very rigid and runs the school on a tight ship, but he is great at what he does."

Kissa heard a slight rumble to her left and noticed her father standing stiffly. He flicked his attention to her. Darkness crossed his features. "I guess there is nothing wrong with that."

She disagreed. Fadel didn't care for her presence in the school and that thought gave way to an inkling of feeling that he would make her stay hard for her.

"Benji, I think room 105 is an empty quarter in the women's dorm. I need to rest my old bones. Can you see Kissa there and provide her with whatever she needs?"

"Of course, Father," Benji said.

After leaving Harmon to rest, Benji gave them a brief tour of the school, emphasizing the important places such as the dining hall, classroom floors, and eventually led them to the west tower. He explained the towers held the dorms of the students. Gender separated the towers, and both maintained 20 floors. The councilors' and instructor's private chambers were on the first floor of the main building, and they took shifts "patrolling" the towers at night.

As they entered the west tower, metal stairs spiraled up its center. Each floor held five dorm rooms, and a shared lavatory and washroom. In addition, the shared space surrounding the stairs on each floor comprised a lounge area with a simple chaise, chairs, and tables. Kissa's room was on the 10th floor.

As she and her father entered her new room, she allowed hope to fill her heart again. The room was simple, with cream-colored walls, bed linen, and curtains. A wardrobe stood against the right wall with a long mirror on its door. On the left, under the only window, was her bed. Kissa's eyes slightly widened at the yellow robe laying neatly across it. The first year robe.

Second-year students wore green, and the third-year donned blue. The fourth-year students wore gray like Benji's, and graduates and above wore the revered white robes—like her mother.

Immediately, Kissa walked over to the small bed, and picked up the robe with a smile. A small feeling of accomplishment flushed through her. Then, she stood on her bed and opened the pale, bland curtains. The sight of the city of Zuberi left her speechless, her eyes wide with amazement.

This was the closest she'd ever been to the sprawling city. The drawings in her books didn't do it justice. At the top of it all, Horus Citadel stood mighty, a guardian watching over the city. She stepped down off her bed, and her father walked up behind her.

"I know you have dreamed of this since you were a little girl. You most certainly deserve to be here," her father said.

Kissa sighed. "But?"

"I think you have already discovered that the path will not be easy."

Stepping out of her land for a day brought so many unexpected events. It opened her eyes to the real world. Kissa still could not wrap her mind around shadow wolves, magic trinkets, and the depth of the sickness ravaging her kingdom. Her parents prepared her as best as possible, homeschooling her with their knowledge, experience, and books, but those things didn't hold a candle to actually experiencing it.

Still, she owed it to them and herself to give it everything.

"Your mother and I didn't have a peaceful time when we married. Many opposed our marriage, fearing others would follow our example and 'taint the blood,' as they said. So, although we earned our positions time and time again, it took twice the dedication and time to receive them."

Kissa's heart flared with indignant anger on behalf of her parents. She, too, would have to work twice as hard to prove herself to everyone else. The world didn't like different.

She turned to her father. "Thank you for letting me go to Sapphire City and for believing in me." She shook her head with a grin. "I know it went against your protective nature."

The Commander chuckled. "I knew the hardships you would face. But your all-wise mother helped me realize I can't hide you from the world nor shield you from harsh realities. It will only hurt you later. Knowledge of our circumstance is how we learn and become strong against it. But I have long known you are a force to be reckoned with. You will soon learn what it takes to control that fire in your heart, daughter." He pointed at her chest where her sundial rested. "And when to use it."

Only embers now, Kissa felt her fire hum against her chest. It would only become more challenging to control from now on. Especially if she had to "fight" as everyone kept warning her. Even more, the things she learned to do at home might not be applicable here. She'd need to find a new routine.

Her father's words dripped with a deeper meaning, though. As he looked out the window upon his kingdom, his dark eyes hinted at sadness, and she wished she could take it away. She could feel his indecisiveness, fear, and love fighting for dominance. She did not understand these new sensations. They troubled her.

"What is it, Father?" She braced herself.

He didn't take his eyes off the capital. "You will discover things you thought all your life were impossible, even wondrous. But there will also be times when what you find may not be what you hoped for. I cannot stop you from trying to find your blood parents." He turned his attention to her. "I just hope they are worth it when you do."

She had thought about finding them, but he didn't seem too happy about that. Was he jealous? No, he wanted her to be happy, and it wasn't in him to be that way. Something else bothered him.

"What do you mean?" She pushed.

Her father gave her a pointed look. "The less you know, the safer you are."

Her brows furrowed. "Didn't you just tell me that knowledge of our circumstance is how we learn and become strong against it?"

"I do not keep things from you to be spiteful. I physically cannot. The Oath keeps my tongue bound. I have already said too much."

Oh.

She didn't know why it still shocked her. He told her as much before. The rigidness of his posture told her he was wrestling with himself. An icy chill gathered at her spine.

He grabbed her hand. "Just be mindful of who you divulge anything to. When it is time, I will tell you. Until then, be watchful, choose your battles wisely, and fight with everything in you when the need arises. Promise me."

The passion with which he said the last words made the ice already coating her spine feel like a heavy glacier. Her stomach twisted in knots, trying to understand what he wasn't saying. Despite how she felt, though, he would never let her stay if he thought she couldn't handle herself.

"I promise," Kissa said.

After putting away her things, Kissa sat on her bed crisscrossed, with her eyes glued to the capital. Her father's mysterious words continued to play in her head. *You will discover things you thought all your life were impossible, even wondrous.*

The sound of the gong made Kissa jump. Again. The sound echoed through her room and through her soul. Once, twice, a third time. Suddenly, the sound of laughter outside caught her attention, and she glanced down towards the landscaped grounds to see students pouring out. The end of classes.

Kissa didn't want to stay in her room any longer, but where would she go? As if on command, her stomach growled in answer. Deciding to go to the dining hall, she jumped up and grabbed her satchel. She opened the door, and a tall girl with an afro-style bob and a green hair bow stood before her.

The pristine girl did not have one hair out of place. Her white toes, perfectly polished and evenly trimmed, were visible in her white sandals that she tied up her calf and disappeared under her green robe. But the perfectly contempt look on her face gave Kissa pause. No introduction or greeting came from the girl, just...

"The High Councilor expects you before the breakfast gong tomorrow."

Kissa raised a brow as the girl handed her a parchment that read the same. The personal messenger seemed a bit much, but maybe that was the way in Serenity.

"What is your name?" She tried to break the awkwardness.

"Lani Fadel." Her chin raised, as if Kissa should already know.

"Okay, Lani Fadel. Thank you for the message." Kissa tucked the message in her satchel. She turned to close the door behind herself and lock it. When she turned back, Lani still stood there, now with a heated glare like Kissa broke every law in the kingdom.

"You cannot roam the halls without your robe."

Kissa looked down at her ordinary clothing. At that very moment, slamming the door in the girl's smug face was tempting, but her last name rang a bell and Kissa didn't need those problems. She swiftly returned to her room to put on her robe.

"Happy?" Kissa closed the door behind her again.

"Why are you wearing that silly head wrap? It's not appropriate school attire," the girl said.

Kissa froze in place. "What is wrong with it?"

"It is unkempt...and suspicious." Her gaze turned skeptical.

She heard her own frustration in her voice as she said, "Suspicious? Do you not have better things to do than question someone's clothing choice?"

The girl's mouth lifted into a wicked smile that felt like it had the power to undo everything she hoped for. Then Lani silently turned on her pretty trimmed toes and walked toward the exit.

Kissa waited a few moments before following her down the spiral stairs. Then left the tower with all the intentions of finding the dining hall. At first, she thought the lingering stares of the students were mere curiosity. She greeted them politely, but they said nothing in return, only wariness lay in their eyes.

Taking a left down a hallway she thought was familiar, she eventually came to a grand staircase centered in a heavily decorated foyer. The aroma of spiced chickpeas and something sweet baking down the hall reached her, but curiosity moved her eyes across the multiple floors above her. *Classrooms*, Benji said.

The second floor landing of the staircase was short, with stairs leading up to it on both sides. Kissa took the stairs closest to her to get a better look. The other levels had long landings with polished wooden railings on each side that led to hallways. Deciding that dinner could wait, she climbed the first set of stairs.

The adjacent halls featured a uniform arrangement of doors to rooms. Wooden plaques above them signified the class. The next two floors were just as uneventful, so she climbed to the fourth level. It was here that Kissa felt a strong tingle within her. Not a warning this time, but more of an urging, if she had to describe it. Less intrusive than the pull she felt from the strange blue eyed warrior at the First Temple. Yet, similar.

Kissa pushed down the image of the half dressed man and the flutters that accompanied him, as she investigated the corridor to her left. She noticed that this hall's paintings differed from the rest of the typical Zuranian landscapes and seascapes that decorated the rest of the school. She slowed to a stop in front of a canvas larger than her.

Her mouth parted as she took in the majestic bird before her. Its black feathers cascaded down the creature's head and body, then blended into various blues of indigo and sapphire to the tips of the wings and tail. The background, a deep purple sky with three moons and countless colorful stars, caused gooseflesh to rise on her arms.

The bird seemed to fly right at her, and its deep amber eyes burned like the sun as it pinned her where she stood. An unexpected pang formed in her chest, for they strangely reminded her of her sister Aya's eyes. Maybe it was because she missed her, but Kissa could not ignore the similarities. Aya's irises reminded Kissa of honey. After a long moment, she tore her eyes away to observe the next painting.

The urging seemed to grow as she stood in front of the next mural. Kissa knew from other portraits that the woman laying peacefully on the vibrant green grass was Zuri in her physical human form. The graceful goddess wore a soft white dress that draped over her lean curves and accented her copper toned skin and deep brown pixie cut. Her head was on the lap of what had to be another goddess.

Kissa tilted her head as she racked her brain, but could not recall this Ancient. The unknown goddess had black, tightly curled hair that was full and ended at her hips, almost touching the grass. The artist captured her staring to the left toward a familiar forest of fall colored trees.

Za Forest?

The goddess had a poise about her as she touched Zuri's head in a nurturing way. Were they sisters? Kissa couldn't recall the Ancients having siblings. Maybe they were best friends? Kissa scoffed at the idea that the fickle deities had normal relationships. That would be way too human.

Kissa walked up close to the painting. The goddess' golden brown skin shimmered slightly in the painting's sun. Her eyes appeared hazel green, and Kissa thought she could see flecks of silver and gold, but couldn't be sure. Something about her felt so familiar, which was odd. She had no clue who she was.

Almost touching the mural with her nose, Kissa tried to get a better look at her eyes. She wished the artist would have painted her looking forward so she could see her irises more clearly. None of the Ancients had Kissa's eye color, though she always wondered why. Maybe it was just an error on the artist's part.

"I see you're finding your way around."

So engrossed in the painting, Kissa jumped and whipped around to see Benji leaning on the wall with an amused look. His light golden eyes appeared cunning and mischievous at that moment. His light brown hair, only a few inches, curled messily and complimented his smooth, terra-cotta skin.

It was at this moment that Kissa remembered where she saw him before. The rider in the forest the other day.

She assessed him with inquisitive eyes now, but it made little sense. He never had a sword with him, and if he did, why didn't he use it with the shadow wolf? What was he doing coming from the First Temple so deep in Za Forest? She didn't want to say something and be wrong. It was too early to test the new friendship blossoming between them.

Instead, she narrowed her eyes playfully. "Yes, I was tired of waiting for you to come save me from my boredom." Then she rolled her eyes.

A lighthearted chuckle escaped him, and his eyes sparkled with a youthful glow. "I didn't know you were waiting for me."

"Clearly!" Then she spun back to the painting at hand. "Do you know who this is?" Kissa pointed to the unknown goddess.

"Ah! Yes. That is a rare depiction of the Ancient of Life."

Kissa's brows furrowed. "I never heard of her." Though she purposely did not study more than the basics of religion, she knew with certainty that the Ancient of Life was not part of *The Seven*.

Benji leaned on the wall next to her. "Most don't. The Ancient of Life didn't make any of us in her likeness, though she created us. She created all living beings, including *The Seven*... a truth lost to time. I always wondered why that was."

Kissa's brows raised in shock. How could she have missed that in her studies? Somehow, she didn't think she did. She suspected that someone intentionally removed it from her learning. But why?

Her mind spun with the new information. She never thought of the Ancients having a beginning, being gods and all. So, to know that someone else created them astounded her. She had to admit that seeing the deity this intimately incited something in her. This goddess was life, and because of her, everything else existed.

So why did no one worship her? Or was she forgotten? Kissa felt an unusual sadness for the Ancient. They should worship her above all others.

Confused by her own feelings, Kissa backtracked to the first mural of the mighty majestic bird. "And who might this be?" Kissa asked.

"This amazing portrait is the only one in all the world. It is Zuri in her familiar form," Benji said.

Kissa sighed with disappointment that it wasn't someone else she didn't know about, but her dissatisfaction couldn't eclipse the beauty of the glorious portrait. However, the longer she stared at the Ancient's long talons, fluorescent wing tips, and eyes as bright as the sun, she grew sad. Zuri alone possessed the ability to wipe out sickness... and she did nothing. Where was her *grace* now?

Kissa's eyes burned from the unshed tears for those dying at this very moment. The Ancient's selfish inaction was precisely why she didn't put her faith in them. Why pray to someone that didn't care?

"Are you okay?" Benji asked. No doubt witnessing her internal conflict.

Kissa nodded as she wiped the unwelcome tear that fell on her cheek. The concern on Benji's face didn't overcome the fact that he loved his goddess. Kissa didn't dare tell him her true feelings. As she parted her lips to tell him she was fine, the initials L.R. on the corner of the canvas grabbed her attention.

"Who is the artist?" She asked curiously, nodding to the initials.

Benji's face turned up at her question. "You want to meet her?"

"You mean she is here?" Kissa did not mask her surprise.

He nodded. "Come." Then gestured for her to walk with him.

Her brow raised at his invitation. She saw a glint of amusement in his eyes. Clearly, this artist was important to him. Curiosity nagged at her as she bit her bottom lip. Honestly, Kissa had little else to do.

9

MURALS & DREAMS

KISSA

THEY DIDN'T GO FAR, stopping at a partly cracked door at the end of the same corridor. At first glance, the art that covered the door reminded Kissa of doodling. Colorful drawings of flowers, stars, and rainbows graced the outer part of the door. In the center, a painting showed a blindfolded man on a wooden chair. He held a harp and tilted his head toward it as if listening to his own music.

"That is a depiction of Miro, the Ancient of Tranquility."

Something itched at her the longer she stared at the painting. "Why does he wear a bandage over his eyes?"

"He is blind. For Miron's, creation is in here," Benji pointed to her heart.

Kissa's mouth dropped. "The Ancient of Tranquility is blind? Then how does he see what he is playing, or painting, or...anything?" She knew the Ancient's primary power of Dream Casting through basic history reading, but she discovered he had a passion for art and loved painting, music, and dancing.

"He feels it."

His words resonated deep in Kissa's spirit and suddenly she was at the meadow on her land, feeling the smooth wood of her bow, and the vibration of the arrow and string between her fingers. Chills crept through her body at the feeling. "I get it."

Benji stared at her with an unreadable expression for a moment, then gestured for Kissa to lead the way. When she walked in and took in the room, she gasped. It felt like she walked into somewhere else entirely.

The walls were a soft green, almost mint. Beautiful landscape paintings of waterfalls, mountains, deserts, and beaches covered each of them. Candles brightened most of the space, giving a soft glow. Fresh-cut flowers in beautiful, various-sized painted vases filled the room. Some vases, half her size, held outstretched plants she didn't even know the name of, giving the space a tropical forest vibe. Even the floor, covered in lush carpet, gave the feeling of standing on white-colored sand.

She didn't even know where to start, so she turned back toward the door to view the wall behind her first. Kissa's breath left her.

Across the entire wall was a lifelike portrait of a mountain she recognized—Aarusha. Her kingdom looked as if she was seeing it for the first time. The perspective from afar captured the kingdom in its entirety. The artist depicted Osmond's light, the harbor, and the boardwalk with painstaking detail. Even tiny fishing boats traversed the waters. The dark leaves of Za Forest glimmered in the sun at the tips. At the very summit, Horus Citadel stood just as perfect as if she were looking at it from her new bedroom window.

Kissa had no words. The skill set to make something like this was far beyond her. As she finally turned to take in the other murals—also painted in fine, precise detail—she wondered if they, too, were different parts of the world. But her curiosity moved her forward to the plants she recognized as purple petals of lavender and clusters of mint mingling with others in the air. A quiet trickling sound of water came from somewhere within, but the mass of plant life made it hard to pinpoint where.

The space exuded tranquility. As Kissa turned fully, she tried to put a name to it all, but fell short. If she did, she didn't think any words could even come close to encompassing the creative work around her. It felt so inviting, and she didn't even realize the tension in her shoulders loosened. Any conflicted feelings she felt beforehand melted away the moment she stepped inside the door.

Maneuvering through the creative forest, she danced from plant to plant, guessing the names and smelling their fragrances. She finally made it to the far wall, where a simple iron bed with a wide wooden dresser with six drawers sat beside it. The dresser had glasses full of various colored paint, all precisely in order by shade. Vibrant reds, yellows, pinks, blues, violets and everything in between. The artist neatly lined brushes from longest to shortest in clear vases. This part of the room didn't fit with the rest. It was... too normal.

To the left, a floor-to-ceiling window with open louvered shutters revealed the darkening sky and the school's gardens. This was where Kissa observed a young girl with a flowing, butter-colored dress staring out into the view with her back to her. Her thick wavy earth-brown hair with lighter brown highlights fell down her back and reminded Kissa of spring soil when life begins anew. She assumed she was in this girl's room since there was nobody else and only one bed.

Intrigued, she walked over to the girl. "Hello!"

When the girl turned, Kissa startled. Two different eye colors stared back at her. The iris on the right was green, and the left beamed an amber brown. Though she reminded her of a doll, she was no little girl, just small. In fact, Kissa gaged her to be only a summer or two younger than herself. Her tawny and fair skin blended into soft rosy cheeks that uplifted her heart-shaped face.

Her eyes did not dart around as Kissa expected, assessing her differences. They seemed to stare through her, not at her. Before she could think more of it, the young lady pinched her brows.

"Who are you?" she asked.

"Oh, I am Kissa." She felt sheepish, as if she crowded the girl's personal space—or all her space since they did not knock before entering. So, Kissa moved back to give her room.

The young woman resumed her stare out the window, wrapping her arms around herself. Then, with a slight accent confirming her origins, she said, "There is a tension in the air. Can you feel it? Something comes."

Confused at her statement, Kissa glanced out the window and stared at the pond and manicured garden that greeted her when she first came. Since she did not know Serenity or the girl well, she didn't know what to make of the perceptive question.

"Benji, your back?" The Miron artist squealed as if she didn't make a profound statement a moment ago, shaking Kissa from her thoughts.

She realized she left Benji at the door and didn't even hear him approach. The girl wrapped her arm around his waist familiarly. He smiled, embracing her back. Kissa thought she felt something not her own, but she couldn't describe it. Only that she sensed the two were possibly more than friends.

"Layla, meet Kissa. She is new to Serenity," Benji said.

Layla nodded, skeptical. Or was that curiosity? Again, she didn't meet her eyes, staring right through Kissa.

Benji gave a look, as if apologizing for the girl's rudeness. "Layla is one of my dearest friends. She is also the artist that painted these extraordinary murals." The artist's rosy cheeks beamed a little brighter at the praise.

"All of them?" Kissa asked in awe.

"Yes, most of the ones in the school, anyway. Layla has lived here most of her life."

Kissa's eyes widened. She felt astounded by both the visual magnificence Layla composed and the strangeness that she actually lived in Serenity. Was she a healer, too? The artist did not wear robes. However, she didn't want to be rude and ask about it. The girl was already looking at her suspiciously.

"You are so talented. It is a pleasure to meet you," Kissa said.

Layla's eyes narrowed, studying her like she couldn't put her finger on something. She never looked directly at Kissa, but she felt the focus all the same. Maybe she was determining if she liked her or not. Or, more likely, if she was a threat. Possibly something else entirely. Kissa cursed her sheltered life.

"Thank you," Layla finally said. Then she glanced up at Benji, who was almost two of her. "Would you two like to play Mind's Eye with me? It should be more fun with the three of us."

Snatching the opportunity to learn more about the mysterious girl who seemed to draw her in, Kissa piped up. "Sure!" She said maybe too excitedly. "You will need to teach me. I am not familiar with the game."

Layla nodded with the beginning of a smile. "It is not difficult."

Benji waved his free arm in a dramatically bored way. "Yes, this is one of the many games the children play in Layla's part of the world."

"I am no child," Layla snapped back, though amusement sparked in her eyes as she looked up at him. "Mirons merely exercise our minds regularly, specifically memory. Something *you* should do more of."

"What have I forgotten now?" Benji asked in exasperation.

Layla looked toward Kissa, then, possibly thinking better of whatever she was about to say, said, "We will talk about it later."

Kissa watched the graceful artist stride to her bed confidently, as if she were a dancer. She wondered if all Mirons glided that way. Kissa paid extra attention to her father's lessons about their kingdom's culture, filled with artists, musicians, and dancers. It fascinated her. She learned their God inspired their creative ideas through dreams. Gazing at all the murals behind them, Kissa wondered how true that was.

She approached Layla's bed and sat at the end as the artist sat at the head, giving them enough room in between. Benji pulled up a chair from somewhere within Layla's forest and sat between them. Then the artist pulled out a small stack of parchment from a drawer next to her. The front image of the stack had a detailed, lifelike painting of a horse that reminded Kissa of Sky.

"May I?" she asked.

Layla handed her some of the small square-shaped parchment, the size of her palm. They felt pressed like the ones she wrote on, but stiffer, as if multiple pressed into one, making it hard to bend. She noticed the colorful illustrations raised slightly on the parchment. The other side felt smooth with nothing on it.

"Did you make these?" Kissa looked through the intricate paintings of various animals in awe.

"Yes, they are called cards," Layla said.

Kissa only nodded in reply as she gave them back. She watched in curiosity as Layla shuffled them nimbly—wondering how she made even that seem wondrous.

"There is an animal on each card. We will lay them face down. The goal is to find the matching cards." Her voice sounded like a lullaby, and Kissa wondered if the girl was a singer, too.

Layla started the game with a brief instruction by flipping over a duck and then a goat. She touched the raised illustrations on both briefly. "See, these don't match. But I must remember where they are when I find their matching pair." Then she flipped them face down again.

As she watched Layla, Kissa's mind flashed back to the Miron symbol on the girl's door. The feeling that something evaded her senses itched at her again. At her turn, she flipped over a tiger and luckily found the other on the first try.

"Very good! We will play until all the matches are found. The person with the most matches wins," Layla said.

They enjoyed the clever game as the three of them played together. Benji was purposefully dramatic, to Layla's delight. He scowled when he didn't find matches and became animated when any of them did. Kissa did not know the last time she ever felt this lighthearted and relaxed.

They chatted about their lives, and she eventually learned that Layla was born with a sick heart. When she was five summers, her parents brought her from Miro to seek Elder Harmon, who specialized in her condition. She stayed under his care at the House of Life. Unfortunately, her parents died from a sickness called malaria, the same as Kissa's mother's parents. With no other family able to care for her with a sick heart, Elder Harmon took her in and brought her to Serenity.

As Layla told the story, the ache in Kissa's chest grew into a full-blown heartbreak. She found it strange since she didn't know this girl or her parents, but she felt it all the same. Confused, she looked at Benji, who now comforted Layla with his arm around her. Kissa knew there wasn't anything that she could say. Apologies would not bring her parents back.

"You are so strong, Layla. I couldn't imagine being alone in a foreign place, but it seems you made a life for yourself here."

She meant that. Layla lived with a sick heart, lost both her parents, and had to live in a distant land with no family. If that wasn't strength, Kissa did not know what was.

Layla patted Benji's arm. "Thank you. But I wasn't alone. Benji and his family made sure of that."

Kissa could not help the yearning inside her. More than anything, she wished for the same. After a few moments of uncomfortable silence, Kissa looked toward the window to see night fall. She didn't want to overstay her welcome.

She glanced at Benji and gave him a nod. "It's getting late. I think I'm going to head back to my room."

Benji stood up with a smirk. "I will walk you to the dorms. I wouldn't want you getting lost."

Kissa had no argument with that logic. She looked at Layla. "It was very nice to meet you. I know we just met, but I hope one day we can be friends."

Layla's face smoothed into a smile so bright it was almost angelic. "Of course we will. I have dreamed it."

***

THE LEAVES ON THE familiar Za trees surrounding Kissa were no longer tipped with color but fully changed with fall. She stood under a sky full of glittering stars, and the full moon sat heavy, bigger than she ever remembered seeing it, with an orangish-red hue.

The Harvest Moon. Unease blanketed Kissa. The Harvest Moon was weeks away.

Something pulled her forward toward her sea cliffs. Perturbed, she walked over and stared out into the sea. Mirroring the heavens above, the sea cast each bright star, and the waves caused the orange glowing orb to resemble flames. A beautiful landscape ready for a gifted artist to capture.

The scene had a serene look to it, but it felt misplaced, like a mirage. As she peered further out into the deeper part of the waters, Kissa saw something move between the reflective stars. As it moved closer, its edges sharpened until a clearer picture settled before her.

A deep black vessel, nothing she'd ever seen, cut through the waters with such velocity that it shouldn't have been physically possible. A warship, she gathered. Though in all her books and history lessons with her father, she never read or seen a warship of this make.

As it continued to wade closer, Kissa picked out massive black sails waving against the wind. Her breath hitched. The ship didn't even have oars to row it, but that seemed impossible. Wasn't that the way of the world—the more oars a ship had, the faster it propelled? How else did this vessel maneuver through the waters with such speed?

The answer ensnared her, captivating and vengeful—a powerful energy. Its unwelcome presence ignited a rebellion within her, her fire rose to expel it like a virus. Kissa felt like a spectator in her own body as she felt the heat soar through her and crash against the unwelcomed energy, expelling the sensation. As if the energy trying to invade her was no match against her hostile fire, it evaporated into nothing.

This was not the first time Kissa felt the fire in her chest rise to protect her. Since she could remember, her fire entwined with her emotions as if they were one, but it was the first time she felt it take precise action. Now, it burned low at the pit of her chest like molting embers—like it felt satisfied to be used at last.

As if by magic, the warship faded away like ashes scattered in the wind. When she finally pulled her eyes away from the now shipless sea and looked up, the night sky only held a sea of white stars.

10

SHADOWS & LIGHT

KISSA

Prior to the wake-up call, Kissa snuck to the communal washroom to shower. She felt on edge, an uncanny feeling she couldn't quite shake. The vividness of the ship, a vessel she couldn't conjure in her wildest dreams, left her uneasy and she couldn't fall back to sleep. The warship reminded her of the shadow wolf they encountered in the forest, how its darkness moved at its edges.

Some gifts, like visions, come without warning. The shimmery light's lilting voice echoed in her mind.

Kissa turned on the water and, as the hot stream trickled down her shivering body, she could not warm the cold remnants the dream provoked. Since when did she listen to glittery blobs from her dreams? *Magic did not exist,* she reasoned. Though unsure of the strange happenings, Kissa remained confident on logical answers. At least, that is what she kept murmuring to herself as she tried to wash the vivid memory of the dream away.

With practiced adeptness, she washed and braided her locs into one long braid and wrapped it into a bun. Before departing the stall, she wrapped her head and body with towels, then quickly padded down the hall to her room. Kissa locked the door behind her. Then she made her way to the mirror hanging on her wardrobe.

Unwrapping the towel from her head, she stared at her red hair with displeasure. Was it her blood mother or father that cursed her, then left her in enemy territory to risk the gallows? Shaking her head, she grabbed the yellow scarf with abstract gray designs from her wardrobe.

Through time, she found creative ways to style her *bindings*. A way to feel good about wearing them, she supposed. Her mother insisted that she would start a trend, but Lani's glare at her scarf last night told her not to lay her hopes on that.

A few summers ago, Kissa tried coloring her locs with indigo dye. She thought it would darken her hair, however, it only turned her vibrant red hair to purple. Though she loved the color, it was a pain to get out. Later, after learning how to make black writing ink, she came up with the brilliant idea of dyeing her hair with it. Her mother all but threw her in the tub. Apparently, the soot used for ink was toxic. A few experiments later, she realized the messiness, constant application, and toxicity of it all weren't worth the trouble. She settled on wearing scarves.

However, another thought crossed Kissa's mind. She grabbed her satchel from the door of her wardrobe and grabbed the ring at the bottom. As she examined the signet, a subtle hum hinted at something more. Kissa twisted her lips in contemplation. The old woman claimed her father had forged it. Honestly, it was the real reason she wanted the ring so desperately.

Her mind tried to conjure his face. *Is he Eashitan? An engineer, or a maker of things?* Yet, the concept of silver eyes and hair didn't feel quite right. Kissa briefly considered an idea she avoided thinking about.

The world admired Sagians before the war, as the world's intellects—scholars, philosophers, scientists, and researchers. They discovered the cycles of water, weather patterns, the sun, and the moon. *Brilliant thinkers,* they were called.

A periodical she read a couple summers ago said that Soris the Wise, a Sagian researcher, discovered the theory of photosynthesis, the cycle between trees and oxygen. The deserts of Sagia, said to be hot and desolate, didn't afford him a great environment to test his theories, so he traveled around the world. However, during one of his quests, Leviathan warriors captured him while traveling suspiciously close to Hell's Conception—the ferocious waters between Osmondia and the Isles of Death. Even more, the warriors found a tome and meticulous notes about sacred magic inside the cabin of his ship. The crew of his ship faced immediate execution, but before Soris met his end, the High Chancellor, Sierra Moswen herself, traveled from the Halls of Justice to stop the execution.

The waters Soris and his crew traversed did not belong to Osmondia. Without delay, the Adels escorted Soris back to Sagia. High Chancellor Moswen kept his research and his books to "protect" the *Natural Order of Life*. Kissa always wondered if there was truth to the claims of Sagian wizards and magic.

Who are you? She stared at the ring as if it held the secrets of her origins. That was her genuine desire, down to the core of her. Yet, Kissa refrained. Facing the truth would be difficult for her if she were to learn that her biological father was some evil sorcerer from a distant kingdom. No, Kissa decided. She was not ready just yet. Her wounds were still too raw.

She turned her attention back to the ring, focusing on her current desire. Sliding it on her right ring finger, she held her breath, then waited. One breath, two...

The face of the ring lit up around her finger. The surface of the face warped and, suddenly, the mountain and tree atop it dissolved, causing Kissa's heart to kick up. In its place, a dark onyx dragon head surfaced. Two ruby eyes appeared glowing deviously, and horns sprouted from its nostrils.

In a panic, Kissa snatched the ring off her finger and threw it on the floor. The eyes dimmed, but the menacing dragon visage persisted. It brought back the haunting dream from the previous night like a striking war axe.

Her heart thundered in her ears as her stomach turned. What did it mean? Was it another illusion from the witch? The walls of her room felt like it closed in on her as she tried to grasp some logical explanation.

She flicked her attention to the window, and the twilight sky looked back at her. The wake-up gong felt eons away, and she needed something to reclaim her nerves and thoughts now. Only one thing came to mind.

Kissa opened her wardrobe and snatched up one of her plain scarves, covering her hand with it. Then she reached down and picked up the Chonda ring and wrapped it thrice over and threw it in the back of her wardrobe. Kissa blew out a deep breath. Then she grabbed the hard lute case leaning against the back wall and placed it on her bed.

Kissa stared at it for a few moments before opening it. Then she retrieved her bow and quiver full of gold fletching arrows. Despite the school's rigid laws against weapons, her father—always protective—told her to keep them close. Nobody would think twice about a musical instrument case.

Kissa could already feel the calm as she gripped her bow. Archery was a vital part of her well-being. Last night, she learned from the god of tranquility that she needed her bow like the air she breathed.

She left them on the bed as she wrapped her silk yellow and gray scarf in such a way that not a single hair was shown. Then she put on a cream tunic, black leggings, and finally her robe and boots. Grabbing her bow and quiver of arrows, she slung them over her shoulder. She then threw on her black cloak to cover it all lest she bumped into anyone.

Kissa quickly donned her hood and silently departed the tower. Not a soul greeted her as she tiptoed through the dim halls, headed towards the entrance foyer. After a few wrong turns, the front doors eventually came into sight, but before she exited, muffled male voices reached her ears.

"For four days, she's been in a coma."

Surprised that anyone was awake, she paused. Kissa searched for the source and saw a low light glowing under Elder Harmon's study. She looked back towards the outside and beyond, wrestling with herself for a moment. Then curiosity moved her feet closer to the door to listen.

"The disease seems resistant to the normal antitoxins. It's like it changes and adapts, then devours the regenerated healthy cells."

That was Elder Harmon's voice. They were speaking about the Sleeping sickness. She moved a little closer.

"What if it's magic?"

Kissa's eyes widened. That voice sounded very much like Benji.

"It would answer why nothing so far has worked. But magic? That is beyond

my expertise."

"So she will die."

The man sounded devastated, and his words squeezed at Kissa's heart. Suddenly, movement followed by rushed boot steps came closer to the door. Her breath hitched, and in a mad dash, she crossed the foyer and pushed through the front doors.

⚬

KISSA PASSED THE FOUNTAINS, crossed the bridge, and ventured into the forest. She continued to look back as she moved, scared to be discovered. Finally, she stumbled upon a small clearing beyond the school's borders, nestled within a dense grove of trees.

She listened around her, checking and rechecking how she came. When she felt confident that nobody had caught her eavesdropping or her botched escape, she picked out a tree for her target. When she took off her cloak, she removed her robe as well. Wearing it while shooting a weapon made Kissa feel conflicted. The cool air brushed against her skin, but it felt good. She folded her cloak and robe on top of her satchel, then attached her quiver to her hip.

In the middle of the clearing, Kissa adjusted her bow and, with a deep breath, drew her first arrow. When she released it, she imagined it was all her troubles as of late. Before the arrow hit the target, she released another and another. By the time the last arrow thunk into its target, a familiar calmness enveloped her, and Kissa allowed herself to exhale.

She walked over to grab her arrows for another round, using the time to reflect. First, Kissa considered the Chonda ring, but her stomach tied in knots at the thought, so she moved her mind to the dream. Was it a vision? Kissa couldn't be sure. She shifted her attention to another heavy thought—her mother's tale of Kissa being delivered to them.

She knew for a fact that her mother believed in her story. But Kissa found it hard to accept that a goddess cared about her enough to visit her mother's dreams long before she was born. Why her? Moreover, who delivered her? The woman who bound Kissa's parents with an oath, keeping her from a normal life, was the object of her spite.

As she grabbed the last of the arrows, she felt a tingle—the familiar sensation of being watched. Taking no chances this time, she nocked an arrow and turned. A cloaked man stood in the clearing, semi-illuminated by the stars above, resembling a tall dark shadow. She cursed herself for being so absorbed in her thoughts that she didn't hear him approach.

A sword hanging from his hip caught her eye. She dared not move and kept her arrow pointed at his heart. "Who are you?" A slight quiver in her voice showed her unease.

"I should ask the same of you."

Startled by the resonance of his husky voice, she narrowed her eyes. Not deterred in the slightest by her nocked arrow, he moved a little closer, revealing his deep sepia skin and unshaven face. Kissa's breath hitched as he fully came into view. His piercing gaze stirred her memory of the day at the Temple, and many countless daydreams since then. Dark circles encased his eyes, as if he hadn't slept since she last saw him. Kissa tilted her head, realizing it was his anguished voice she had heard in Harmon's study.

Despite the mysterious dark cloak and short sword, she only felt empathy for the blue-eyed stranger. But if she met him once already, was he still a stranger? *Familiar stranger*, she decided.

Kissa didn't lower her bow, but cocked her head to the side. "Do you like what you see?"

A hint of a smile graced the familiar stranger's lips, and a flutter swept through Kissa. She scowled at her body's inappropriate response to a dangerous situation. She recalled the drums that lured her to him. Kissa needed to keep her wits about her.

"Do you always follow helpless women into the woods?" she asked.

This made him chuckle. "I am a Scorpion. It is my duty to investigate suspicious activity." He took another step closer. "Like, for instance, why a student healer is so adept at archery?" He nodded at her bow. "You don't seem very helpless to me."

Though Kissa felt relief that he confirmed he was a warrior of the kingdom, she didn't like how he catalogued her robe, her eyes, and her bow—multiple things that didn't fit.

Kissa lifted her chin. "Not that it is your business, but I didn't think there was a law against practicing archery in the early morning."

He shifted his eyes upward to glance at the sky. "Is it morning?" He shook his head. "My days blur together sometimes."

Kissa pulled her eyes from the warrior to see pink streaks across the dark expanse. She needed to end this—whatever this was—and head toward Serenity. She lowered her bow.

The warrior lifted a brow and gestured toward her bow. "I thought your people vow against violence and all that."

He had a certain air about him, but she couldn't pin it, which irritated her further. Kissa cursed her sheltered life for the hundredth time. She felt like a guilty child under his watchful gaze.

She scowled. "As you so clearly see, I'm where I am supposed to be. Why are you visiting Serenity in darkness cloaked in shadows, following women into the forest?" Kissa snapped before thinking better of it.

His hint of a smile fell, and darkness crossed his face. Kissa stood tense. All she needed was to be stabbed on her first day of school. It would make Fadel's life more agreeable, but she wasn't about to give that uptight prude his wish so easily. Kissa moved toward her belongings, but she paused when the stranger gestured towards her chest with a gleam in his eyes.

"I'll tell you why I'm here if you tell me about that peculiar necklace," he said.

Kissa glanced down and found her necklace out in the open. Again, she cursed herself. Tucking it in her tunic now would only appear like she was hiding something.

"It is a sundial."

His brows wrinkled in confusion. "Sundial?"

Now it was Kissa's turn to feel confused. "Does nobody else carry a time keeper on their person?"

The warrior shook his head, confusion still on his face. Kissa's brows furrowed. She always thought her father gave it to her, a warrior's gadget. Now she realized she didn't know who gifted it to her.

She slung her bow over her shoulder, then lifted her necklace. "I'll show you how it works if you promise not to stab me."

He chuckled and raised his hands in surrender. "I promise."

She beckoned him closer. He towered over her, and she had to look up to meet his gaze. The darkness of the sky turned his eyes to a Prussian Blue. His hand slightly brushed up against her and a zip coursed through her.

Kissa gathered her focus and pointed to the lines at the outset of the sundial. "These lines represent the hours, and this is the gnomon. When the sun ascends, the gnomon's shadow moves around the dial plate. Each line represents an hour."

As she continued, the smell of him—subtle spice, sandalwood, and a hint of sweat—reached her senses. Kissa felt enamored as his brows sharpened and his almond-shaped eyes danced with intrigue at her words. At the Temple, he had a light dust of stubble on his face, with his hair tied up in a warrior's bun. However, his beard grew thicker and a few locs peaked out from his cloak, heightening his allure.

Excitedly, he said, "That is fascinating. This invention could change everything. Imagine no need to wait for bells to tell the hour!" He looked over at her with a smile. "Did the Eashitans make it? Where did you get it?"

The Eashitan's god, Desire, was the Ancient of Ambition. They made many modern mechanizations, such as the tolling bell, warships, and weapons. Her father told her that their kingdom had buildings as tall as mountains, and Sapphire City had nothing on their trade harbor. During the war, Osmondia wanted to keep their inventors, but Eashitans used the opportunity as a chance to gain their own independence.

"I am not sure who gifted it to me. I've had it since I could remember," she said honestly.

His brows raised in surprise as he gazed into her eyes, as if searching for something. Kissa felt like she could fall into those dreamy blue depths and stay there forever.

"Where are your mother and father?"

The loaded question snapped her out of the trance. Now she knew how her father felt when she "interrogated" him. Though the familiar stranger intrigued her, she didn't feel ready to divulge the chaos of her personal life. Kissa didn't even know his name.

As if he sensed it, he said, "I'm sorry. I let my inquisitiveness get ahead of me."

"What is your name?" Kissa asked.

His brows raised for a moment before a smug grin played on his lips. "Someone told me that to give someone their name is to give them power over them."

His husky whisper caused a flutter in her again. She smiled as he cleverly used her words against her. He cleared his throat again and turned his attention towards Zuberi. She followed it and saw a few of the city's lights flickering through the trees.

"You asked why I'm here." His face darkened again, and she saw his reluctance. "My mother has the sleeping sickness and is in a coma. I hoped Elder Harmon made progress in his research."

Kissa felt his deep pain as she listened. Her face fell. The coma signaled the end of their days. Nobody ever awakened from it and so they named the plague the Sleeping sickness.

Her eyes welled up and Kissa couldn't tell where her sorrow ended, and his grief began. She realized with clarity that it was the stranger's suffering she felt. Kissa inhaled and blinked back her tears. "I am so sorry."

She hated those useless words. The need to console him, to make it better, overwhelmed her. Without thinking, Kissa reached out and touched his hand. Abruptly, a strange spark ignited at the harmless touch and startled them both. Then the strange glow from before enveloped her hand.

When she healed Elder Harmon, it was a faint glow on her fingertips. Now the light expanded past her wrists and the light became more significant as it encompassed his hand. Kissa felt something leaving the core of her, like string pulling from a bundle of yarn. Stunned, she pulled her hand back. The light dimmed until it was gone completely, leaving a tingle in its wake. She looked up.

The warrior's eyes mirrored her own shock. "What did—What was that?"

"I—I don't know. I—"

Kissa's answer died off when the sound of gongs sounded, startling her. The wake-up call. Suddenly, she realized the impropriety of standing so close alone with a man she didn't know in the dark. Kissa needed to return her bow and arrows to her room, and she knew the High Councilor would not tolerate lateness.

"I'm sorry to leave like this, but I must go. Maybe you can come visit me at Serenity another day?"

He stared at her, still with shock. He opened his mouth to say something, but gave her a curt nod instead.

"I don't know what happened just now, but can we keep it a secret until I know more?" Kissa searched his eyes for his answer.

The warrior's brow raised, but he gave another nod. Kissa did not know how she knew, but she felt his sincerity.

"It was nice meeting you...again," she said. Though it pained her to leave him speechless, she didn't have a minute to lose. She pulled on her robe and cloak and ran back towards Serenity.

"Wait!" He called out right before she left the clearing. This time, she turned her head. "Who should I ask for when I call on you?"

A smile graced her lips. "Kissa."

11

BEFORE THE STORM

KISSA

KISSA'S BLOOD FROZE AS she eyed the marble plaque outside of Councilor Fadel's door. She realized this man most likely read all submissions. At the very least, it passed Fadel's desk for final approval. Or in her case, rejection. She felt it in her bones. This would not be a quick or joyful meeting.

She ensured her robe was on straight, her sundial necklace tucked in, and then checked her head wrap. Eager to finish the meeting's agenda, she inhaled deeply and tapped on the door.

On the other side, a curt voice echoed. *"Come in!"*

Kissa opened the door and saw the High Councilor in deep focus at his desk with a stylus. Scrolls lay all around him, and he wore a scowl on his face. Either he had a resting piss face, or Fadel didn't care to hide his disapproval since he dwelled in his own space. Probably the latter, as he continued writing on his parchment and didn't greet her.

Kissa took the time to look around. Fadel's office spoke of wealth. The wooden desk and chairs, made of solid Za, had intricate designs engraved in them. A deep red velvet rug accented the room, and matching drapes adorned the windows. A contrast to the flimsy curtains in her room. Even the sconces on the wall shined from its pure gold.

Paintings lined the walls of temple-like buildings similar to the House of

Life. She noticed, however, that none of the portraits portrayed people. Was the Councilor without a wife or children? Her thoughts drifted to Lani, and she wondered how they related.

They both have the resting piss face down expertly, Kissa chuckled to herself.

The Councilor glanced upwards, disturbed. Her eyes went wide as she realized she had laughed out loud. His eyes narrowed on her as if taking in her measure and finding her insufficient. With a sigh of disappointment, he put his quill aside and motioned towards the chair. Kissa's smile fell.

Once she sat down, he looked at her for a long moment. "Against my sound advice and decision to reject your submission, Elder Harmon accepted you into Serenity. I must ensure you don't make a mockery of it."

Hello to you, too. Something else he and Lani share, Kissa thought.

Unsurprisingly, he didn't want her here and revealed his true feelings at this moment. She felt like an awkward mouse that landed in a hawk's clutches and felt her parent's absence keenly.

"I expect you to be in your classes on time. You are not to leave the school grounds." He stood and walked around his desk to lean in front of it. His average height felt imposing. "The gong sounds before the city toll. First gong is the wake-up call. Second is the first meal. Third and subsequent prompts are for class attendance." He paused, studying Kissa.

"If you hear the city toll bell and are not in class, you are late. The 7th gong means classes are done for the day. After supper, you are to return to your room. Lights out at the 8th gong, no exceptions."

Kissa only nodded her understanding. Fadel reached over and grabbed a parchment from his desk and handed it to her. She stared at the parchment as long as her. A list of rules, but the very top was her schedule. Immediately, she realized her surname on the paper said Bau—her mother's maiden name.

Before she could ask about it, he continued. "I do not blame you, of course, for your parent's folly. You are just a victim of circumstance. However, you owe your presence here to Elder Harmon's grace. I swore an oath to protect this school's reputation. So, we find ourselves at a crossroads, so to speak."

Folly. Though Fadel did not hide his contempt, he tried to cover it with self-righteousness. She'd bet he was the one who wrote her rejection letter. As if Kissa's parents' love was a mistake. Or that her mere presence would throw Serenity into disarray, but Harmon said that was what the school needed, didn't he?

"My surname is Ashtar, not Bau."

The High Councilor's eyes flashed with anger. "It must have been an oversight."

Kissa nodded, though she didn't believe him. Anything to cover up her Osmondian heritage. He didn't even know the half of it. She wondered how he would react if he knew her mother adopted her or that she had Sagian blood running through her veins.

He looked at her pointedly. "Kissa, I suggest that if you don't want your stay to be short-lived that you learn to blend in."

A veiled threat. Her ears burned, and the hum in her chest instigated the flames that flourished in her chest. Whatever this strange hum was, it didn't seem to take too kindly to intimidation. Despite her parentage, she had the right to be at Serenity as long as she could heal naturally. Who cared if a few snotty kids didn't like her last name?

Her father's words flashed in her mind. *Be watchful, choose your battles wisely, and fight with everything in you when the need arises.*

Although she longed to tell the High Councilor where to stuff his misplaced superiority and stupid gongs, she understood it would only confirm his opinion of her. His view of the Osmondian people. No matter her origins, she was Osmondian. This was her kingdom.

Her father's words settled on her shoulders. She needed to choose her battles. Fadel was important to Serenity and had the power to make her life miserable. Kissa blew out a silent breath, centered herself, and let her fire cool.

She smoothed her face. "Anything else?"

He narrowed his eyes at her, then gestured toward her scarf. "Yes. The dress code does not allow for any outside accessories."

Kissa stiffened. "This is part of my attire. It is not an *outside accessory.*"

"Do you have a medical reason to wear it?"

Despite wanting to say yes, Kissa anticipated the need for proof. Worse, he may even want to see the "medical issue." The time it would take her mother to write a "reason" would take days. She wondered why she did not warn her of such things. Then again, she did not need to worry about such concerns.

"No."

"Very well. Class starts soon, and I have no choice but to allow this horrid thing today. We have high standards in Serenity. Tomorrow I expect you well groomed."

Did he think she didn't want to do her hair? Kissa nodded at the remark. It seemed better for him to think her lazy than to know the truth.

"Enjoy your day, High Councilor." Kissa left the office, reluctantly accepting the constricting directives meant to trap her in a bubble—her new gilded cage. Except this one felt much closer to a dungeon with a jailor who loathed the sight of her.

She didn't feel hungry after their meeting, so instead she made her way to the grand stairs of the academic floors. According to her schedule, her class was on the third floor. When she found it, the plaque above the door said, "Anatomy."

She was the first to arrive. The room felt airy from the cracked windows in the back. Only flapping parchment scattered on a simple wooden desk made a sound. Rows of matching small desks attached to metal chairs filled the rest of the space.

Crossing the herringbone slated floor, she picked a desk. Kissa unraveled the parchment Fadel gave her, scouring for a way out of her predicament. Toward the bottom, there was a section for dress code.

"Students are not to wear external clothing. No armor, shawls, cloaks, hats, scarves or head covering of any kind unless the student has a medical excuse. A signed letter from the healer must be obtained and submitted to the Shadora Council for review.

Kissa's spirit dimmed further each time she read the lousy rule. What did it matter if students wore any of those things? Worse still, she did not know what to do about her hair and only the rest of the day to figure it out. She rolled up the paper and stuffed the wretched thing back into her satchel.

She looked up and noticed a shorter table she had missed in front of the long desk. Multiple jars with something floating inside lined the table. As usual, her old friend, curiosity, caused her feet to stride over and pick up one of the glass containers.

A heart, she realized. She read the parchment that lay underneath. *Osmondian Female.* She thought audibly as her whisper echoed around the empty room. She turned it in awe as the organ floated in the preserved fluid that kept it from decaying.

"Those are not toys to be played with!"

The voice snapped her attention to the door. At first glance, a small, unassuming man wearing a white robe walked in. His long beard and short, thinning hair exposed his age, but it was his probing beady eyes the color of sulfur that gave her pause. Narrowed and scrutinizing.

He walked behind the long desk, saying nothing else. Then he ignored her completely as he shuffled through his books and notes. The man left her feeling confused, like he summarized everything he needed to know in that one sharp look and didn't seem impressed with Kissa.

Was every Elder in Serenity this rude? No polite greetings, no introductions, just brittle indifference?

No, Elder Harmon was the warmest person she ever met. She remembered his thoughtful comments about her eyes when they first met. How he held her hand. Family, he said.

Laughter and chatter floated from the hall. Kissa quickly put the jar back on the table and returned to the small desk she chose earlier. She watched the students filtering in wearing yellow robes like her, though a couple had green robes.

Many of them studied her openly, and she felt naked as their gazes cataloged her scarf and not gold eyes. Kissa kept her chin up and face neutral, despite wanting to disappear under their watchful stares. Her facade faltered slightly when a familiar face walked in.

Lani Fadel.

She wore her hair differently, tied up in a bun, but the same glower lined her features. A tall and lithe girl beside her with thick twists through her hair looked straight at Kissa with contempt in her eyes. She strode right up to her and stared her down with expectation.

Kissa rolled her eyes. She wasn't in the mood. "Can I help you?"

"You are in my seat!"

She looked over at the beady eyed man, who watched the encounter from his desk with what seemed like a purposeful aloofness. Not wanting to argue over something so trivial, Kissa quickly grabbed her things and stood in the back near the windows.

She waited until everyone sat down before picking an empty desk near the back. As she gathered her quill and bound parchment, whispers around her made her ears burn. She could only make out a few words, but one question stood out among the others...*Is that her?... the Half-Breed?*

Rumors were already circulating around the school, and she hadn't even finished her first class. Kissa barely heard the city bell ring through the buzzing sounding in her ear.

"From the whispers around the room, I gather you noticed the fresh face in our class." His attention briefly rested on her, and she felt her cheeks warm. "If you have questions for Ms. Bau, please ask them after class. Now, we will—"

Anger rose within Kissa. "Ashtar!"

The beady man stared at her with a heated gaze. "Pardon me?"

"My name is Kissa Ashtar, not Bau." A few students snickered at her outburst, but Kissa held his glare.

"It makes no difference to me what your name is. Unless you have another urgent outcry to make, I will resume teaching my class." Kissa saw the loathing in his eyes.

All the students stared at her. Some with distaste, others with apprehension. You don't belong here, their eyes said. Her heart hammered in her chest.

"No, that's it." Her reply earned some laughs.

Kissa felt hot with embarrassment. Did she need to say that? What difference would it have made to the opinions of those around her? No, she made the right choice. Kissa was proud of her father's Osmondian heritage, and his integrity was next to none. From what she saw from the Elders thus far, her father had set a high standard.

Eventually, she learned the beady, sulfur eyed man's name was Elder Bowman. When he was not addressing her, the elder was warm and answered thoughtfully. Despite their heated interaction, the instructor had a way with words that drew her into his lecture. Kissa stayed quiet and took her notes for the rest of the morning.

The remainder of the day was more of the same. Kissa learned quickly to make herself small and fade into the background. However, it seemed her stupid scarf made her stand out like a sore thumb all day and the suspicious glances thrown her way made her feel uneasy.

After her classes, she raced up to her room and locked the door behind her. Now, Kissa stood in front of her mirror again. Unwrapping her scarf, she stared at the bane of her existence, the coiled locs of the enemy that framed her face. The reason for all the stifling rules and conflicts in her life.

Even if wearing her scarf wasn't a breach of conduct, she was tired of wearing them. She was tired of being different, standing out. Kissa felt ostracized by everything and everyone. She wanted to live a normal life and go where she wished without the constant threat of being exposed.

Kissa pulled the ring from her wardrobe and unwrapped the scarf from it. She held it in her palm, staring at it with uncertainty. Though she feared the dragon head on its face and what it possibly represented, she could not deny the connection she felt to the trinket. The same hum emanating from it flowed through her veins.

Was she imagining it? Desperate to feel something from the man that created it?

Since her birthnight, strange things kept happening, with no logical answers to how they came to be. Kissa pushed the thoughts of magic aside and slid the ring on her right ring finger. She closed her eyes and drew in a breath. She already knew the color she wished for her hair.

In her early teenage years, when she still had an inkling of hope for the Ancients and understood the dangers her locs posed, she prayed for them to be the color of her favorite flower.

Feeling for the hum inside her, she conjured the rare iris in her mind. She whispered the name of the perennial gem with sword-like foliage and vibrant black flowers, with a hint of bronze at its edges.

Before the Storm.

A tingle in her scalp caused her heart to skip, and Kissa's eyes popped open. She stiffened, as her heart did the same. In the square mirror before her, a stranger stared back at her. Long black locs framed her shocked face. She dared to blink, in case it dissipated like every other anomaly lately.

"It worked!" She pulled on a black strand near her face, scrutinizing it. The end had a hint of bronze at the tip. She checked her fingers, but they came away clean.

Kissa huffed a laugh as she twirled in the mirror. Then she swirled her head around, watching as her newly black hair swayed across her face. For the first time in 18 summers, she no longer had to cover her hair. A weight lifted from her chest. Nothing could shadow the excitement that burned through her now.

A knock on the door startled her. She took one last look at herself, then Kissa tiptoed to the door. She went to reach for the lock but froze in place. "Who is it?"

"Benji. Are you indisposed?"

The muscle that tensed in her shoulders released. Though she did not know him for long, she felt a warmth around him. He was the perfect person to see her new hair. Kissa opened the door and stepped aside, out of view from the hall.

Benji walked in with a hesitant manner, but relaxed when he saw her dressed. He took a few moments to appraise her. His brows raised in surprise.

"What?" She couldn't help the smile that bloomed. Her heart thundered in her chest.

He tilted his head to the side. "It's strange to see you with your hair down.

I'm not sure what I expected, but it is very becoming on you. You should stop wearing the scarves."

Kissa's eyes lit up. "Thank you. Um, I'll keep that in mind."

Benji's stare didn't waver as he said, "Anyway, I came to get you for supper. The Shadora Council have an announcement and asked everyone to be present at the dining hall."

"Do you know what it is about?"

"Most likely updates on the Sleeping sickness," he said.

"Okay. Let me get my satchel."

When she returned, Kissa caught him staring again with a probing look. "What is it?" she asked.

"You look so much like her, it is almost crazy." Fascination glinted in his eyes.

"Like who?" She immediately thought of her mother's onyx hair. It was one of the main reasons she used to pray for the color.

"The Ancient of Life," Benji said.

All the air shot out of Kissa's lungs. She wanted to laugh and tell him to stop teasing her, but the intensity in his fascinated gaze made her feel like he actually meant it. Kissa didn't expect him to say she looked like a deity.

"Really?"

He nodded with pensive eyes, as if trying to put the pieces together. "Your golden skin, your eyes, even your hair. You are an exact replica."

It was only last evening that she stared at Layla's painting of the goddess, desperately trying to figure out the exact color of her eyes. Was that why she felt familiar? Maybe? But Kissa's hair wasn't truly black, so she pushed the thought away.

"Well, I'll take that as an upmost compliment." She gave him a grin.

Benji smirked, then turned toward the door. "Let's go. We can't be late for these things."

Just that quick she forgot what he came to get her for. "Right. Let's go."

Kissa skipped supper and the first meal, so this was her first time witnessing the dining hall in action. It was a sizeable space with multiple long tables with chairs taking up most of it. Students lined the tables, chatting away with their fellow students or eating their dinner. The rest of the students formed a queue in a designated area where food was being served by the kitchen staff.

Kissa got in line with Benji and eyed the dinner on display. There were various vegetables: squash, glazed carrots, sweet potatoes and others. A pang of disappointment hit her when she remembered Zuranians were vegetarians. Chickpeas, white beans, and boiled eggs were the protein. Kissa decided on chickpeas, glazed carrots, rice and a roll.

For the first time that day, no one noticed her as they moved to a table near the back. It may have been the buzz of the Shadora Council, but she would take any reprieve from the blatant stares.

Kissa assessed the beautiful forests and waterfall tapestries covering the walls and wondered if Layla had made them. She loved the one of a dove flying across the world. On the far side, a massive floor to ceiling window overlooked the gardens. Benji led her to an empty table next to it.

"So, how was your first day?" Benji asked, as they started eating.

"Eh, nobody wants me here. Do you think Fadel told others who I am?"

Benji's brows lifted. "Everyone knows who you are, Kissa. You are the daughter of a well-known High Healer. Your mother is one of the reasons Serenity even exists. Not to mention, your parent's marriage is epic and before our time they were the talk of all of Osmondia and Zurania and probably beyond. Then add on the fact that nobody—and I mean nobody—knew they had a daughter. If someone doesn't know who you are, they will soon enough."

Kissa thought about that. Once she applied for the Healer Apprentice program, she exposed herself to the world. In hindsight, she wondered if that was the real reason her father denied her request for so long.

Benji wasn't done. "There is nothing to be ashamed of. Onya and Omani were the first to marry outside their blood, and their strength speaks volumes because of it. Believe it or not, despite my father not knowing of your existence, he is very proud of you. Stop worrying about what others think."

Easy for him to say. He was practically a prince at Serenity. He didn't receive the glares and contempt that she did. She was about to say as much when a gong sounded, interrupting supper. Then a woman appeared on a raised platform Kissa now noticed near the entrance.

The woman was quite beautiful with Osmondian locs in her brown hair with twisted white flowers woven in between—a tribute to the people she served. Kissa liked her already. Her presence commanded attention with her deep purple robes. Royal Healer robes.

Mira Harmon, Kissa realized. She glanced at Benji to find him smiling at his mother's presence. Her amber eyes swept the room with an expectance, but her warm smile reminded her of Benji's. Her attention shuffled through the room and eventually settled on Kissa. She thought her eyes widened slightly in recognition, but Mira swept her gaze away so fast she might have imagined it.

This woman was not only Benji's mother, but she raised her mother, too. What would that make her to Kissa? *Nothing now,* she supposed. A pang of loss accompanied the awe of seeing her for the first time.

"I hope everyone is enjoying their meal this night." Her voice boomed through the hall. Everyone quieted immediately. "The Shadora Council has received your letters and concerns. We are here to answer questions and encourage confidence in the arduous work you do."

Wrapped up in the presence of Mira, Kissa didn't see the six others sitting in wooden chairs behind her. She recognized Fadel and Elder Harmon right away. Elder Boman sat to the left of Fadel. She didn't recognize the woman who sat to his right, nor the other three men.

These individuals formed the Shadora Council. Kissa always imagined a group of skewed faces seeing her application and rejecting it right away. Now she knew the process was more complicated than that. Most likely, a debate ensued and then a vote. She didn't know why, but she breathed easier knowing that the council comprised at least two people she knew had integrity.

Mira joined the Council and sat down. Elder Boman took the platform and asked a question Kissa didn't hear. A blue-robed girl with loose, curly brown hair and a sharp nose raised her hand.

"Yes, Tarha." Elder Boman said.

"Well, we know the people have been developing the sickness rapidly, and it's only worsening. So what should we look for in our work? How do we protect ourselves?" Others mumbled their agreement throughout the hall. Kissa sat up straighter in her seat.

"That is a brilliant question. But first, we want you all to know facts, not rumors. The sickness's origins are unknown, though Elder Harmon continues to research it. The sickness appears limited to the Osmondian people, but caution is still necessary.

"No particular class of people is targeted by the sickness. As you well know, the sickness afflicted Osmondia's queen. Unfortunately, she may pass any day now."

The mention of the Queen made her mood sadden. That the Sleeping sickness seemed isolated to her kingdom puzzled Kissa. That meant something specific to Osmondia made her people sick.

"After interviewing and observing those inflicted, we found it starts with an onset of a bloody nose. Then, within days, the patient feels fatigued and has aching joints, followed by a cough and fever."

Elder Bowman sketched the list of symptoms on a huge board behind him as he spoke. Kissa pulled out her ink and parchment, and wrote them down, though they burned into her memory.

"They no longer have the energy to complete simple tasks. Within a week, the cough eventually builds liquid to form in the lungs, causing pneumonia. Despite our progress, current medicines for pneumonia don't work for these patients. Then, they eventually slip into a coma to never wake. The patient appears to waste away until death."

"Masks are required in the clinical area on the first floor to prevent sickness. Though only third and fourth-year students have access to the area, I suggest all of you keep a cloth on you." Bowman finished as he lifted his as an example.

Kissa's thoughts went to her mother at the House of Life, surrounded by sickness. Her mother was smart, though, and she knew she would take every precaution. As she grabbed the cloth a few blue robe students handed out, she thought back on the conversation she overheard in Harmon's study that morning.

What disease resisted antibodies, but yet only inflicted one nation of people?

As the rest of the meeting concluded and the Shadora Council left, Kissa had one thing on her mind. They needed to find the origins and a cure.

12

HIDDEN WITHIN

TAJI

TAJI CLUTCHES HIS MOTHER'S hand as she brings him to his favorite place, his only tell. Shelves filled with hundreds of books tower over him and excitement fills him to the brim. But even at the tender age of three, he has learned to control those outbursts. He searches through the section of the picture books. Spotting a book with a golden lion on the front, he picks it up with both hands and turns to his mother.

Her contagious smile brightens as she looks at Taji with sparkling indigo eyes. "Knowledge is a gift, son. Keep searching for it."

SADNESS WASHED OVER TAJI as the memory of his mother faded away. She played a significant role in his love of books. He missed engaging with her as he discovered something new and exciting. Now, as he left the barracks, as he did most nights, he searched for an answer he didn't have a question for. A feeling...an urge of something he hoped to understand once he found it.

Taji pushed past his heartache as he heaved open the double Za doors. His favorite scents wrapped around him, a faint hint of vanilla, burning candles, and ancient parchment. The Grand Library, or Bibliotheca, as scholars called it, still triggered a bit of eagerness inside him. Yet, he only scratched the surface of wisdom that beheld the hundreds of stonewashed stone shelves lining each wall.

He approached the polished double wooden stairs in the library, which ascended several floors on either side. Avoiding those stairs, he grabbed a torch from the wall and descended to the hidden ancient history section.

The first king, Malachi the Great, started this deeper part of the library as the citadel was being built from the ground up. The ancient catacomb held scrolls and tomes of his reign and those of his successors. To Taji's pleasure, it also held timeless texts regarding each of the Ancients.

As he reached the bottom landing, he lifted the torch to illuminate the space. Darkness greeted him. From memory, he lit the sconce on the entering wall and the one across from him. Then several torches on each wall lit up consecutively—an early invention by the Eashitans.

Unlike upstairs, this space lacked divided sections and levels. Instead, it extended deep, possibly the length of the citadel. Alabaster ambries built into the limestone lined both walls along the catacomb, protecting the ancient scrolls, and tomes.

Above the ambries, murals depicting the Ancients adorned the smoothed limestone walls. Taji lifted his torch as he strode past *The Seven*. Zuri, Miro, Raven, Justice, Desire, Sage, and finally he settled in front of Osmond. It was a custom for Taji to recognize each of them respectfully, though he served only one.

He stared up at the Ancient of Strength, his people's God. Among the various portrayals of Osmond in the kingdom, this painting was Taji's favorite. It was the oldest known painting, but it looked so lifelike that Taji thought it was an actual depiction. A famous Miron artist from centuries ago, Lotus Maltaki, created it. He named it *The Devine Warrior*.

Osmond stood on a cliff wearing white leather armor with gold edging and sandals that tied up his calf. His pauldron only covered one shoulder with a symbol of a mountain and a tree. The symbol of creation. A massive sword sheathed on his back gleamed in the light of the two suns beaming around him. The gold pummel had intricate writing etched in it—the Divine Language.

Osmond's skin, a deep chestnut brown, slightly shimmered. His dark Jata locs, like any Osmondian, was pulled up in a warrior bun. Despite his God's tense expression, his blue eyes held a captivating spark.

The painting always brought a sense of reverence to Taji. Despite Osmond's power and significance, he looked... human. Of course, he knew this was not his true form. All the Ancients were pure ethereal energy, but they chose human forms, and most even shape-shifted into majestic creatures. Somehow, looking at his God this way made him personable. It made Taji want to draw closer to him.

Shaking off the chill that skated across his arms, he looked down at the ambry below the painting. He hoped to find something new regarding magic. Ever since seeing that strange girl at Serenity, he became infatuated with the light she emitted...among other things.

"Kissa." He rolled her name off his tongue, as he did many times since she revealed it. He smiled as he rubbed his hand where he could still feel the echoes of her touch.

That morning, he felt hopeless when he stormed out of Harmon's office. He'd hoped his old friend found a cure or something for this horrid curse on his people. As he started toward the citadel, his attention snagged on someone running into the forest. Though tempted to ignore it, the warrior in him couldn't resist the urge to investigate.

In all honestly, he expected to see some silly student smoking ogerleaf. Or perhaps a lover's secret meeting. It would have been interesting to witness, as Zuranians often exuded a holy-than-thou attitude. However, he didn't expect to see her.

He swore his eyes deceived him as he watched her strip down to her tunic, holding her familiar bow. Then, with the practiced ease of any warrior, she released six arrows consecutively at breakneck speed. Built like a warrior, tall and toned, she did not have the lithe physique of most Zuranians.

Taji recalled how his heart quickened as she turned toward him and pointed an arrow straight at his heart. Her unique eyes held a threat, but he saw the trace of intrigue in their depths. Even when she spoke, her voice held a hint of melodic inflection, though her actual words conveyed an unspoken warning of a quick death.

He recalled his traitorous heart skipped a beat, and he thought briefly that she could not be from this world—she was too perfect. Taji knew then, as he stared at the extraordinary woman before him, he'd let her pierce his heart right where he stood.

Later, when she no longer threatened his life and showed him the workings of the sundial, as she called it, it took everything in Taji to focus on her words. Up close, he spotted freckles dotting her nose, the silver and gold flecks in the hazel depths of her irises. He still smelled her scent of jasmine and a whiff of cocoa butter.

Then she touched him...

In retrospect, she appeared as shocked as he did. The light seemed... *magical?* He dared to say. Taji did not know what magic looked like, but the energy felt pure, almost blissful. All he really understood was that he no longer felt weighed down, and even more, the heartache he'd felt in his chest since his mother fell sick... just dissipated. Though he knew it was only momentary, Kissa's touch gave him that respite.

As she left him standing flabbergasted for the second time, he resolved to learn more about her. Unfortunately, as he stared at the few textbooks he gathered on the reading table, there was very little about the supernatural. Not for the first time, Taji wondered if that was intentional.

Clearing his mind, he put the torch he held in an empty sconce on the wall beside the ambry dedicated to Osmond. He heard a faint click and flicked his attention to the torch. Suddenly, the wall next to the ambry moved.

Taji jumped back and drew his sword in reflex. However, nothing came running out of the darkness beyond. Curious, he grabbed the torch out of the sconce, ready to explore the secret corridor, but as he did, the wall immediately moved back into place.

What the...

It looked like a normal wall to the eye, nothing amiss. Sheathing his sword, he went to grab another torch. Then he returned the other one to the sconce.

Just as he thought, he heard the click, and the wall slid open again.

Taji raised the torch in his hand, the other on the hilt of his sword, as he peered into the dark space. It was a small room covered in a thick layer of dust and on the ground lay a black leather tome encased in a glass box.

He carefully stepped into the room and approached it. Gold script across the front of the tome read, *Sword of Osiris*. With his brows scrunched, Taji lifted the top of the glass. Then he pulled out the black leather book and dusted it off. When he opened it, a faint drumming sounded, similar to when he meditated, practiced or battled in challenges. He closed the book, and the drums ceased. Then he opened it for good measure, and the drums started again.

Excitement washed over him. Could this be what he was searching for? The book promised a fascinating read, at the very least.

Taji quickly carried the tome to the reader's table he studied at. He cautiously sat down and pushed past the rhythmic beat to explore the book. Oddly, the pages were crisp, with no creases or wear. He focused on the first page and recognized the writing inside, the Divine Language. But why? No human could translate the language of the gods. His excitement quickly turned to disappointment as he flipped through pages. After confirming it was all in the same language, he closed the tome with a huff.

"That writing predates Haava. It is called Ceepsun."

Taji whirled in his chair to find the Bibliotheca's Keeper leaning on his cane as he stood in his soft, white robes a few paces away.

"Elder Mif," Taji said, gathering himself. "I didn't hear you approach."

"I heard your frustrations." Elder Mif chuckled softly. "I knew it could only be you. Nobody else visits this part of the library."

"Did you know there is a secret room down here? I found it by chance." Taji shook his head in wonder.

"You did not find it by chance. It was *Fate*," the elder said.

Taji's brow raised in skepticism as he watched the aging man slowly shuffle over to the table and sit beside him. For at least three generations of Taji's family, Elder Mif had been the dedicated keeper of the library. His knowledge was unparalleled. So when he spoke, Taji listened.

"I've been the Keeper for a long time. I am the only one who knows the book's location, as the one before me knew and so forth. This text is many, many centuries old and I believe Osmond wrote it himself."

Taji's eyes widened, unable to mask his surprise. He studied the aging keeper. Elder Mif had taught him gems all his life, and for the longest time, Taji didn't think there was anything the man didn't know.

"How can you be sure?"

Elder Mif opened the tome to the first page, and the drums started again, but this time Taji focused, eager to know if his God's words were before him. He studied the style of the script—perfectly lined and spaced. The curves gave an elegant tone, and the ink was gold, like the title. The writing reminded Taji of something whimsical.

The Elder's finger rested on the word *Doortay*. "This word means chose or handpicked," then he read the full passage: "Osiris ayaa doortay gacantiisa. Osiris chose his hand."

Confusion washed over Taji. "Who is Osiris?" He only knew of one Osiris, the voice inside him.

"Osiris is the name of Osmond's divine sword." The elder replied with a smile and a glint in his eye. "It is a secret passed down from keeper to keeper."

Taji's eyes wandered back to the painting, specifically the sword. He trailed the words on the pummel. Unable to read either, he still discerned they shared a common language. He couldn't ask what he really wanted to know out loud.

Is the voice in my mind and the sword the same? Impossible.

His brows furrowed. "Why would Osiris choose another when he is Osmond's blade?"

"Why indeed? That is the real question," Elder Mif said as his eyes transformed into the teacher Taji grew to know, discerning. "If you recall our history lessons, then you remember that long ago, when the seven different nations established themselves, we inherited the role of warriors and protectors, like our God. The King's Tournament wasn't a flashy custom as it is today, but a competition for the title of Protector of the Realm. It was a big ordeal. Ancient kings conducted a ceremony to bestow the title of protector and pass down the

Blade of Isis."

Taji recalled that after the last Protector died in the war, King Keysia stopped bestowing the title, instead promoting warriors to commanders of his military. He didn't deem the other nations worthy of Osmondian protection, and instead became obsessed with strengthening the Leviathan and Scorpion ranks. The mad king vowed not to allow Osmondia to fall again.

"What's the connection to Osiris?" Taji asked.

For the first time, Taji saw the age of his old friend. The tired lines of his eyes, the slight slump to his shoulders. "As Keeper, I hold many secrets. Usually because nobody ever asks and I will perish only telling my successor. However, there are three guarded secrets that are important to the future of our kingdom, our world. Osmond's sword, the tome, and then the prophecy. You know of it, but not its entirety."

Elder Mif pulled out a small tome the size of his palm from his robe pocket. He opened it to a specific page, then turned it to him. Taji held his stare for a moment before flicking his attention to the small book. Age had weathered the leather, even the parchment was no longer standard.

"When the moon sits full, basked in an orangish glow, the hidden one will reveal herself. Enemies will bring the Age of Fury, and the downfall of two kingdoms shall be its outcome."

Taji's shoulders bunched up as he read the passage. He spent most of his younger life fearing this prophecy when his mother taught it to him. Shortly after, the king order anyone speaking it to the dungeon. Now Taji enforced swift punishment to anyone spreading it. Despite the King's wrath, people in the kingdom still continued to whisper the prophecy from the First Mother.

"What does this have to do with anything?" Taji asked.

"Continue reading," Elder Mif said with a nod.

"With her light, she will gather with her seven others: The Protector, the Dream Walker, the Shaman, the Scholar, the Engineer, the Adjudicator, and the Enchantress from all seven kingdoms. Together, they will enforce the Creator's will and usher in a new era...the Age of Redemption."

Taji's eyes widened as the drums within him picked up speed. He read the passage again. Though there were rumors it existed, this was the very first time Taji read the full version. So many questions rose in him. If this was, in fact, the full prophecy from the First Mother, then part of it was already fulfilled. There were indeed seven kingdoms now.

"Seven others..." Taji said to himself out loud.

"From every kingdom. My duty is to the *Protector*." Elder Mif looked at him patiently.

Taji's heart hammered as he realized what the man was saying. "I am no Protector, old friend."

Elder Mif gazed at him thoughtfully. "You inquired about Osiris and the connection to the old kings' bestowal of the title Protector of the Realm. The first Keeper, Saul the Shrewd, deemed it so. He and King Malachi created the King's tournament as a test of strength and courage without revealing the secret to those unworthy." He sighed, and a sadness settled in his eyes. "But we have lost our way. The Divine Warrior would not leave something so majestic and sacred among mad and unjust kings. Our faith has weakened as a kingdom. But I have watched you all your life, Taji. Your faith is rare and strong, like a budding flower amongst the weeds."

The drums in Taji's mind seemed to reel at those words, sounding louder than ever. He couldn't tell if they were from his hammering heart or the tome. He closed the tome swiftly. When the drums ceased, Taji let out a deep sigh and dragged his hand down his face. Elder Mif lifted a brow at this action. He said nothing, though a hint of amusement shined in his eyes.

"How do you know no other has read this book?" The elder was up there in age. Maybe his memory was not as profound as it once was.

"Because the keepers made it so. Only the chosen can find it. Or...stumble upon it." Elder Mif said with a smile.

"If nobody can read it, then why hide it?" Taji asked.

Elder Mif's face became serious. "No human can translate it. Only the Divine. The Ancients and their children... *Celestials.* There are also those that wish to find Osiris and they do not wish to use the divine sword with selfless intentions."

A shiver ran through Taji. There were accounts of Celestials in the earlier history of Haava. Some thought of them as guardians that worked on behalf of the Ancients. However, no one had written sightings or accounts about them since long before the war. When he was a boy, his mother read him a story about a unit of sea warriors stuck near Dragon's Cove during an incoming storm. Allegedly, a Celestial appeared and, using powers to move the wind, saved the warriors from a drowning death.

Taji wondered if there was someone specific the keepers hid it from.

He looked up to see Elder Mif staring at the text that had started this impromptu history lesson. "It was an honor to be its keeper... but it seems it has found a new one."

Taji scowled. He was no keeper of divine books and he was certainly not the Protector spoken of in the prophecy.

He ignored the statement. "What could a human with no magic do with an unreadable tome or his sword? It makes no sense." Taji shook his head in disbelief. "According to history, no one has seen Celestials in over two centuries."

Elder Mif arched a brow at him. "The Ancient's ethereal energy is in everything around us. Is it so far-fetched that if one of them wanted to gift someone magic or a powerful weapon, they could make it so? I know you have heard the rumors that the Sagians gained sorcery from their God, the Ancient of Wisdom." A darkness passed over the Elder's eyes. "The scrolls say that Sage is the *Original Sorcerer*, the *Saaxir*. I do not hold all the answers, but the tome will shed more light on that reason."

Even though Taji didn't know the full implications of that title, *Saaxir*, he heard the claims of Sagia. But why would Osmond give up Osiris just to fight the Sagians? If that were true, the conclusion of the last war would have ended differently. Even if the Sagians wielded magic, they were still human. Something wasn't adding up.

Taji sighed, biting back all the engrained denials he wanted to utter. *Magic doesn't exist,* he wanted to say. But the light from Kissa's hand surfaced in his mind, and the tight hold on the things he grew up believing started to unravel.

"There is a reason for that tome... for Osiris. It is time you find it. It is time for you to embrace your cloak of duties," Elder Mif said.

The bluntness of the statement took Taji aback. The Elder always spoke with matter-of-fact truth, and Taji was no longer a naïve boy uninterested in the on-goings of the world around him. He felt overwhelmed with what he now knew and what he still didn't. Like a strategic game, he only had some pieces and needed to find the rest.

And beneath it all... he did not feel worthy.

The thought of Osiris choosing him was a hard concept to accept. To think himself deserving of something so majestic. He'd never even slayed a human enemy, let alone a powerful unknown entity that he would need Osmond's sword to defeat.

As if reading his mind, Elder Mif's eyes softened. "That book appeared to you for a reason. It is not for me to know that reason, but I can tell by your questioning and eagerness about the subject that you know it. You are now its keeper. Continue having faith, and you will discover everything. Listen, even to the impossible."

Taji stared at the Elder, filled with wisdom and kindness, always surrounded by ancient scripts. He yearned to tell him about Osiris in his mind and the drums in his veins. Taji wished to confide in someone many times, but... he couldn't risk it.

Instead, he asked, "Where do you think the sword is?"

"Keep your mind, eyes, and heart open, and Osiris will reveal himself." Elder Mif said. Then he stood and clasped Taji's back. "I enjoyed this talk. It reminds me of when you were young and full of questions." He smiled wistfully. "I've given you much to sift through. There are some books upstairs I need to rebind. I'll be in my den if you need me."

Taji nodded. He couldn't read the "magical" book, but he could get more answers about his kingdom's history, about the Protector of the Realms of old.

As Elder Mif shuffled away, he filtered through the onslaught of information he dropped on him. A gust of wind brushed against Taji's skin, and he swore he heard a faint scream. With narrowed eyes, he looked toward the catacomb's opposite end. He had yet to explore how deep the tunnel went, and a sudden urge of action peaked in him.

He grabbed the torch from the sconce that revealed Osiris' tome. The wall closed immediately. Then he grabbed the ancient book and placed it in his rucksack. As Taji reached the threshold where the torchlights that lined the walls no longer ventured, he pulled the hood of his cloak over his head.

It was time to unearth some more secrets.

13

BELONGING

Kissa

Every color surrounded Kissa. Gleaming reds, blues, yellows, and in between. Something inside her knew these were the true colors of the stars.

This had to be a dream. How else could she explain her current ability to drift through the Cosmos? With a smile, she embraced it all with an adventurous spirit.

Before too long, a specific star caught her attention. It seemed to drift off by itself, not clustered like the others. On closer inspection, gold and silver flecks swirled within its crimson starlight.

She felt the wandering star's loneliness just as she knew its aura was feminine. Were stars sentient beings? Kissa thought of the shimmery light that visited her dream on her birthnight. She said she was a star.

As she pondered the thought, something gripped her heart and resonated deep within her. It wasn't simply a feeling. The star wandered, seeking something. It mimicked Kissa's own hidden feelings of being lost and wanting to belong. It felt profound somehow.

Drawn to the lost star, she glided closer and watched curiously as the star swarmed in an elegant, yet powerful whirlwind. The dance reached a crescendo, then halted with a burst, causing Kissa to startle. The dazzling tiny fragments settled into a heap, suspended on nothing.

Kissa dared not move toward what looked to be an unassuming pile of glitter.

A few breath-holding moments passed like this. Then, thinking it did whatever it would, she looked away to continue exploring.

Kissa felt a tingle, an urging, and turned back toward the fragmented star. The specks rose from the glittering ashes and formed whole again. Instead of a star, though, a woman stood before Kissa's eyes.

She stood almost six hands tall, with a firm body resembling a warrior. Her wild Jata locs fell past her shoulders, and blazed in varieties of red and streaks of gold. She wore black leather armor that formed around her curves like shadows, with a familiar bow on her back and a quiver of arrows strapped to her hip.

Kissa dared to breathe when the star woman turned her way. Her eyes, hazel-green with bits of gold and silver, blazed with confidence.

She waded closer as the female warrior continued her search, undeterred. Kissa noted the familiar freckles that peppered her glittery golden brown face and the long, dark lashes that accentuated her perceptive eyes. Before she could speculate further, their surroundings changed from the Cosmos to an unfamiliar land. Thick trees and wild vines surrounded them, and Kissa felt the warm humidity caress her skin.

As if by magic, seven cloaked warriors appeared out of thin air and walked toward the female warrior. Kissa tried to identify them. One glided like a dancer and Kissa thought the warrior was female, but she and five of the others rushed ahead without a word, their cloaks obscuring them.

The one who stayed wore the same leather armor as the star woman, and a massive sword with a pure gold hilt adorned his back. Determination filled his stark blue eyes, and his deep sepia skin reminded her of the acorns that fall with the leaves of autumn.

The familiar stranger.

The swoon-worthy smirk he gave the female warrior caused a flutter in Kissa's core. Familiarity between the two warriors spoke volumes as their gazes met. Then, the blue-eyed warrior nodded and led ahead, while the female warrior prepared her bow, watchful. Catching up with the others, the group moved like a cohesive team and a sense of belonging wrapped around Kissa. She yearned for it.

It seemed none of the warriors noticed her, so she followed along with the group as they moved deeper into the jungle. Kissa had never experienced a jungle, per se, but decided this was precisely what one would look and feel like as she wiped the sweat beading on her brow.

A warning tingled down Kissa's spine, reminding her of the night of the shadow wolf. She turned her head to the right and saw someone with long, deep black hair with matching robes creep out of the deepness of the uncultivated trees. Kissa felt the woman's dark intentions—slick with ominous resolve.

"Witches!" the star warrior shouted to her companions.

Her team unsheathed their weapons and spread out. The familiar stranger already wielded his majestic sword, and the powerful weapon released a rhythmic sound. The war drum called to Kissa's spirit and wrapped around her in a protective embrace.

At the front, he stood beside the female warrior, who had already nocked an arrow. Upon being made out, the witch whistled, and five more, just like her, appeared from the brush. All six of the witch's eyes were black as an abyss, just like their hair and robes. Their sinister look caused Kissa to shiver. Then, as if the witches moved as one, they pulled silver balls from their robes and threw them in the air with expert accuracy.

"Silverlight!" the familiar stranger called out.

Kissa didn't know what a Silverlight was, but she watched, transfixed, as he spun his heavy sword with both hands so fast it stilled in a blurred motion. Lightning emanated from the tip, the shade of his eyes, lighting up the jungle. Three erratic strikes branched out from the sword and hit the Silverlight balls, evaporating them into nothing.

Beside him, the star warrior drew and released her arrows, one after the other. Kissa only saw a blur of movement as she took down a silver ball and then aimed at the witches, dropping them one by one. However, these were not regular arrows. Kissa stood slack-jawed as she regarded the crimson light surrounding them as they released into the air.

But even with all their otherworldly speed, lightning, and glittery arrows, she watched in horror as one of the Silverlight balls slipped through their defenses. She opened her mouth to warn them, but the shuddering burst of sound swallowed her *cry. Kissa didn't even have time to throw up her arms as the release of energy hit her full-on.*

EXHAUSTED, KISSA ENTERED THE dining hall. She observed a few people already eating and tried not to be annoyed. The breakfast gong had not even sounded yet. Kissa decided she would take her food to the gardens. Sluggishly, she got in line.

Fatigue, hunger, and irritation seeped into her senses. Right away, Kissa realized they weren't her own. While she sensed something different about herself since her birthnight, she ignored the trickles of emotions she felt here and there. However, they seemed to grow more prominent with each passing breath.

Her "gifts" were becoming stronger at an alarming rate and she wished to know how to turn the damn things off. Between that and the strange dreams at night, Kissa could barely keep her eyes open.

She observed the morning food displayed. Cream of rice, various nuts, toast, a fruit medley, and some poached eggs. Kissa wrinkled her nose. She wasn't sure if she'd be able to sustain the meatless diet Zuranians lived by for much longer.

Some bacon would be nice, she thought, as her stomach growled in misery.

At least they didn't restrict the coffee that Kissa generously poured into her mug. Choosing nuts, eggs and toast, Kissa made her way toward the garden. Then, like a premonition, the gong for the morning meal sounded. She closed her eyes and sighed. Kissa's shoulders tightened as if preparing for a battle.

On cue, she felt the sea of students making their way towards her moments before she heard them. *Happiness, irritation, sleepiness, and hunger*, mixed with many others, slammed into her as more students made their way to the dining hall. Kissa couldn't distinguish one feeling from the next, as they seemed to blur together when more students poured in. She clutched her food tray, trying to stay steady in the onslaught.

Kissa needed to get to the gardens.

She focused on the garden door. Head down, she made a beeline for it as casually as possible, but right before she reached the door that promised her reprieve, a pair of laced-up sandals with trimmed toes entered her vision. She looked up to see a familiar sly smile, green robes, and fierce gold eyes.

"What is it?" Kissa asked.

She didn't have time for this girl's snide remarks right now. Two other girls accompanied her. One girl to the right with green robes, hair in a top bun, with eyes too close together. Kissa thought she might be in her biochemistry class. To the left was Tula. The girl who confronted her about her desk on Kissa's first day.

Behind them, a blue-robed male leaned on the wall with a hint of a grin. A grin that Kissa didn't like. She didn't know their problem but felt their antipathy toward her like a storm pouring over her now trembling body.

Kissa decided she didn't care what they wanted. "Excuse me!" She tried to push past them to get to the gardens, but Lani's next words stopped her.

"You see? She's like the rest of them!" The four of them nodded, as if Kissa confirmed something they had already discussed.

"You are in my way. Please move," Kissa said as politely as she could muster. The growing emotions blooming in her mind threatened to undo her.

Lani said, "Taking what you want is in your nature. You can't be content with your grand kingdom, weapons, and ships. No, you take what is ours, too. I do not know how your father bullied Elder Harmon into accepting you, but we have petitioned the high court."

Kissa felt taken aback by Lani's statement. She was not talking about petty student issues, but about Osmondians. Her people. The agreement felt by Kissa revealed a shared sentiment. She scanned the few faces watching the encounter, taking in their amused looks before looking at Lani once more.

"I don't know your issues with the kingdom you *serve*, but you are the only bully I see. Now let me pass." Kissa straightened her shoulders as her mind tried and failed to block the heated moods of those around her.

Rage flashed in Lani's eyes. "You don't belong here! Why don't you do us all a favor and leave?"

Others started circling around them. Kissa's embers ignited, but her mouth watered from the nausea settling in. Her breathing quickened as more students approached the group. She tried to push the feelings from her mind, but it felt like trying to catch water with her arms. Despite her desperation to avoid humiliation, she swayed. But she held tight, refusing to give satisfaction to those who wished for her downfall.

Collecting what little thoughts she could, Kissa said, "My mother is—"

"*A traitor!*" Lani cut off her reply with venom.

The tray Kissa held shook as she tried to control her trembling anger. "You know nothing about my family or me!"

The male in their group straightened up from the wall and walked over to Lani. "I think that is enough, sis," he said.

Lani ignored her brother. "I know you are an Osmondian half-breed who does not belong in our school. You should be at the barracks with the rest of your kind."

Kissa dropped her platter of food all over the ground, splattering eggs on Lani's trimmed toes. She shrieked, expounding the thrumming in Kissa's head. She felt herself about to collapse as the edges of her vision closed in on her.

Just then, firm hands clutched her arm and kept her upright. Benji. His other hand moved to her back. Darkness crossed his face as his amber eyes assessed her, his mouth turned down at the corners.

He turned to Lani's group. "*That is enough!* Take your sister and go, Maron!" Without even a glance to see if they listened, Benji helped Kissa to the nearest table.

She could have imaged it in the ragged state she was in, but his presence felt like a cool breeze on a sweltering day. Her stomach still clashed against her ribs, but the emotions battering her felt pushed to the recess of her mind. She could breathe and didn't feel like she was on the cusp of death anymore.

Kissa shook her head. "*Gardens.*"

In truth, she wouldn't even make it. Her legs felt unsure, like a newborn giraffe. Instead, she listened to Benji's silent encouragement and sat down, putting her head down between her legs, and closing her eyes. Her nausea and dizziness lessened some.

"Drink this water." Benji handed her a cup.

Kissa knew that all the students were watching her. She could feel their curiosity at the edge of her mind. She just wanted to run away.

Benji held up the cup for her as she took a sip. The water felt cool gliding down her parched throat. Kissa saw exhaustion in his eyes and sweat on his forehead. She was in no state to ask him what was wrong, but he sat down next to her with a heavy thump.

Suddenly, she felt the relief fade and emotions swarm around her like an angry mob. Her vision swam, and the edges of her vision darkened again. Kissa groaned. She was about to pass out.

Please no!

The pressure caused her to collapse between her legs again. It seemed she could not win this. Tears fell down her face, and she didn't have the strength even to wipe them. Exhausted, Kissa surrendered control.

As the blackness behind her lids tried to consume her whole, the bright shimmery white door with the red knob from before appeared. It was wide open, with tendrils of various shades of dark and light mist seeping across its threshold.

I am in your mind's eye, Kissa remembered the star woman said.

As she watched the mist roll through the door unimpeded, shrouding the sparkly white frame, she knew they were the other student's emotions. The door—a gateway to her mind.

All doors close, Kissa thought.

Her fire sparked at that thought, giving her newfound energy. She allowed it to grow, warming her from within. It left the den inside her chest and moved through her torso, then her legs and arms. When it reached her fragile mind, Kissa felt the power mend the damage within.

Kissa glared at the mist as it tried to overtake her mind. *You will not control me.* Her fire roared with conviction, building her confidence.

For this is my mind.

With the scrounged up energy left in her, Kissa slammed the door shut. The onslaught of emotions stopped, and she shuddered from the effort and relief. Kissa slouched between her knees. Her fire calmed. Nothing but embers now.

Kissa heard voices, and she struggled to lift her head and open her heavy eyelids. Then the blanket of warm relief that seemed to accompany Benji wrapped around her once more, and everything went black.

14

BELATED TIES

KISSA

KISSA GROANED AT THE effort of opening her eyes, aggravating the splitting ache in her head that throbbed in tune with her pulse. She reached up and massaged her temples, which did nothing. She looked around, finding herself back in her room. Her window revealed a night sky.

She removed her cover and quickly inspected herself. Still dressed in her robe and clothes from earlier, she wondered who had brought her to her room. On instinct, she reached for her hair and found it bare. She shot up in her bed, then remembered it was now black. Her shoulders relaxed.

Bladder full, she slowly moved to get up. Kissa winced at her body's stiffness. She felt weak, and her legs trembled. Using the bed to steady herself, she eventually shuffled to the hall. Thankfully, it was quiet, with everyone sleeping. She made it to the shared lavatory as fast as her wobbly legs allowed.

Though she had a headache, Kissa checked her mind's door. She found it closed tightly as she left it. If she could conjure bolts and extra locks to keep it shut, she would have.

Finishing up, she washed her hands at the basin. She looked up in the mirror above the sink to check her reflection. Kissa yelped. Blatant red and gold locs framed her face. Her heart fell to her feet. Kissa quickly shut off the water and ran to her room before anyone could see her.

She rushed through her door and whipped it closed. Locking the door, Kissa collapsed to the floor in a painful, exhausted heap.

"Kissa?"

Her heart jumped in her throat. She looked up, and her scattered brain slowly processed a woman dressed in purple robes standing in her room. Her flawless terra cotta skin and dark hair braided in one plait. The same white flowers weaved between the braids.

"Mira."

Oh, this is not good. No-no-no-no-no-no!

With a calm demeanor, Mira reached down and helped Kissa stand and guided her to her bed. "Are you alright?"

Am I alright? Is this woman color blind? Kissa thought, but did not say. She nodded instead.

Mira chuckled softly and patted her hand. "I am glad that I was visiting Marquis when word came you fainted."

"Oh?" Kissa croaked, as her cheeks heated with all kinds of embarrassment.

"Come, it's night and you've slept all day. You are dehydrated and likely hungry, so I brought you healing tea and soup." She gestured to a bowl and glass sitting on a small table Kissa swore wasn't there when she woke up.

"Thank you." Every nerve in her body was on alert. Kissa felt unsure.

"Benji carried you here. I accompanied him because I wanted to attend to you myself." Mira gave her a warm smile.

Kissa's cheeks heated more. The idea of Benji carrying her to her room was humiliating. Then she wondered why a Royal Healer would care for someone like her.

"Thank you for that. I understand more important people need your attention."

Mira's eyes softened. "Oh, Kissa. You are my family and though you may not know it, you are very important to me." Sadness settled in the older woman's eyes.

Despite closing her mind, Kissa felt the urge to know how Mira was feeling. Kissa summoned up the door of her mind and opened it just a crack. She immediately felt a hint of sadness, smothered in... *love? That can't be right.*

It reminded her of her mother's warm pastries, fresh out of the oven with a dash of cinnamon. Kissa's shoulders relaxed slightly at the discovery.

It was then that Kissa's stomach growled. Mira chuckled as she reached for the bowl of soup off the table and handed it to her. As Kissa stirred the soup, a question had gnawed at her since she saw the Royal Healer in the dining hall.

"Mira, why did you never visit?" Her father told her, but she wanted to hear it from her.

The Royal Healer's brows shot up as if surprised Kissa asked, and she didn't answer immediately. Feeling the woman's conflict at the forefront now, she didn't want to push, so Kissa ate her soup to give her a moment. She detected ginseng with various vegetables in the broth, and the heat felt soothing on her dry throat.

Mira started pacing the floor. "I knew it was for your safety. I don't want to overstep, because your father would be furious. But I must confess something. I was aware of you."

Now it was Kissa's turn to look shocked. She didn't think anyone knew of her outside of her home growing up.

Mira nodded her head and smiled sadly. "Inka was my closest friend." An ache formed in Kissa's chest to hear the name of her grandmother. "Because of that, Onya is like a daughter to me."

She sat next to Kissa on her bed. "I saw your mother every day, and then poof." Mira exaggerated a poof of smoke with her hands. "She'd visit me occasionally, but I had my suspicions. One day, I knew your father was on duty, and I came to the cottage. I let myself in and saw Onya sitting in a rocking chair, singing and rocking a baby back and forth. At first, I was furious. I thought, why would she keep a baby from me? But then, when she lifted you up, I saw your red curls.

"Fear overwhelmed me for you and your mother that day. I knew the consequences if anyone knew. So, I kept you a secret all this time." A tear ran down her cheek. "Every day, you've been in my thoughts. Wondering what you looked like, what games you played, if you were happy. Hoping that one day I'd see you again. Then I received news that Marquis accepted you into Serenity. I had many questions, of course, but my heart soared."

Kissa stared at her, dumbfounded. Mira wanted to be in her life. Someone other than her parents caring about her, even in secret, soothed a part of her soul. When her mother read Mira's letters, she felt like a stranger looking through a window of a home she didn't belong to.

Family, Elder Harmon said the day she met him.

Kissa sat the bowl down. "Well, I painted on all the walls, played hide and seek with Mama, and when I was 12, my father made me my first bow."

Mira burst out in laughter and it wrapped around Kissa's heart. "I can just see your mother's face when he brought that home."

Kissa chuckled. "Yes, initially she was very cross. But that's the thing. Mama let me be who I am. I love archery just as much as I love healing, and she understood that."

Mira nodded in silence for a moment. "I wish everyone had your mother's mind about life. But our societies are complex and weighed down with tradition. I'm afraid my son suffers because of it."

Kissa thought about Benji and his mischievous smile. She did not know him well enough to comment on it. However, his personality seemed too big to fit the restricting air of Serenity. His closeness to Layla told her exactly what he thought about society and tradition.

"Benji thinks I don't know of his long love of swordplay. He grew up in the Citadel watching your father train the young warriors. I hate he has to hide it."

Kissa's brows raised in complete surprise at Mira's confession. She thought of that day in the forest, the rider. It was Benji. Now she understood why he didn't have his sword with him the day they encountered the shadow wolf. Most likely hiding it from his father as she hid her bow.

"That's our secret. When he is ready, he will tell me." Mira said with a wink.

Kissa smiled and nodded. Changing the subject, she gestured towards a large white leather bag with intricate rose patterns on the front that she now coveted. "That is a beautiful satchel."

The Royal Healer smiled thoughtfully as she reached into its contents and pulled out a small square glass case and a cream in a sealed bowl. The case opened up into a compact mirror with golden brown powder. Kissa's brows raised in interest.

"I brought this for you. This is to cover the dark circles under your eyes," Mira said. "May I?"

Kissa nodded, then sat still as Mira applied the cream first to her full face. It felt soothing and smelled lovely, like bergamot.

As she worked, she said, "I noticed that your hair was black earlier. I don't mean to intrude, but I only know of one magic that can accomplish such feats. Dark Magic."

Kissa stiffened. She opened then closed her mouth again, speechless. Was the Chonda ring dark magic? Even more, how did Mira know of this Dark Magic?

At her loss for words, Mira said, "Whatever it is, I will not pry. Just promise me you will be careful, Kissa. There is much you do not understand in our realm and beyond. Things that can hurt you if you do not understand its origins."

Kissa looked up, and Mira's amber eyes burned into hers. She wanted to share about the witch in the market and how she probably traded her soul for the useless ring. But Kissa wasn't ready to reveal that. She appreciated Mira's worry for her, so she nodded her understanding.

Disappointment showed on Mira's face, but she let it be. Then she dabbed the golden powder under Kissa's eyes with her fingers. "Though they are training, they are not healers yet. We told the students that you passed out from exhaustion because of your long travels. Hopefully, that should keep them from asking questions."

Kissa didn't really care about the other student's unease. They didn't care about how she felt being subjugated by Lani's hateful words. They just watched. Kissa felt targeted.

"Why do they hate me?"

Mira paused, her eyes softened. "They don't hate you, Kissa. They don't know you. It is what you represent to them." She put down the cream and the compact. "After the war with Sagia, Osmondia closed its doors to the other nations, along with their protection and support. King Keysia declared the other nations fleeing as desertion and treason. When they tried to return to their homes, the King did not permit them. For those that stayed, he ordered them killed in retribution for those that fled. It was a very dark time for our world.

"Some nations, like Zurania and Miro, took centuries to develop their small kingdoms into their current states. Some resent that Osmondia solely protects their own, despite their divine obligation to safeguard the world."

Kissa's heart broke for the other nations. Zuranians and Mirons fled in fear. She knew some of the story of King Keysia. The other nations felt inequality under the Osmondians before the war. However, none of the history books she read spoke of genocide afterward. It seemed Osmondians wanted to erase that part of their history. They even went to the extent of banning books from other kingdoms.

"Why serve in Osmondia if they feel that way? Why not choose another school?" Kissa asked.

Mira lifted a brow. "Why disturb a sleeping bear when you can live long and at peace otherwise? Queen Safiyah negotiated peace treaties and bridges, so to speak, between the nations. She lifted the ban, and now other kingdoms can visit their ancestral home. Serving Osmondia is our tribute to her hard work to make it happen. The relationship may be complicated, but there is one because of her."

The Royal healer looked away, glassy eyed. Kissa knew it hurt her to speak of the dying Queen, her friend. Kissa grabbed her hand. Mira smiled at the gesture and squeezed Kissa's in appreciation.

"The point is to compromise and reciprocate. Only time will heal old wounds. Zurania must extend an olive branch if they desire Osmondia's protection. That is what political peace is."

Kissa never really cared for politics. She felt everyone should help everyone, but of course, Haava was not a perfect world. The mention of the war made her think of her dream of the warship. It was a warning. She felt it in her spirit.

Mira lifted the compact mirror to Kissa, pausing her thoughts. Her brows rose as she stared at her reflection. The dark smudges were gone, and she had the distinct feeling it was the cream. Now that she thought about it, her splitting headache was gone, too. Kissa looked down at her empty bowl of soup in wonderment.

Then Mira reached over, grabbed her satchel, and placed the cream and glass case in the inside pocket before giving it to her.

"My gift to you. Happy late Birthnight, Kissa! I'm sorry I couldn't spend it with you," she said.

Her eyes widened, and her heart squeezed. "Wow! Thank you, Mira."

She put her bowl of soup on the table and walked over to her dresser. She returned with the mortar and pestle her mother gifted her, then placed it inside her new satchel. Kissa felt equipped by the women who inspired her most.

Mira beamed. "It is my pleasure." Then, all too soon, she stood. "I wish I could stay longer, but I need to return to the Citadel."

Kissa nodded her understanding and gestured to walk her out. As they reached her door, she remembered something. "Mira, can you give my father a letter?"

"Of course!" Mira said.

Then Kissa walked over to her dresser and grabbed a blank parchment and quill from her top drawer. She wrote a quick note, then Kissa folded the parchment and handed it to Mira.

"Thank you," Kissa said and watched Mira put it in her cloak pocket.

"You're welcome, my dear. Benji can deliver missives too, when he comes to the Citadel to visit. Remember that."

"I'll keep that in mind."

Before the Royal Healer turned to go, she grabbed Kissa's hands. "I won't pretend that this journey will be easy for you. There will be times you will question yourself, question your dreams. Don't give up! There are far more than you know that are hoping for your success. Remember that."

Tears sprang to Kissa's eyes. She didn't know how much she needed to hear that. As she watched Mira depart, inspiration flowed through her veins. She would not give up.

MIRA'S SOUP REALLY WAS a miracle. It worked so well that Kissa couldn't sleep again. The Royal Healer also gave her a lot to think about. Between secretly knowing about her and her parting words, her mind whirled from one thing to the next.

Giddiness made Kissa laugh out loud. Benji was a swordsman! The confirmation of what she already knew satiated her mind. Oh, how she wished to practice with him. But Mira was right, it was not hers to tell. If Kissa wasn't good at anything else, she knew how to keep a secret.

As the moon set high in the dark sky and twilight made itself known, she tried to figure out why the stupid ring wasn't working. Her other secret. Kissa examined the face and the outer band. Physically, there was nothing wrong with it...other than the ominous dragon face.

She flipped it around between her fingers when something engraved on the inside gave her pause. Kissa couldn't see it in the dim light, so she brought the ring over to the candlelight. Her heart quickened. Examining it closer, she saw tiny words, barely visible to the naked eye, etched on the inside of the band.

"As the world turns, so too will your desire." She repeated it in her mind, dissecting each word and their meanings. This was what she loved to do—figure out things, their meaning, and how they worked.

As the world turns...

There were many occasions as of late that she wished she took her father's lessons more seriously. Luckily, this was not one of those times. She remembered learning that Haava constantly rotates on its axis and that is why the sun rises in the east and sets in the west. Legend has it that the Ancient of Wisdom designed the system to ensure that the entire realm would have its share of sunlight, creating the seasons.

Her heart warmed at the memory of her father, her history and science teacher. Their mutual love of the sun kept that lesson rooted in her mind. Haava completed a full rotation in a day, if one could believe it. She remembered thinking it was impossible for a world so massive to only take a day.

"Then why does it take a full four seasons for the sun to orbit our world?" Young Kissa debated her father during a lesson. He chuckled, then clarified that the sun's apparent size from her cliffs was deceptive, as it was actually millions of miles away. Even a thumb length closer, Haava would not be habitable. She remembered being blown away by that discovery.

A day.

Was that the limitation the witch purposely did not warn her about? Did her wish only last a day? It made sense. Her hair most likely reverted just before dinner, when she had made her wish the day prior. Did it mean she could not use the wish again? Or did she need to reapply it each day? She needed to find out.

She stood in her mirror, examining herself as she wished her hair to change. Missing it the first time, Kissa watched closely. She felt the tingle in her scalp, then from the ends to the root, red transformed to black. No light, glow, or anything special, really. Just the continual hum that connected her to the ring somehow.

A sudden pang of loss for her red and gold locs hit her swift and hard. Something she didn't think she would ever feel. Maybe it was her dream of the confident version of herself that didn't exist.

She stared at the fictitious girl before her. The version that didn't want to be different. The version everyone else wanted her to look like. She barely knew the girl before her. It wasn't just her hair, but the anger growing inside her, and the ugly secrets that were now making up her world.

Why did she care so damn much about what everyone else wanted? The answer blazed in her mind like a desperate song with no ending.

Kissa Ashtar wanted to belong.

15

SHADORA COUNCIL

KISSA

KISSA AWOKE FEELING REFRESHED, free from any strange dreams or encounters with mysterious lights during the night. With a smile, she got ready for the day, putting on her satchel, robe, and boots before stepping outside.

However, as she opened the door, she let out a surprised yelp. A girl she had never seen before, dressed in blue robes, stood before her. The girl had a bun atop her head and her golden eyes blinked at Kissa with the same suspicion that seemed to be directed towards her by everyone else.

With narrowed eyes, Kissa asked, "What is it?" If they were going to treat her that way, she was prepared to respond in kind.

With a bored air, the girl said, "The Shadora Council summons you." Without another word, she handed Kissa a parchment and walked away.

As she watched the girl retreat, her heart sank in her stomach. She knew the incident with Lani undoubtedly reached the Council's ears. Holding the parchment in her hands, she scanned its contents. The meeting would take place in Elder Harmon's study, and only moments away. With a sense of urgency, Kissa hastened her steps.

As she stepped into the Overseer's office for the first time, she noticed two things. First, his office was even larger than Fadel's, which had a purpose. Occupying more than half of the space at the back was a laboratory. Peering through the secure window, Kissa observed the glass tubes and beakers arranged on long tables, each containing different mixtures. Though it was empty, Kissa's curiosity ignited, urging her to explore whatever research Harmon was conducting.

His den also served as a council chamber. The back room showcased an immaculate white stone table adorned with several lavender cushioned chairs. Zuranian landscape paintings covered almost every inch of the walls. Positioned behind the head of the table, a beautiful tapestry depicted a radiant white castle that seemed to emit a gentle glow. The pristine castle stood in stark contrast to the dark stones of Horus Citadel. Manicured gardens and a stunning waterfall backdrop surrounded Primrose Castle.

Naturally, a council room wouldn't be complete without its members. Eight individuals sat at the table, their eyes fixed on Kissa. Nervousness crept into her stomach as she felt the weight of their scrutiny, their various shades of gold intensifying the sensation.

"Kissa, I'm glad you have joined us. Please take a seat." Elder Harmon stood and gestured a seat near him at the head of the table.

His kind eyes gave nothing away. She nodded her thanks and sat down next to Mira, who sat to the right of her husband. She gave a warm smile in greeting and Kissa returned it.

Her mood darkened as she turned her attention to the rest of the table. Lani sat between Elder Fadel and another woman. Kissa remembered her from the dining hall. She sat with the same pompous look as Fadel. Though older, she had the same facial structure as Lani, and the same almond-shaped eyes that held a loathing gaze as she looked down her nose at Kissa.

Definitely related.

"Before we begin, I'd like to introduce everyone present. This is the first time Kissa has formally met with the Shadora Council. Of course, you know I am Marquis Harmon, Overseer of Serenity and the House of Life. This is Mira Harmon, Royal Healer to Queen Safiyah. To your immediate right is Krane Bowman, also your anatomy instructor. Pamu Nerayo, our physics and biochemistry instructor. He also teaches chemistry and genetics. Next is

Yosif Beru, our renowned surgeon. He has since retired and now mentors and conducts clinical work at Serenity."

Kissa eyed the members as Elder Harmon introduced them, searing their faces to memory. Each of them, important to Serenity.

"You have already met Ruben Fadel, our High Councilor, and next to Lani is Rekik Fadel. She also serves as our ambassador to our King, Tor Cithrali."

Kissa's eyes widened. Not because as ambassador, Rekik had the ear of the Zuranian king himself, though that was eye opening, but...*Ruben* Fadel?

It could just be a coincidence. Kissa was sure there were many Rubens in the world, of course. But with such a high standing among the Zuranians? She thought about how he stared daggers at her father when they came to Serenity. His uptightness. How he called their love a "folly". It seemed personal. Kissa had a strong gut feeling that this was the same man that asked for her mother's hand in marriage.

"Kissa, do you have anything you would like to ask the council before we begin?" Elder Harmon addressed, interrupting her thoughts.

"Not at this time," Kissa said. She let the information settle within. This was not the time to think about *Rubin*. She needed to keep her wits about her.

"Very well. Elder Fadel?" He gestured.

"It has come to the Council's attention that an incident took place in the dining hall during the morning meal yesterday. First, I want to note that at Serenity, we do not tolerate bullying of any kind."

Was the High Councilor implying that she bullied Lani? Kissa's mind whirled and the fire in her chest rose from its slumber. As if the conversation in the room peaked its ears and tuned in. Kissa sat up straighter in her chair.

"Lani, please explain to the council your account of what happened yesterday." Fadel said.

She snapped her attention to Lani. In dramatic fashion, the girl straightened up while her eyes glistened as if holding back tears. Kissa held back her eye roll.

"I went to get my morning meal in the dining hall when I saw Kissa seemed unwell. Tula and I stopped to ask her, but she became enraged and started screaming at me and my friends to move out of her way. The look in her eyes told me she wanted to move me herself. I felt threatened."

Elder Fadel nodded. "What else happened?"

"I told her that behavior did not belong at Serenity. She threw her tray to the ground, splattering food all over me. That is when I left."

Kissa closed her eyes, if only to stop the fire that threatened to burn down the room. Her fists clenched underneath the table. She didn't dare say a word, less she look like the deranged lunatic Lani made her out to be. She opened her eyes to find everyone staring at her. With every fiber of her being, she gathered herself.

"Thank you, Lani." Elder Harmon said. "Does anyone have questions?"

It was Mira who spoke next. "Lani, you said Kissa was visibly unwell? Can you clarify that? How so?"

Kissa swore irritation flash behind Lani's eyes, but it disappeared just as quickly. "She seemed upset about something. I am not sure if she didn't feel well, but she could have just said that. Kissa has always been rude to me. She snapped on me her first day when I gave her the missive to meet with my uncle. I found it odd that she wore a scarf and inquired about it. In so many words, she told me to mind my business."

So Fadel was her uncle. Kissa heard a scoff down the table. Elder Bowman. His head shook with a sense of certainty, condemning Kissa as guilty in this foolishness.

It was then that Kissa opened her mind's door. Sending her senses out, she felt nothing but concern from those closest to her, as expected. Mira was worried, and it deepened Kissa's own dread. However, she felt disgruntled energy from the other five members at the other end of the table. As if they truly believed in Lani's words and they were rallying behind her. Kissa closed her senses down.

"Thank you Lani. Kissa, can you tell us in your words what took place?" Elder Harmon asked.

Kissa glanced at Mira, and her look implored her to tread carefully. She thought about the words she imparted to her. These members didn't know her. Kissa represented the kingdom that took everything away from them. She thought of being honest, but would she really be? She very well couldn't tell them of her empathy gift. Kissa said a few choice words to Lani, too, if she were being honest.

As she stared out down the table, she realized it didn't really matter what she told them today. They will always come for her. It didn't matter how small she made herself, or what color her hair was, or that she worked twice as hard as everyone else just for subpar grades. This was bigger than Kissa and Lani—pawns in the bigger scheme of politics.

Kissa cleared her throat. "I wasn't feeling well because I haven't been sleeping or eating as I should. On my way to the gardens for fresh air, Lani and three others stopped me. I admit I wasn't the kindest that morning. However, I never once threatened her, and I dropped my tray right before I fainted from exhaustion and lack of sustenance. I am very grateful that Benji Harmon was present. I think I would have landed on my face had he not intervened." Kissa forced a timid smile.

"And are you feeling better now?" Elder Harmon asked with concern.

"Yes, I am."

Mira said, "I confirm Kissa was in a state of dehydration and exhaustion. Most likely from her travels and adjusting to the new environment. "

The burning looks from the others down the table told her they expected Kissa to scream and rage about lies and unfairness. She felt grateful Benji was there because she relied on the fact that Lani wouldn't want Benji to be summoned to tell the Council the truth.

However, it was Elder Harmon's words that made her rethink her entire life.

"It is my observation that there was an unfortunate misunderstanding between these girls. But misunderstanding or not, you two are supposed to represent Serenity's core values: kindness, selflessness, and duty, above all else. Do you think that either of your behaviors reflected any of those qualities?" Elder Harmon admonished.

Kissa bowed her head at the truth of those words. Since she learned how to walk, those qualities had been engrained in her by her mother and father. Along with integrity, respect, and loyalty. She did not display any of those qualities during that incident, and shame gripped her.

"No, I did not, Elder Harmon," she said. Down the table, Lani sighed and shook her head no.

Fadel glared at Kissa before saying, "I don't think the act should go undisciplined. The students witnessed the ordeal, and it is important that they do not believe it is acceptable to mock the behavior we work hard to uphold in our school."

"What do you have in mind, Fadel?" Harmon asked.

"Kitchen duty for one cycle after class," Fadel replied.

"Everyone else agrees to this?" Harmon asked the other members. Kissa looked around the chamber at the rest of them, nodding their heads. "Very well. Lani Fadel, Kissa Ashtar, you are to report to the kitchens after class. This will be your duty for ten days. Hopefully, you two can learn to get along during that time," Elder Harmon said.

"What?" Lani protested. "Why do I have kitchen duty?" She looked at the woman next to her. "Mother, this is not fair. You said *she* was supposed to be punished, not me!"

"Quiet, Lani. You will not rot away in the kitchens." Lady Rekik said with an annoyed look. She turned to Elder Harmon. "Is this meeting resolved?" Elder Harmon nodded, concluding the meeting. Then she stood up and yanked Lani with her out the door.

The rest of the members took that as their cue to leave. Kissa did not care for kitchen duty, but felt all the better knowing Lani hated it more. Although their plan to have Kissa expelled failed, she couldn't help the feeling blooming inside her.

Maybe, perhaps, this was not her destiny after all.

16

FATHOMLESS PIT

TAJI

AT THE READER'S DESK deep under the Grand Library, Taji pored over the books that Elder Mif lent him of the warriors of old.

Protectors in the past upheld the Natural Order of Life, a set of laws enacted by King Malachi, the Halls of Justice, and the High Elders of the other five nations. Back then, there was only one king, but Malachi was a just and fair and each nation had a representative that made up the council.

After the war and the nations went their separate ways, each kingdom established their own laws for their kingdom, but the Natural Order of Life still stands. When other laws clash, it takes precedence as the supreme law.

Treat others as you want them to treat you.

Do not murder.

Refrain from taking what doesn't belong to you.

Do not lay with someone's husband or wife.

Do not give false testimony.

Worship only The Seven and avoid any other deities.

Do not interfere with Essence, for it is the domain of the Divine.

The seventh law was one Taji researched before and knew well. Following the war, King Keysia swiftly punished anyone who even slightly violated this law.

If he discovered anyone to be Sagian or Ravenian near their lands, he promptly had them executed. Unfortunately, even those from Osmondia judged mentally unstable were incarcerated.

Osiris remained a secret known only by his mother, who cautioned him at a very young age never to share the voice in his head with anyone. The pure fear behind her sparkling blue eyes scared him enough to never tell a soul. Not even Benji, though he considered him like a brother.

In Taji's search for any texts that might shed light on the Celestials that visited during King Keysia's reign, he came across a book titled "Guardians" written by Elder Mif's great-grandfather, a former Keeper of the sacred scrolls. In truth, it appeared at his reading table when he returned the next morning.

According to the text, Celestial's core duty was to guard the Gateway between the human realm and the realm of the Ancients. In the days when they still visited Haava, they took their human form or the form of their familiars if they had one. Taji couldn't find anything on why they stopped visiting the human realm so suddenly or why the gateway seemed to vanish.

Furthermore, none of the small selection of texts he found on supernatural gifts or magic shed any light on Osiris or the drums that coursed through him. He knew that only one book held that information.

His eyes flicked to the black leather tome with bold gold scripted letters scattered among the rest, mocking him. Unfortunately, Taji still could not translate a word of it. He felt like he was missing vital pieces that connected it all. He rubbed his face in frustration. Having the answers in front of him but unable to retrieve them felt vexing.

He rose and approached the mural of the Ancient of Strength, fixating on the Sword of Osiris. *What am I missing? What would you have me do?* Taji implored.

He needed to unlock the secrets of the tome, but was unsure how he was supposed to accomplish that. He also needed to find Osiris, though he did not understand how it tied to saving his people or ridding the kingdom of the sickness.

The sound of boot steps making their way down the stairs from the upper library caught his attention. Taji cleared his books from the table and put them to the side, except for the Sword of Osiris, which he put in his rucksack. Despite his protests, it seemed he was the tomes keeper now, especially since the answers he sought were in it.

A giant of a man, dressed in black leather armor and concealed by his cloak hood, strode over to the table. Armed to the teeth, he carried throwing knives and his long sword. He threw back his hood, revealing short dark locs that hung around his ears. His thick, bushy eyebrows and deep-set eyes, highlighted by a black band pulling his hair away from his face, gave him a permanent, glowering expression. They called him The Mountain to his amusement, but his size was only a facade. Chase moved swifter than light itself and Taji was proud to call the deadly warrior his friend.

Taji gave him a nod. "How many are in the inner ward?"

Unlike Benji, who hid his sword abilities, amongst other things, Chase was a warrior through and through. He was the only other person Taji trusted. The perfect person to take to the Fathomless Pit.

"Too many. Commander Ashtar is at the barracks." He raised one of his bushy brows. "Amon is the High official on guard tonight. We need to be discreet."

Damn. Amon was the Commander of the Elite that served as the King's personal guard. Cunning with an aptitude for stealth, he was the King's eyes in everything, and it wouldn't bode well if they crossed paths with him. Taji thought it unusual that he would be the one guarding the Pit. Amon normally questioned the enemies of war. Unease worked through him. He didn't want to witness that.

They debated going through the common prison held in the Leviathan keep—the direct way to the dungeons and pit. But if everything went to shit, they didn't want any witnesses seeing them enter. Taji flicked his eyes towards the dark tunnel, calculating. Something within him urged him to consider it.

That meant going through the tunnel of the catacomb, an alternative last-minute plan Taji thought up after he explored the other night. Despite the risks, the scheme was sounder than Chase's crazy plan to spike all the guard's supper with curare—Taji didn't need that on his conscience.

"I agree." He finally said.

"It's too late to drug the bastards now." Chase said with a smirk.

With mirth in his eyes, Taji said, "We will go through the tunnels."

Chase's eyes lit up. Taji already explained what he found the other night. They had planned to explore it more when they had time, but as with all things in Taji's life, nothing ever went as planned. It seemed now was as good as any.

Sporting his own usual black leather armor and cloak, he picked up his rucksack that held Osiris' book, tools, and "borrowed" map he found. In addition, a schedule of the prison and dungeons he came across in Commander Ashtar's study. To his delight, their commander was also in charge of the schedule for the Pit.

However, Amon was not on the schedule tonight, which only made Taji more curious why the Elite leader was guarding it.

Signaling him to lead, Chase grabbed an unlit torch from the wall. After lighting his oil lamp, the pair journeyed deeper into the catacomb. Once they well and truly exited the catacomb, a draft settled in the air. While the underground library had polished stone on the walls and smooth floors, the tunnel they entered had a natural cavern feel, rugged and unfinished.

When they reached about midway, they left the main pathway, diverting into one of the branch tunnels. Taji paused along the right wall, lifting his torch. Chase stared at him inquisitively and Taji gestured for him to come closer. Empty sconces lined the walls of the tunnel, and Taji gave the face of one a twist, revealing a spyhole underneath.

A clever discovery. At some point and time, someone built a spy network throughout the citadel. He wouldn't be surprised if it was the mad king himself who built it.

Chase raised a brow before looking first. He pulled back with a grin on his face. Taji peeked next and spotted Crow, an old prison guard, sleep in his chair with a book resting on his chest. Behind him was dark, but he could just make out the cells. Taji turned back to Chase with an accusing brow.

The looks said, *Did you drug him?* Chase's shoulders vibrated, holding in a laugh, but thankfully he shook his head no.

Twisting the sconce back, Taji took the lead further into the underground passage. After a few turns, the tunnel descended, confirming their entry into the dungeons. The darkness seemed to swallow them, and the air turned humid. They kept alert, with light footsteps the rest of the way. They couldn't be certain that nobody else knew of the hidden network.

Taji pulled out the map, checking and rechecking. Soon, they plateaued, then went even deeper, where he estimated the Fathomless Pit entrance began. That is where Amon would stand guard while two trusted Scorpions patrolled the inside. A bridge overlooked the pit where he and Chase planned to post, hopefully avoiding Amon and the Scorpions altogether.

A steep incline lifted them above the pit, guiding them towards another wall. Taji was sure it led to the alcove just before the bridge. Lifting his torch, he searched for the mark he left the other night. Upon finding it, he twisted the sconce near it, revealing the spy hole.

Taji had only made it this far. From here on out, he and Chase would uncover what lay beyond together.

In the darkness beyond the spy hole, Taji heard faint footsteps. Chase listened next while he went over the map one last time. He set his oil lamp on the ground near the wall.

Chase nodded, confirming that it was clear as he twisted the sconce back, then handed Taji the torch and extinguished the fire in the lamp. His heart hammered, causing the drums to emerge. Then he placed the unlit torch inside the sconce. A soft click, then the wall section slid right.

Taking a moment to listen, Taji used it to steel himself. Then he slipped into the blackness, Chase close on his heels. Unspoken, they left the wall open, just in case they had to make an unplanned, hasty escape.

The air shifted. It felt hot and oppressive, even more so than the dungeons. Now, a strange sensation simmered inside him, a slow pull, as if something was being taken from inside of him.

The pair moved toward a dim light at the end of the hall, pausing before the bridge. Both of them tilted their heads and listened for anything that would help them locate the guards on duty. It was then that he realized that though his heart thundered against his ribs, no drums accompanied it. Taji was unsure what it meant, or how it was being caused. Deciding he could do nothing about it, he pushed it aside to focus back on the task.

Chase stared at him, waiting for the go. Creeping low, Taji scouted the entrance of the bridge. When he saw no movement or guards, he nodded and led the way. They stayed low while observing the layout. Chase stiffened beside him, pulling his attention below them.

Two rows of six all-black caged cells lined opposite each other and were barely a quarter the size of the common ones in the Leviathan tower. Empty save for three. Only two torches lined the stone walls around the cages, giving no light to the unmoving lumps of the prisoners shackled to the stone walls within. Taji couldn't identify them, but the smell of decay invaded his nostrils. Either they were dead, or soon would be.

He flicked his attention to the far end near the entrance, where sets of shackle chains lined the wall. More torches illuminated this space. Tingles of unease broke across Taji's shoulders. Right between two well-lit torches was a woman with long, black, unkempt hair hanging forward at her wrists and ankles. She had on a dingy shift that scarcely covered her, or the marks that marred her fair skin.

Taji searched, but the Pit was empty. No guards. Nothing. It didn't feel right. He looked at Chase, whose eyes wore their own shock. Despite not knowing the Pit's protocol, he sensed something amiss.

Multiple bootsteps stomped from the entrance, and as one, he and Chase moved closest to the inner wall, shrouded by the darkness of the alcove before the bridge. They stood flat against the wall and stayed completely still. Taji dared to breathe as he strained his neck to see who had entered.

Shit.

Dressed in royal armor, including a helm, as if preparing for war, King Lan himself strode in. Flanked by two of his Elite, his entire aura exuded command. With a sneer on his face and a hand on the hilt of his saber, he faced the woman. Amon and the other Elite, Tyson, illuminated the space even more with their torches.

"Naomi!"

The King's snarl echoed around the Pit. When the chained woman didn't move, he nodded to Tyson, who then splashed a liquid substance on her. She came to with a sharp growl. When she lifted her head, the torches illuminated the woman's scarred face, and her onyx eyes narrowed on the King.

Taji's body stilled. The same dark eyes he watched fade from life in his nightmares. He felt sure he watched her die before hundreds of witnesses. How? What was the reason for the king's decision to keep her alive? It couldn't be good.

He lowered into a crouch, staying in the shadows and unseen. A glance behind him, and he noticed Chase doing the same, with identical inquiries in his gaze. Taji wished they could get closer, but he dared not risk it.

The King's voice commanded obedience, filling the space. "Where is the tome?"

The woman looked at him, then bellowed a shrill laugh, grating on Taji's ears. He flinched as the King slapped the woman hard with his gauntlet-covered hand. The sound echoed through the chamber.

This seemed only to antagonize the witch as she laughed harder, then spat at the King's feet. In the next breath, Amon pressed his dagger under the woman's chin. Her laughter ceased as a dribble of blood trickled down her neck.

Black blood.

"You will tell me, Witch!"

Her nostrils flared in disgust. "I smell the fear on you. Poor King Lan's afraid of war." She made a sound between a giggle and a snarl. "But it is not the weakling Sagian king you should fear."

Amon shifted in front of the King. "You will answer my king or..."

"Or what?" She snapped forward. The shackles rattled as they restrained her. "You will kill me?"

"I know how to end your kind," the king said. "You are only alive after all this time because I allow it!"

The witch laughed again, dark and foreboding. "I am not afraid of death. I have seen my end, and it is not by your hand. My brother comes and I will live long enough to see your very ground crack open, and your renowned mountains crumble. I will laugh in glee as the waves of the seas block your skies and wash away your shores. Your precious kingdom will fall."

The air snapped. The fires on the torches flickered. Taji felt like time had stopped. The prophetic tone in her words staggered him. A moment passed, then two.

Then, without taking his eyes off her, the King said, "End her."

Taji watched wide-eyed as Amon unsheathed a long sword with a blade as black as midnight. It seemed to absorb the surrounding firelight as they swayed toward the blade. With no hesitation, he sliced through the witch's neck in one swift movement.

A light flashed before Taji could look away, stunning his eyes. He whipped his head away, shielding his face with his arm. Bile formed in his throat. Spots danced across his vision.

Expecting a headless corpse, he reluctantly looked back at the woman. Only to find her gone. She vanished.

"Impossible!" Amon said. His blade still mid air.

Tyson turned to the king with fear in his eyes. "My Grace, s-she's a Celestial!"

"Quiet!" Tension rolled off King Lan's shoulders. "She served her use. We need to find that tome. Then it won't matter what divine scum roams this realm. Even the Gods won't be able to stop us!"

Chills gathered up Taji's spine. It was time to go.

He and Chase crept back toward the tunnels. Taji passed the torch back to Chase, and the wall closed. He picked up his oil lamp and relit it. Then they moved as one to return to the library.

The scene repeated in Taji's mind. A Celestial sat right under everyone's notice, but the King did not seem perturbed by it as his Elite. Like he knew. A storm of questions brewed through his mind, only adding to the plethora of worries already sitting unanswered. What tome was he searching for? Muddled with his thoughts, Taji barely heard the faint whisper of Osiris, stopping him in his tracks.

Now that they were outside of the pit, Taji's drums returned, a hum he could barely feel, like raindrops pattering a window. He lifted his right hand, signaling Chase. Then covered his oil lamp with its cap, smothering them in darkness. As quietly as he could, he pulled out his short sword. Without looking, he knew Chase donned his hunting knives, his preferred weapon.

Taji felt the inflection of air, ducking just in time as a sword tip scraped the stone wall above his head. He dropped his lamp, but sparks formed, allowing him to see where his attacker stood. Taji launched forward with his right shoulder, throwing his assailant off his feet. His eyes hadn't adjusted to the dark yet, but he could hear Chase joining in with a quick succession of grunts and blows.

The absence of sound before the attack meant it was an Elite. His chest tightened. Though he had full confidence in Chase's abilities, they were more assassins than warriors. But as soon as it started, the scuffling stopped and to his relief, a faint light appeared, showcasing a bloody Chase standing over a body with his oil lamp relit.

The attacker wore all black attire, including a mask. Only his eyes were visible—lifeless, staring into nothing. Chase stabbed the attacker directly in his sternum. His comrade pulled his knife out, then wiped it off on the Elite's pant leg and sheathed it back into one of his many slots.

"The others will come. We need to make haste."

The pair moved further through the tunnels. When they reached the intersection that led to the library's catacomb, he stopped. His eyes flicked down the dark tunnel opposite to the library. Something was pulling him that way.

Taji realized then that through the rush of escape and survival, his drums returned fully. Though a familiar comfort, the deafening silence outside of it alarmed him. Again, he smothered the light, blanketing them in darkness.

When he explored the tunnels the other night, Taji searched the tunnel in question. He found an unused exit that led out into a cave within Aarusha. He couldn't determine its exact destination then. It wasn't on the maps, but now, with the Elite on their trail, it might be their best chance.

Taji closed his eyes and tilted his head left, toward the library, listening.

Then he tilted right, leading to the cave exit. He waited, even though his body screamed to move.

Right. Osiris whispered, clear and true.

He felt the ancient sentient guide him toward the cave exit. Chase stayed on his heels, and, as instructed by Osiris, they made their way through the right tunnel. With no light, they used their hands against the walls to navigate. Along the way, they occasionally paused, taking the time to listen. When he heard nothing from Osiris or their pursuers, they kept going.

Eventually, they reached a dead end. Taji knew it to be the exit. He grabbed Chase's unlit torch and felt around for the sconce. Once he found it, he placed the torch on the sconce. The wall opened as expected. They waited until it gully opened, then grabbed the torch before rushing in as the wall closed behind them.

Taji relit his oil lamp and assessed the cave. It was empty, damp, and musty, but water trickled in near the ground from the lone exit. They must be near the ravine. With no other choice, they followed it.

Keeping the lamp lip, they did not speak until they knew where it led. The path went deep and closed in, making them creep low in some parts. Eventually it opened up, then inclined, finally leading into another cave.

He let out a long breath as he looked around at the familiar markings on the wall. *"The First Temple."* Relief flooded his veins.

Taking it as his cue, Chase slid to the ground and leaned his head against the cavern wall, letting out a deep sigh. His friend just killed a man for the first time, and Taji wasn't sure what he should say to comfort him. If the roles were reversed, he would have done the same for him. Surprisingly, that fact didn't trouble him, because that Elite would have killed them both. They were wading in uncharted waters, and a heavy silence hung between them.

One thing was absolutely certain. This night would change their lives indefinitely.

17

Homesick

KISSA

LEAVING THE DINING HALL line, Kissa looked around for a place to sit. Disregarding the heated stares, she made her way to the back table by the window, which overlooked the garden. She pulled her anatomy notes out, an action that carried no thought behind it.

Stirring the milk in her coffee, Kissa gazed out the window, barely present. It was a beautiful morning. The kingdom awakening as the sun ascended, casting a golden glow that illuminated every corner. Autumn's arrival was evident as the forest transformed into a vivid tapestry of crimson, orange, and gold.

Kissa found the golden landscape didn't reach the dark hollowness inside her, a dreadful chasm that dug its claws into her on her birthnight, and grew each day as her misery unfolded. Ever since her confrontation with Lani, she received nothing but unsavory looks from students and instructors alike.

The failing grades in each of her classes so far only fanned the fire, burning her dreams and leaving ashes in its wake. A tear slipped through and ran down her cheek, and she wiped it away. Kissa felt so alone. It made her mood sour, which only influenced everyone's thoughts of her more. So, she ignored them altogether, content with just being present for class—a vicious cycle breaking down her resolve. Though she lived her whole life without friends, she always had her mother.

For the Stars, I miss my mother.

Yesterday, she received a letter from her. Amid the gloom, Kissa cherished her one source of joy, taking in every detail with delight. She felt her mother's passion through her words as she spoke of her theories about the sickness and the small things that inspired her. Then she read it again and again.

When she tried to write back, Kissa could only think about her mother's clear joy with her newfound purpose. She didn't want to spoil that with her melancholy. So she had yet to return a letter.

Kissa had too many secrets. Her life felt like a facade that weighed on her. Even if someone had the courage to befriend her, she couldn't bring herself to unveil her true self. She imagined telling Layla or Benji that she could sense their feelings. They would never speak to her again. Just the thought broke her heart.

It was better for them if she stayed away.

Practicing to seal off her mind made it easier for Kissa, much more manageable than suppressing the fire in her heart when she felt slighted. Kissa learned to choose whose thoughts she wanted to sense—a useful side to a gift dumped on her she didn't even want.

She wished to understand how and why she received magic. No shimmery light revisited her since her birthnight, and the library at school didn't have books on magic or supernatural gifts—at least not on humans. There were plenty of books on the magic the goddess Zuri wielded. Apparently, she had the gift of healing, shapeshifting, and transcending between realms.

If only I could turn into a majestic creature and visit a different world.

As Kissa tried to focus on her notes, she felt a tingle. Someone was watching her. People stared at her all the time, and she didn't want to ruin her breakfast and the last tethers of sanity she had left, so she ignored it.

The tingling persisted as she took a bite of her oats. Kissa chanced a glimpse and locked eyes with Benji walking toward her table carrying a tray of food with an unabashed smile. Kissa sighed. She wished to be left alone, undisturbed.

When he reached the table, she said, "I would like to eat in peace."

She regretted her sharp tone. Since finding out he carried her to her room, Kissa had been dodging him. It was for all the better. Benji didn't need her secrets and notorious reputation weighing him down.

Ignoring her request, he sat down right across from her. He still had a smile plastered on his face. Kissa refused to look at him, rolling her eyes with a hint of a grin—his infectious smile irritatingly spreading its good cheer.

"Everything alright with you?" He asked. "I heard about the meeting with the Council."

Ugh. She didn't want to think about that, let alone speak about it. The echoes of the council's hateful thoughts still jarred her mind. "I'll be fine. I'm just having a rough start."

She looked back down at her notes and continued eating her oats. Kissa hated to push him away, because honestly, she felt drawn to Benji. Pure friendship, of course, but he was like a brother she never had—she wished she had. Yet, when she thought of the future before him, the choice became easier.

"I have a letter for you from your father," he said.

She whipped her head up. Kissa almost forgot she'd written to her father. Benji handed her a rolled parchment, and she practically snatched it from him and immediately opened it.

Dear Firebird,

*I hope this finds you well. Your dream
confirms our existing knowledge, and
I'm waiting for the sunbird's return
for a precise time frame. I must say,
I am happy to know you are finding
your path.*

*As for your question, it is true. We
have long known of their treachery.*

After reading, burn this letter. Please,
keep silent about your revelations.

We will speak soon,

COA

The letter conveyed so much in those few words that Kissa didn't know where to begin. Firebird and Sunbird were nicknames given to her and her sister when they were children. The mention of Aya made her breath quicken.

The only thing grounding her was knowing that if her sister died, Kissa would know. The bond they shared surpassed time and space, but it didn't stop her from worrying that Aya lay in a cold dark ditch hurt somewhere. However, her father seemed certain that she would return. So Kissa made herself push those dark thoughts away.

She felt taken aback by her father's casual mention of her "vision". Even she still struggled to believe it, but he didn't seem surprised at all. Most likely something the oath forbade him to say.

Her father also confirmed what she thought. Sagians had magic. The answer only prompted more questions. How did they receive it? What were they using it for? The most burning question: Was her blood father an evil sorcerer as she feared?

Kissa shook her head. Hopefully, when she saw the commander again, he'd have more answers for her. She thought about his request for her to burn the letter. Were the "snakes" in Serenity part of the Council? She wouldn't put it past them. Were they working with the Sagians?

The thought triggered a cautious feeling within Kissa. She needed to be more aware of her surroundings. Something was unfolding.

Kissa found Benji looking at her with furrowed brows. His smile vanished, replaced by a look of deep concern.

"Everything okay? You seem a bit...anxious," he asked.

Kissa looked down at her trembling hands clinching the letter. Her father's words still occupied half of her mind, and the question caught her off guard. The sincerity in his amber eyes evoked the desire to share her deepest secrets with him. That she missed her mother and sister and felt alone in the world. Or that she had weird gifts she couldn't explain, but they did absolutely nothing to save their kingdom from the sickness. Or maybe that she wouldn't graduate as a healer because absolutely everyone in the school hated her and was determined to see her fail...

Yet, she didn't say any of that. Instead, she forced a smile and said, "It's nothing to worry yourself about, Benji."

He threw his spoon down on the table with a hard clink. "Why do you care what they think?"

She raised a brow at his pointed tone of voice. Kissa looked around them for listening ears. Students were on their way to class and the dining hall was almost empty, but a few stragglers turned their way.

"Who are you referring to?" She felt the heaviness of opening a door she wished to stay closed.

"The ones that think their shit smells like roses. Their narrow-mindedness is stifling both our culture and kingdom." Benji's eyes could have leveled the citadel. "You know exactly who I speak of. The ones who are afraid of a girl that will outshine them, so they put her in a little box to control her."

Kissa's eyes widened, and her mouth partly opened. Though she'd been adamant about keeping it closed, she cracked open her mind's door and allowed her senses to brush up against Benji. For the first time, she saw a faint shimmer of a strand that connected her to him. A spicy, potent sensation that wrapped around her quickly overcame her shock.

Passion.

The future of Serenity sat upon Benji's shoulders. However, he appeared determined to resist those he would eventually lead. She thought of him riding hard in the forest with his sword. Before, she couldn't even imagine Benji being that rider with his quips and jokes. Now, as he looked at her with a fire lit behind his eyes, she knew. Benji was a warrior at heart.

When she woke up that morning, Kissa didn't expect to divulge her feelings for breakfast, but deflecting was an art she was skilled at. "You will be an amazing and compassionate leader, just like your father. Hopefully, when you are an overseer, things will be different." She meant that with everything in her. Her eyes burned with the truth of her next words. "You don't need someone like me dimming your light."

Kissa wanted friends, family, maybe even a lover one day, but as it stood, she could not.

Benji's eyes hardened. "You think I give a shit about being overseer?" He ran his hands through his curls, heated, uncertain. *"We are family, Kissa!"*

Family. A whirlwind of emotions hit her with full force, and it was her own. Family didn't give up on one another—didn't push each other away. They accepted each other, flaws and all. It was what she really wanted, wasn't it? Kissa blinked back the tears that threatened to fall. He was making this so hard.

As her emotions settled, she focused on what Benji didn't say. Now she felt conflict rumble through him. Part guilt, the other part...resolve.

Kissa put her notes down and sat up. She looked around before saying, "You don't want to be overseer?" It felt almost like blasphemy to even utter it.

He simply stared at her with a pensive look, as if no one had ever asked him that before. Maybe no one did. Until now, Kissa always saw him as Serenity's future. Now, as she stared at the first person who ever befriended her, she realized the smiles and jests were just a facade. Underneath it all, something else burned within.

"It is better that I show you. Come with me to the capital," he said.

Kissa looked around again. She dropped her voice even lower. *"Right now?"*

Benji smirked, and Kissa found she missed it. "No, this endcycle."

It was two days away, thank the Stars. Serenity's class cycle was seven days, then a three-day endcycle. However, this endcycle began the Harvest Festival and most students already received permission to go home to celebrate with their family. Ten complete days of… well, she didn't know just yet. Her mother sent a request to the Shadora Council for permission for her to go home. However, Kissa still had heard nothing.

"You are not going to Zurania?" She asked.

"No, I haven't visited our homeland since I was 14. Osmondia is my home and I celebrate at the capital. It's a sight to behold. Besides, my mother needs to be with Queen Safiyah and my father will stay by her side."

Kissa sat back in her chair, eyeing Benji. "I am restricted from leaving the premises unless I am going home. Remaining here is part of the stipulations of attending Serenity."

Anger flashed in his amber eyes. "Did Fadel make that rule?"

She nodded. "When I lived at home, I couldn't leave our lands."

Benji furrowed his brows. Then his face softened as understanding seemed to dawn on him. His attention paused on her hair. She stiffened in her seat.

Kissa didn't think about the fact that Benji most likely saw her red locs when he helped his mother care for her the other morning. Why didn't he say anything? Then again, Kissa spent the last couple of days avoiding him.

"Relax. Your hair could be green and I would still find you irritating," he said.

Her shoulders relaxed. Benji's lip curled up into a sly smile. Kissa rolled her eyes. *Troublemaker.*

"We won't wear our robes. Wear your cloak so we can remain inconspicuous," he added.

She turned her attention to the window to sort out the various feelings that clashed within her. It was one thing to sneak out and practice archery. She stayed near the school when she did. Yet she couldn't help the powerful urge for freedom that burned within her when she stared at the city lights through the break of trees every morning. She didn't care about Fadel, but she cared about breaking her father's trust.

Kissa blew out a long breath. "Let me think about it." She continued to stare out the window, fearing he would see the genuine answer deep within her, but his silence made her look at him.

Benji's smirk widened and victory twinkled in his eyes. "Make sure you wear comfortable shoes."

Troublemaker indeed.

18

SACRED LAW

KISSA

As Kissa soared through the iridescent night sky, now pastel pink with blue fluffy clouds, she felt more content than she had in a while. The inverted scene had no ending. No below or above, just clouds and sky all around as she glided within the cloudscape of her mind.

When the glistening white door appeared unbidden, and the glittery gold and emerald star from before appeared, it didn't shock her this time. Her eyes narrowed, though. Kissa was sure she had shut her mind before falling asleep.

"Hello, Kissa. I have something to show you. Come." The light turned back to the doorway and drifted through, like strolling into a shop.

Kissa sputtered. She never thought the door led to anywhere else other than her mind. Floating closer, she timidly stepped onto the puffy walkway shaped like stones. She never stood so close to the doorway.

What she thought was a random white glittery door was actually white, gold, and crimson light shaped into a door. The crimson and gold zipped throughout the white like tiny lightning rods. Its arch shape, much like the door of her cottage, gave the impression that she subconsciously designed it herself. On the other side, swirling starlight stared back at her. It reminded her of the beautiful, colorful stars in the cosmos from her vision. It hummed within her, beckoning her forth.

She hesitated. Though curiosity burned within her, there was no sign of the glittery light woman. Kissa cautiously reached her hand into the whirlpool of starlight. She felt a tingling sensation as her hand slid to the other side. When she pulled her hand back intact, relief coated her. With a deep breath, she gathered her courage and stepped through.

It felt disorienting at first, like all the cells in her body rearranged themselves within that breath. As her surroundings changed, her senses did, too. Immediately, she felt like she could breathe and her body felt looser, stronger even.

Her eyes now lit up with a newfound sense of wonder. The unfamiliar place was unusually bright, and though it was a dream, Kissa found she had to close her eyes against the burst of vibrant colors. With her eyes shut, the gentle rustle of wind whispered in her ears, a soothing melody that drowned out the silence of her aching heart.

Throughout her life, Kissa had always felt restricted, but now she found she could finally breathe.

Brine and sea salt hung in the air, and the sound of crashing waves hit her intimately. She opened her eyes and her mouth fell open. Though she found herself on top of a sea cliff, it was not her own. Kissa stared at the sea that seemed made of amethyst quartz as it glittered brightly from...

"Is that two suns?" Kissa breathed. The sky itself was a blinding bright teal, almost green, with hints of dazzling yellow and coral. Breathtaking.

"It is." The light said with a chuckle from the side of her.

When Kissa turned to find the voice, it was no longer a shimmery light from before that welcomed her. A woman as astounding as the two suns above her stood before her. Her skin was golden brown, much like Kissa's, except it shimmered as if made from a burning star herself.

The lovely woman's long curly dark hair reached her hips and blew around in the wind just so. She wore sleeveless armor around her breast and torso, made from a dark green material similar to leather. The bottom flared out into a flowy skirt that billowed in the wind like her hair. She held a staff, made of entwined branches of a Za tree and at the top, the tendrils held some type of crystal orb that glowed bright all around them, even amongst the bright landscape. It felt and looked ancient. The artifact hummed across Kissa's senses, calling to her.

"You are the Goddess from Layla's painting!"

The woman smiled vividly. It almost hurt to look at her. "Layla. She is a favorite of mine. She is pure, and her light reminds me every day of why I created humans."

Her voice was exactly the same as the aura, and Kissa realized suddenly that they were the same. Not knowing what to say to a goddess, Kissa shifted awkwardly as she looked away. She scoffed in the goddess' face on her birthnight. She internally cursed herself for her ignorance.

Then her breath hitched as she watched curious creatures swimming within the sparkly purple waters. Whales? But these whales had shimmery powder blue blubber and wings instead of fins, and when they broke through the waves, they glided several lengths before diving back into the sea. Kissa's heart sang.

She realized everything shimmered in this place, including the brilliant sky and the cliff under Kissa's feet. She lifted her hand and gasped at her shimmery fingers.

"Am I- am I in Nibiru?" Kissa dared to ask.

"Yes, this is the Ancient realm." The Goddess held a sad smile.

Kissa's brows shot to her hairline. "Am I dreaming?" There was no way she was in Nibiru. The thought itself seemed impossible even to imagine.

"In a sense. The physical part of you still sleeps in Haava. However, your Essence is here," the goddess said in her singsong voice that sounded like a melody and commanding all at once.

Her Essence. That astonished Kissa. She wondered what magic was at play. She marveled at how the Ancients really had the power to do anything they put their mind to.

"You spoke of this Essence before. What is it exactly?" Kissa asked.

"It is spiritual energy. Every living creature I created, including humans, possesses a spiritual energy that I imbued within them. However, those who are gifted, such as the Ancients and Celestials, tap into it to use their gifts. Some can manipulate it to turn into their familiars. Others can bend elements to their will. It is unique to the user."

Dumbfounded, Kissa only nodded. She sensed there was more to it, but since she didn't even know the basics, she let it be. "Why am I here?"

"We are at war. Unfortunately, your world is being used as a pawn, and there are those who wish for its demise. Osmondia is just the first kingdom."

Kissa felt a deep sadness emanate from the Ancient. It felt uncanny that she could feel such a thing from someone so powerful. Then, as she processed what she said, her anger blazed at the thought of something happening to her kingdom, her people.

"Then why not do something about it? You are more powerful than any human."

The Ancient of Life shook her head as she looked out at the waters, as if she saw more than just its purple depths. "It is not that simple. I cannot interfere directly. It is the first Sacred Law that governs our realm."

"You can't, or you won't!" Kissa shocked herself with her audacity. However, the Ancients had the power to do anything they wanted, but they did nothing.

The Ancient turned to Kissa with a look that made her anger waver under such scrutiny. "I give all creation the gift of choice. I will not interfere just because I don't like those choices or the consequences. If I step in for one, then I have to step in for all."

Though she looked to be no older than her, Kissa felt the eternal power emanate from the Ancient and her ageless gaze. She created life. How old was the goddess, exactly? Kissa felt lost in her eyes for a long moment. Wisdom and discernment lined their hazel-green hues with gold and silver specks.

Just like her own.

Then the Ancient's melodic voice snapped her to the present. "What kind of life is it to be governed by us? Commanding how and when to do things." The Goddess's question hung in the air. "How will humanity learn if they don't make their own choices, good or bad? That is not why I created life."

Kissa tried to wrap her mind around that. She thought about her own life. All she wanted was to make her own choices and control her own path, whether wrong or right. The Sagians rebelled against Osmondia for that same reason—an independent spirit. Though she did not like it, she understood the Ancient's mind on the matter.

Then the goddess said, "I created and enforce the Sacred Law that governs our realm. If I break them, why should any others keep them? "

"Someone must have broken them. How do the Sagians have magic?" Kissa asked.

A darkness passed over the Ancient's stoic face. "I did not create humans with the ability to tap into their Essence. When an Ancient or even a powerful Celestial gifts a human magic, it is called Divine Magic. The Ancients regard it with such gravity that they had never attempted it before. It is not the gifting of magic in itself that is unlawful. It is in how it is done and the motives behind it."

The goddess stood in front of her. The immensity of her presence made Kissa take a step back, but her intense gaze held her in her thralls.

"Certain events were already in motion prior to the creation of Haava. One of The Seven deviated from their path. Despite being condemned, the path he created from those choices has far-reaching and long-standing consequences."

Kissa felt a bit irritated at the Ancient's cryptic words. What events? Who was condemned? Just speak plainly, Kissa thought.

As if hearing her thoughts, the Ancient's face became severe. "I told you on our first encounter that I cannot reveal too much. The Sacred Laws govern this. The balance of Fate and destiny is a fragile thing. It can tip the balance in favor of the enemy." Her face softened. "I have foreseen the many ways this plays out. You are at the heart of it all. Trust me, you will understand it all in due time, Kissa."

A chill crawled up Kissa's spine. The center of what? A powerful Ancient broke a Sacred Law. Which law, and what would stop another self-righteous god or goddess from breaking it again? Kissa felt that whatever the Ancient before her was asking her to do was an impossible endeavor.

"You will not be on this quest alone. Layla is what we call a Dream Walker. The Shaman and Protector are closer than you think. It is their destiny as part of the seven gifted to walk alongside you. Find them. Open up, and you may find that there are many, gifted and non-gifted, that share in your destiny. They will help you turn the tides. Together, you are most powerful."

Shaman and Protector? Kissa felt confused. How was she supposed to find these people? She didn't even have friends, let alone allies. She tried to think of all the people she encountered in her life, which weren't many. Layla's heart-shaped face *came to mind, and Kissa felt guilt lace through her heart. She hadn't visited her since that first day.*

"So, who is this shaman and protector? Do they have Divine Magic?"

"Yes," the goddess said. "Although we cannot intervene directly, we chose them specifically for different reasons unique to them. But most of all, we know they will use the Divine Magic gifted to them with pure intentions. We will guide all of you on your individual paths."

Of course, the Goddess wouldn't tell her directly who the other gifted were. It seemed Kissa would have to find out on her own.

"We?"

The Ancient of Life smiled. This time it was not sad, but brilliant and warm. "The other Ancients, of course. We will be watching."

THE ANCIENT AND HER dazzling beautiful world disappeared, and Kissa stared at the back of her eyelids. She slowly opened her eyes, and for the first time, the air around her felt heavy, as if it carried the weight of her suppressed existence. The other realm felt lighter and more fluent somehow, and she wondered why.

Kissa sat up in her bed. The moon sat high in the night sky. After experiencing two suns, purple oceans, and a goddess, she was wide awake. Her mind turned to the dream she had about the warriors in the jungle.

Were they the other gifted? She mused.

That explanation felt right. But how would she find them? Their faces were hidden in the vision... except one. The familiar stranger. He was one of them. She wondered what his gifts were.

Memories of the drums that had captivated her resurfaced, causing her to scrunch her brows. What kind of gift was that? He hadn't called on her since the morning in the meadows, and she wondered if intrusive Ancients visited his sleep too. She doubted Osmond was that dramatic.

Before thinking better of it, Kissa was on her feet, throwing on her robe. She put on her boots and left the tower. Though it was a rule to stay in her room during the night, she found herself in the academic wing, climbing the stairs to the fourth floor, drawn to Layla's paintings.

She stood in front of the mural of the two goddesses in the meadow. Again, she stared at the Ancient of Life. Now marveling over the fact that Layla painted an exact replica of the goddess. Her hair, eyes, skin, and build were so spot on, as if she were there herself. Kissa wondered about that, but it was the middle of the night and she didn't want to disturb Layla's sleep.

Kissa tore her eyes away, ready to go back to bed, when she yelped in surprise. Layla stood there with her head tilted. Kissa swore, and the girl smiled at the reaction. Being the object of her heterochromia eyes felt unnerving. A moment passed like that, and she was about to open her mouth, but Layla spoke first.

"My inspiration for my art comes in dreams. Sometimes I dream of places in the human realm I have never even visited. I've seen the waterfalls deep in the Zuranian kingdom and the marble pillars of the Halls of Justice. Even the jungles of Ravenia and the desert dunes of Sagia."

"Okay?" Kissa tried to wrap her mind around the fact that Layla's paintings were of other kingdoms she hadn't traveled to or seen. *Dream Walker.*

Did she just say the jungles of Ravenia? Kissa flashed back to the dream with the warriors. The sweat on her brow. Silverlight. Her death.

"But my favorite dreams are of the realm of the Ancients. Their world is not like ours. They have three moons called sister moons and two suns that orbit their world. They have the most beautiful horses, striped like lions, with horns and wings," she lilted.

Every time Kissa thought she wanted to say something, her mouth closed in astonishment. She just came back from visiting those two suns and definitely understood the awe in Layla's statement.

Finally, she asked, "You dream of Nibiru?"

Layla nodded, then turned and walked to her room. Curiously, Kissa followed. When they entered the artist's room, Layla skipped past her haven of plant life and paintings to the dresser next to her bed. She pulled out a book from the top drawer.

"Sometimes, I have multiple dreams, so I try to draw them while the memories are fresh." She explained. "When I first met you, you felt familiar, but I couldn't figure out why. By the time you left, I had already realized why, but I waited until you visited me alone."

This peaked Kissa's interest. She sat on the edge of her bed while she flipped through the pages of her book of drawings. Kissa could only see that some had color, and some were black and white—unfinished, maybe? Finally, finding the page she had searched for, Layla handed it to Kissa.

She excepted it, and when she looked down, Kissa stared in disbelief. Right before her, as if taken from her own vision, the star warrior stood. Black leather armor, fiery locs, and the familiar bow. Kissa stared at her future self, astonished. It felt so surreal, and it took a moment for her to regain her bearings.

Her mouth parted to say something but clamped closed. She looked back up at Layla, who smiled whimsically, a juxtaposition to the chill climbing up Kissa's back.

"How is it you dream of me?" A quiver in her voice gave away her unease.

Layla's face turned serious as she said, "Our dreams are a gift from our God that inspires our creativity, and all Mirons have them. I was born blind, but I see everything in my dreams. When I turned four, I started dreaming of the Ancients, and my mother told me I was one of only two in existence with the gift. Sometimes I dream of more." She tapped on the depiction of Kissa with her finger.

Kissa shook her head. "I don't understand."

"I can't answer the why. I wish I knew. But I can tell you I do not dream of humans. That is why you do not see them in my paintings. However, I do, from time to time, dream of *Celestials*." Layla raised a brow at Kissa.

"*Celestials?*" Kissa mouthed. Her fire stirred at the statement and the hum within her seemed to come alive.

Kissa scoffed. She was human. An unimportant human at that. Why the girl dreamed of her, she didn't know. However, she had to admit Layla was amazingly gifted beyond understanding, and there had to be a reason she dreamed of her.

Then her head whipped up at Layla with wide eyes. "*You're blind?*"

Layla chuckled. "I was wondering when you would catch that. Yes, all Dream Walkers are blind like our God."

"There are others?"

Layla nodded. "One other that we know of for sure, a famous artist named Lotus Maltaki."

Kissa heard of the artist. He gained fame in his time for his paintings of the Ancients, but that was many centuries ago in the days of the first ruler, King Malachi.

"The painting in the hall with the two goddesses. Did you dream that, too?"

"Ah, *The Birth of Autumn*. That is my favorite. I am merely a spectator, but I get to experience unique moments. The Ancient of Grace and The Ancient of Life are very close. I felt this unbreakable bond between them. I rarely see such an intimate moment, and even rarer, that I see the Goddess that created all life. She seems to like to be in the background of things." Layla lilted wistfully.

Kissa didn't think her eyes could be any wider. It was difficult to imagine the Ancients being intimate like humans. "The trees in the painting were Za trees. Were they here?"

Layla nodded her head enthusiastically. "Yes, there was a time that both the Ancients and Celestials visited us. They stopped coming as frequently long before the War of the Great Divide. Then suddenly, nothing at all. At least, I have not dreamed of them being here in the present. Though that could be purposely." Layla's smile fell as she looked out toward her window. "What I have gathered is that the Gateway has disappeared. It is the portal between realms. From my dreams, I gathered it was in the Lochlan Mountains in the Farrow Desert."

Kissa scrunched her face. She never read of any portal. Kissa assumed that with their magic, the divine could just appear. "Farrow Desert? That is in the kingdom of Sagia, correct?"

Layla's voice became lower as she said, "It is now. Before the war, there was nothing there. It makes you question why the Sagians chose that land to build their kingdom."

As Kissa contemplated this, Layla's next words cast her thoughts to the wind.

"You know, the Ancient of Wisdom was in love with the Ancient of Life, but she did not return his feelings."

Kissa imagined the creator of the sun to be a beautiful being and wondered why the goddess did not return his love. These things seemed complicated. "Really?"

Layla nodded. Then she whispered, "In the glimpses I saw, it seemed to me like he became obsessed, like a jilted lover."

Kissa's jaw dropped. She never imagined in her wildest dreams that she would hear gossip about the Ancients. "A jilted lover? Do tell."

Layla chuckled. "I don't know this part for sure because I don't read minds, and in some dreams, I can't hear sound. But I think The Ancient of Life knew Sage only coveted her gift to create life."

That would be a reason not to return his feelings. Many times, Kissa felt like the Ancient of Life felt her emotions and possibly even read her thoughts. She answered questions Kissa didn't even ask out loud, as if she already knew. If anyone knew someone's true intentions, it would be her.

"All I know is the story only gets darker from there, and I was not privy to witness any of it. I only get snippets in dreams, but I know that the unrest here in Haava mirrors the contention in Nibiru. I can feel it in the air in the far in between times I get to visit in my sleep."

"So your dreams show you times of the future and the past?" Kissa asked in wonder.

"I am no oracle, if that is what you mean. But yes, they are random crumbs of the past and occasionally the future. Even the present. Sometimes, I have no real way of knowing which. I am just a witness that records it in my art." Layla gestured at the colorful drawing of Kissa.

Kissa thought about her next words. If anyone understood or had clarity, it would be Layla. "I had a dream tonight. I think- I think I was in Nibiru and spoke with the Ancient of Life." Then she pointed to Layla's sketch. "This drawing, I dreamed this version of me, too. There were others. I think you are one of them, Layla."

Layla nodded knowingly. "I know it seems impossible, but you are special,

Kissa. You have gifts of visions for a greater purpose. I wouldn't have dreamed of you otherwise."

Kissa wished she knew what this 'greater purpose' was exactly. She was about to scoff, but the truth was, she believed Layla. Maybe because she felt the sincerity emanate from her. Perhaps the joy the Miron artist exuded when she spoke of these temperamental deities that stirred something within her. Or even the words the Ancient of Life spoke of her. Either way, Kissa knew within her that Layla was true.

She also felt relief that someone else experienced gifts as she did and knew her secrets. Kissa did not have to push Layla away to hide herself. She already knew. Her whimsical personality made more sense now. Though Kissa still felt lukewarm toward the Ancients for their abandonment, she couldn't argue with the fact that she understood them a little more from Layla's eyes.

"Do the Ancients have insignias?" Kissa dared to ask. She needed answers, and there was no use hiding from them.

"They do. The kingdoms adapted some of them. Miro's is called Hope. That is the painting of the man with the harp on my door. The Adels have Justice's scales. The Sagians adapted their god's black dragon."

A shudder racked through Kissa as she thought about the Chonda ring in her satchel and her vision of the warship treading through Osmondian waters. But that was not why she asked about the Ancient's insignias.

"Do any of them have a symbol with a mountain and tree atop it?" Kissa asked.

Layla's smile brightened. "Yes. The Ancient of Life."

19

UNBIDDEN SECRETS

KISSA

KISSA FOLDED HER TUNICS neatly in her case. The action was in the foreground as she battled with her heart and mind. She finally received permission to go home for the harvest break. Benji delivered it personally. Her heart soared when her friend delivered the news. She promptly turned down going to the capital. Benji handled it with only mild disappointment.

"You deserve to go home. It has been a hard first class cycle." He'd said. "Promise me you will return."

Though she knew he intended to be well-meaning, his words chaffed at Kissa, immediately dampening the joy of going home. She had only been at Serenity for one class cycle and her friend worried if she would return. She didn't even tell him the truth of it all, and yet he knew she hated being there. But that was not what upset her most. Now she felt exposed for the coward she really was.

When she opened herself to the truth of magic and finally accepted the gifts given to her, she acknowledged her part in something bigger. Bigger than disparaging classmates that didn't want her at their school. Bigger than her own feelings of rejection.

She'd carried a foreboding feeling since meeting with the Ancient of Life, and her restlessness had nothing to do with the Fadels or the council. Threats jeopardized her world, rendering her feelings irrelevant. How could she save the world if she couldn't handle other's opinions? Her challenges at school were nothing compared to what might await her, and that thought raised the gooseflesh on her arms.

Shaking it off, she grabbed her satchel and put on her cloak, bow, and quiver from the closet. She glanced in the mirror and her breath caught. Despite her unusual eyes, she looked very much like an Osmondian warrior.

The vision of herself, a star warrior, and the seven others traveling the jungle surfaced in her mind. The confident, fierce, and determined version of her surpassed this current shell of a girl.

Kissa sighed. Even if she went home, the things that truly mattered were elsewhere. Her mother just started her duties and could not take leave. Her father was at the capital, overseeing the patrols during the festival and Aya still had not returned.

Her heart squeezed, and her eyes burned. Aya was on a mission, risking her very life, while Kissa pouted about petty instructors and students. Every person she loved or held in high regard did something that mattered.

Regardless of her role in the larger outcome, she would never find the other gifted by staying sheltered. The origins of the sickness would not reveal itself by hiding about on her sea cliffs. She felt the rightness of her decision as her resolve settled over her shoulders.

She flicked her attention out her window toward the city. Benji was most likely halfway there. She needed to leave now if she wanted to catch up with him. She stared at her student robe neatly folded on her bed, next to her case of clothes. It represented the lifelong dream of following in her mother's footsteps.

Taking control of our destiny is worthwhile, but occasionally...Fate has other plans.

Her mother's words wrapped around her mind like an embrace, and for once, she understood the meaning with deep clarity. There were things Kissa needed to discover, and she wouldn't find them at Serenity, nor in the safety of her lands.

She left her case and robe on the bed. Then, without another glance, she left. Kissa didn't understand the emotions in her just yet, but it felt a lot like she was laying her childhood dreams to rest.

When she reached the forest's edge, Kissa allowed herself a moment's rest as she heaved out of breath. Sneaking through the brush made her feel elated and guilty at the same time. Glancing back at Serenity, she caught sight of the west tower. She considered returning, but dismissed the idea, determined to follow through.

Anxiety rose from the pit of her stomach. Or was it excitement? Kissa breathed in, trying to collect herself. Her eyes locked on Benji as he casually strode across the Tantara Bridge that overlooked a ravine separating the forest from the capital. Relief mixed with a bit of envy for his carefree spirit and ability to go where he wished surfaced. But it all fell to the wayside as she looked beyond the bridge.

The sturdy dark stones of Horus Citadel stood overlooking the cavernous city that spilled down both sides of Aarusha. Surrounded by an obsidian wall at least twenty hands tall, the towers and peaks seemed to reach the Ancient realm itself. Blue Osmondian flags of a serpent and scorpion wrapped around a silver sword topped the towers and keeps. Wispy clouds wound around the citadel like a slithering snake.

Kissa pulled the hood of her cloak tighter. As her foot crossed the edge, she glanced back towards the forest one last time. If her father caught her, she knew that he'd take away her only freedom.

But it isn't freedom, is it? She only exchanged one cage for another.

With that thought, Kissa crossed the clearing and walked over to the Tantara bridge. As she crossed it, she assessed the gate. Scorpion warriors patrolled the outside grounds and wore metal armor and swords at their hips. Above them, archers stood inside the towers with nocked arrows, ready. Kissa wondered if they always guarded the gate so heavily. Nervousness bubbled up. She doubted they would recognize her, yet only as she passed through unstopped did she breathe again.

Entering the city proper, her eyes wandered as she took in the homes, temples, and markets carved into the mountain. The limestone caves, fissures, and rocks held the natural beauty only found in her kingdom. Vines of violet passion flowers grew wildly everywhere, climbing the exterior of the grottos and rooftops alike. Royal blue and silver banners adorning the Osmondian crest snapped in the wind.

Some steps in the city appeared random, while others wound through houses, shops, and cobblestone roads. Unsure of the way, Kissa zoned in on steps that led through the middle of the city.

She took a breath or two to trail where it would lead her and found Benji midway. Her shoulders relaxed a little at the sight of him until she realized the extent of the steps. The number of them was endless, and that was just what the mist didn't conceal.

Bracing herself, she focused on where she placed her feet as she hiked up the steep steps. Up she went, as her legs burned from the exertion, eventually developing a slight cramp in her side. Every so often she tracked Benji moving fluently up the incline, and she cursed her lazy bones.

Kissa noticed that despite the randomness from afar, there was order to the city's architecture. On some rooftops, thatches of grass grew with little gardens. Signposted poles marked occasional step landings. They led to cobblestone paths that encircled the mountain on either side. Roads. Markets, cobbler shops, forges and anything else a city would need lined these cobblestone roads.

Kissa's curiosity beckoned her, but she stayed the course. When she made it to a landing that led to a road named *"Baker's Way,"* the smell of fresh baked rolls and other delicacies hit her nose. Her stomach grumbled, reminding her she had left without eating.

She looked up, and with sudden panic, she realized Benji was nowhere in sight. Somewhere between paying attention to her clumsy feet and sight seeing she lost him. What tickled her mind even more, not one soul greeted her since she entered the city. She expected crowds of people, according to her father's tales, but the city appeared abandoned.

Where did they go?

She did a full turn around and her stomach dropped. *"Good Goddess!"*

The steep steps below her felt like a drop to her death. She eased down on the step before her, so she could catch her breath and figure out a plan. As her heart and breathing settled, a thought crossed her mind. Kissa closed her eyes, summoning the shimmery white door to her mind. She'd practiced for days, keeping it closed, only allowing sentiments as she deemed necessary. Kissa grabbed the crimson knob in her mind's eye and slowly opened it.

Just a little...

A blast of overwhelming excitement hit her like a hurricane. Kissa fell over in her mind's eye, and literally as she bent over and clutched her head. It felt like the ocean burst forth and smashed through the flimsy barrier of her mind. Kissa's heart beat erratically as she tried to calm her scrambling thoughts, but the fear of passing out and being left vulnerable and alone took over. She couldn't seem to catch her breath and the fuzziness at the edges of her vision seemed to increase the panic.

If she continued this way, she'd surely pass out. While taking small breaths, she focused on rebuilding the barrier. Eventually, the ocean current lessened to a lake, then a bubbling stream, then finally just a trickle of sentiments came through. Fortunately, she now knew the citizens were within the bailey of the citadel. Unfortunately, it didn't tell her where Benji went. Perhaps he was with everyone, but she felt certain that whatever he wanted to show her wasn't there.

Kissa flipped through the things she learned about her magic in such a few short days, hoping to find something that would help her locate her friend. Her Essence was something she thought of often since learning of it. She still hardly believed she visited Nibiru—the world of the Gods. Was it a stretch to think that if her Essence could transcend realms, it could reach other places?

Deciding there was no time like the present to test her theory, Kissa closed her eyes. However, words from the Ancient of Life lilted in her mind unbidden.

You must not drain your Essence entirely, for you will lose your gifts permanently. Consider the consequences before casting any magic.

Kissa remembered laughing in the Ancient's face at those words. To be fair, she did not know she was a goddess then, and until recently, she felt bitter about being given such gifts. Now, she didn't know how she felt exactly. But she would be lying if she didn't find them useful, especially if Kissa took the time to master them. She needed to practice.

With her eyes still closed, Kissa opened her mind's cloudscape. Billowy, fluffy clouds surrounded her, as if her mind only waited for her instruction. She summoned up images of Benji's willowy build, his smile, his mischievous golden eyes. She was unsure if this would truly work. Kissa was winging it, but if her theory proved correct, she...

Her breath hitched. *There.* Somewhere below her, like a beacon, she felt the familiar emotions of passion and determination she came to recognize in Benji. She slowly opened her eyes and the shimmery line that she saw between them before materialized. It seemed attached to her heart, her Essence. It trailed down the cobblestone road on the right.

Somehow, her magic was connected to Benji. Something told her that if she followed the magical thread, she would find him at the other end of it.

Listening to herself, Kissa followed it past the shops and around the bend of the mountainside. It grew darker as the tall trees cast shadows along the pass. Up ahead, a copse of trees stood before her, so thick she would have missed the cave entrance between them if her Essence didn't guide her.

Kissa hesitated. The cave was dark, and she could only see descending steps leading toward more darkness. But Benji was in there somewhere. Gathering her courage, she took the steps, leading her into the bowels of Aarusha.

When she reached the bottom, thankfully torches lit the cave, and she took in her surroundings. It was empty, a tunnel leading somewhere else. Ignoring her uncertainty, she followed it, descending deeper when Kissa heard the distinct sound of scurrying and scratching.

By the Stars! She hoped the cave-dwelling rodents would keep their distance.

Finally, she approached another bend to the left, lit up by more torches that widened out into an open space. Despite the dimness, the flickering torches showed a large space. An underground cavern.

While her eyes adjusted, the odor of human waste and death invaded her senses and nearly made her retch. A deep cough startled her, and she looked down to see the silhouette of a man slumped against the wall by her feet. Beside him lay another, too still for Kissa's liking.

As her eyes amended to the dim light, she stared in shock at the crowd of people, sitting or lying on cots or the ground. It puzzled Kissa why anyone would choose to be in such a place. The air felt humid and stale. The candlelight and handful of torches made the room lighting so dim, she could barely see the windowless cavernous walls surrounding them. Trash littered the ground and Kissa jumped out of her skin when a rat skittered over her boots.

A stone's throw away, a little girl caught her eye, laying across a woman's lap. Her little flower dress frayed at the seams, and she wasn't wearing any shoes. The woman, most likely her mother, lay against the wall with her eyes closed. Dirt caked the mother's face and through her locs, and her lips cracked to the point of bleeding. Kissa's heart squeezed as she saw the little girl's arms wrapped around her mother's neck. Black veins peaked from underneath her sleeve to the tips of her fingers like ominous tree branches.

She straightened as realization kicked in. These unfortunate people had the sleeping sickness. Her heart stammered. *Why are they here and not the House of Life?* Then her memories answered for her. All the sick waiting outside the hospital for a bed. Even more, most of them wouldn't make the journey to the coast.

Surely, they needed healers to help them. Kissa's whole being roared in anger at the despicableness of it all. She scanned around and found Benji in the far corner. She stomped over to demand answers, but her pace slowed as she heard him speaking gently to a woman laid out on a cot.

The poor woman was barely older than her mother and her face contorted in such agony, Kissa felt her pain. Some of her ire softened as she watched the woman's body tremble as if even taking a breath hurt too much.

Benji took the woman's mottled hand that spread across her entire body, inside his own. "Show me where it hurts," he said.

The sick woman licked her lips, wincing with the effort. Then, she pointed to her chest, where the black veins were darkest, creeping toward her neck. Kissa quietly watched Benji lay his free hand on the woman's heart. A faint glow permeated the tips of his fingers, and the woman's face slowly relaxed as her trembling ceased.

Kissa knew her eyes did not deceive her. Benji relieved the woman's pain with no visible remedies. Only the glow of his fingertips, just like her own when she healed his father.

The now relaxed woman gazed at Benji, eyes filled with tears. A smile formed on her splintered lips. "Thank you, *Shaman*."

Chills crossed over Kissa's entire body. *Shaman*. Where did she know that term from?

Benji replied with a shake of his head. "It is the least you deserve. I wish I could do more."

He moved to the next person, and Kissa observed again, but this time, she sent out her senses around the cave. The feelings of despair and anguish that accompanied agonizing pain surrounded her. She found it hard to breathe. It was so thick in the air. Slowly, she shortened her scope to just the man before Benji.

His muddy brown eyes were hard as steel. His locs, up in a warriors bun, made Kissa think he was a Scorpion. He sat on the floor, slumped against the wall. Kissa felt his excruciating pain in his chest as she gasped and clutched her own. Feeling the agony made the sickness more real. Her people were suffering in the worst way.

The warrior's hands clenched into fists beside him, and his legs stiffened, but he wouldn't utter a sound. Benji crouched before him and whispered something. The man pointed to his chest with a grunt. Her friend laid his hand over the man's heart, just like the woman. As his finger tips glowed, Kissa felt the relief flooding through her as the man's face smoothed out and his body loosened. She exhaled, just as he did. He closed his eyes and rested his head back.

A woman reached out and clasped Benji's hands. Her eyes appeared swollen and red from crying. Kissa sensed the bone crushing grief overwhelming her. "He is stubborn and watching him suffer is so hard. Thank you." She dropped her head as tears fell from her face.

Benji's glowing hands encompassed the woman's. She raised her gaze and her relief reflected in her brown eyes against the soft light. Kissa felt the relief on her mind as the woman's shoulders relaxed.

She knew this feeling as she wiped the tears from her own cheek. She felt it before. "Benji."

Benji turned, and his eyes widened when he recognized her. For a breath, he seemed lost for words, so Kissa walked right up to him and wrapped her arms around his midriff. He stiffened.

She leaned her head against his shoulder. "It was you."

The morning Lani confronted Kissa, her empathy gift overwhelmed her, and she remembered distinctly the relief that pushed the feelings to the outset. She knew now that her compassionate friend eased it for her.

He didn't reply, but his body loosened, and he rested his head on hers. When they broke apart, he didn't smile, but his eyes held wonder. "I'm glad you came, Kissa."

Many questions whirled through Kissa's mind. Things she wished to know about his ability, about where they were, but she asked none of those things as she gestured for him to continue. Her attention rested on the people as she accompanied him.

Kissa helped pass out water, food, and blankets alongside Benji. He knew most of the sick by name, and she burned them to memory. They listened to the stories of those forgotten by the world. They mourned with those grieving, and they laughed with those attempting to ease the suffering with jokes. Whatever helped them through their sorrow.

She discovered two important things that morning. Gratitude filled her heart as she reflected on Benji's invitation, grateful that she listened to her intuition and came. To glimpse a peak of what fueled her friend's passion was an honor to be a part of. It reignited her love of healing and reminded her why she chose this path. And though she knew that Serenity was not part of that path, it didn't change her desire to help her people.

Second...Benji was one of the gifted. She knew it in her spirit as she watched her selfless friend ease one person's pain to the next. The connection to him she couldn't explain before felt more prominent now. As if a wall between them she didn't know existed was now broken down. Kissa knew whatever bonded her to Benji would reveal itself in time.

She found three of the gifted. Layla, Benji and the familiar stranger. Now she needed to find her place in the world.

20

HARVEST FESTIVAL

KISSA

BY STAYING HIDDEN UNDER her cloak hood and not attracting attention to herself, Kissa avoided standing out. At least, that is what she muttered to herself, as she and Benji walked through the massive gates of the citadel.

She swallowed down her fear as children giggling immediately grabbed her attention as they ran around the pair. They were chasing one another with wooden swords, their joyful expressions contagious as Kissa's face lit up.

So many people. Women were tending to their little ones and laughing with their husbands. Men were shouting at their comrades. Osmondians embraced and danced, played games, and enjoyed delicious food. Music, laughter, and ale hung heavy in the air.

It was overwhelming to process the scene before her. Kissa's attention jumped between the people, the decor, and the citadel itself. Decorative festive banners were everywhere. Some of the Osmondian crest, some of autumn feasts, others with garlands of flowers designed around them. Lines of purple and blue lilies twisted around the lantern poles, while silky fabric of fall colors draped the inner wall.

The organizers placed the stands along the inner wall to leave the center open to dancing and games. Different sections separated the food, games, and wares. In the game section, right on the cobblestone, a few people played quiet strategic games with groups of spectators surrounding them. Further back, Kissa saw people playing darts, while others talked amongst themselves.

A commotion in the game section snagged Kissa's attention, and she pulled Benji over to see. Amused, she watched as one group pulled the other with rope, causing them to topple like fallen trees in a muddy pool. Tug of war, Benji told her. Raucous laughter permeated the air, and they both chuckled at the mud splattered grins on the people's faces.

A little girl with bright brown eyes startled her as she ran up and gave Kissa a flower crown made of pink fireweed.

The little girl squealed. "Your eyes are pretty!"

She gave the girl an exhausted smile of thanks and watched her skip to the next woman. Putting her flower crown on underneath her hood, Kissa looked around. "Where to?"

Her stomach growled in answer to her own question. She still hadn't eaten a thing since she left Serenity. As Benji led her to the food section, many choices grabbed her attention. Stands selling fruit filled pastries, fresh produce, and different roasted meats. Keo's Fresh Kebobs, advertising ale, shish kebabs, and satisfactory service moved her feet.

She made a beeline to whom she hoped was Keo. "Hello."

"Happy Harvest, what can I get you?" The tall man shared a warm smile, reminding her of her father.

She didn't bother looking at the menu. "Chicken, pineapples, and green peppers!"

The man nodded with mirth in his eyes and said, "I make them fresh. It will just be a bit."

She noticed Benji standing off to the side. "You are not eating?" She asked.

"I like a little less meat in my diet." He said with his hand on his stomach.

Kissa's eyes widened. "Oh, I forgot! If you want to eat somewhere else, we can."

She chided herself for her insensitivity about the vegetarian diet of Zuranians. Now Kissa felt selfish about her food choice. She scanned for somewhere else for them to eat.

Benji chuckled, "Eat, Kissa. There is a special place I go. I'll meet you at the benches shortly."

"Are you sure?" she said, still feeling bad.

"It is fine," he said with a reassuring smile. Then he walked a few stands down to the stand that sold fresh produce. An older Osmondian woman owned it and her face lit up upon seeing Benji. They quickly began speaking in what looked like exaggerating gestures. She admired how her friend could feel at ease anywhere.

Feeling better now, Kissa focused on the man preparing her meal. She watched Keo—as he told her—oil the grill and lay fresh chicken on one side. He seasoned it, then flipped it over and sauteed the peppers and pineapples on another grill. He told her it was a favorite that he served at the Harvest Festivals, making the bulk of his earnings for the season.

Before too long, her food was ready, and she paid with one of her three coins. Thinking better, she gave him the other two as a tip. Kissa smiled at the action. It felt good to buy her own food.

After thanking Keo, she found an empty bench with a clear view of the festivities. Her mouth watered at the seasoned chicken, and she took a bite before sitting down. She moaned at the flavors that burst across her taste buds. It was savory with a bit of tang.

While she ate, she watched the next groups play tug of war. The initial thrill died down and, with a moment alone, Kissa's thoughts eventually returned to the sick in the cavern. Celebrating was difficult with that on her mind. Despite the joy in the atmosphere, people were dying.

Did the mothers running after their children play like it may be their last? Did the young couples prancing around know of the sick hidden away underneath their dancing feet? Which cheerful face will succumb to the sickness next?

This was most likely their sole opportunity to escape from these thoughts. Their reprieve from the realities of life.

"Are you okay, girl?"

Kissa whipped her head up to see a woman with ochre skin and long silver Jata locs, watching her with concern.

She blinked back the tears, trying to get ahold of herself. "I'm sorry."

"Is anyone sitting here?" The woman gestured toward the empty seat next to her.

Her hair color and slight wrinkles near her eyes gave away her age, but she stood strong and hale. Her dark eyes reminded Kissa of the Calla Lilly that grew around her lands. She looked over her shoulder and saw Benji deeply engaged in a discussion with the stand's owner.

"No, please sit."

"I'm Lilly." The woman settled beside Kissa. Her gaze filled with wistfulness as she watched the festivities.

"I'm Kissa."

"*Kissa?* What an unusual name." Lilly grinned, and Kissa couldn't help but smile. "Why are you sitting by yourself? Where is your family?"

"My mother and father are on duty. I am here with a friend." A twinge of yearning that liked to accompany her thoughts of them tightened her chest.

"Ah. I know how you feel. My son is part of the royal guards, so I don't get to see him much either. I brought my grandmuffin this season." She pointed to a little girl with pigtails being chased around the cobblestones by a tall woman with long, dark hair.

Despite her previous mood, Kissa could not help but smile. Though strangers, Lilly and Kissa fell into chatter like old friends. She felt lulled out of her negative mood by the older woman's words as she talked about her late husband's love for the festivals. They were once both Scorpion warriors who enlisted during King Levi's reign—Queen Safiyah's father. A time when lots of women were warriors, honing their skills alongside men.

"They have to find their sea legs if they want to be warriors these days," Lilly said.

"Why do you think it changed?" Kissa asked, confused of why only Leviathans accepted women in their ranks.

"The prophecy, child."

"Prophecy?" Kissa could not remember any prophecy mentioned in her studies that would cause the repression of women. She'd remember something like that. She always thought the Scorpion leaders were being chauvinistic. It seemed stupid to keep capable women from strengthening the military over a potential event that may not happen.

Lilly shook her head. "To even speak of it is *treason*."

Kissa's eyes widened, but she quickly dropped the subject. She had enough problems and didn't need to add treason to the list. But it stirred something within her, just like seeing the sick in the cavern.

"Can I ask you something?" Kissa asked.

"What is it?" The woman's brows furrowed as her eyes studied Kissa's.

She almost hesitated. Unsure how to approach the topic. It was something she wanted to ask Benji when he returned, but Lilly's openness was refreshing, and Kissa felt at ease. Even more, she longed to understand the public sentiment.

"The sick. Why are they hidden underground?"

The woman's countenance shared a painful awareness, as her eyes glossed over with unshed tears. Kissa felt maybe she pushed too far, but Lilly moved closer to her on the bench. "The kingdom is not as glamorous as it seems. The cursed are not the first secret tucked away to be forgotten and most likely not the last. There are even darker places that exist."

Cursed. An odd term for the sick. Kissa wondered why they were called that. Lilly's words felt personal, as if she had experienced those dark places herself. Kissa shivered at the thought of worse places than the underground cave.

"They don't deserve to die that way. Or to be forgotten," she whispered, though her indignant fire within wanted to scream it to the world.

"Secrets are a dictator's most powerful weapon. For it is wise not to seek them out," the woman said pointedly.

Kissa knew all about secrets, but using it as a weapon? She didn't believe Queen Safiyah would do that. So what 'dictator' was she speaking about? Just as her mind started to go down that rabbit hole, Lilly's voice brought her back.

"My family is expecting me. Will you be well?"

Kissa forced a smile before saying, "Yes, I think so. Thank you for keeping me company...and for your insight."

Lilly stood. Her kind eyes locked onto hers before she said, "You be careful. In my long life, I've learned that our essence lies in what we desire most. Inquiries unveil true intentions. Sometimes, it is best left alone."

Kissa watched as Lilly walked away. Her mind spinning from the conversation. The woman's words rubbed her the wrong way for the same reason Benji's words chaffed at her. If everyone stayed safe and looked the other way, then nothing would change. Kissa refused to believe Queen Safiyah knew about any of the travesties and did nothing about them. She needed to find out more.

Suddenly, a horn blew and startled her out of the bench. Kissa looked over toward the food stands, specifically toward where she saw Benji last, but he was not there, nor the woman he was speaking to. Keo shut the curtain and placed a closed sign on the window ledge of his stand. Others did the same. As if on cue, everyone around her started hurrying toward the right side of the inner bailey in whispered excitement.

She tried to look for Benji amongst the crowd, but didn't see him. Before Kissa could ask a passerby where they were going, a familiar sensation gripped her—a cadence that called to her soul and spirit. A flutter coursed through her, and a smile spread across her face. The familiar stranger was here. The tempo pulled her in the crowd's direction.

Captivated, Kissa smoothly navigated the bustling crowd in her trance. As the mighty cadence echoed, it carried a hint of sadness, reminding her of the warrior's grief for his mother the other morning. Kissa feared the worst.

The crowd moved towards the back of the citadel to a newly constructed extension to it she hadn't noticed before. Its stone appeared brighter than the citadel, and the outer walls had a rounded shape instead of rigid and straight like the rest. The superstructure was over half the height that of the fortress, hidden by inner walls to the outside.

She halted before what appeared to be a tunnel entrance. Kissa moved out of the way as citizens rushed past her and entered. Though the urge to follow surged through her, the logical worry of coming across her father stopped her. In the growing chaos, she couldn't find Benji anywhere.

By the Stars, she muttered to herself as she watched the last few citizens from the bailey entering the tunnel. She didn't hike millions of steps to stand all alone in an empty bailey. Surely, Kissa could blend in with the crowd as long as she kept her hood on and her wits about her. Right?

The cadence coursed stronger through her being, urging her to come. Its persistence, along with her curiosity of the what event was about to take place, finally won her over. A group of five chatting animatedly among themselves walked past Kissa to go through the entrance. Without second-guessing it, she blended in with them.

Sticking close to their group, she followed them through the tunnel and beyond.

Kissa didn't know what to expect as she entered, but as she took it all in, her mouth fell agape. The morning sun beamed down on her from the open top. The superstructure had no roof. She turned completely, taking in the ongoing rows of elevated stone steps that stopped at the outer wall and wrapped around the entirety of it like a ring. The people rushed toward the steps, some sitting down.

Amphitheater, she heard a man say to another as they walked past her.

This was the amphitheater her father mentioned. Kissa remembered trying to picture what it was as he explained it, but her imagination didn't come close to what lay before her. She turned to the center of it all, an enormous pit with packed dirt inside, where a small assembly of musicians played. The melody of the music had an upbeat tempo, but Kissa knew it was not the song that tugged on her spirit.

Feeling exposed, she lowered the cloak's hood to conceal her unusual eyes and followed the rhythmic pull across to the other side of the pit. She watched the musicians perform energetically as she strolled past and thought it odd that they performed on dirt. She wondered if some type of musical concert was about to start.

As she rounded the pit, she came upon two Scorpion warriors guarding an alcove that blocked the other side of the arena. On the other side, a wide balcony lined up on the outer wall of the citadel, with an opening in the center. From the balcony, a flight of steps that split around a massive gate at the bottom led to the pit. Beyond the closed gate appeared to be a dark tunnel. That was where she needed to go. The source of the beautiful sad tempo came from there, she was certain.

What would she say upon finding the familiar stranger? What if he didn't desire to see her, and she only imagined the intrigue in his striking blue eyes? She steeled herself. There really was only one way to find out. While contemplating her words for the alcove guards, another horn blew. She turned and saw everyone hurrying to the higher seats.

As Kissa scrambled to decide what to do, her eyes fell on a group of Scorpion warriors entering the tunnel entrance. Her heart froze as she recognized the commander leading them. Her father.

"Ancients!" She ducked so fast that she knocked into a woman beside her. Sheepishly, she apologized and slipped past the scowling woman into the crowd.

Thankful that a lot of them were standing, she hid from view. She wound through the throng, making her way to a higher level, and stood between two hefty Osmondian men. They paid her no heed while she glanced past the man on her left. Her father stood in the first row. Though dressed in his usual warrior leathers, he seemed different. His brown eyes held a calculating gaze, assessing everyone and everything around him. He was on duty.

She sighed at the tension that left her shoulders, feeling grateful that she didn't stand in the empty bailey to wait for Benji. Kissa imagined her father dragging her home in that instant, never to see daylight again. The cadence still lulled her, but she couldn't risk getting caught. Kissa would have to find the familiar stranger later.

The King! Whispers around her grew animated.

She stiffened as her eyes swept around to look for the said King. The musicians played a dramatic melody. Everyone's attention was on the much grander area with balconies cut off from the rest. There, amid a dozen warriors, a poised man stood, wearing a velvet royal blue robe and a golden crown that graced his head.

Two black-clad warriors, reminding Kissa of assassins, broke off from the rest and flanked the Osmondian King as he gracefully descended the steps to the pit. He was a handsome man. His dark brown Jata locs braided into an exotic design didn't seem feminine in the slightest. His build was warrior-like, tall, with broad shoulders and a two-handed sword that looked mighty and heavy, slung from a scabbard at his waist. Kissa recalled her father saying that before he was king, he was the Scorpion General for over two decades.

She searched the balcony for someone that might resemble the Crowned Prince, but only the Scorpions guarding the area remained. Kissa cursed again when she realized everyone around her was kneeling. She hurriedly dropped her head, feeling awkward and clumsy, not at all sure if she was doing it right. All the while, her eyes swept around. Amidst the flurry, she failed to notice the Leviathan Warriors occupying the first few rows in her section.

When the King made it to the center of the pit, he raised his arms. The dramatic music stopped immediately and all she could hear was her own heart thundering in her ears. Kissa wondered what event she had stumbled upon that the King and almost all the military were present.

"*Rise,*" he boomed across the space.

The musicians quickly packed their assembly and left through the right alcove. The pit was now empty, except for the king and his two black clad warriors standing in the middle.

The king smiled and said, "Welcome to the 150th Harvest Festival and the long awaited King's Tournament!"

The crowd roared its approval. She heard banging on shields by a magnitude of warriors. In the row her father sat, Scorpions shouted proudly, lifting their swords. Below her, the same enthusiasm blared from the Leviathans with their axes and short swords in the air.

"I hope you are enjoying the new amphitheater!" The King smiled and once more, the audience shouted, and Kissa couldn't resist the excitement. "I know you are as excited as I am."

Her father told her stories of the Tournament and his battle in his challenge to become Commander, long ago. She remembered being confused and feeling the tradition was brutal. But now, being enveloped in it, a thrill seeped into her.

"Although my wife, our queen, cannot be present, we must uphold the tradition in her honor." The King's voice turned grave and not a sound echoed among the crowd at the mention of their queen. "We will honor Queen Safiyah the Great and keep her in our hearts as we discover the next Champion of Osmondia!"

The people roared louder this time. Across the pit, the gate opened under the king's balcony. Where the familiar stranger's cadence urged her. A warrior entered, fully armored, with an enormous axe raised in the air. Kissa couldn't see the armor's insignia, but the surrounding Leviathans clamored at their shields in answer and the crowd stomped.

"From the depths of the Den of Serpents! Osmondia's current Champion and our favorite Commander of the Mighty Leviathaaaans... Maru, The Axe!"

Kissa shouted with the crowd this time, feeling lost in the feeling. She felt like she knew Commander Maru from all her father's stories. Whispers of anticipation for the Challenger filled her ears. Kissa wanted to know, too. As the crowd died down, the King raised his hand. Silence blanketed the audience.

The King's smile beamed brighter. "Now, the long awaited challenger. A young Scorpion warrior!"

Loud clamoring and deep hoots made Kissa peek over to where her father stood. The rows and rows of Scorpions standing, pounding their shields, and calling out made Kissa smile.

"This warrior has rightfully earned his place here. He enlisted at 12 summers old so that he could one day lead his *kingdom to glory!*"

Kissa gasped with everyone else. *Who was this challenger?* The whispered excitement turned frenzied around her.

If the King's smile could get any wider, it did. "Yes, Osmondia! Help me introduce the 150th Challenger, your Prince and heir to the throne... *Taji, theeee Slayerrrrr!!!*" He bellowed across the amphitheater.

Kissa's breath hitched. She couldn't believe the Crowned Prince was taking part in the King's Tournament. The surrounding noise became deafening, and she thought her eardrums would bust. Her whole body shook from the crowd's stomping. The gate opened again, revealing the prince and possibly the next Champion of Osmondia.

Kissa didn't think she breathed as her eyes followed his tall frame, long dark locs that reached his midriff, and that familiar determination in his steely ocean-blue eyes. Eyes Kissa daydreamed about every day since the First Temple. Her heart hammered along with the cadence of drums that called to her like a siren. Stronger now as the source grew closer. Her mind tried to wrap around what she was seeing and feeling.

Amidst the surrounding chaos, Kissa only saw *him*. The familiar stranger was the Crowned Prince of Osmondia.

21

OSMONDIA'S CHAMPION

TAJI

SITTING CROSS-LEGGED ON THE ground with his sword on his lap, the Crowned Prince's eyes fell closed as he listened to the roar of excitement from his people. Despite it being one of the most monumental days of his life, his heart felt heavy as it stayed with his mother lying in a coma, fighting for her life.

Taji couldn't seem to muster the same level of enthusiasm as his people. He wondered how she stayed with them for so long, fearing his mother's last breath was imminent. The torturous wait, a reminder of life's fragility.

Focus, Osiris whispered.

Taji knew he should. In a moment, the horn would sound, marking the beginning of his most important battle. But it didn't matter. Nothing mattered if his mother died. Everything good and right in their kingdom would perish with her. The crown overwhelmed him. Her dreams felt impossible.

How am I to fulfill it?

By its own accord, Osiris' drums filled his spirit. His brows furrowed in confusion. He was not practicing or meditating, nor had he opened up the book that continued to vex him. He listened to the gentle and steady melody emerging, reminiscent of a sacred song—far from the usual beat of battle. Yet, he swayed to its rhythm, giving himself to it and the tears he fought back for what felt like a moon cycle fell.

Osiris mourned with him.

Focus.

The ancient voice sounded softer as he wrested Taji's burdens from him. Sounds and time faded, as if he weren't physically present. Then, as if by magic, a sword appeared upright before him.

Taji thought his heart stopped. The pummel, hilt, and cross guard gleamed with a golden hue, while intricate divine script adorned every inch. As he gawked at the sword in his mind, he could feel a slight tingling sensation, as tiny blue and white electrical currents flowed through the metal.

He cautiously reached out for the sacred sword. It pulsed twice—a silent consent.

Despite his thoughts of unworthiness and every other emotion bombarding him, he couldn't resist being drawn to it. As his hand gripped the hilt, the sword beamed even brighter. Approval hummed through Taji's hand, vibrating through his shoulders and chest until it settled in his core.

Aware it was a figment, he couldn't deny the sword's rightness in his hand. He wondered how much grander it would feel to actually wield Osiris in battle. His mind slid to an absolute focus that surpassed anything before and with it, something deeper unlocked within him. The crescendo vibrated with the light within and moved through his body and his spirit and filled him with something he couldn't quite comprehend.

Wisdom?

Maybe, because before him, something started taking shape. As if the board and pieces of the frustrating game played by the gods finally revealed itself. A thought came to him, clear and true. He may not fully understand the path before him, but winning the tournament was a crucial step.

Then the horn sounded.

Taking stock of his senses, he opened his eyes. The subtle noises around him sounded crisp even while the drums thrummed. He carefully stood up with his short sword and grabbed his shield. Though the tunnel was dim, he knew his sight sharpened as he took in every detail around him. For once, he experienced a sense of wholeness.

Taji heard his father's voice boom through the small tunnel as he announced Commander Maru. A sliver of doubt passed through him. Outperforming him won't be easy. There's a reason Maru was a two-time champion.

Courage...

The tunnel to the gate pulled open. With a deep breath, Taji steeled himself and entered the pit. The bright sun pierced his eyes, and it took a moment for his vision to adjust. He heard the crowd's deafening cries and stomping of feet, along with the familiar sound of swords hitting shields.

He took in his Scorpion brethren, lifting their shields in salute. The crowd started chanting his name. A trickle of pride filled his heart, not for himself, but for his people who filled the arena to watch him. These were his people, and he needed to win for them.

He eyed Commander Maru's massive arms as he tossed his mace axe from hand to hand, spinning it as he did. A dangerous weapon that bashed heads in. If the Commander felt surprised to fight his prince, he didn't show it. His smug look signified that he wasn't worried in the least.

Taji's focus was on keeping Osiris's drums in his mind front and center and winning this tournament. Deep within him, he felt that if he didn't win, all would be lost.

Moving to his stance, the horn sounded, and Maru charged with purpose, wearing a wicked grin. Clearly, confidence was not short among the Leviathan warriors or their commanders. Taji kept his cool, listening to the rhythmic beat course through his body. Now in battle mode, he felt his mind expand and his surroundings slow. The noise surrounding him became background chaos.

He watched Maru fight in the last two tournaments, and he knew how he moved. The commander moved forward, swift as if he were not an enormous block of muscle. Taji ignored his inclination to move and waited patiently for his massive ax to swing forth before he sidestepped and spun with momentum, elbowing Maru in his nose.

Taji heard him grunt, then Maru swung his ax upward with lightning speed. Not trusting to move fast enough, Taji parried, now on the defense. A move the commander expected because he turned his axe forward, aiming for his torso.

Taji jumped back. Maru grinned, unfazed by the blood dripping from his nose.

Taji assessed the Commander. He spun and heaved his axe as swiftly as a sword. Fortunately, he did not have Taji's reach or his swift footwork. So, he moved to the outside, circling him.

Maru's grin grew as he spat blood on the ground. "Is the Princeling scared?"

The Commander followed through with a swipe to the right side. Taji spun to the left, but the axe still nicked his outer forearm. He barely registered the sharp pain as he bounced back from Maru's reach. Now the Commander looked amused, and his dark brown eyes reflected a predator. And just like a lion pouncing on his easy prey, he charged after Taji, swinging his axe around his head at a quick speed like a propeller.

Taji knew this move. It was how Maru received his name, The Axe.

With no opening, he lifted his shield, blocking the haymakers that pushed him back with potent force. A powerful blow caused Taji to slide backwards on the packed dirt and his shield to splinter. For an instant, he wavered as he saw his approaching options. He was close to the edge of the pit and knew one well-timed blow would cause him to stagger outside the pit and losing by technicality, or even worse, lose his head.

As he attempted to step to the left side of him, Maru met him with his axe, smashing what little left of Taji's shield into pieces. Fear danced along his spine. Warriors died in challenges all the time, a glaring fact. The people did not need to mourn both their queen and prince.

Taji grappled for Osiris in his mind as the cadence boosted alongside his adrenaline. It seemed almost an impossible task in the throes of battle. Now he used his short sword to parry the hefty axe, but as the weapons connected for a third time, Maru's axe cut through his blade like water.

Shit.

Shieldless, with a broken sword in his hand, Taji bounced back out of Maru's immediate reach. The Leviathan Commander barely took a moment to catch his breath and was prowling towards Taji again. He bunted his axe toward his chest. The Prince spun to the right of him, barely avoiding the chest crushing hit, but as the commander continued forward with the force of his momentum,

Taji whipped around and stabbed the back of his exposed right thigh with the broken blade.

Riding the moment, he pulled the broken blade out, stepped to the side, and slid into his stance.

Maru grunted in pain, but he refused to fall. However, he took the moment to collect himself. Taji used the time to fasten his connection to Osiris, then braced into a crouch. Both warriors watching closely as they crept in a wide circle around one another.

Then Maru lunged towards him. This time, his axe swung forward in a wide arc as he aimed for Taji's vulnerable chest. With his feet rooted to the ground, he arched backwards, bending back so far, he braced himself with his free hand. Taji felt the force behind the swing as the wind blew across his face.

With his injured thigh, the force of not connecting staggered Maru. Seeing the opening, Taji bounced forward, and with his broken sword clutched tightly, unleashed a forceful uppercut, striking the Commander directly on the chin. Maru's head flew back, and the rest of his body followed as he dropped hard into the dirt, still clutching his axe.

To the prince's relief, Maru did not get up. Blood leaked from his mouth, thigh, and nose now as he lay unconscious. Taji observed the shards from the pieces of his shield and sword littered across the pit. He shook his head in disbelief.

The crowd's shouts flooded in as his mind wrapped around the fact that he actually defeated the commander. He didn't allow the high of his people to fill him with pride, as if it weren't the narrowest win in history. He nearly died twice.

Instead, he closed his eyes and gave thanks to Osmond and Osiris for this favor. Then he released the drums.

"Well done, my son!" The King beamed proudly as he clasped his shoulder, causing Taji to grimace. He quickly reminded himself that he did this for his people, his kingdom. He forced a smile and nodded to his father, keeping up appearances.

His father walked to the middle of the pit with a glint in his eye as he gestured him forward. He raised his hand, and the crowd fell into obedient silence. Grabbing Taji's wrist of the hand with the broken sword, he lifted it in the air.

"Our new Champion of Osmondia, Prince Taji Isaiah Lan!"

Warmth spread through his chest as the crowd screamed his name and the banging of his fellow warrior's shields and war cries reached his ears. Commander Ashtar gave his nod of approval. Clearly, they did not care that he almost lost. Taji let out a long breath he didn't know he was holding.

I did not fail my them.

His eyes caught on a few Leviathans and healers running across the pit to assist their fallen commander. When Maru sat up, now conscious, he stared daggers at Taji that could have slit his throat where he stood. He didn't return the gesture, of course. Commander Maru was more than a worthy opponent. Instead, he nodded to the man in respect.

Then Taji strode out of the pit as Osmondia's new champion.

TIME SEEMED TO FLY by as Taji greeted his people, who rushed towards him no sooner than he exited the pit. The moment made all the previous seven seasons of challenges worthwhile, despite the exhaustion and pain. He realized, as he watched his people look upon him with appreciation and shout their praise, that this was the hope they needed.

"Well fought!" Commander Ashtar clasped his shoulder. A glint of pride in his eyes provoked a smile from Taji. "It feels like only yesterday that I put your first sword in your hand."

Taji remembered that day clearly. At twelve summers old, he told himself that he would one day gain the prestigious title of commander and lead a legion just like him. "Thanks, Commander. I couldn't have done it without you."

As he spoke, Taji knew he truly cared nothing for his father's superficial praise. It was this man's approval he sought. The commander's fierce dedication and sharp guidance made this moment possible.

With a genuine smile, he shouted. "*Scorpions!*"

"*Scorpions!*" His brethren called out en masse. Swords hit against shields clamoring throughout the amphitheater, exciting the crowd. Taji laughed and felt lighter than he did in a long time.

Hundreds of greetings and thanks later, the sea of people finally parted ways to enjoy the rest of the season's festivities.

"Brother, that was the shortest tournament in history. The people had no time to enjoy it!"

Taji turned to Chase and gave him a knowing smile. "It is not my fault the Leviathans can't stay up long enough for me to get in a few good moves!"

They both laughed as Chase clasped his shoulder in a warm greeting. "It is true. I almost died from laughter when you laid him out snoring. An epic fight! They will speak of it for centuries to come!" Then he cupped his mouth like a horn. "CHAMPION OF OSMONDIA!"

It still had not caught up with Taji that he won the fight. Feeling spent, he decided it was a good time to go to the barracks and freshen up. Tonight was the Feast of Champions, and he needed a moment alone. He had to prepare himself mentally to deal with his insufferable father.

As he turned to head that way, he spotted Benji down near the entrance tunnel. Taji decided to go speak to his friend, but someone snatched the back of his friend's cloak and pulled him into the dark tunnel. Taji started. He went to grab the hilt of his sword and gripped nothing but air.

Shit.

As he jogged down the rest of the stairs, prepared to pummel anyone trying to hurt his friend, he caught sight of Benji pressed up against the tunnel wall. But all fight drained out of him as he recognized his attacker.

Though the tunnel shadows snd her dark cloak covered most of her, part of her golden-brown face showed as it shimmered just slightly in the sunlight rays from the entrance. She wore her bow on her back as usual.

Kissa?

Humor replaced the urgency as he chuckled at Benji's startled face. An unusual eagerness filled him as he walked over. Kissa's eyebrows were sharp and her eyes narrowed as she frowned at Benji, saying something he couldn't hear. They didn't notice him approach, too deep in their intense exchange.

"Benji!"

It was the first thing he could think of, though his eyes stayed rooted on Kissa. Benji turned toward him and grinned. He whispered something to her, and she tensed up. When Kissa finally turned toward him, Taji thought he saw her cheeks flush.

Benji exited the tunnel with a smug grin. "I knew it! Champion of Osmondia! What will you do now with a legion under your command?"

Taji smirked. "I haven't had time to think of it."

"Bull-dung! You have thought of nothing else since we were toddlers, thrashing around our wooden swords."

It was true. But now Taji felt a larger purpose on the horizon. A purpose he was still trying to sort out. "I guess we will have to see."

His attention swiftly turned toward Kissa, who joined them. She bowed stiffly and awkwardly. "Prince Taji, congratulations on your victory."

He couldn't help his disappointment in her refined, albeit clumsy, courtesy. Her behavior seemed uncertain upon discovering his status. He felt a little guilty keeping it from her, but it was refreshing to speak to someone who didn't want something from him. Taji kept his demeanor neutral.

"Thank you, Kissa." He emphasized her name as if trying it out on his tongue for the first time, making her blush even more.

Benji watched the exchange with a lifted brow. "Am I missing something? Have you two met?"

"We met a time or two. I had the pleasure of encountering Kissa at Serenity when I was there." Taji grabbed his heart in mock pain. "She almost struck me square in the heart with an arrow."

Kissa cheeks turned a rosy color. She opened her mouth to deny it, but clasped it closed. Now that they stood fully in the sun, her eyes reminded him of the morning sunrise over the tip of the forest, giving it a golden-green hue. Her allure felt captivating, and he knew she had no clue. That only drew him more.

Benji scoffed as he swiped a hand down his face. "Kissa! I wish you would have told me. I would have warned you to stay far away from this scoundrel!"

Her laugh was a tinkling delight to his ears.

"Did you enjoy the tournament?" Taji asked with a smirk, ignoring Benji all together.

Her eyes glinted, making his heart quicken. "Yes, your Grace. You fought bravely."

"Okay now, we have more important matters to attend to." Benji teased. Then he turned to Taji. "Congratulations on your win, brother."

"If I'm not mistaken, it sounded like you desire to be part of my legion." Taji jested.

"Indeed. The gods made a mistake and placed me in a Zuranian body."

They laughed at the old joke between them. Zuranians didn't believe in any bloodshed unless it was part of some healing process. Of course, Benji actually knew his way around a sword. But Taji knew his friend had the compassionate heart of a healer and he knew secrets, too.

"You know your father would never agree to that, Shaman."

With widened eyes, Benji looked at Taji as if encountering him anew. He looked at Kissa, who wore the same shocked expression. They shared something unspoken. A foreign feeling washed over Taji at their familiarity.

He knew their friendship wasn't romantic. Benji was in love with the Miron artist that lived in Serenity. Maybe, more likely, Taji just missed his best friend.

Clearing his throat, he looked at Kissa. "I'll call on you at Serenity after the Harvest Festival. If that is still okay?"

Her brows rose higher in surprise. She opened her mouth to reply, but Benji cut her off.

"Absolutely not! All Serenity needs is for the Osmondian Champion to come calling on her. It would be all the talk. Fadel would have a heart attack." Then he pondered a moment. "On second thought..."

All three of them laughed at the same time. Taji's eyes brightened at seeing Kissa so carefree. Her laugh sounded like a musical chime he could listen to forever. But all too soon, a throat cleared behind him.

He turned to see Chase and registered his friend's grim face and slight slump to his shoulders. "Brother, King Lan requests your presence." Then he leaned in to speak against his ear. "It is your mother."

Taji's smile fell just as his heart did. All the heartache Osiris soothed in him returned like a cyclone smashing against his chest. The prince made no excuses to part as he immediately ran toward the citadel, leaving Kissa and his two friends in his wake.

22

QUEEN SAFIYAH

KISSA

KISSA SENSED THE AGONY in the prince as he took off toward the citadel. She knew it was about his mother by the frantic way he left them without a word. Her heart tore, and the worse came to her mind as it did when she felt his sad cadence.

Her eyes burned as the feeling that followed her for days now crept its head up. Just when Osmondia's heir gave everyone hope, darkness wanted to snuff it out. The kingdom would mourn their queen when they needed strength for what lay ahead.

Benji stared after his friend with a torn look. "We should go to him. He needs us right now."

Kissa hesitated. She felt awkward following the prince into his home. A girl he barely knew. However, the sensation she had come to refer to as her fire compelled her to follow the broken prince.

She gazed at Benji. The prince hinted at knowing his friend was helping the people in secret. She wondered if he knew of his wonderful gift. "I'm with you. Don't leave me this time."

Benji winced at the admonishment, but agreed as he led the way. Thankfully, most of the crowd dispersed to the festivities in the bailey. Unimpeded, they walked through the now empty pit to the alcove attached to Citadel. The same two Scorpions guarded the entry. Both of their eyes washed over Kissa, taking in her regular clothing, then paused on her unusual eyes.

"She is with me. We are here to aid my mother," Benji said.

The guards clearly recognized him, but they hesitated. They didn't have their healer robes and Kissa sensed they didn't trust her. Before they could bar her entry, another voice called out ahead of them.

"Erin, Law, they are with me. Let them through." The strapping warrior that relayed the summons to the Prince. He was even bigger than her father, and though he had a no-nonsense face, Kissa felt grateful for his timely intervention.

"Chase." The guard to the right, Law, nodded. Then signaled the other guard to let them through.

"Thank you, Brother," Benji said.

Chase nodded in reply and led them swiftly through the alcove. It turned out that it was a short tunnel that led them to various entry points of the Citadel. She felt turned around by the maze of hallways and doors. Eventually, they reached what appeared to be an atrium.

Kissa stared in blatant wonder. The lancet windows with colored glass, had casings surrounding them that looked like vines of flowers. The stone walls, designed in a herringbone pattern, met the ceiling with gold crown molding trim that reminded her of waves with jewels on the crest. A glass mural of clouds and sunlight beamed from the domed ceiling above them. A woman with a white, flowy shift floated in the middle of the sky. Her dark hair floated around her, cascading over her face and obscuring it. She gripped an orb in her palms that showed like the sun.

"At night, the dome fills with stars, and the orb becomes a moon." Benji whispered next to her.

"It is beautiful." She wanted to ask who the woman was, but Chase kept a quick pace and they soon exited the impressive room.

The atrium set the tone for the rest of the citadel. Though they did not enter any rooms and kept a fast pace, the corridors leading to the grand stairs had murals and gold-framed portraits covering their herringbone themed walls. Above the grand staircase wrapped in lush, navy blue carpeting, a high fan-vaulted ceiling shaped like a star held the same lancet windows as the atrium.

The Prince crossed the landing at the top of the magnificent staircase. He glanced back, locking eyes with her briefly before continuing. Another set of guards kept guarded the landing, but upon seeing Chase, they allowed them through.

Down a lengthy corridor, grander than her own home, Kissa sensed waves of sorrow assaulting her mind. Guards, servants, healers, and others stood outside an overly decorated double door with a tense presence. The Queen's chamber.

Benji nodded to the polished wooden benches across from the doors, one of the many decorating the hall. "I'm going to check on my mother."

Kissa nodded and sat in solemn silence while he and Chase entered the chamber. Her attention traveled to the paintings on the walls, searching for a portrait of Queen Safiyah. Several were family impressions, but the majority were of old kings—no women. As she contemplated this, Mira exited the chamber with a grim face.

"Mira!" Kissa stood.

"My dear, I'm glad you are here," she said. "How are you feeling?"

"I am not sure."

Mira nodded. "Since your grandmother's passing, Safiyah is the closest thing I have to a sister. And the prince..." She sucked in a breath. "He asked for you. Once the King leaves the chamber, I will take you in."

"*Me?*"

Kissa's mouth suddenly felt dry. Surely, there were others he wanted with him during this time. Could she even deny the prince?

The queen's chamber doors opened before she opened her mouth to protest. The warriors stood stiffer, whispers suddenly silenced. King Lan, flanked by two black-clad warriors, exited. He wore the same royal robes as earlier, though his enthusiastic countenance changed drastically.

Everyone crouched on one knee. Kissa was unsure of what to do. As if hearing her question, Mira pulled on her cloak sleeve. Kissa saw the Royal Healer bow her head and did the same.

As the King passed, curiosity incited Kissa to lift her head just enough to see him through her lashes. She opened her senses. He appeared guarded and regal, as if accustomed to concealing his feelings in public, yet Kissa felt a peculiar satisfaction from him. Similar to the sated feeling she felt when her arrows met their marks—not the grief a man should feel when losing his wife.

The King swept away down the hall, not sparing a glance or a word. The tension in the hall ebbed away with him. Benji and Chase walked out a moment later, whispering to one another in deep conversation.

"I will walk you in," Mira said as she handed Kissa a cloth to cover her mouth and nose.

Kissa wanted to tell Mira she couldn't go, but words failed her. She put on the cloth, though she knew she didn't need it. When she spared a glance at Benji, his brows knitted with concern. He nodded at her, an assurance that he wouldn't leave.

Taking a breath, she stood and reluctantly followed Mira inside Queen Safiyah's room.

⚬

WHEN SHE LEFT SERENITY that morning, not sure where Fate would take her, visiting a royal chamber never crossed her mind. An enormous fireplace on the farthest wall nursed a small fire. Intricate windows on the right wall were open, but the room was dim. It even *felt* dim.

She noted the Queen's massive canopy bed with huge posts on the left wall. Thick plum drapes hung over the canopy, with white roses woven at the bottom seams. Prince Taji sat on an oversized chair beside the bed, holding his mother's hand. His face was grim, and the sourness of his grief caressed her.

Queen Safiyah lay tucked under covers with her eyes closed, and her dark brown hair was loose in waves around her head. As Kissa followed Mira closer, the frailness of the queen made her heart speed up. She seemed thin and the dark veins marked her everywhere.

Anxiety filled Kissa, and she felt stuck, not willing to move any closer. Tears welled in her eyes as she tried and failed to block the sadness out. Unfortunately, the feelings were her own. It was too soon for her to witness another death.

She heard a rattled breath and gasped. The queen's chest rose slightly. She was in the last stages before death.

"Kissa is here, your Grace. I'll be right in the hall if you need me." Mira's words broke the heavy silence.

Her shoulders stiffened as she watched Mira leave the chambers, not realizing she wouldn't be with her. Standing awkwardly, Kissa looked down at the beautiful woven carpet matching the canopy drapes. Despite being summoned by the prince, she couldn't shake the feeling of intruding on something very private. She wished to be anywhere but there.

Prince Taji turned to her, gesturing for her to come closer. She obliged, sitting in the empty chair next to him. "She was always strong with purpose. It's hard to see her this way. It's as if she is holding on to us."

His words wrapped around her heart and settled there. This was not about her. Her duty as a healer was also to console those in need. Kissa squared her shoulders, taking in a deep breath. "What do you need from me, my Prince?"

His leg bounced nervously, so unlike the confident warrior he portrayed. "At first, I thought I had imagined it. I don't even think you knew what you were doing. But that day, when you touched me, you healed something inside me."

Kissa stiffened. "I did?"

"I hadn't slept in days and I was a broken mess that morning. After you touched me with your light, I felt...*renewed*."

She reflected on that morning, the light that emanated from her palms. It seemed so long ago now. She lifted her hands, now curious of the ridges that lined her palms.

A smidge of hope filled Kissa at the Prince's confirmation. She thought about Benji's gift to take away pain and grief. Was that her gift, too? But that didn't sit right in Kissa's mind. She healed Elder Harmon's broken leg, not his mind. From what the prince was saying, she healed him physically.

"I have a healing gift." Kissa said to herself, finally confirming her thoughts. It was not an ability that the Ancient of Life explained to her, and she wondered why.

The prince raised a brow. "I figured that part out. I'm still trying to understand how." He stared at her with something in his eyes. Wonder maybe? "I've thought about it ever since, and I want to know if you would do the same for my mother."

Kissa's mind swarmed with his request, and why wouldn't he? She was his mother and the queen. If she were in his shoes, she'd ask the same. "All I knew was that I wanted to console you that morning from your grief. I don't even know how I did it." Suddenly, she felt the weight of his request fully. Uncertainty filled her.

The prince turned back to his mother. "It can't be any worse, even if you can't heal her. Maybe she can pass to the *After* in peace. I hate the thought of her being in pain or being stuck in the in-between because she is holding on to us."

"I don't want to give you false hope, your Grace."

His face softened as he looked back at her with his warm sapphire eyes. *"Taji."*

Kissa just stared at him. He wanted her to call him by his name, but was it appropriate? Did he consider her a friend? Her cheeks flushed, and she looked away. Why did speaking to him now seem so difficult for her?

Hope trickled from him and something else she couldn't identify. "I think it starts with the desire."

The way his deep voice rumbled made her forget what he was speaking about. Everything about him made her mind sputter and her heart quicken. She chided herself. Nothing would ever happen between them. He was the next ruler of Osmondia, while Kissa remained uncertain of *who* she was.

"There is no pressure, Kissa. I understand the gravity of what I'm asking," he said.

Kissa realized he took her silence as reluctance. Her eyes widened. *"No!* By the stars I want to... but we are not speaking about a superficial injury. This disease is a mystery to even those who have been studying it since the start. I'm just—I'm trying to think of how."

She wanted to heal the queen, not just for Taji but for the people of Osmondia. For Mira, and all those close to her. If there was a way, she would do it, but Kissa was not supposed to use her gifts outside of empathy and visions until she understood them more. Her hands clenched, her mind at a crossroads.

She was just a human girl from the forest. Insignificant, curious at best. The Ancient of Life gave these magical gifts to her, but neglected to teach their purpose or how to use them. Only a promise that she would watch over her.

That doesn't help me now, Kissa thought.

She closed her eyes, trying to feel for her Essence as she did that very morning. The thought of how Benji effortlessly took away pain from the sick, like a lifelong honed instinct, didn't help any. She felt similar to a fish out of water as she tried to learn her gifts on the whim.

Grasping at straws, she thought of Lilly's words. *Our essence lies in what we desire most.* Did she mean *Essence*? Surely not. But Kissa had no time to ponder the statement in its entirety.

You are much greater than you think, Kissa. However, consequences arise from using great power, often unseen until revealed. Choose well.

Kissa startled at the voice in her mind, almost falling out of her chair. She licked her lips, not sure how to reply.

Choose well.

What would be the consequence? Kissa couldn't think of any at the moment. If she was successful, the queen would live. The kingdom wouldn't mourn and Taji would have his mother back. Regardless of the potential outcomes, she was certain it was the right thing to do.

She opened her eyes to find Taji patiently gazing at her. With newfound confidence, she reached her hand out, palm up. "I'm ready."

With no hesitation, he took his mother's hand and placed it in Kissa's palm. The minor act felt significant. He trusted her completely with his mother's life.

As the Queen's hand lay delicately in Kissa's palm, she searched her core for her Essence. She didn't have to look hard—it wanted to be used, *urging her.* Instantly, her fire rose to the surface. Tingles started from her chest to the tips of her fingers, followed by an intoxicating warmth.

It felt different now that she was consciously directing it. Though it still seemed strange, it also felt like an instinct she had all along.

The light covered her fingertips, reminding her of little stars firing in the night sky. She took notice of the odd sensation of her Essence leaving the core, like a thread of yarn being pulled from the skein. Kissa clung to the queen, determined to heal her.

Taji sucked in a breath with wide eyes as he focused on his mother. Kissa saw the stunning blue in his eyes with clarity as the light from her hands grew brighter. This felt right to her. Maybe even her destiny, if such a thing were true. As if her life path followed a delicate pattern woven by something greater.

The light expanded to Queen Safiyah's hand, wrist, then arm. Her eyes widened as she saw past skin and flesh into the frail woman's internal body. She didn't think she could ever get used to that. The light flowed like liquid. *Her* light.

The dark veins disappeared as Kissa's light touched the black substance—otherworldly and foul. By instinct, she closed her eyes and tuned into her power, feeling it flow from her core. Light flashed in her eyes, and humming reverberated through her entire being.

Kissa gasped as she opened them. She and her light were one. How is this possible? Her light was not pure white, but crimson and gold specks whirled throughout it—like her vision.

The disease seemed to invade every crevice of the queen's body, and sadness for all those suffering settled in Kissa. The darkness surrounding her was invading them. She did not know how she would rid her kingdom of this affliction. Even now, fatigue settled in at edges of her mind.

Without warning, she and her light came to an impasse. A dark mass of ominous clouds enclosed the space. Thick and towering, it rolled through like a coming storm. A room? But that made no sense. People did not have rooms in their body. The space seemed familiar in an eerie sort of way. It reminded her of...

Kissa's heart ceased to beat for a moment.

Queen Safiyah's mind. An uneasy feeling wrapped around her, along with confusion. *How did I get in here?*

The difference between the night sky and the puffy clouds of her own mind and the horror before her was so vast, it didn't feel right. Dark and cold surrounded her, causing her to shiver as if it touched her physical skin. Even more, the dark clouds felt alive, like an awful, evil sentient.

As if suddenly aware of her light, the dark clouds moved towards her. A smaller tendril broke off, reared up, and latched on to her light. Pain flared through her, unexpected and brutal. A freeze so cold that it burned.

Her fire flared in response, sensing her danger. Like the night of her first vision, a burst of power repelled the darkness with crimson light. The tendril withdrew as if in pain, fleeing to the farther reaches of the queen's mind.

These were not clouds. They were shadows.

She didn't second guess it as she forced her inner fire toward them. Kissa ignored the burning sensation that accompanied it and flung her light with everything in her. *Leave her!*

The shadow withered against her light, thrashing and trying to flee, but her light only grew more vast as it pulled deeply from her core. Just when she felt her core was nearing empty, her light pulsed and swallowed the receding darkness until it was nothing. Like dark clouds receding after a storm, a soft light returned to the space, revealing a woman crouched in the corner with her arms wrapped around her trembling body.

Kissa's heart splintered. She walked up cautiously, not wanting to scare her, then crouched down. "Queen Safiyah."

The frail woman's head snapped up, meeting Kissa's gaze. Her eyes were blue like Taji's, though not as brilliant, as if the darkness she suffered snuffed them dull. "I-Is it gone?"

She held back her tears and gave the queen an exhausted smile. "It is. Your son is waiting for you."

Before she could say anymore, Kissa slammed back into her physical body, a jarring sensation. Feeling weak, she opened her eyes. Her Essence still wrapped around Queen Safiyah like a cocoon, making her appear angelic.

Anxiety enveloped Kissa, leaving her unsure of how to stop the process. Her hand remained tightly clasped with the queen's, while darkness began encroaching on the edges of her vision. The fear of losing consciousness and being defenseless filled her with dread, prompting her to release her grasp.

It happened too suddenly, and Kissa didn't even have a moment to react. Before she knew it, she was falling, unable to muster the strength to cry out or save herself. She heard Taji call her name, but it sounded muffled and distant.

Then everything went dark—again.

23

SULKIEST MOODS

MARU

MARU KNEW HIS BROODING mood wouldn't make for the best company. The concussion, the wound on his leg and his broken nose helped none to assuage it. The Zuranian healers stitched him up and applied salves, but it still pained him to walk. Every wince was a constant reminder of his defeat. His loss of title. Now, he must ready himself for the upcoming Feast of Champions.

Maru growled. He only wanted to be alone and brood, but that wasn't in his cards today.

"Brother, it could have been worse. If the prince lost, I think we'd all be in trouble. You took one for the kingdom."

Sabu wore a goofy look that he just wanted to slap off his face. Maru tried and failed to ignore the untamed mop of black curls on his younger brother's head, allowing him his phases of rebellion. He even named him his second mate, thinking with a proper title and more duties, he would grow out of it all. Now Sabu wore a stupid pastel green tunic and knee-length pants, of all things. He treated everything as a joke. It was beyond annoying.

Maru didn't even respond to his brother as he mugged the side of his head and pushed past him to exit the healer's tent. As the cool air greeted him, he took in the arena. Most of the people left for the festival and it was almost empty. He'd sent his brother to tell his fellow warriors he'd see them at the feast. Thankfully, they listened. He didn't know what to say to any of them.

His eye caught on three young children playing in the pit. Only a few summers old and full of energy, they playfully clashed wooden swords in their own made up tournament. He stepped toward them.

"Shani!"

The only girl in the group stopped abruptly and looked at him. She had her mother's big brown eyes and a smile that could melt the hardest of hearts...or the sulkiest of moods.

Her eyes lit up. "Ba! I saw you fight. You were so strong fighting the Prince!" Then she glanced down at her dusty slippers and tried to hide her wooden sword behind her back as if just remembering them.

Maru couldn't help the soft chuckle that slipped. Ignoring the stabbing pain in his leg, he picked his spirited daughter up. "Did you now? Come, let's find Ma. Tell your cousins you will see them later."

Leaning over her father's shoulder, Shani waved at them, careful not to drop her wooden sword. Maru only walked a few steps before spotting his wife, Corah, speaking to her sister, Rena. She looked up as she saw them coming. Her countenance made Maru falter. Not with pity, as he expected, but with pride and love. He pushed his shoulders back, lifting his chin a little higher.

Corah walked toward them, moving her hips in a way that, even a decade later, made him pine after her. "I had my eye on her, my love."

She wore a soft blue tunic and brown leather tights. Her dark dreads were up in a braided design, keeping her neck and shoulders clear.

Maru let Shani down, and she immediately ran to her uncle Sabu. His brother picked her up and walked off, giving them a moment. Maru seized the opportunity, wrapped his arms around his wife, and kissed her deeply. His heart sped up, and the world felt like it was finally in harmony at that moment.

When they broke apart, Maru stared into her fierce brown eyes. "I know you did. I didn't want our little girl to get lost in the crowd."

Her lip curled in a steamy way that made his fire burn. He always admired her strength, but her loyalty was next to none. Corah was the positive energy to his negative.

He leaned into her and grabbed her hips with mischief in his eyes. "Are you sure you don't want to leave tonight? We could leave right now. Just give the word."

Corah chuckled, a sound that ignited his heart. She twisted her lips as if contemplating it. "I'm sure we can wait a few days."

Maru let out a dramatic sigh and playfully scowled with disappointment, making her laugh more. All too soon, the pleasant moment faded, leaving behind the harsh reality of his defeat.

Knowing him well, Cora did not allow him to brood. She grabbed his leathers. "I am proud of you. You fought well, and you gave it your utmost. You are one of the most respected commanders in the greatest military in the world." She rubbed his chest as if soothing his pride. "Even if you had none of it, you will always be *my* champion."

She passionately kissed him, her lips easing Maru's lingering frustration. Moments passed, and he wished to hold her longer, but he saw Sabu stride up with Shani and their mother in his peripheral.

"What would I do without you?" He reluctantly let his wife's hips go and turned to his mother.

He winced as she pulled him down to her level to kiss his forehead. "You fought well, son."

The Commander managed a smile as he hugged the woman who only saw the good in her sons. He valued all of their efforts, truly, but this was something he needed to face on his terms. Unfortunately, that would take some time.

He addressed them all as he said, "By first light, I must visit the coast to oversee my warriors."

Corah palmed his cheek with concern in her eyes. "Everything will be fine. You need rest," she said.

He grabbed her hand and kissed it. "I will rest once I'm there."

Despite not wanting to worry his family, he felt conflicted after leaving Sapphire City with less than his intended patrol. Before the harvest, he expressed his concerns at the Council of War after a few scouts warned them of an unidentified ship departing Dragon's Cove. With Commander Ashtar's support, the king agreed to five hundred Leviathans in Sapphire City.

Then, the night before he left the coast, the king sent an order that all warriors were to attend the festival. King Lan spoke of some gibberish about fearing Osmond's wrath, but the commander sensed a deeper scheme. Lan held his cards close to his chest, and it was impossible to decipher his actions.

Maru was livid, and he had an uneasy feeling about it all. So, he ordered half his personal warriors to stay behind. Those more loyal to him than the impetuous king.

He pushed the foreboding feeling aside and glanced at Corah. He knew she didn't like his decision, but his worries were valid. She said nothing else, but her pensive look meant Maru would hear it tonight.

With an impatient huff, he said, "Let's get ready for this bloody dinner."

24

FEAST OF CHAMPIONS

TAJI

TAJI PLACED HIS MOTHER's hand in Kissa's, not knowing what to expect. The pure light from her fingers moved its way to his mother, mesmerizing him as it also stroked fear in his heart. The ethereal energy flowing from her felt like whispers from the sun, reviving and nourishing, but Taji feared the unknown. He still knew next to nothing about magic.

Eventually, those fears laid to rest as he watched his mother transform before his very eyes. The dark veins dissipated as Kissa's light smothered them in its wake. His mother's chest expanded as the light reached her lungs, now taking full breaths. When his mother's face smoothed out, no longer grimacing from pain, Taji thought his heart would burst.

While Kissa's eyes were closed, as if she were in a trance, he stood, hovering just above the warm rays encasing his mother. Kissa jolted, and his attention immediately snapped to her. Her face scrunched up as if in anguish.

Concern rode him. Neither of them knew what to expect for his mother nor for her. *"Kissa!"*

She didn't respond. Eventually, though, her face returned to normal and his panic settled for the time being. Taji felt helpless to stop or encourage the magic, but his attention continually flicked between Kissa and his mother, watching.

When she finally let go of his mother's hand, he noticed her trembling in the chair. Then her body gave way from underneath her and Taji caught her just in time before her face hit the unforgiving stone floor.

Her eyes stayed shut, and fear clawed across Taji's chest as he moved her onto the lush area rug as gently as he could manage. Checking her pulse, he confirmed its presence as he pondered what to do.

There were only a few he trusted, but only one wise and understanding enough to advise him and help Kissa. As he decided, a screech came from his mother's window. An enormous bird perched on the sill. Its golden brown and white feathers glinted in the sun's light, while scrutiny and intelligence radiated from its intense gold eyes. Its keen attention moved from Taji to Kissa's lying form on the floor. Golden eagles were rare, and he had never seen one with actual gold in its feathers, nor such brilliant amber eyes.

With no time to speculate, Taji rushed to the door and poked his head out. Various sets of eyes landed on him, but he only looked for one. He nodded toward her and silently Mira stood and followed him inside. When they reentered the chambers, he immediately looked toward the window, but the mysterious golden eagle was gone.

Mira's face fell upon seeing Kissa and she rushed to her, kneeling down on the floor to check her for injuries. "Your Grace, what has happened?"

Taji felt conflicted. He was uncertain if he should tell Mira Kissa's secret. Since that morning at Serenity, he felt the urge to keep them, but without knowledge of the ailment, Mira couldn't heal her. He was uncertain if she even could. "She fell unconscious."

Mira narrowed her eyes. "From what?"

Taji rubbed the back of his neck, acutely aware of the eyes and ears around the citadel. He crouched beside her and lowered his voice. "She used healing magic."

Mira breathed in sharply as she flicked her attention behind her to his mother. She mumbled something under her breath about someone not being ready. Then she returned her attention back to Kissa. Her touch was gentle, as her brows knitted together, surveying Kissa more throughly.

Eventually, she said, "Kissa is in a restorative, deep sleep. The duration of her sleep is uncertain, depending on the extent of her magic. It may be days.”

Taji gazed at Mira anew. She listed the diagnoses as if it was a common occurrence. He watched as she nibbled her bottom lip in worry, as she fussed over Kissa, moving her hair out of her face and straightening her cloak. She cared for Kissa.

“You know her?”

Mira’s brows shot up. “Of course! She attends Serenity.”

Her response felt forced. She said nothing else as she stood and walked over to assess his mother. Her clear avoidance of the topic told Taji everything he needed to know. She, too, was a keeper of secrets. He decided not to press it.

As she gaged his mother health, Mira’s face brightened. “The black veins are gone!” Tears of joy fell from her eyes. “Her fever has broken, she is no longer fighting, and her breaths are even and steady.”

Mira’s confirmation eased some of the tightening in his chest. “Did Kissa rid her of the sickness or...?” He let the silence finish what he couldn’t say.

“Only time will tell. We will have to wait for Safiyah to wake up to know for sure, but I would say she cured her. *It is a miracle.*” Her eyes closed as she said the last part.

Amidst the hope of his mother’s recovery, dread crept its ugly head up. His father would become suspicious. Taji would never tell him of Kissa’s healing power, but he was cunning and would start asking questions. Her magic was powerful and if he thought he could use her...

Images of the witch shackled in the pit came to mind, and anxiousness burrowed its way in his chest. “Mira, if my father walks in-”

Her eyes snapped up from his mother, burning with a fire in them he hadn’t seen before. *“You must protect her!”*

Anger flared within him, and he was unsure where it was coming from. The impulse he had felt ever since he first saw Kissa, to protect her, seemed to possess a will of its own. “You doubt me?”

Mira’s eyes softened its fire. “No, I don’t. But there are so many things you don’t understand yet. We don’t have time for me to explain them, but know it is dire that your father does not find her.”

He'd been thinking of a safe place for her to recover. He considered his chambers, but he always slept at the barracks. It might seem suspicious if he suddenly slept in his chambers now. Yet, it appeared to be the only location he could discreetly bring her at the moment. He eyed his mother's wardrobe. A secret passage lay behind it, directly to his rooms.

Though he was curious about what she was referring to, she was right. There was no time. "I will take her to my chambers."

Mira's professional demeanor returned, though the passion didn't dull. "Very well. Take her now. We cannot raise suspicion. Send Benji in, and we will watch over them both until your return. You have a feast to prepare for, Champion."

***

The skillful musicians, elegant decor, and banquet of food that could feed the entire kingdom fell to the background. As Taji sat on his throne to his father's right, pushing his perfectly roasted duck and root vegetables around his plate, his mind wouldn't leave the girl lying unconscious in his bed.

Why did he have this unsettled feeling deep within him? A need to be with her and ensure her safety. It seemed beyond him somehow. Yet questions swarmed around his mind, unanswered. How did she come to possess magic? Who were her parents? He decided that when he returned, he would have a long talk with Mira.

A backdrop of Za forest stared at him from the glazed walls of the throne room. The deep orange sunset gave the trees a golden-green hue that immediately made him think of Kissa's unusual eyes.

"What is it? You have not even taken a bite of your food or sipped your wine. You should be celebrating." His father gruffly said, pulling his attention.

"I apologize. I am just thinking about the future of our kingdom, among other things," Taji said dryly.

His father smirked, an unusual expression for him. "Ah, welcome to my life."

Taji kept his retort to himself. The man never cared about anything other than himself for a day in his life. For the feast, his father wore a satin white tunic under his royal blue waistcoat, similar to his own. The gold embroidered emblem of the Osmondian Crest—a sword with a leviathan and a scorpion entwined around a blade—adorned the front of his coat. His gold crown glinted in the light.

"Come now, no sulking. Tonight is for celebration." He said as he sipped from his chalice.

He looked at his father suspiciously. Something about his mood didn't sit right with him. He was up to something. However, his words did as attended, snapping Taji back to the present.

The prince's eyes swept the heavily decorated throne room. The King's Elite lined all four walls with calculated attention. Amon stood to the king's left, his focus on the tables holding important people.

Every commander was present, including Leviathan High Commander Eshu and Scorpion High Commander Henne. Taji nodded to Eshu, his great uncle and closest advisor to his mother, who loved to irritate his father, standing up to him at every council meeting. For that alone, he was one of Taji's favorite people. The only reason his uncle still had his head was the real threat of a Leviathan rebellion if the King ever thought to follow through. However, Henne's loyalty to the king was unwavering. His yes man. A cowardly man that Taji couldn't stand the sight of.

Further down that table, Commander Maru sat brooding next to his wife, looking like he would rather be anywhere but there. Taji didn't know if his sour mood was because of his injuries or his loss of the title. Most likely both, but this was the Feast of Champions, and Maru was nothing if not a champion.

For the first time, the feast included ambassadors from ally kingdoms. Though only a few of them, their presence felt vital. A statement.

Chancellor Sierra Moswen of Adel sat composed, wearing a hunter-green dress that complemented her ebony skin and dark brown hair currently braided up into cornrows. Being Adel, she served the Ancient of Justice and their province—The Halls of Justice. The sect governed international law between the nations. Taji met Justress Moswen one other time, a couple summers ago, when she intercepted an execution on a Sagian researcher, Soris the Wise.

Beside the Chancellor sat Odion Ata from Eashita—a renowned shipbuilder with whom the King had close ties. He wore his silver locs down, and his argentine eyes raked over everything and everyone, probably assessing new prospects to line his already wealthy pockets.

Taji never met the ambassador for Miro sitting across from Odion, but knew her by name, Criaesia Tutu. She worked on creative projects throughout the realm and was best known for her astonishing sculptures. Tonight she wore a white dress. Her chestnut hair waved down her back, and her severe eyebrows shadowed one blue eye and the other green. She caught his curious gaze and gave a respectful nod, and Taji returned it.

The members of the Shadora Council had their own table. High Councilor Fadel and his conniving sister, Rekik, had identical looks of disgust. Everything about them made Taji's blood boil, but for whatever reason, Elder Harmon trusted them and it was not his place to intervene in the other kingdom's politics as long as it didn't interfere with Osmondia.

"Father, why are the ambassadors here?" Taji asked.

"They are here to celebrate you." His father nodded to his attendant, and servants rushed in to clear the table in front of them.

All conversation ceased as King Lan stood in front of his throne, prompting everyone else to stand with him. Taji's attention caught on the empty grand throne to the left of his father's. As everyone else seemed captivated by the king's poised demeanor and raised chalice, his thoughts drifted to his mother. Uncertainty leaked through. If the queen did not awaken, the prince would be the one to shoulder the responsibility of assuming the throne.

The king's voice echoed across the room. "I thank all of you for coming to celebrate our new Champion! Taji Isaiah Lan!"

In practiced grace, he nodded and smiled, masking the nervousness that racked his body as everyone enveloped him in their attention. Though he expected it, as with every tournament season and responsibility as the only prince of the kingdom, it still unnerved him to be the jewel of the crown.

"For the first time in Osmondian history, an heir to the throne took part in the King's tournament. People must know their future ruler is capable, fierce, and courageous in battle." The king smiled as if it were his idea.

Taji scoffed internally. His father was adamantly against him being chosen as Challenger. Whether it was because he didn't believe in him or it was unconventional, he didn't know. It wasn't until recently, when it benefited him and seemed to line up with his own schemes, that he relented.

"That said, we will do things differently this season." The king raised his arm toward the tables of ambassadors. "Our foreign allies accompany us from Miro, Eashita, Zurania, and the Halls of Justice. There is a reason for that. Over the past two hundred years, our Champions have consistently risen to commander, leading legions and fleets."

His father looked over, smiling at him as if he were actually the light of his life and not the thorn in his side he was. "While I have complete faith in my son's ability to lead a legion of warriors, let us return to the tradition of the old kings."

The keen faces of the High Commanders and Ambassadors differed from the surprised guests and Taji's rattling insides. As his eyes swept the room, he zeroed in on Commander Ashtar. He wore the same knowing look as his seniors, and he couldn't help the frustration that his own commander kept him in the dark, too.

"You see, before the great war that divided our realm, everyone had their place in the Osmondian Kingdom. Eashitans were our astounding inventors. Mirons created sophisticated art and entertainment, Zuranians gave their unique gift of healing, and the Adels kept everyone in line by enacting fair and swift justice. Even the Sagians were our philosophers and instructors, while Ravenian scientists studied the Cosmos and made life-changing cures."

It was completely silent, not even the sound of breathing. As the King glanced around, he proclaimed, "Osmondia's duty is to defend its people from threats within and beyond the kingdom. Unfortunately, in our quest for revenge, we forgot our place in the realm. Though your queen is not present, I speak on her behalf when I say that we take full responsibility for the rift it created between our nations. It is my role as king to remember my people's duty to the realm."

Taji's blood boiled. His mother was fighting for her life, and he dared to utter that he spoke for her. She knew nothing of his schemes, and his father never cared about anything outside the kingdom unless it threatened his comfort and prestige. Then he acted swift and harsh. Eashitans were arguably the closest allies to Osmondia, but even they would be hard-pressed to get King Lan to give warriors to their cause.

A publicity stunt. His mother, the true matriarch of the kingdom, was the only one who cared. She set the foundation for peace between their allies. Anger burned through Taji as he watched his father take all the credit. He clenched his fists to keep his face neutral. Confronting him now would show discord within.

King Lan paused and swept his eyes around the room in exaggeration before saying, "So, with great deliberation, I reenact the duty of Protector of the Realm!"

Taji felt like the floor dropped from underneath him and struggled to rein in his surprise. How his father received the backing to do so, he didn't know. His sole knowledge was that only his mother could. Even more, the realm had changed in the last two hundred summers, and so would the duties of Protector.

He clenched his jaw to keep his composure. His father couldn't possibly be trying to...

"Though Taji is the youngest to be given this title, his powerful will to learn and fierce heart will serve him well. I am assigning my best to train him during these upcoming seasons. Commander Ashtar, Commander Maru, and Elite Commander Amon," his father said as he clasped his shoulder.

In an instant, the prince's world felt flipped upside down. They should have presented the responsibility to him, allowing him to decide if he wanted it. In which Taji would have promptly said no. He glanced at Maru to find him just as puzzled as him. The commander looked at him with the same question on Taji's mind—*what fuckery was the king up to?*

The King glanced at the ambassadors and announced, "In addition, Taji will learn from the world's finest: Odian Ata from Eashita, Chancellor Moswen from the Halls of Justice, Lady Tutu from Miro, and of course my good friend, Elder Fadel from Zurania. It is time we mend the rifts between our nations. It is Osmondia's duty to defend not just our own lands or interests, but those of our allies."

Taji watched the ambassadors bow in agreement, clearly a prearranged one.

His father just solidified the kingdom's alliance with the other nations in one fell swoop.

The throne doors opened, and everyone turned towards two Elite warriors carrying a long golden rectangular box with gems decorated on top of it. They stopped in front of the king and bent to their knees. When his father opened it, all the breath whooshed out of Taji.

There, on satin cloth, rested a remarkable sword. Even the royal blade his father wore seemed dull in comparison. The golden weapon gleamed against the mundane ornate box that held it. It was almost a replica of the sword Osmond carried in his paintings. Almost.

Taji eyed its pommel, free of the divine language that confirmed it was not Osiris. *The Blade of Isis.* The old kings must have forged the blade to resemble the divine sword. Knowing that fact didn't take away from the fine craftsmanship poured in to create it. Osiris' war cadence urged him forward.

Protector.

He pulled his eyes from the *Blade of Isis* and looked up. So wrapped up in the moment, Taji must have missed something because everyone's attention was on him. His father pierced him with a gaze—a command. Taji couldn't reject the title and sword at this point. It would not only undermine his mother's hard work, but disrespect the entire kingdom.

Reluctantly, Taji kneeled before King Lan, and the triumphant smile on his father's face sent ice down his back. Then he raised the magnificent golden straight sword and placed its tip on Taji's right shoulder, reciting the ancient words, "Taji Isaiah Lan, I hereby anoint you as the Protector of the Realm, the first of your kind in over two hundred years. You are now a member of the esteemed order of Queen Safiya the Great and King Lan of Osmondia. Do you vow to defend the Osmondian Kingdom, its interest, and its allies who stand before us—Miro, Eashita, the Halls of Justice, and Zurania?"

"I do!" Taji felt like a stranger said those words.

His father gently placed the tip of the sword on his left shoulder. "Arise, *Protector of the Realm,* and be recognized!"

Despite the king's scheming, the prince felt the words reverberate through his entire being. Sacred words he could not give back, even if he wanted to. An overwhelming sense of honor washed over him. He stood up, careful to steady himself.

His father held the golden sword laid across his palms, gesturing it to him. When he finally touched the *Blade of Isis*, his drums sang its approval. Taji gripped the pommel with both hands, lifting it and surveying its weight. Perfect.

"Taji Isaiah Lan, our new Protector of the Realm!"

The audience met king's boisterous declaration with thunderous applause. Taji turned to see every one of them bend to a knee. To *him*, he realized. As his nerves settled, Elder Mif's words played in his mind.

It is time for you to embrace your cloak of duties.

He was supposed to give some type of speech, but every word Taji attempted to utter disintegrated into dust on his tongue. However, in an unexpected stroke of fortune, he found himself relieved of the burden as the grand doors of the throne room swung open with haste. Mira dashed into the throne room, coming to a sudden halt. Gasping for breath, she seemed as if she had just sprinted the entire way. All eyes turned to her.

"What is it, Mira?"

The king's brusque tone didn't deter her. A glimmer in her eyes accompanied her wide, beaming smile. "The Queen has awoken!"

25

ISLE OF SHADOWS

TAJI

TAJI FOUND HIMSELF PACING back and forth in front of his mother's window, burdened by a whirlwind of thoughts. A glimmer of hope sparked within him when she briefly woke up, but quickly faded as she fell back into slumber. Deep down, Taji was afraid that it was just a fleeting moment, and he would never have the chance to see those beloved compassionate blue eyes again. Determined, he made a firm decision to stay by her side, refusing to leave.

To his relief, she continued to be visually better. With the disappearance of those awful black veins, her complexion regained its vitality. Her revival was already igniting hope within the citadel, and his father planned to announce it to the people at first light.

However, his father's reaction to his mother's waking seemed strange. He appeared withdrawn. Maybe it was fear of the unknown. Taji knew the agony of crushed hopes. None of them knew what to expect. When his mother closed her eyes, his father quickly left, as if on a mission.

"You will wear a hole in the floor, your Grace," Mira jested, as she entered the chambers.

He turned toward her with a smile that didn't quite reach his eyes. She glanced at him knowingly as she walked over to assess his mother. She did not leave his mother's side either, except to check in on Kissa at his behest.

"How is she?" Taji asked.

"She still sleeps. The healing drained her. It may take her days to recover, but she will."

Mira's reassuring smile did nothing to quench his anxiety. He held a short meeting with those in his close circle, those he trusted implicitly—Mira, Benji, and his royal guard, Chase. At the start, Mira and Benji were adamant not to tell Commander Ashtar or Elder Harmon. Taji did not feel right hiding something so critical from either of them, but their duties would conflict, so he digressed.

They listened as he told them about his first encounter with Kissa at Serenity. How she touched him and how he knew in his heart she could heal his mother. If Chase felt surprised, he didn't let it show. However, Benji blamed Taji for Kissa's well-being. Rightfully so. Ultimately, the four of them devised a plan together. Chase agreed to guard his room, while Benji would come periodically to stay with Kissa under the guise of visiting his mother.

Rubbing his temples, he said, "Mira, get some rest. I will watch over her."

"Are you sure, your Grace? You need sleep, too." Her warm gold eyes watched him warily.

"I will sleep when you wake up. My mind is like a storm, unable to calm. I will alert you of any changes." He felt like he hovered between riveting waves of guilt and hope—either could crash down on him at any moment.

Mira nodded. "I need to do something. I will be back soon."

When she left, Taji walked over to the chair next to his sleeping mother and gently took her hand. Despite his sluggish mind, he attempted to devise a plan for Kissa. She couldn't stay in his chambers for long. Not able to complete their duties, servants would become suspicious. Mira said Kissa was supposed to be home until Maantag. If she didn't wake up soon, he would need to get her home undetected somehow.

It felt weird that he knew so little about Kissa. He didn't know where she lived or who her parents were. When he asked Mira, she said she'd ask her husband, but again, her answer didn't sit right with him. She seemed to know more than she revealed. Benji, too, for that matter. They were both keeping secrets from him, and Taji wasn't sure how to feel about that.

His mind drifted off, and he barely registered the hand he held move. He looked over to see his mother quietly watching him and abruptly stood up.

"Ma!" He gently kissed her forehead. "Are you okay? Do you need water? Do you need me to send for father?"

She said nothing when she awakened the first time. He hoped he was not asking too much to hear her voice this time.

Tired-eyed, his mother gazed up at him. "Water, please." Her voice rasped softly from disuse.

Taji walked over, poured a glass of water for her, and then helped her drink. She eventually drank the whole glass, gesturing for more. They sat in silence for a while. He tried not to overwhelm her, though his adrenaline rushed through his veins as his heart swelled.

"I heard you." His mother eventually whispered.

His face lit up with surprise. *"You did?"*

Taji did not know what happened when someone fell into a coma. Nobody woke up to tell the tale. He read to her everyday just in case she could hear him. His surprise quickly turned to concern. His mother's eyes, once filled with light, now appeared troubled. He would give anything to see the spark in her return.

"What is wrong, Ma?"

"It was so dark," she said. Tears fell down her cheek, and he wished to take them away. "Your voice kept me here."

He sat next to her on the bed and grabbed her hand again. Her fingers, warm against his skin with life, settled his heart somewhat. Taji didn't press to know her thoughts. He waited until she was ready to speak again.

"It is unnatural... a place of nightmares. The shadows showed me unspeakable things. I saw you dying from the sickness and I could do nothing. All the while, I could feel my spirit being ripped from me." Her voice broke.

Shadows?

He opened his mouth, but she continued, "I heard your faint cry for me to wake in the far distance—a cruel torture. Others were there, too. Unable to bear it any longer, I pleaded for the After, but it eluded me. Our people are in that place, Taji. We need to save them."

Taji stiffened. He did not understand what all she was telling him, so he stayed quiet, rubbing circles on the back of her hand. More for his own sake.

Then a faint smile crossed her lips. "Then a bright light appeared. I felt its goodness as its rays brightened the darkness. The shadows feared it. The tug on my spirit ceased, and I felt like I was drifting closer to your voice." She palmed Taji's cheek. "I used it as an anchor to find my way back."

Though she managed a sad smile, his mother's hand trembled on his cheek. Saying nothing, he pulled her into a gentle embrace. Taji decided not to make her relive the horror with questions. Instead, he held her closely as he tried to process what she had revealed.

"I wish I knew who she was," she whispered against Taji's chest.

"Who?"

"The beautiful goddess that saved me," she said.

Taji thought maybe she assumed Osmond saved her, a blessing. It didn't surprise him one bit if their god had his hand in it. It was a miracle. An answer to his deepest prayers. However, his mother's next words stiffened him like a board.

"I'll never forget those beautiful hazel, silver, and gold eyes. Her voice sounded like music and her locs reminded me of rubies and carnelians bathed in sunlight." His mother looked up into his eyes. "She told me you were waiting for me."

Her eyes closed and her breaths became steady. Taji did not let her go. Instead, he slid his boots off and stretched out, pulling the blanket over them both. He laid her head on his chest while rubbing her back in small circles.

On the outside, he controlled his emotions—calm and steady—whatever his mother needed. Inside, anger flared through Taji as his heart tore in half. She mentioned "others."

What is happening to my people?

WHEN MIRA RETURNED, SURPRISINGLY, she brought coffee. Even better,

Elder Harmon accompanied her. Pleased that he did not have to summon the Overseer from his sleep, they met at a small table in his mother's room.

Taji relayed his mother's words. Unfortunately, Harmon had more questions than he could answer. At Mira's insistence, he couldn't tell the overseer about Kissa's involvement, and it was a waiting game for her and his mother to recover.

"Whatever it is, I fear that those inflicted are not even given the peace of death." Taji said heavily.

Elder Harmon turned to Mira. "Do you believe this is the *Isle of Shadows?*"

Mira shook her head. "The Isle of Shadows is not supposed to be filled with nightmares, as Safiyah said. It is an ambient place."

"What's this Isle of Shadows?" Taji asked.

Elder Harmon answered. "An in-between that stands as a gatekeeper between life and death. The Zuranian's greatest duty is to help the dying Transition. Before the After, humans journey to the Isle of Shadows, governed by the Ancient of Chaos. There they reform, readying their souls and spirit for the After. Before the war, Zuranians worked closely with the Ravenians in this ritual."

"How am I not aware of this?" Taji asked. His mother or Elder Mif may have spoken of such things, but Taji felt he'd remember something so important. As it stood, the Keeper of Ceremony conducted rituals for the deceased, but none of the recited words mentioned this place in between.

"It is not the Divine duty of the Osmondians to perform. It is ours. When the war divided us..." She turned her glassy eyes toward the window, letting her words hang.

"Are you saying that when King Keysia threw the other nations out of our kingdom, our dead no longer reached the After? My people have been trapped on the Isle of Shadows for two hundred years?" Taji hissed.

"There is no certainty. Since the Healers returned, we resumed the rituals and have been assisting in the Transition." Harmon replied. "But this...this is something else entirely. It seems the sickness traps them somewhere," Elder Harmon remarked.

"It feels evil." Mira said as she wrapped her arms around herself as if she could feel it on her skin. "*A curse.*"

That was what his people called it. A curse. It seemed fitting. "You think it is magic?" Taji breathed more to himself.

Marquis and Mira looked at one another. A mutual understanding shone in their eyes, hinting that they knew something he didn't. Mira was the one to speak.

"We are certain now, but caution is necessary without tangible evidence."

Taji understood her meaning. It was treason to go searching for things involved with Essence. They needed complete secrecy. It was crazy to think that If Kissa hadn't cured his mother, they would have never known.

"I have no idea where to start searching for the curse's origins. On our way back from the House of Life, we faced a black wolf. When Commander Ashtar killed it, the beast bled black blood, just like the victims of the Sleeping Sickness. We know there is a connection," Elder Harmon said.

Taji's eyes widened. In the Fathomless Pit, the witch bled black blood, and the Elite believed she was a Celestial. There was a connection between it all.

Harmon closed his eyes and clenched his fist. "Our son was correct in his assumptions that this sickness has magical origins."

So much silence prevailed in that moment between them. The cost of even speaking about Essence was death. So, the three of them contemplated until the pieces came together.

Elder Harmon mentioned that testing would be necessary to discover how Queen Safiyah broke the curse. "I know it is not ideal, but the lives of the rest of the kingdom are at stake."

Taji looked at Mira, who slightly shook her head. A warning. "I agree. My mother will be more than willing to assist you in that, Elder Harmon." Then he stood. "I think I'm going to my rooms now."

To keep down suspicion, Taji left through the main door instead of his mother's wardrobe. Walking towards the west wing, where his room was situated, he suddenly heard faint whispers emanating from one of the partially ajar laundry rooms. The servants and guards were working diligently late into the night.

"Did the Elite question you?"

Most likely a maid, but his attention peaked. He moved closer to the door.

"They asked me and Cindy about the people who entered Queen Safiyah's chambers yesterday. It is all suspicious,"

Suspicious indeed. Taji continued walking down the hall, tossing the new information around in his mind. To learn the Citadel's secrets, you asked a servant. Attentive, blending into their unassuming tasks, they saw everything. Unseen and unheard.

The King was searching for someone. The pressure of protecting Kissa became tenfold, and a sick feeling overwhelmed him with suspicion. There was no doubt in his mind that his father had some secret agenda.

When he noticed Chase standing outside his room, he acknowledged him with a nod. "All is quiet?"

Chase then said, "Too quiet."

Too quiet. Taji gestured for him to come into his rooms. As he entered, he spied Benji sleeping on the overstuffed ottoman near the fire. His attention flicked to Kissa, sleeping on his bed.

In his window over his bed, the golden eagle from before perched. Its keen attention on Kissa. He walked over, checking Kissa's forehead and pulse. All the while, the eagle watched his actions, then cocked its head as if studying him.

"She is having nightmares." Taji turned to meet Benji's tired eyes.

"Nightmares?" He looked back at Kissa. She seemed at peace.

"I helped her through them. She sleeps dreamless now." Benji said.

"Alright." He said, ignoring that his friend kept secrets just as deep as he did. "Has the eagle been there the entire time?"

"She comes and goes." Benji said.

"She?" Taji asked with a quirked brow.

"I suspect she is one of Kissa's forest companions," Benji said, sidestepping the question.

Taji merely nodded at the crazy notion. Odd. As he inspected the windows and wardrobe, he said, "Your father is here. We found something and I know he will want your input on it."

He gestured Benji and Chase over to his desk and ran down everything his mother told him, Elder Harmon's thoughts, and what he had overhead from the maids. He also informed Benji about what he and Chase witnessed that night at the Fathomless Pit. The three of them were quiet as they let the heavy information settle.

"I suspect it won't be long before the Elite move on to questioning warriors and commanders." Benji said with a worried look. "Someone will say they saw Kissa entering the Queen's chamber with my mother."

"We must align our narratives and remain consistent," Chase emphasized.

Taji nodded as he rubbed his chin. "Where will we take Kissa?"

"Home." Benji said.

"Yes, but do we know where it is?" Taji asked. Both Benji and Chase's expression looked stuck. None of them knew where the girl lived.

"I can find out." Benji said.

That was a start. Clearly, they wouldn't be doing anything until morning, and that gave Taji more time to solidify the plan. He wouldn't be getting any sleep tonight.

"Chase, discover what the Elite know. I'll arrange Kissa's way home once we know where."

Chase nodded, then silently left through the door. Benji gathered his cloak resting on the chair. Taji felt the urge to mend the rift between them.

"Benji, if I would have known that all this would happen, I-"

The healer held up his hand, cutting him off. "I'll be back in the morning to relieve you." Then he turned his back on the Prince, slipped inside his wardrobe, and disappeared.

26

MISSING SHIPS

MARU

FROM THE GALLERY OF Osmond's Light, Maru gazed at the horizon, captivated by the sun's golden rays dancing on the surface of the sea. As he took a sip from his coffee, lost in thought, he couldn't help but acknowledge the majestic allure of the rolling waves beckoning to his soul.

He had gotten very little sleep since the tournament, and everyone around him insisted that this day was meant for "rest." However, as the sun serenaded the sea, he couldn't shake off the uneasy sensation that gnawed at him. As he leaned on the rail, the nip in the air prompted him to wrap his cloak tighter around himself. The season seemed too cold, like winter was approaching rather than the start of fall.

Despite the lack of stairs and the option to warm by a fire, he forwent sleeping in his family's grotto. It felt empty without his family. Instead, he took over the living quarters in the lighthouse. Maru paid dearly for his stubbornness, opening up his stitches to his thigh from the long climb. Each shooting pain, a reminder that he was not infallible.

He heard rumors of the princeling's skill in swordsmanship, but it was his footwork and adaptability that ultimately won the battle. He moved like lightning and was dexterous in an annoyingly inspiring way. If he were anyone else, the commander would contemplate recruiting him in his personal crew,

Scorpion or not. But as it stood, the wound to Maru's pride hurt worse than a lacerated leg or broken nose.

Boot steps clamored up the stairwell, and Maru didn't bother to look. His entire crew was at the coast with him, comrades who joined him before he even thought of becoming a commander. He appreciated their unwavering loyalty.

However, that meant his second mate, or mother hen, depending on the hour, was there, too.

Maru didn't bother to turn. "Brother, I'm fine. There's no need to hover over me."

He didn't want to be bothered, and the rest of his crew knew that, giving him space. For some ungodly reason, his brother never listened. Maru could feel his assessing eyes raking over him.

Sabu scoffed. "You are supposed to be resting, but it seems you know more than the healers now. Though I can see how you cling to the rail that your leg is re-injured."

Maru kept his eyes straight ahead on the sea. He didn't have the energy to argue with him. He was right, of course. His leg throbbed so badly he could barely think.

"I came to tell you King Lan announced a celebration feast in Queen Safiyah's name on the festival's last day. He summoned us to be there... all of us."

Maru knew he should feel hopeful and excited about a celebration for his queen. Queen Safiyah was the rightful ruler of the kingdom, a direct descendent of Malachi the Great. She was a compassionate ruler who negotiated peace with Zurania, providing Osmondia with a school, hospital, and now healers. Morale within his legions had been hard-kept because of the plague. Now there was a chance to eradicate the deadly sickness once and for all.

He turned to Sabu. "Did you say he summoned us all?" The king knew he left warriors against his orders and now he was blatantly commanding him to abandon the coast.

Sabu strode up next to him. His face turned serious. "They say it is a miracle, brother. There is hope for a cure."

Of course, his people hoped, but they didn't have the resources of skilled

Royal Healers tending to them day and night. They were lucky if they could even get inside the hospital. He hated to be the pessimist, pissing on the expectation of his people. But King Lan never did one helpful thing about the sickness. He did not care for the lower class, and he outright loathed the Leviathans—despite his public demeanor to the contrary.

It didn't sit right with the Commander. This felt more than a power check on Maru's refusal to follow orders. Why was he so adamant about leaving the coast unguarded?

He needed to think and simmer in his thoughts, and there was only one thing that helped him do that. He turned to his brother with a glint in his eye.

"You and Tomeri round up our crew. It's time to take *Yemanja* out."

⸺◆⸺

A hidden den lay tucked away,
exposed for the Gods to see.
If you dare cross the squall's sway,
go deep inside the ageless key.
There the defenders of the kingdom lay,
stalking the depths of the sea.
They hiss cast away! Cast away!
For only the Serpents roam free!

⸺◆⸺

Sabu's baritone voice washed over Maru as he reached the walkway, entering the harbor of the sea cave. To his annoyance, he stood on the quarterdeck playing his lute, tapping his foot as the crew clapped and danced around him. Singing was always his younger brother's pursuit, even as a boy. Maru would jest that he was Miron, switched at birth, because he was quite a talented singer.

Obviously, the Commander would never inform him of that. Or that this song was his favorite. But as he neared his ship, the song hummed through his veins with truth.

Leviathans, often overlooked, were the true defenders of the realm—despite what the bloody Scorpions thought. Nothing but sea surrounded Aarusha, and in the event of a siege, their kingdom relied on their mighty warships.

However, the true secret lay in the size of its force.

The sea cavern walls surrounding them, made of eroded limestone, reached at least half a league deep into Aarusha's bosom. Large enough to house the entire battle fleet of warships. The Den of Serpents was the true secret of the Osmondian Kingdom, remaining hidden in a sea cave far to the northeast, where seafarers and emissaries didn't venture. It was only accessible by the sea or the underground passage.

Each warship sat at least a hundred feet long. Bronze-clad rams decorated the front of each ship, while three rows of oars complimented both sides of each. They named the sea beasts *triremes*, and Maru was proud to command two of them.

However, this day, he was boarding *Yemanja*—his pride and joy. She was smaller than the warships, a sailing vessel with lateen sails made for speed and easier maneuvering of the shallow waters near the coast—an old caravel and the first ship Maru ever owned.

Before embarking, he stood near the bow, rubbing the fin of the seductive sea goddess decorating the front, a habit since his young days to bring forth good fortune to his ship and crew. He now wore his brown leather armor with a Leviathan insignia embedded on his chest and his preferred axe at his hip. He styled his dark locs into two braids, parted in the middle, and tied them back with a queue.

As Maru boarded, he cleared his throat. The music stopped abruptly and his crew snapped to attention.

"Captain!"

"Standby to Cast off. Tomeri!"

His first mate and his friend since childhood stood ready, waiting for orders. Tomeri was taller than most men, and her sharp brows framed chocolate eyes that would cut you down as fast as her twin blades at her hip. She wore her locs plaited with a tight bun at the back. Though he named her acting captain long before becoming a commander, when Maru was aboard, he was the Captain.

"Report."

"Captain, five ships are missing from the Den," she said.

"Five?" He peered around the Den, inspecting. Sure enough, every few berths lay empty. Someone took them out methodically. Unaware, one may not notice at first sight. Thankfully, Tomeri was his hawk.

"The reports contain nothing about it, Captain. Not who may have ordered it or the warriors manning them."

Commander Maru knew nothing of any orders. Did they deem him too injured to accompany them? No, this had furtive scheming written all over it. Tomeri fidgeted just enough for him to notice.

"Speak freely, Tomeri."

"When we entered the underground tunnels that lead to the Den, we noticed many fresh boot tracks coming from Up Top."

Up Top, was the term they used for Zuberi. Mad King Keysia made the network of tunnels for wartime when the military needed to move unseen to either get to their ships or move Scorpions by foot under the enemy's notice. Whoever ordered the mission discreetly moved the warriors through the underground tunnels. They came directly from the Citadel and only one person could give that command.

But why go through so much trouble?

Clues eluded him as he scrutinized the ledgers. He saw no warships sailing while at Osmond's light, and none of his warriors that stayed back to patrol reported such activity. To move a sea force that size, someone would have witnessed it. That meant they must have gone around.

Maru scoffed. It wasn't even a long shot. It was impossible. Nobody dared go that way. It was foolish to do so. The treacherous water between Aarusha and the Isles of Death was called Hell's Conception, for a reason. Williwaw winds struck with little or no warning, causing death to many seafarers.

Someone went to significant efforts to remain unnoticed. It reeked of desperation. But why?

"Cast Off!"

They had only a few remaining hours of daylight. Despite being unaware of the secret mission, Maru saw no problem in scouting farther out.

"Ready!"

Pride filled the Commander as he watched them—all of them proven masters of the sea. He tried to calculate a plan as they sailed out of the Den of Serpents. They would not go through Hell's Conception. He would not risk his crew's safety.

The sun bathed Yemanja in an orangish light as they navigated east around Aarusha. Maru continued to bellow orders as he stood with his hand on the tiller, masting the rudder. The hum of the salty sea filled his spirit. Despite the gnawing feeling and the strange news, he felt better than he had in days. His place was on his ship, on the waters.

"Brother, are we going to Dragon's Cove?" Sabu asked, pulling him from his thoughts.

Maru's attention stayed on the cliffs they needed to navigate around. "We will check the outer perimeter of the inlet. If it seems suspicious, we will investigate further... that is, if it's safe to do so," Maru said.

Sabu turned serious. "You know nothing about why the order was given or the mission. What if we come upon a battle? What if we reveal the mission to the detriment of our brethren?"

His brother was right. In his haste to investigate, Maru didn't even bother to think the King might actually be defending the kingdom. But If he planned to act against the ship the scouts discovered, why the secrecy? The mission seemed too underhanded. Since scrubbing decks as a boy, Maru learned to trust his gut.

"We need to know what lies ahead. Something is coming, brother. I can taste it in the air."

Everyone knew King Lan held the land force by the balls. Regardless of the title change, he still controlled the Scorpion military, overseeing its daily operations. However, for Leviathans to be sent, the order needed to come from the Queen or High Commander Eshu. Something else was at play.

"Alright. If you say so," Sabu looked towards the water. "We follow your lead."

Maru knew this, of course. His company would go wherever he ventured without a second thought. The sobering feeling that he may lead them into danger always settled his impulsive nature. But as warriors, it was their duty to protect their kingdom, their home. Maru refused to allow his brethren or his city to be an afterthought.

He pulled out his field glass. The rare spectacle allowed him to observe all boats and ships before they entered the harbor from afar. He always stationed watchers at Osmond's Light, but it would never replace scouting directly on the sea.

Sabu waved his hand. "Regardless of what it is. We can't let the Scorpions continue to look down their snotty noses at us. We may have lost the tournament, but we will win the war."

Maru's brow raised at that. "What?"

Sabu laughed in his usual annoying manner. "*You* may have lost the tournament, but we will see to it that you win your dignity back!"

A hint of a smile played on Maru's lips at his brother's jibe. Determination settled in his veins along the hum of the sea.

"Whoever it is coming will know Maru, the Axe, and his valiant *Sea Masters*," he shouted. Then he unsheathed his axe and held it in the air for emphasis. "Maybe we will even allow the lightweights to live to speak about it." His voice echoed across the ship.

"Leviathans!" His crew shouted, raising their own weapons. "Yemanja!"

Maru smothered the smile and settled for a determined look as he observed their progress. They were leaving the harbor, spilling out into the sea. As they moved forward, Osmondia shrunk in the distance, taking with it everything he held dear. However, this mission was now their sole focus, and they were determined to see it through.

27

ANCIENT POWER

THE AIR FELT TOO dry and too hot, an oppressive heat. High up, higher than the towers of the citadel, Kissa looked down and saw nothing but a crimson-red sea, with waves as high as buildings that seemed to glide instead of crashing.

A desert, she realized as she watched the sands shift. Looking up, she found the source of the unrelenting oppression—two scorching suns. Was she in Nibiru again? This part of the Ancient realm differed vastly from the tranquil sea cliffs. No sight of animals or beings for miles, just sand. The burning heat made Kissa feel like she was inside her mother's stove.

By the Stars! Who would live in such a place?

She assessed her surroundings. She seemed to stand on a balcony. When Kissa turned around, a spine-chilling sensation crept over her skin. It hummed, a distinct vibration than the one inside her, but similar somehow with deep ageless power. A man on a red rug in a nearby room startled Kissa. A familiar orb suspended on nothing hung in front of him.

His hair was ginger red, brighter than his dark honey skin. Freckles sprinkled his face, and fierce eyebrows framed his closed eyes. They furrowed as the man meditated deeply. His lack of facial hair made him look no older than Kissa. Yet she sensed his overwhelming presence, evoking a primitive familiarity in her.

Who was this man?

A knock sounded behind him, and his eyes popped open to show deep emerald green irises staring back at her. So green they seemed unnatural, and a burning cognizance and cunning stirred within them. Kissa froze on the spot as bitter frustration smashed through her senses, causing her to buckle. He didn't seem to see her as he gracefully stood to open the door, leaving the orb.

A vision.

Kissa remembered a similar orb in the mural in the citadel atrium. An obscured woman held it in her hands, and it beamed like the sun. Kissa moved closer to it, silently stepping into the room. It didn't beam like the sun as the one in the citadel painting, but lightning moved across it, obscuring something swirling in the very core.

"Father, we are waiting for you."

Her attention flicked to the door, and Kissa did a double take. Both men were tall, with lean frames, nearly identical. However, the visitor possessed eyes of deep black with some sort of specks in his eyes like her own. She couldn't make out the color from the distance.

Now inside, the room reminded her of Elder Harmon's laboratory. Multiple tables held ancient scrolls and tomes, and there were beakers and glasses next to them. Cages lined the outer walls covered in white sheets, while smaller orbs hung suspended above her.

What in the stars had she stumbled into?

Kissa tiptoed to the far wall near the cages, careful not to knock over any of the glass. Settling on the other side of the lab, she had a strong feeling that she was meant to see this.

The father flicked his emerald eyes around the room, agitated in thought. Then, as if it were a mask he easily slid on, he smiled. "Let your brothers and sisters know I will be down shortly."

Kissa jerked as the cage next to her rattled. She didn't dare lift the sheet. When she looked back at the men, the visitor moved closer and locked eyes with her. Her mouth dropped as her heart flipped in her chest.

The specks inside his eyes were...stars? They swirled just so like she was looking inside the cosmos themselves. The visitor's brows furrowed and Kissa stiffened with fear, but in the next breath, he flicked his attention outside the balcony doors as if he hadn't seen her at all.

His father waved his hand, and Kissa felt a familiar hum surround her. A ward. "You have been doing well in your training, Moorice. You are strong in your sorcery and your mother's abilities, so I have an important mission for you."

A wariness settled in Moorice, but his eyes stayed focus on his father as if waiting for a command.

"You will visit Haava and teach the Sagians wizardry."

Moorice's shocked reluctance rippled through Kissa. "That is our magic. Father, that is forbidden. They are human."

Molten anger rose from his father. Kissa had to clench her tunic to keep her hands from trembling. She felt all ranges of emotions since understanding her empathy, but this man seemed to be filled with impossible rage.

His voice boomed like thunder across the den. "Are you uncertain of your abilities, afraid of being punished? You are my firstborn, my protégé—expected to lead in greatness beside me. You dare question me?"

Moorice grew rigid. He didn't even blink.

His father frowned in disappointment. Another mask, because his anger continued to pelt Kissa. "Maybe I was mistaken to think you were ready. Your sister would never question my reasoning."

She didn't know why, but Kissa felt a hint of pity for Moorice. His father was manipulating him.

Moorice peered out the window, contemplating. Kissa sensed the fear and guilt battle within him, but smooth determination seemed to win. "No, I am ready."

His father paced in front of Moorice, fiddling with a ring that he twisted around his finger. "We protect our people, including our humans. Sagians lack the strength of the Osmondians. The other nations cower under their rulership. They need their own extraordinary abilities, and I intend to bless them with it."

"What are we protecting them from, Father? War has not touched either realm."

Kissa muffled her gasp. This scene took place before the Great War of the Divide. Kissa Ashtar stood in the Ancient realm over two hundred years ago.

Agitation flared within Moorice's father, wrenching Kissa's breath away. "Do you not trust my wisdom? I am the Saaxir. I know and see all things!"

Moorice stood straighter. "No, Father. I am ashamed to have questioned you." His eyes lowered to the floor in submission. "I will go."

The Saaxir took his time piercing his son with his gaze, letting him squirm under his scrutiny. Then he walked over to the orb that floated on nothing. His hands cupped around it, not touching directly, but an emerald glow emanated, causing the orb to spin.

"Let my worshippers know their God has heard their cries for independence. For this, I am blessing them with sacred magic that will live on through generations. They are not to share their powers with any other people, bound by oath."

"What if I encounter another Celestial?" Moorice inquired.

A sly smile crept on his father's lips. This time, it was genuine. "If the need arises, eliminate them."

Moorice's face reflected his uneasiness. Conflict raged in him, but just as quickly, he smoothed his features out. "I will leave in two turns."

Then he left, and the Saaxir resumed sitting in front of his orb. Kissa stared at him, curiously. What did the self-given title mean? She was sure nothing good. She felt anger, loathing, and spite underneath his cunning beauty.

Kissa sucked in a startled breath as dark tendrils of shadow emerged, billowing like smoke and forming around the Saaxir. It eerily reminded her of the shadows she banished from Queen Safiyah's mind. They slowly solidified, and a woman appeared. With straight raven-black hair to her waist that shined like finely polished obsidian, she wore a seductive form-fitted black gown that hugged her curves, then fell into shadows around her ankles. Her smooth tawny skin was flawless, and her lips, painted black, curved into a sultry smile.

Despite her perfection, that was not what stole Kissa's attention. Her almond-shaped eyes were black with colorful specks swirling through them...just like Moorice.

The woman trailed her fingers with extremely long black painted nails up the Saaxir's chest. "Is everything in place, my love?"

His reaction to the woman was less than welcoming. His eyes never left the orb.

"Yes, but your son is stubborn. I will send Naomi with him to see that the mission is done."

The woman's smile fell just a touch, and something glinted in her otherworldly eyes. "I thought we agreed that I have my own plans for Naomi."

"Then you have two turns to prepare her. I have made my decision."

The woman sashayed away from the Saaxir, who seemed content to ignore her. She paused in front of the balcony doors. Her shadows swarmed around her ankles in an agitated way. "You are impatient. We have spent centuries planning this. I will not allow you to be reckless."

Oddly, Kissa could not feel her thoughts or emotions, but she suddenly felt like a firestorm engulfed her from the pure rage from the Saaxir. With fear clear in the woman's onyx eyes, her chest lurched forward and her head snapped back. Kissa saw nothing tangible, but felt the incredible power surrounding them as her bones quaked in fear.

The Saxxir stood. Somehow, he seemed larger than the room, imposing now. He lifted the woman with a thought. Her long onyx hair dragged behind her as he pulled her to him, only a breath away. She didn't dare fight back or say a word, but the Saaxir's voice snapped like thunder.

"Do not speak to me of patience and plans, Chaos, as if you care. Centuries pass in the blink of our eyes. Moorice questions my commands because you coddle him. I will send Naomi early to guarantee our success. If this part of the plan does not happen, then we are all doomed to the Chasm."

Kissa watched in horror as he lifted the woman of shadows higher, almost reaching the vaulted ceiling. A whip-like crack echoed, and the woman plummeted towards the floor. With a whip of her hand, her shadows wrapped around her, hovering her mere inches above the floor. Shaking with suppressed anger—or possibly the use of power—she glared at the Saaxir with deadly intent. But she said nothing.

The Saaxir laughed with a crazed look as his emerald green eyes glowed within. "Allow me? You, nor that bitch or her lapdog, the Divine Warrior, can stop me!"

As they locked glares, Kissa shook from the energy constricting her, stealing her breaths.

Finally, the seductive woman acknowledged her defeat with a simple request. "Call for me when it's done." Then her shadows wrapped around her again, and in the next blink, she was gone.

28

LINES DRAWN

TAJI

THE SECRET PASSAGE BEFORE *him was familiar, yet what lay beyond terrified Taji. Urged onward, he felt time against him. With Isis already unsheathed, he steeled himself and pulled on the sconce that allowed him entry. His drums rushed up to meet him, and Taji allowed them to settle him and focus his mind. Then, alone, he crept into the shadows without a sound.*

Immediately, the eerie feeling from before washed over his skin. His drums quieted. Disregarding the feeling, Taji went towards the bridge entrance leading to the Pit. He poked his head around the corner. Nothing.

Everything felt...off.

With his sword raised, he pushed forward anyway, and when Taji reached the middle of the bridge, he met silence. The Fathomless Pit was empty. No prisoners. No Scorpions on patrol. Unsure, he crossed the bridge and descended the steps to the cell floor.

Taji crept through the pathway in between, searching each cell. Empty. Dread filled his gut. Did his father kill them all?

He swept his eyes above him again towards the bridge, then rechecked the cages, seeing if he had missed something. When he turned back towards the entrance, his blood went cold. A woman hung limply with shackles around her ankles and wrists. Her wild, red hair mirrored the flames that danced around her.

His senses betrayed him. Unable to see her face, he still sensed her—a hum that beckoned him and an unyielding need to protect her, no matter what.

"Kissa?"

She did not move, and Taji's heart hammered as he tried to make sense of what he was seeing.

Was he too late?

He rushed toward her, then braced himself as he reached out and lifted her chin. Her eyes stayed closed, and a heaviness engulfed him. His father found her.

He could not stop the burn in his eyes—the burn in his heart.

Then her eyes snapped opened, and Taji gaped as he stared into those hazel-green eyes with gold and silver specks. Relief washed over him.

"Don't let them take me." Her voice was a melodic caress squeezing his heart.

Confused, he growled. "I'm getting you out now!"

Her features softened. "You will wake soon. Then we must go!"

⸺◆⸺

Taji jolted up, immediately looking to his left. Then let out a breath as Kissa's sleeping form still lay peacefully on his bed. The faint glow right before first light showed from the window above her.

He looked down at the book before him and the gold letters stared back. He must have fallen asleep trying to decipher the Sword of Osiris at his desk.

Taji stretched his neck to both sides as he thought of the dream. The feeling was unsettlingly real, like a warning that it would occur unless he saved Kissa from the Citadel at once. But Benji hadn't returned, and he did not know where she lived.

The First Temple.

Osiris' voice felt like a cool breeze to his scorching thoughts. The suggestion fit perfectly and felt right. He would carry her to the temple, using the underground tunnels.

He picked up his oil lamp and walked over to Kissa. Throughout the night, he checked her for fever and a pulse, purely out of paranoia. Without being a healer, it was his only method to calm his mind. He used his oil lamp to scan over her form, when shock struck him true and hard.

This was not *Kissa*. This girl had red hair draped over her face. *Enemy*. The engrained thought blazed through his mind. He reached for the hilt of a sword not on his hip. Shit. He stumbled backward as if to avoid being bitten by a viper. Kissa's sea of black locs that usually swathed his pillows were now red.

She had beautiful hazel, silver, and gold eyes, and her voice sounded like music. Her tresses reminded me of rubies and carnelians bathed in sunlight.

His mother's words hit him like a sledge hammer. Conflict rose in him swift and hard. The girl he thought of constantly was the enemy? Before Taji could wrap his mind around it all, cold steel rested against his neck and he stiffened.

Every irrational thought imaginable raced through Taji's mind. This was all a trap to get the enemy inside the citadel. Now he was about to die. How could he be such a fool?

"Tell me why I should not kill you where you stand?"

The familiarness of the assailant's voice struck Taji to his core. He turned his head just so. "Commander Ashtar?"

In his peripheral, the commander said nothing, but his stare felt distinctly like blades ready to slice him to the bone. Not the proud look from the Feast or tournament victory. No, his eyes spelled the intent of murder.

Confusion flooded Taji. Was this a joke? The steel at his neck said otherwise. Taji tried and failed to harden the fear that rippled through him.

He looked at Blade of Isis by the door, unassumingly leaning against the wall near his armor. Shit. Taji lifted his arms as if in surrender, slightly turning to face the commander and get a read on him.

"Stop there!" The commander growled.

Taji stiffened. He felt a sense of unease as he faced his mentor, knowing that defeating him, even with a sword, seemed impossible. As Omani stared at him silently with death in his eyes, a hint of amusement crossed his features.

He knew it, too. The look dared him to try.

Why was the commander threatening him? He hadn't even seen him since the Feast. The only thing Taji could think of was...

Kissa.

Heading Mira's request, the Prince had not told his commander about Kissa. In truth, he had his own reasons. It was solely his fault and his duty to fix. A sudden fear for her grew in Taji. Would the Commander deem her a prisoner of war and kill her? He felt torn between his duties and what he felt was right.

Desperately, Taji tried to calculate a way to his sword—his only advantage. His room suddenly appeared larger than ever before.

Without another thought, he sprinted toward his lifeline. In his peripheral, he saw the moment the commander swung his sword. Time seemed to come to a crawl. The wind whipped past him as he ducked and rolled underneath the heavy blade.

Staying low, he scattered swiftly towards Isis. Almost there. As the golden sword came into arm's reach, beckoning him, Taji felt a flutter of optimism. He extended his arm to grab the hilt. Snatching Isis up, he twirled around to face the commander. The tip of the commander's sword touched Taji's unprotected chest.

"Your first mistake was not having your sword next to you."

A mistake he deemed never to make again if he made it out of this mess alive. Taji flicked his attention back to Kissa in his peripheral. Then, with sheer determination, he used Isis to knock the commander's blade away. Then he lept forward into battle mode. The commander was a blur of blocks and swings, but Taji kept up, blocking the steel aimed at his neck.

His drums flared up with indignation. Why is he trying to kill me? Ice danced along his spine. His minuscule life flashed before him as he parried another swing. Their swords clashed and Taji pushed against the Commander's blade to throw him off balance. Instead, their blades crossed into a deadlock.

He used his weight to push Taji back. "Your second mistake was thinking you're the only one who knows the passages. Enemies roam these halls. I taught you better than this."

He was larger than Taji, and he felt his boots sliding back little by little, closing him in against the wall. He spun around, breaking away from the Commander, and leaped to the right. In his stance, he braced for another attack.

"She is not the enemy," Taji heaved. "She healed our queen." Even though he didn't understand Kissa's purpose just yet, that fact was still true. The Commander said nothing, so he continued. "I am your Prince and I order you to stand down. I will not allow you to take her."

The Commander did not kill him yet, and that had to mean something. He wasn't sure if Osiris gave him the confidence needed, but Taji found that his fear, uncertainty, and preservation meant nothing at this moment. Despite his conflicting emotions regarding Kissa, his overwhelming desire was to protect her from the man who had been like a father to him.

Commander Ashtar raised a brow in surprise. "So, you would protect this girl, knowing she may be the enemy?"

"I will!" Taji didn't have to think about it.

Omani narrowed his eyes. "Even from the King? Your father?"

Despite lacking time to think, Taji knew he would. So he raised Isis higher. "Even from the King! Now stand down!"

Omani stared at Taji hard, studying him. He thought he saw something like relief behind his stern eyes. Then the commander lowered his sword and sheathed it. "Good!"

Taji did not lower Isis, the urge to get Kissa far away from danger pumped through his blood. *"Good?"*

"Amon watches my every move. So, I used the secret passages get here. The Elite swarm the tunnels. You wouldn't know anything about that, would you?" He lifted a brow knowingly.

Taji hesitated. He didn't know what the Commander was playing at.

Omani relaxed in the chair by the desk as if he hadn't threatened his life a moment ago. "Now, tell me why my daughter is in your bed."

<hr>

Taji felt like he had been in the center of a relentless tempest for two days, with fleeting respites disrupted by forceful surges. He stood there, bewildered, his raised sword still in hand, as he tried to process the fact that the commander wasn't trying to kill him anymore.

My daughter...

That was not what he expected Commander Ashtar to say. *"Your daughter?"* Taji repeated incredulously.

"Yes, Kissa is my daughter."

"But..." Taji looked back at Kissa's sleeping form in his bed. "She is Sagian."

"She is more than that!" The commander growled. "She is our future, gifted in ways beyond even my understanding!"

Taji stared at his mentor like he never knew him at all. Countless questions formed on his lips, yet he didn't know where to begin. Finally, he sheathed his sword, then deeply inhaled, trying to gather himself. He walked over to the empty ottoman near the door and slumped on it.

Commander Ashtar stared at him. "Start from the beginning."

With a relieved breath, Taji told him how he stumbled upon Kissa and her healing touch. "She was the hope I prayed for. I did not think beyond that, and now my father hunts for her."

The Commander said nothing as he listened to Taji's version of when Kissa healed his mother, what his mother had experienced, and what he and Chase witnessed at the Pit. Once he finished, silence descended around them.

Taji felt like a weight lifted from his shoulders as he waited for judgment. He would accept it. Whatever anger the commander felt, he would suffer it bravely.

However, it never came.

Instead, the Commander stood and walked over to Kissa's lying form. He brushed her cheek as he looked at his daughter with a softness he had never seen in the man. His look turned solemn as he stared out the window. "So, your father knows Queen Safiyah didn't wake up without magic. Now they are on a headhunt. Does that not seem strange to you?"

It did. A thought that Taji pondered on since finding out they were searching for Kissa. How did his father know the curse was of magic origins? Unless...

"Where do you think the witch went?" He knew it in his bones that she was the source.

The commander looked back at him with a mirthless smirk. "You and I both know she is no ordinary witch. I believe she will make herself known soon. There are also scouts who've seen an unidentified ship on the seas. Care to place a bet on the likelihood of it heading in our direction?"

Taji's chest tightened. He attended the Council of War, but hearing it from the Commander hit him differently. It awakened a primal need in him. Protect his kingdom, protect his mother...protect Kissa.

He couldn't understand his feelings for her. It conflicted with his duties. He knew nothing about her, yet he couldn't push the feeling aside.

"Did my father finally give orders to confront the ship?" He asked, holding on to a slither of hope.

Commander Ashtar shook his head gravely, squashing any redemption. "You are Protector of the Realm. Ancient protectors displayed bravery and unwavering integrity. They upheld the Natural Order of Life. They not only defended their own but all the nations within the realm. And sometimes...sometimes they had to make very difficult choices."

Before now, Taji always chose to ignore his father's actions. He knew one day he had to confront his father, but he always imagined it when he became king and had the power. He lacked evidence and power to take action against him now.

But his father allowed their people to suffer. He knew the source and did nothing. Aware of the imminent threat, but choose idleness? This was beyond something he could ignore.

"What would a Celestial gain in poisoning a kingdom?" Taji asked.

Omani's brow lifted, signaling another thought for Taji's mind. "The same reason the Ancient of Wisdom granted his human worshippers magic. What do you think?"

To defeat Osmondia? But they already did that. There had to be something more.

However, the Commander took his unspoken fears and spoke them into existence. "The Ancients are at war."

Taji's chest tightened. People deemed it blasphemy to speak about such things. However, he knew others shared the same thoughts. The Ancients and Celestials had been absent for at least two-hundred years. Now suddenly, one was poisoning his people and another would reach their shores soon. If Naomi's last words to his father were true, he would destroy the kingdom.

"We humans are just insignificant pieces caught in the middle. We can only do our part to win the human part of this war. The gods may doom us, despite Kissa's ability to save our people."

Taji felt like the world crumbled beneath him, and he only stayed upright because he was sitting. How were they to fight against the Ancients? He woke from a nightmare, only to find a darker one.

Strength, Wisdom, Courage...

He stared at the girl he needed to protect from his own father. She was the sunlight casting its rays on his kingdom, divulging all the dark truths. He stood tall, meeting the Commander's gaze. "At least one god is on our side because they gifted us Kissa. I don't know which one yet, but you cannot convince me that Osmond would watch us be destroyed. We are his people. There must be a way."

Taji felt his drums respond to his conviction, strengthening his courage. Though he did not tell the Commander about Osiris, it was Taji's definitive proof that Osmond was still with them.

The Commander silently watched him—a flicker of pride showed in his eyes. Then a light knock at his wardrobe broke their unspoken thoughts. Omani was already up, covering Kissa's form with the blanket. He stood with his sword ready, then nodded.

With Isis secured in his hand, Taji crept silently to the wardrobe door. "Who is it?"

"*Chase.*"

The Commander nodded for him to open it. His royal guard walked out and behind him, Benji.

"What has happened?" The three of them agreed that if something went wrong, they would knock on the wardrobe door, alerting the others to their approach.

It was Benji who answered. "They questioned my mother and searched for me at Serenity. They are looking for a girl with black hair that entered the queen's chamber with my mother. We shared the agreed story, but Amon will soon uncover it. We need to get Kissa out now."

Their story was that Kissa was a student healer, coming to assist Mira and Benji. In their story, she left with Benji and was now home. A home none of them knew the location of.

"What about Mira and my mother?" Taji asked. He didn't know what his father might try now.

Commander Ashtar approached the three of them. "Mira will keep watch over Safiyah, and I will keep watch over both of them. The King's announcement ensures the Queen's safety for now. Opposing him now will only lead to all of you being imprisoned. Benji, return to Serenity. You are our eyes there. Taji, Chase, you will leave with Kissa and Chase will be our messenger."

"Yes, Commander." The three said in unison.

The Commander's face softened. His hand lay on Taji and Benji's shoulders, and Chase stood beside him. "I have watched the three of you grow up into the passionate, honest, loyal men you are today. I am proud of each one of you. Watch out for one another, lean into your strengths, and do what feels right. Even when you don't understand the things happening around you with your eyes." His attention lingered on Taji with that statement. "Mira and I knew the consequences long before today, and we are more than ready to accept them, at any cost." Omani's eyes swept over the three of them, imploring them. "Watch over my daughter."

Benji's face became severe as tension rolled off his shoulders. Taji knew it pained him to leave his mother in the clutches of the King, just like it killed him to do the same. His hand clenched in a fist and he held it up to his chest. "I will do so with my life!"

A solid understanding settled around the three of them. A line drawn in the sand. As complicated and unsure as Taji felt, this was his Fate. He would protect Kissa at all costs.

29

BROKEN

DREAMS OF ORBS, STARS, and magic filtered through Kissa's mind while she slept. Voices swam in and out, though her mind could not fully grasp any words. When her eyes finally opened, they felt heavy, like an iron door rusted around the edges. She barely kept them open. Everything was hazy, and she just made out flames flicker across from her.

Cold.

She groaned from the ice seeping through her. A blanket covered her, but its material did nothing to stave away the chills that took root in her bones. Kissa had never been this cold before.

"You are awake?"

She heard relief in Taji's deep tone, and Kissa snapped her head to the side of her. Her vision swam.

"Take your time. You have been asleep for three days," he whispered.

Three days?

Taji was in his familiar black leathers and cloak. Leaned back against the wall next to her, he held what looked like a book in his lap. He appeared tense, but his brows creased in worry as he watched her come to.

Kissa closed her eyes and slowly rolled her head around, trying to loosen her neck and clear the haze lingering in her mind. Three days. The last thing she remembered was holding on to his mother's hand desperately, hoping to heal her.

When she finally opened her eyes again, Kissa took in the small cavern that surrounded them. Faded engravings marked the walls. Her eyes drew to them like a moth to a flame. The impressions seemed ancient, made up of both illustrations and words—writing that seemed familiar, but her hazy mind couldn't grasp it.

She licked her dry lips. "Where are we?" Her throat sounded hoarse from disuse.

Taji handed her a waterskin. "We are in the First Temple. We arrived yesterday. Chase is keeping watch outside."

As she guzzled down the water that tasted like sweet nectar to her dry throat, Kissa thought about the first time she met Taji near the Temple. She didn't get to explore like she wanted, but she thought all that remained was a landscape of rubble. Her brows furrowed.

"Benji and I found this part still intact when we were about ten summers old, playing in the woods. Something always drew me here. We are underneath the ruins, a hidden cave," he said.

Kissa imagined Taji and Benji running around like the children she saw playing at the festival, playing with swords and passing around flower crowns. The familiar hint of sadness followed. She did not grow up exploring temples with them as she should have.

Focusing on the present, she asked, "Tell me what happened and why we are here."

His eyes lit up, making her heart skip. "Because you healed the queen."

She gasped. "She lives?"

Taji nodded. His smile was a breath of fresh air to her soul. "She is awake. I've waited days for you to wake up so I can thank you. It seems the kingdom owes you a great debt, Kissa Ashtar."

"There is a no debt. I would do it a thousand times again."

It did not escape her attention that Taji used her surname, nor the golden two-handed sword leaning against the wall between them. Apparently, Kissa slept through a lot. She remembered the fear that seized her when his sword broke during the tournament. Though beautifully made and gold, this was not the blade from her vision. It didn't sing to her spirit.

"Nice sword," she said.

"Ah." He peered at the sword in question. "Perks of being Protector of the Realm, I suppose. It is the Blade of Isis."

"Protector of the Realm? Isn't that an ancient title?" She remembered reading about it during her history lessons with her father. They hadn't named a Protector in centuries, not since the last one, Isaiah the Brave, died in the war.

Taji nodded. "You are correct. One of my father's schemes I haven't figured out just yet." Then he knocked the breath from her lungs as he said, "My mother thinks a fiery-haired goddess saved her."

He watched Kissa fight the urge to touch her hair, clinching her hands into fists at her side. Three days. It felt like someone had pulled the rug from under her. Her attention filled with anticipation. She was sure he said the comment for a reason and she was waiting for the other boot to drop.

Honestly, Kissa wasn't sure how she felt about the Prince knowing about her origins. Did he see her differently? He didn't seem angry or repulsed by her, but that didn't mean he still wanted to be friends with her.

Then his face became serious, and he grabbed her hand casually. The action ignited something in her as she felt his rough palms against her own. Kissa felt fuzzy inside, lightheaded. A strange feeling she never felt before. It made her feel a tad subconscious, but she didn't take her eyes off his piercing gaze as he spoke.

"I felt shocked, of course. Even a bit hurt, but it wasn't like you had time to lay all your secrets to me. Thankfully, your father explained everything."

He did? She wondered what her father thought about her healing gifts. "How is he?"

"He and Mira stayed back at the Citadel. We are waiting for him to send word that it is safe to take you home."

She sat up and scooted herself against the wall. Was she ready to go home? She still had things to uncover. Even more, why didn't her father take her home immediately when she fell unconscious?

"If it is all good news, then why are we here?" She asked.

Kissa watched the conflict behind Taji's eyes. He was warring with something. "Saving my mother has brought certain truths to light," he said.

She listened intently as Taji explained everything that had transpired after she fainted. Her cheeks burned to discover he hid her in his chambers and that her father saw her lying unconscious in his bed. However, her embarrassment quickly dissolved into anger once he confirmed Kissa's thoughts about the origins of the sickness. Now, the King hunted her.

With his hand still holding Kissa's, Taji asked, "Tell me what happened?"

It may have been three days ago, but to her, it felt like it had just happened. The rolling shadows inside Queen Safiyah's mind made her shutter. All those sick in the kingdom suffered the same infliction, and she had no idea how to save them all.

"It's hard to explain. I could see inside her...even inside her mind. It felt cold and dark." She shivered from the memory. "A black taint was everywhere inside her. When I reached her mind, I found a storm of sentient shadows sucking the life force from her. When I finally fought it off, I found your mother hiding in the far reaches of her herself, holding on."

A tear fell down her cheek. She didn't know the strength it took for the queen to hold on that long. Most died within a few days of slipping into a coma. The pain in the Prince's eyes at the mention of what his mother went through, at what others in the kingdom were enduring, squeezed her heart.

His jaw clenched as he looked away for a moment to gather himself. She used the engravings on the wall as a distraction to give him time. Neither Kissa nor Taji experienced such a thing, and it felt like grasping at straws of how to eradicate it. She passed out for three days and was unsure how to use her powers to save the rest of the kingdom.

Something bothered her. Before she could think it through, Kissa blurted it out. "When I waited outside your mother's chamber that day, your father walked past me. I felt his sentiments, and they were not of someone grieving for their wife."

Taji narrowed his eyes. "How so?"

Kissa licked her lips. "It reminded me of what I feel when I complete something important. Like a sated feeling. Not of sadness or even anger. More like a satisfied feeling."

Taji looked at her, even more bewildered. "What do you mean, you felt his sentiments?"

Oh right.

Kissa blew out a breath. The Prince knew of her gift of healing, but he did not know of her empathy gift. Now that she exposed it, she had no choice but to explain it. She contemplated how best to describe the impossible.

"I have multiple gifts. One is healing, but another is empathy. I can sense other's emotions." She winced as she said it, ready to embrace his shock and question whether she intrusively felt his feelings without his knowledge.

Taji stared at her incredulously. He gave her a slow blink, then asked, "So, you can feel what I feel?"

Kissa nodded. "I mean, I can if I choose to."

"What am I feeling now?" He asked. Wariness crossed his face.

Kissa stared at the prince, shocked by his request. Now that he knew, she felt conflicted about delving into his private emotions. What if she felt something she didn't want to know? Maybe there was a way to even sift through someone's sentiments. However, she didn't know how to do that yet.

She summoned the pristine white door with the crimson knob in her mind. Surprised to find it closed, she opened it. Then she reached out, only to be met with an empty icy breeze across her senses.

Her brows furrowed in confusion. She tried again...nothing. In a silent panic, she reached for the familiar fire that normally rested within her chest. Her core felt cold and empty, as was her sundial necklace as she touched it. Now that she focused, the hum in her veins was quiet.

Fear engulfed Kissa.

Taji read the fear in her eyes. "What is it?"

"My Essence... it's gone." She said, trembling. It was so cold.

"Maybe it depleted from healing my mother and it takes time to rejuvenate," Taji said, raising his brows. "It must have taken great power to fight against another magic."

"Maybe," she croaked. "But the Ancient of Life told me that if I emptied my well, I may lose my gifts forever."

Taji's eyes grew wide and a sharp swear fell from his lips. "The Ancient of Life?" He stood up immediately. "You spoke to the Creator?"

She nodded solemnly. "She is the one who bound my gifts as a baby and unlocked my gifts on my birthnight."

"Kissa, that is incredible! Did you see her? What was it like?"

He was so excited, Kissa almost forgot what she was upset about. Feeling bitter, Kissa said, "Intense and intrusive!"

Taji's eyes softened. "I'm sorry. That was insensitive of me." He dragged a hand down his face, then sat back down beside Kissa and picked her hand back up. "Alright. Let's think about this. How would you know if you emptied your well completely? Did she say?"

Kissa shook her head. "I don't know. That's the thing. She gave me these gifts with a few basic warnings. No instruction on how to use them or what their purpose is."

"I see. We just have to wait then. But Kissa, I don't think the Ancient of Life would grant you something so special to lose so easily." His eyes held the spark of one who believed in such things.

Kissa huffed, stopping the curse that wanted to rip from her lips in response. She was inside the remains of the First Temple. It wouldn't bode well to say such things about the Ancients. Silence settled between them.

But as she thought about it, she realized it wasn't fair to be angry at the Ancient of Life. She was not the others and Kissa knew she cared deeply for humans. She created them.

"She is magnificent." Kissa finally said, earning a stunned glance from the Prince that made her smile. "I think I met her pure form first. Her starlight is a brilliant emerald green and dazzling gold just like her eyes. Her voice, it has a melodic lilt to it, like notes of a violin."

She scrunched her lips. "She is intense, though. But...but her smile is scintillating. It will blind you if you stare too long. Honestly, she is not at all what I expected." Kissa gazed beyond Taji as she thought of something.

"What is it?"

"You said you never seen eyes like mine," she said. "They are hers."

"Kissa, that has to mean something. Nobody has her eyes because she didn't make any of us in her image. Mine are blue like Osmond's. Only the Crown and heirs have them."

When she first met Taji, she remembered his eyes triggered a memory of something. She realized now that his eyes gave a clue to his lineage—Royal Lineage. And yet, his hand still encased her own. A silent statement that no matter their origins, he was her friend.

His laugh lines deepened around his eyes as he stared at her. His smile was infectious and Kissa found she could not look away. She remembered how the future of him in her vision stared at her. Like nothing else existed.

"I heard a story about the Ancient of Life from the library keeper when I was young. It could be just a myth, but I like to think it is true." Taji said.

His rumbling voice and how his intense blue eyes searched her own caused flutters in her stomach. Kissa looked at him expectedly.

"It is said that the Ancient of Life loved the Divine Warrior. But another Ancient coveted her. This Ancient loathed Osmond, and it caused strife within their realm. So, selflessly, the Ancient of Life chose not to be with either to keep peace in the Ancient realm. Which meant she did not birth any Celestials of her own. When Haava was created, she asked for the others, and together they built our world. Then... she created us out of love."

Taji's tragic love story moved her, and ever since she learned of the Ancient of Life, something drew Kissa to her. She chose not to make humans like her and gave all beings choice and love despite her own predicament. The Ancient seemed humble, though putting "Ancient" and "humble" in a sentence felt strange. Yet, Kissa realized she knew next to nothing of the Ancients, only opinions created out of anger.

"I do not worship any of the Ancients." She let that settle for a moment. When Taji nodded for her to continue, she said, "When my father taught me the history of the war, I felt angry that they abandoned us. As I grew older, I didn't feel they deserved my prayers, my faith. But the Ancient of Life explained why she did not intervene. She told me of the Sacred Laws."

Taji nodded. As royalty, he most likely tutored in all things about the Ancients and the laws that governed the divine. "You are not wrong in your feelings, Kissa. It is just misplaced. When my mother was dying, I felt lost in my grief. I still had a tournament to win, and the weight of the crown loomed over my head like an anvil, ready to drop at any moment. My people were still dying. I was so angry that Osmond would allow my faithful mother to die."

Kissa's chest squeezed. She never felt that type of emotional pain, but the echo of his grief still lingered in her mind from the morning at Serenity. He moved closer and Kissa's breath stuttered. She could not help staring at his perfect lips as he spoke.

"But then I met you." His eyes pierced her with its intensity. "You renewed the faith of a broken-hearted prince that morning and didn't even know it. You gave me hope in the darkest of places. Then you healed my mother, and I realized it was you all along."

Kissa's mouth suddenly felt parched again. She licked her lips as her heart hammered in her chest at Taji's vulnerability and words. "Realized what?"

"That you are the answer to my prayers, Kissa Ashtar. The Ancients are with us, and you are proof of that."

Kissa was stunned by his words, finding it difficult to believe that she could be considered an answer to anyone's anything. All she did was what she thought was right. The kingdom didn't owe her anything.

"Get some rest. I'm going to check in with Chase and send word to your father." He said before he pulled back his hands from hers. Kissa mourned his touch.

She watched him leave, then reached up to touch her hair with a trembling hand. Her finger tips touched silky fabric, wrapped around her entire head. She blew out a breath of relief. Looking around, she found her satchel, bow, and quivers against the wall to her other side. She grabbed her satchel and reached in to find the Chonda ring to find it wasn't there.

Kissa upturned her bag. Jars of healing salves, wraps, and her mortar and pestle fell out on the ground before her, but no Chonda ring. Did she lose it? Did someone take it? But why? Alarm flared inside her.

She stood and checked the deep pockets of her cloak and came back empty-handed. Kissa wrapped her arms around herself, trying to calm her heavy breathing and the whirlwind of thoughts as she checked the ground. Worry clouded her mind.

Though the ring held little intimate value, it was dangerous if it fell into the wrong hands. She had her scarf for now, but when she had the chance, she would ask around and retrace her steps. Maybe Mira or her father found it. She hoped.

Finally, realizing there was nothing more she could do, Kissa sat back down against the wall and returned the items back to her satchel. Her body still ached and the search for the ring exhausted her. She settled to get some rest and closed her eyes again.

Summoning her door as she always did before she slept, Kissa realized without her gifts, she felt empty. Like her very spirit was missing, and even though she complained her gifts were thrust upon her, she discovered that her very being wept for its loss.

A wail ripped from her chest as tears fell down her face. Kissa felt broken.

30

SWORD OF OSIRIS

Taji

WHEN TAJI RETURNED FROM sending word to Commander Ashtar that Kissa was awake, he found her sitting cross-legged on the ground, staring at the engravings on the wall. The fire that normally burned within her eyes seemed snuffed out. The usual hum he felt around her, urging him to act, was now silent. Accepting it was difficult, but now seeing it fade like a dying candle felt even harder.

"What do we do now? We can't lie low and do nothing," Kissa said. She clenched her fingers with nervous energy.

He sat against the wall with his open tome. Like her, he wanted to act, but they had to await her father's message. "We are waiting."

Kissa stood. With a hand on her hip, she turned to him. "There is a ship coming and a Celestial on the loose somewhere. We should be warning our people."

"Warning them about something that we ourselves don't even really know sounds counter-productive," he said before thinking.

Kissa's eyes hardened. "I refuse to sit here and do nothing when we can be—I don't know—preparing?" Her arms flared up in the air.

He didn't need to have her empathy ability to feel the determination in her words. Yet, her intentions were not in question. No, what Taji truly feared was the powerful capability of her gifts. That she entered his mother's mind and divulged that she could feel other's emotions left Taji on edge. If his father discovered it or she ended up in his custody, there was no way to predict his actions. Since his dream of her chained and lifeless, he felt the need to be extra cautious.

"Would you say *something*?" Kissa snapped.

"I understand your need to warn others, but the tunnels are not safe while Amon searches for you. We must go through the forest, but not blindly. We need to wait for word from your father."

Kissa huffed, but said nothing more. She wrapped her arms around herself and returned to probing the wall. He understood her need to do something. As a warrior, he felt restless too, but knew they had to strategize.

He watched silently as Kissa observed three different-sized circles engraved on the wall. The largest sat in the middle and the medium-sized one just above it. The left side held a small circle with unreadable words to Taji. Kissa touched each of them, examining them intently. After she finished, she turned to him with a sense of wonderment in her eyes.

Taji stood and walked up next to her. "What is it?"

"This is Haava." She touched the largest circle. "This is the moon," she said to the smaller one above it. Then she moved over to the smallest one. "This is the orb at the Citadel. The one I saw in my dream."

Taji thought hard for an orb at the citadel, but drew a blank. Before he could ask her about it or the dream, she said,

"When the moon sits full, basked in an orangish glow, the hidden one will reveal herself. Enemies will bring the Age of Fury, and the downfall of two kingdoms shall be its outcome. With her light, she will gather with her seven others: The Protector, the Dream Walker, the Shaman, the Scholar, the Engineer, the Adjudicator, and the Enchantress from all seven kingdoms. Together, they will enforce the Creator's will and usher in a new era...the Age of Redemption."

The fire of the torches dimmed, then flared around them. Taji stared slack jawed as the full prophecy flowed from her lips. He was certain Kissa read it word for word. Something about her saying it out-loud sent tension rolling through him. Like she spoke it into existence.

She turned back to him. "It's a prophecy. What do you think it means?" Her brows scrunched in puzzled amazement. Then, her voice softened as she said, "It is the reason women can't be Scorpions, isn't it?"

Taji nodded. "It is the oldest prophecy taught by the First Mother. It has yet to come to pass." He let out a heavy breath. "It is the reason my father banned women from the military. We're ordered to send anyone caught spreading it to the dungeons."

A flicker of fire flared behind her eyes. Just a trickle of the usual inferno he'd come to know within her. For a moment, Taji wanted nothing more than to beckon it and bask in its burn.

Her eyes flared. "So it is the king repressing women? What a coward!"

Taji felt like Kissa slapped *him* in the face. Though his father gave the orders, Taji followed them like a senseless puppet. Like his uncle, he should have been standing up to his father instead of making excuses and putting it off. The sting from her words, he realized, was shame.

Suddenly, Kissa's eyes grew wide, shaking him from his thoughts. "I think I figured it out! She told me there are other gifted. Others like me who share the same destiny. She told me of the Protector, Shaman and Dream Walker. These others are new to me, though."

Kissa was speaking so fast it was hard to keep up. "Who told you?" He asked.

"The Ancient of Life." She closed her eyes. "Layla is the Dream Walker, Benji is the Shaman and you..."

When she opened her eyes, she stared at Taji with conviction. He straightened up before her, looking down into her unique eyes, knowing the words before they slipped from her lips.

"You're the Protector. I dreamed of you in my visions. You held a majestic sword," Kissa said.

Taji's mind soared as his heart hammered against his chest. Protector. Visions. Sword.

"You saw me wielding Osiris?"

"Who is Osiris?" Confusion lined her features.

"The majestic sword. He belongs to Osmond. He hid it in the human realm for the chosen to find," he said.

Even now, the words felt strange leaving his mouth. Taji found it hard to accept that he was Osiris' chosen. But Kissa's eyes lit up with understanding, and Taji's treacherous heart skipped in eagerness.

Her eyes lifted in a wistful gaze. "The sword was magnificent. It hummed ethereal magic, and you wielded it with purpose like you and Osiris were one."

Since finding the tome, he felt like a failure for not figuring out the Divine language. She didn't know it, but Kissa's words poured life into him. That she had visions, another gift, astounded him, but he took notice of something even more profound.

"You can read the Divine language."

Kissa tilted her head. "Divine language?"

Taji approached the wall and gestured towards the scribble-like inscription. "Ceepsun, language of Ancients."

With a tilted head, she simply said, "Huh," as if it was nothing sacred and unimaginable.

Taji's thoughts tangled up in his throat. He walked over to where he was sitting earlier, where he had tried to decipher the Sword of Osiris as he waited for her to wake. He picked up the book with trembling hands. Wordlessly, he handed it to her.

She stared at him with a bewildered expression before looking down at the book. Her eyes brightened before she gently touched the inscription in awe. "I've never seen ink in gold." She examined the leather and first page. Then she read it out loud:

"Osiris, the mighty blade of the Ancient of Strength, will choose its wielder. The chosen warrior must encompass wisdom, courage, and strength. When the chosen is worthy, he will unlock the secrets of this scripture."

As she read the words, Taji's heart hammered against his ribs. Osiris's drums began immediately, a tune of urgency. Kissa gasped, clutching her chest. She seemed to arch into him. He looked down into her face, into eyes that reminded him of the leaves of the forest bathed in the sun's rays. His arm brushed hers, the book between them.

"Your drums call to me," Kissa said. "Outside of the Temple, and right before the King's tournament, I felt them."

Suddenly, everything else fell away, and Kissa was the only thing in his world. "Nobody has ever heard them before."

"What does it mean?" Kissa asked.

"I-I don't know." That seemed to be the answer for everything as of late. He looked down at the book, then cleared his throat and straightened up, trying to regain himself. "Does it tell us where Osmond hid Osiris?"

Smirking, Kissa glanced down at the book and read through the pages. She seemed to get a thrill that he needed her. She paced around the cavern slowly, in her own world. Taji said nothing and allowed her to read, all the while admiring her from where he stood. Even without her gifts, Kissa was a sight to behold.

"Oh, no!" she said, shaking her head.

"What is it?" He asked. His heart pounded against his ribs.

"Osiris is on the Isles of Death."

Of course it was. The only place impossible to get to. The Isles were unknown territory. Infiltrating the Sagian Kingdom seemed a walk in the park in comparison. Hell's Conception, the sea between the islands and Osmondia, gained its name from the unpredictable storms that favored it. He met no one who lived to tell the story.

So close, yet so far. Frustration bubbled up. "Are you sure?" But even as he asked, he knew it to be true.

Kissa nodded, then continued reading. She explained Taji needed to read the book in its entirety to understand the magic of Osiris. There were sections for each ability, such as those connected to Osiris's sentient.

Sanbanyi, the drums Taji felt in his being, finally had a name. FoKus and Heightened Senses, gifts Osiris gave him in his time of need. However, another section outlined his abilities once he brandished the sword, which was completely new to him.

Foresight, Speed, Invisibility, and something called Ngurumo.

"Ngurumo?" Taji paced, lost in thought.

As Kissa read, her brows furrowed in concentration. Occasionally, she would look up, stare out in contemplation, and bite her bottom lip as she did. When she turned abruptly and caught him staring at her, her brows lifted. "What?" Her cheeks reddened at his open gaze.

He reached out toward the head wrap Mira put on her before they left the Citadel. When he discovered her hair that day, it was dark in the room and he only had moments before Commander Ashtar confronted him. He was curious, to say the least. "May I?"

Kissa blinked, clearly caught off guard. When she realized his intentions, her eyes widened with a storm brewing behind him. He was sure she would say no, but then she gently placed the book on the floor and reached up and unraveled her scarf herself.

As the scarf came off, Taji stared intently. Vermillion, titian, and gold tresses that made up her locs fell down her back. They reminded him of the different colored Za leaves during the seasons of autumn. Her locs were wild, untamed. Her hair was...

"Stunning!"

Though her hair was red, it was unlike the rust color of the Sagians. Her hair was vibrant, maybe even too vibrant. Her father was right. Kissa was more than Sagian. So much more. He only wished to be by her side as she discovered it all.

Though he knew she needed to conceal this part of herself, it felt wrong to hide something so exotic, beautiful, and uniquely hers. He wished to see Kissa like this always. Yet, the thought of his brethren harming her made him irrationally furious.

When he tried to meet her eyes, he found Kissa staring at the floor, fiddling with her sundial. Taji lifted her chin to see her better—really see her. He saw the innocence of a sheltered life, the uncertainty of her place in the world, the mysteries that even she was unwinding. Taji didn't understand the connection to her that burned so fiercely between them.

"You are the most stunning woman I have ever met, Kissa. Never be ashamed of your true nature."

She gave a watery smile as her eyes misted with tears. Then Taji looked down at her hand clinching her necklace. The engraving on the back of the sundial caught his eye. His extensive understanding of the Ancients enabled him to recognize all of their symbols.

A tree on top of a mountain. The insignia for creation. Osmond wore it on his pauldron. His eyes hardened in thought. He remembered asking Kissa where she had got the necklace from.

I am not sure who gifted it to me. I've had it since I could remember.

Suddenly, the pieces clicked in place, locking it all into a perfect picture. Her hair and eyes, her unknown origins, her gifts. Her light beamed brighter than all the light in the world. She was... hope.

"Kissa!" The air rushed out of him.

She looked at him expectantly, looking back and forth between his blue orbs he saw reflected in her irises.

"The Prophecy is about you." He didn't let her startled eyes sway him in the least. He grabbed the trinket on her neck, revealing the symbol. "You are the Ancient of Life's warrior. It is *you* who will reveal yourself."

31

DAUGHTER OF ZURI

KISSA

"THE ANCIENT OF LIFE'S warrior?" Kissa repeated.

Kissa looked down at her keepsake. When Layla told her whose symbol it was, she didn't make the connection. The awe and confidence in Taji's eyes took her back. He didn't doubt his words for one breath.

She scoffed. Kissa was anxious, awkward, and stubborn, challenging her father at every turn. Her temper blazed over the simplist things, often out of control. She shook her head. No, he had to be mistaken, though Taji's look told her he knew her doubt, but it didn't change the fact.

A prophecy about me?

But wouldn't she feel *chosen* or whatever she was? Wouldn't something inside her tell her that? Even more, why didn't the Ancient of Life say that in her intrusive visits to her dreams?

She threw her hands up in irritation. "There is nothing special about me. Stop looking at me like that!"

He curled his lip into that insufferable smirk. "You healed the queen. Today alone, you interpreted the Divine language and the Sword of Osiris. You wear the insignia of the Ancient of Life close to your heart," he said. "The Creator of Life herself unbound you and visited your dreams. I don't think anyone else can say the same." Then he raised a brow. "You seem pretty special to me."

When he put it like that...

Taji's eyes held her captive. She knew he said the last part to prove a point, and yet... the way he looked at her simultaneously caused shivers and heat to shoot through her. Why did the Prince have to be so frustratingly handsome? He was so close, she could feel the warmth of his body.

He chose that moment to lower his head even closer, their breaths mingled between them.

Those insufferable lips...

Without warning, the floors beneath her shuttered, causing her to lurch forward. Taji's firm hands wrapped around her as she fell against his chest. They stared at one another with wide eyes.

She was the first to blink. "What was that?"

"I'm not..."

Before he could finish his statement, the walls of the temple shifted. Taji gripped her tight. Kissa watched wide-eyed as cracks formed in the walls and cut through the ground right before her. Dust and debris fell down on them, ready to bury them alive.

Breaking from his grip, she quickly reached for her bow and quiver, throwing it over her shoulder, along with her satchel. Then a loud rumble echoed around them.

"We need to go now!" Taji pushed her in front of him, steering her through the cave toward a tunnel leading out.

Kissa's heart raced as she followed the path, coughing up dust. Suddenly, a giant silhouette stood before her, blocking the broken exit. Her body froze, then Chase's face came into view. He reached for her and pulled her toward the exit. When they made it outside into the night air, Kissa breathed it in hastily.

"Come, it is a quake," Chase said. "The horses are there. We need to pick up the pace." He pointed to a copse of trees where two warhorses stood in the meadow.

Kissa tried to take in her surroundings, but the entire mountain felt like it was shuddering. She stayed between them as they ran, trying her best to keep up. She could hear tree branches breaking in the distance from the force. Animals cried out as they skittered across the ground, and she heard birds flocking above them.

More than once, the ground cracked open, and they had to maneuver around fissures. Kissa fell twice, but Taji's and Chase's powerful arms kept her from face planting.

Then it stopped.

The silence seemed to swallow them. In a stance, they surveyed their surroundings, ready to run if required. Kissa gazed up at the night sky, and her jaw dropped. At the center of it all, the moon, bigger than she ever seen it, illuminated the surroundings with its magnificent orangish hue.

The Harvest Moon.

The vision of the lone warship blanketed by shadows surfaced in her mind, stark and clear. "He's here!" Kissa said.

Taji walked up to her, his brows furrowed tightly. "Who is here?"

She had a strong feeling about who commanded that ship, but Taji was a warrior and needed facts. A feeling alone wouldn't satisfy him. She closed her eyes to think. Shifting through all the things she learned in the past moon cycle.

"Layla mentioned a gateway for the Divine to transcend between realms. It's now gone. But I saw a vision of the past. Just before the war, two centuries ago. The Ancient of Wisdom sent two Celestials here to teach the Sagian people magic. What if..."

Both of them looked at Kissa like she grew two heads. Taji recovered first as his look grew contemplative. "They were already here." He finished.

"The witch has to be one of them," Chase said.

Kissa looked between them. Taji told her about the witch her father apprehended, that the King kept in the Fathomless Pit, and her last words before she disappeared. Ice slid down her spine. Deeply buried memories resurfaced from the past. She shook her head to rid her mind of it.

Chase and Taji locked eyes, something unspoken between them, something she was all too familiar with. Kissa's hands clenched with impatience. This was not the time to hide things from her. But to her relief, Taji spoke up.

"It's her brother. We must return to the capital and warn the people," he said, approaching the two horses.

What he said made sense. It clicked in her mind and felt right. Naomi and Moorice were Celestials, siblings and never left the human realm. But why wait until now?

Kissa planted her feet right where she stood. "What about Sapphire City?"

Taji whipped around toward her. "Sapphire City? My father summoned the citizens to the capital for my mother's ceremony. Nobody is there, not even a patrol." His eyes widened at his own words. "Shit!"

Kissa lifted her chin. "I'm not leaving them. My mother's there and I'm not leaving her." Anger flared within her that the king would leave the sick to their own detriment. She knew without a doubt her mother wouldn't leave them either, summoned or not.

Taji looked torn. She knew it was his duty to protect his kingdom, and the majority of the people were in the capital. It also didn't slip her notice that he missed his mother's ceremony to stay with her. Even so, Kissa would not abandon those at the coast, even if she had to find her own way there.

She observed Taji's moment of resolve. Her heart thundered in expectation.

The Prince faced Chase. "Go warn Commander Ashtar and High Commander Eshu. We need to prepare for what comes. Tell Ashtar to gather about twenty from our legion and meet me at the coast." He looked at Kissa. "Let us hope we are not too late."

Chase nodded, mounted his horse and took off toward the citadel without another word.

Taji grabbed the other horse. Then turned to Kissa, taking her in. He extended his hand. "This won't be a simple mission."

Kissa still stubbornly stood with her arms folded, concealing the deep relief that she was not alone. Ignoring his offered hand, she climbed on his black stallion with ease. She looked down at his amused face. "Then let us go, your Grace. We're wasting time."

He smirked before he mounted and settled behind her. The warmth from his chest and thighs around her tingled down her spine. She felt acutely aware of his closeness. The aroma of sandalwood wrapped around her and settled her nerves, melting away any stubborn thought that lingered as Kissa relaxed against his chest.

She felt the warmth of his breath against her ear, sending shivers through her body as he said, "Where ever your light takes you, I am there, Kissa Ashtar."

THE JOURNEY TO THE coast was taking longer than expected. They came across fissures along the forest floor that made it difficult for Taji's horse—Cosmo—to trot steadily. Za trees, broken clean off from their stumps, lie across the ground as if they were just mere plants uprooted. Turned up stones obstructed the centuries old trail beneath them.

To make matters worse, droplets of rain pelted them. Though it wasn't heavy, the cold air from the summit seemed to follow them through the forest, making the rain feel like ice shards against their exposed skin. They wrapped their cloaks tighter, underdressed for what appeared to be an approaching storm. A long night was ahead of them.

The silence of the forest felt eerie. Usually, Za's forest flourished with birds, animals, and wildlife, but there was nothing but the sounds of wind whipping through the trees for leagues. It made Kissa feel uneasy. Every once in a while, she spotted the harvest moon through the breaks in the trees. It felt like an omen.

With a serious face, eyes constantly scanning the brush, the Prince's mood seemed to sour the further they traveled. He hadn't said over two words since they left the Temple. His worry was clear to Kissa, and the unknown only intensified it.

She sat in her own whirlwind of thoughts. Most glaringly was the cryptic prophecy that seemed to shake the kingdom. Literally. She pondered her parents, their hidden secrets, and the untold truths. What else haven't they told her? Then, her mind drifted to the lost Chonda ring.

It had been four days since she last saw it. She pondered asking Taji, but wished to evade the expected questions he undoubtedly would ask. Kissa decided she couldn't dwell on what she couldn't control and didn't know. The ring could be anywhere now. She had to just hope it wasn't in the wrong hands.

The urging of her bladder overwhelmed her. She turned to Taji. "I need to...you know. Relieve..." Kissa's cheeks burned.

The Prince's brow raised in that questioning way, a change from the face of stone since they left the Temple. "You will need to use a tree or go into the bushes. There are no privies here." He gestured to the forest.

Kissa narrowed her eyes at him. "I know that!"

"Be quick about it."

Kissa rolled her eyes. That he mentioned a tree, and told her to be quick about it, said he knew nothing of a woman's anatomy. Cosmo stopped, and she dismounted, stomping into the hip-high brush. She only relieved herself once she felt far enough from the prince's eyes and grumpy mood. Kissa finished and started back, but stalled midway at a familiar presence.

A bird-like screech broke the silence. Kissa looked up, and her mouth parted.

Aya?

I am here.

Aya's sing-song voice lilted in her mind. Then, she gracefully maneuvered the treetops as she came down and landed on Kissa's now outstretched arm. Not believing her eyes, she stared at the golden eagle for a long moment. Then she reached up with a trembling hand, praying for the first time that Aya was real, before stroking her.

Kissa wept uncontrollably when she felt the smooth sensation between her gold and white feathers. Aya waited patiently, gazing at her with her molten amber eyes. Kissa finally found her voice.

"You are really here!"

Her joy surpassed everything in that moment. Her sister was alive and well. Aya was here. It filled a crack within the hollowness inside her, and Kissa shuddered at the relief. As she wiped her tears, Aya tilted her head as if regarding Kissa.

I'm sorry that I could not return before your birthnight. I found you in the citadel, unconscious.

"My birthnight! Aya, I was so afraid I wouldn't see you ever again!" It was just like her sister to leave on a dangerous mission than come back and care that she missed her birthnight.

He is here, Kissa!

A chill crossed Kissa's shoulders. "Who?"

Aya's feathers bristled. *He is not of this world. A Celestial with great power born to the Ancients of Wisdom and Chaos. His greatest strength is kinetic. He also commands the winds and shadows. They call him Wind General in the Sagian Kingdom. He and his sister have been here since before the war's beginning.*

So it *was* Moorice, as Kissa feared. A lump formed in her throat as goosebumps crossed her entire body. He was a spitting image of his father, but with his mother's eyes. Kissa did not get to observe his power during her vision, but she knew if he had even half of the ancient magic she felt from both the Saaxir and Chaos...

"What does he want?" She feared the answer as she looked into Aya's eyes.

Their unusual bond since children allowed them to sense each other's feelings. Kissa sensed a subtle inner urging, suggesting Aya's reluctance to express something.

"What is it, Sister?" Kissa stroked Aya's soft feathers.

I felt your magic when you healed the Queen and I was not yet near the kingdom. It was powerful. Three nights before, I felt something else that I never felt before.

Kissa looked away pensively. What was she doing three nights before? Then she gasped in realization. *The Chonda ring.* When she first put it on her finger and it changed its face. Kissa wasn't sure what to make of it.

Her sister's anxiousness felt palpable. It melded with her own dread, causing her to feel even more disparaged by the coming trouble. The Ancient of Life warned her of consequences when using magic. Kissa didn't truly understand the depth of that warning until now.

There is much you do not know. He comes for you. Aya said.

"He? As in Moorice? But what does he want with me?"

No! The finality in Aya's voice made fear climb up Kissa's throat. *Moorice is but a pawn, sister.*

Kissa thought about how his father manipulated him to travel to Haava and teach the Sagians magic. Was Aya speaking of the Saaxir? But before she could ask further, Aya tilted her head.

We have company.

Kissa stared at her in confusion. "What?" Then, as her sister's words caught up to her, she snapped her attention toward the path. The Prince stood only a stone's throw away with startled eyes and mouth ajar. Kissa stiffened, wondering how much he had witnessed. Too much, judging by his shocked expression.

"Taji. This is my sister Aya."

His expression didn't change. "We have met."

Feeling Kissa's confusion at the statement, Aya said, *When you were unconscious, I came to his rooms to check on you.*

Oh. Kissa turned to Taji, taking in his astonished look. "We speak within our minds." She tried and failed to sound casual.

The Prince's brows raised even higher. "You mean *telepathically*?"

Kissa bit her lip as she nodded. This was going downhill fast, and she didn't know how to recover it. She chided herself for not staying alert or at least thinking about the fact that he would worry when she didn't return right away.

"I know this may seem peculiar, but..."

Something else snagged Kissa's mind. She whirled her head back toward Aya, still perched on her arm. Her eyes became pointed. "Wait. How do you know of my gifts? Moorice's power? You said you felt my power, and you were not in Osmondia. How can that be?"

Again, Aya tilted her head in the way birds do as she regarded Kissa with her brilliant eyes. *Because I am your Guardian.*

Her pointed look turned puzzled. "My Guardian?"

In reply, Aya flew off her arm and hovered gracefully before her and the prince. A light flared, bathing the dark forest with gold and white starlight. Kissa and Taji closed their eyes against the richness of the light. When she opened her own, a woman stood before them.

Her white chiffon dress with lace showed off her delicate bronze shoulders and draped to her bare feet. Her skin shimmered brightly against the night, causing Kissa to squint as her eyes adjusted. Gold and white hair pulled up in a loose braid, swept over her shoulder and spilled to her hips. Kissa stared into her molten amber eyes with her mouth agape.

Aya smiled, and it was radiant. "We bonded the moment you were born."

Her voice sounded just as it did in Kissa's mind—a sing-song inflection in it. As the surprise faded, and the questions bubbled up, Kissa could not help the hurt and confusion that surfaced.

"I had a feeling you were more than just a bird," Taji said.

Aya smiled at the prince, nodding in respect. "Protector."

No. Kissa shook her head in disbelief. Surely, she would know if her sister was a Celestial. Maybe the telepathy was a telltale sign. That and the fact that Aya was exceedingly more intelligent than any human, let alone a bird. Why did she never think more of it? She allowed others' expectations to blind her. A magic-less world where humans did not have gifts and Celestials were mere myth.

A facade.

"Why would you not tell me?" Hurt laced Kissa's whisper.

Aya leaned in to touch her cheek, but Kissa pulled away. "It was not time. You would not have understood as you do now." Her sister's eyes saddened. "Nothing has changed, Kissa. We are still sisters, and I love you as I always have. This is my greater purpose, to guide you and those with you."

She wanted desperately to accept Aya's explanation for keeping such an elaborate secret, with all the gloom in the world at the moment, but her hurt overshadowed it. Aya was the one Kissa trusted the most in the world. There were supposed to be no secrets between them. It was as if everyone she knew and loved didn't really exist.

"So, what are you, exactly?"

The abrupt question made her look at the Prince. He seemed to take all this exceptionally well. Despite the bluntness of his question, he looked at Aya with reverence.

She chuckled, sounding like a plucked note from a harp. "Isn't it obvious? I am a shape-shifter and a transcendent like my mother, Zuri."

"Zuri, is your mother?" Both Taji and Kissa blurted in unison.

Aya's focus fell on Kissa. "I have so much to tell you, but we have little time. Please believe I would never hurt you intentionally. I would give my life to keep you safe. In time, all your questions will be answered."

That seemed to be the motto of Kissa's life lately. Nobody seemed to have time to explain themselves. She felt the familiar trickle of Aya's warmth across her shoulders. Still, it wouldn't reach the growing sea of hollowness within her. Everyone seemed to be lying to her these days. Hurt grew right next to her feelings of confusion, strife, and bitterness. "We need to alert Father."

"He already knows." Aya addressed them both now. "He's not alone in this knowledge. The Commander plans to meet with the King half past first light. I do not have high hopes. For the King's agenda is not with his people."

"How do you mean?" Taji moved closer.

"Your father's eyes are on something that does not belong to him." Aya gestured toward the Prince's rucksack knowingly.

Understanding lit in Taji's eyes. "I need to go the Citadel and help the Commander convince my father. Our kingdom, our people are at risk!"

Aya's eyes softened. "You cannot stop what is already in motion, Protector. Your father made grave mistakes. As your forefathers recklessly did in the past. You must find Osiris before him, and only then can you change the outcome for the other kingdoms."

Taji looked like Aya had stabbed him in the heart. "You mean Osmondia will fall? I can't..." He shook his head. "No, I won't accept that."

"It is prophesied, Prince. A kingdom is more than just stones and riches. When the Mad King cast the other nations aside, they rebuilt. Your people will rebuild too, but only if you listen. Do not leave Kissa. Testing the Fates will only bring serious consequences."

Her sister's candid tone and Taji's devastated look crushed her heart, but Kissa knew all too well the implications of not heeding consequences. She knew it was something Taji must come to grips with on his own. Hopefully, it would not end with him losing his gift, or worse, their people.

Aya then looked at Kissa. "You must make haste to Sapphire City. I feel

Mother and those inflicted are in danger. We will train in your magic when the hour is no longer urgent."

She shook her head, trying to hold back the tears at the mention of her lost power. "My gifts are gone."

Though she was not much older than Kissa, Aya's face softened, giving her a sensible look. "They are not gone, Sister. When we use significant amounts of power, our bodies naturally shut down to protect us from emptying our well. It takes time to refill when we've used so much."

She reached out again, and this time Kissa allowed her. Aya touched the sundial, and it flared to life. Kissa felt the familiar fire fill her chest, moving through her veins, causing the humming sensation to return with vigor. Though the Ancient of Life told her, Kissa knew with certainty now, that the erratic fire she battled all her life within her was her Essence.

When Aya's hand retreated, Kissa felt complete again, as she took in a full breath since waking up.

"Nothing is indefinite, including your Essence. Pace yourself. If you feel a strain, that is your body telling you to rest," Aya said.

Kissa nodded, this time fully understanding the risks and consequences.

"I will see you soon, Sister. Tread carefully in these parts."

Then the flash of energy bloomed again. The golden eagle Kissa thought she knew so well immediately took to the skies, leaving her with far more questions than answers.

32

STORMS

Taji

As they journeyed along the rugged coastline, Taji's gaze remained fixated on the vast expanse of the sea. Uncertainty clouded his thoughts, yet he remained attuned to his surroundings. The violent earthquake had ravaged portions of the once-sturdy boardwalk. The bustling market that used to teem with life now lay in ruins, with shattered poles and torn fabric scattered on the ground.

This led them closer to the grotto homes, where humble dwellings stood nestled against the lush forest. The sheer force of the tremor had reduced some of his people's homes to mere rubble, a heartbreaking sight.

The silence that hung in the air was suffocating, disrupting Taji's concentration and leaving him unsettled. Yet, an urgency thrummed through his blood. His mission was twofold—reach Osiris before his father and safeguard his world from the looming threat of the two dark Celestials.

The rain stopped, but it didn't appease him any. Only the sound of wind whipped through the air as the prophecy rolled through his mind like a forbidden whisper. Taji looked down at Kissa. He knew she was the center of it all, and he couldn't help the anger that simmered at the thought. His kingdom and everything he loved would soon fall, but the energy that filled his veins with a need he never experienced before consumed him at the look of her.

The softness to her curves and the way she leaned against him, wrapping her jasmine essence around his being, didn't help his turbulent feelings any. He knew he wasn't doing a great job concealing his mood, but trying to find words to express the chaos in him felt fruitless. So he stayed silent.

Taji slowed them down near the harbor. Rows of ships of all sizes and fishing boats swayed stationary in their berths. Despite the brief absence of rain, the chilled air from the forest only seemed to pick up.

They stared at the orange globe that hung impossibly low in the night sky, casting the sea in mesmerizing coral hues. It was beautiful in a haunting way. An eerie stillness settled over the landscape, as if nature itself held its breath in anticipation of the impending tempest.

"We need a powerful ship to reach the Isles of Death. None of these will work."

Taji's brows lifted. Kissa's random mention of the mission and accompanying him made him pause. She was right, of course. None of the sailing ships before them would make it through Hell's Conception. He needed a ship from the Den of Serpents. However, getting there was another difficult task.

"And someone crazy enough to take us," Kissa said.

Frustration gnawed at him. By birthright, he should have been a Leviathan warrior like his mother and the long line of kings before her, whose strength and valor echoed through the ages. In some foul pre-marriage agreement, his father asked for a Scorpion successor. The choice ripped from him before he was even born.

Taji sighed. "Let's get the people to higher land first." He pulled on the reins. Just as he was about to continue forward, the wind picked up, carrying with it a distinct creaking sound.

Kissa pointed toward the hull of the nearest ship. "Look!"

The vessels that swayed lazily just a moment ago were now pulled taut on their line towards the sea. Taji's heart picked up as he dismounted for a closer look. Kissa scanned their surroundings, staying close as he crouched near the edge of the walkway.

His brows scrunched as he watched the water underneath the dock reverse towards the sea like a fast-moving low tide. A very low tide, as the moon's light illuminated the rocky terrain underneath.

Kissa stood, looking toward the sea. "The water is moving toward the deep." The wind snatched up her words and grew stronger with each passing moment.

In the distance, lightning illuminated the sky, followed by the rumbling sound of thunder that vibrated through the air. The heavens suddenly opened up and released a downpour of rain.

Go! Osiris echoed right before his drums flared within him.

Taji grabbed Kissa's hand with a blazing need to get her to safety. As they reached his horse, he scouted the waters again. Despite the darkness and relentless rain, the moon's glow illuminated the harbor, creating a brighter than usual night sky. A distinct and dense dark line emerged at the junction of the sky and sea. With it, a roaring sounded in the distance, growing louder as the moments ticked.

Kissa swung up on the saddle, Taji right behind her in the next breath. They trotted down the path, veering west toward the hospital.

"It's getting closer!" Kissa said.

Taji chanced a look behind them. The line on the horizon continued to expand. "It's some type of tropical storm. We need to get to higher ground." His mind whirled as his horse to gallop faster.

As the rocky landscape of the House of Life loomed ahead, the roaring sound caused vibrations to resonate through his entire being. Then an ear piercing creak echoed across the coast. They both whipped their heads around.

Taji's eyes widened with both fascination and horror as the dark line emerged in the ethereal moonlight. Moving fast, a massive wall of water, at least thirty spans high, surged forward. It lifted the berthed ships within its jaws of rushing water and crashed into the harbor with magnificent power. The sheer force of its movement caused the wooden dock, pier, and walkway to crush under its path. It continued inland, carrying ships, buildings, and anything else with the misfortune of being in its way.

"We'll never make it!" Kissa's fear blended with Taji's.

He squeezed Cosmo's flank with his calves, and they burst into a breakneck gait across the broken terrain. The rushing waters nipped at their heals. The steps to the hospital gate were just a few spans away. He wasn't sure how his horse would handle climbing the slippery steps. There was no time like the present.

Before Cosmo's hooves even touched the first step, the wild waters caught up to them. One moment, they were upright on the saddle, and in the next, everything turned upside down as the wave mercilessly collided with them, crashing them into the stone steps.

Taji reached out, trying to grab the branches of the tree surrounding the steps, but his hand slipped and he whirled upside down into murky waters, trying and failing to straighten up and break through for air. Something smacked him in the head and his vision became woozy. He reached up for anything to grab hold of, and his hand caught onto a piece of driftwood above him.

His head broke through the rushing water, but Taji soon realized the current was pushing him away from the hospital gate, ready to smash into the broken grottos ahead. He reached out and grabbed a branch dangling above him, this time finding purchase. He used it to pull himself above the water, but his leathers, sword, and rucksack were weighing him down.

"Taji!" Kissa's shrill cry stabbed him like a dagger in the heart.

He looked around and found her near the stone steps. Kissa's arms gripped a broken stump for dear life, while the current of the water dragged her lower body along. Her hair, now unbound, whipped around in the turbulent wind. She wouldn't be able to hold on much longer.

His drums intensified. Realizing the branch he held was part of a tree inside the courtyard of the hospital, he pulled himself to a higher branch, wrapping his legs around it, praying it would hold. He was hanging above the water, gurgling and roaring right under him. He simply had to reach the next one, climb down, and rush to Kissa from above.

With his legs around the branch, Taji reached for the next above him when Kissa's scream curled in his gut. He looked up to see her arms slipped, and the current snatched her under. He felt like his heart fell with her.

The rushing water and rain pelting his body became background music as he catalogued Kissa's movements. Just as she was riding the current under him, her head dipped back underneath the water. Taji reached down and gripped her cloak floating above the water and heaved up. Her head finally broke the water as she took in frantic breaths, reaching for his wrist to stay above the water.

He looked dead into her eyes. "Don't you let go!"

As Taji pulled Kissa up, his drums intensified. The sound of rushing water filled his ears, blending with the pounding rain, and mingling with the sharp scent of adrenaline. His muscles strained with every effort, and his heart pounded in his chest as he fought against the turbulent current trying to sweep Kissa away. The tree branch dug into his legs, and Taji prayed for it to hold.

Finally, her trembling fingers found purchase on the branch below, and she mustered the strength to pull herself up. Taji's relief washed over him, entwining with the lingering fear that still gripped his heart. Together, they clung to the tree, their bodies battered by the elements.

Breathing heavily, Taji gazed into Kissa's eyes, a mixture of relief and gratitude passing between them. He led the way toward the base of the towering tree. Solid ground beneath his boots brought a wave of relief. Its firmness grounded him. He assisted Kissa down, the sound of her deep exhale resonating in his bones.

Realizing her hair was no longer covered, she quickly braided them into one and pulled up her hood. Selfishly, Taji felt a twinge of disappointment. For the first time, Kissa appeared vulnerable. She stared up at him, searching for something. He brought his arms up around her shoulders, and to his surprise, she melted against him, resting her head on his chest.

Taji exhaled, feeling a profound sense of need for her. He had almost lost her, and his fear lingered, as if it were still a possibility. When he reluctantly let her go, the rest of the world seemed to fade away. The storm raged on, but the near death struggle strengthened their bond. Her tear-filled eyes glistened, reflecting the moonlight, as her bottom lip trembled. Taji gently brushed it away with his thumb and her mouth parted slightly.

The rain continued to pour relentlessly. The raging waters below threatened to engulf their world, but at that moment, Taji didn't give a damn as he slammed his lips against Kissa's.

33

GUARDIANS

KISSA'S BODY IGNITED IN a fiery blaze, the heat spreading through every inch of her being, as the Prince's lips, tantalizingly sweet, met hers. The crackle of desire filled the air, mingling with the rage of the storm.

Her eyes closed and a soft moan erupted from her, seeming to fuel Taji's urgency as he pressed her back against the tree. Bracing himself with one hand on the trunk, the other palmed at her nape, pulling her closer as she arched in. The feel of every hard line of his strong warrior body, even with his leathers on, made her cheeks flare with warmth of timidness.

None of her dreams could have prepared her for the overwhelming desire that the prince ignited within her heart, mind, and soul. Her arms reached up, wrapping around his shoulders, needing him closer, but the interruption of a loud neigh of a horse sounded beside them. Kissa's eyes popped open, and they both stiffened as the world around them slowly crept its way back in.

Taji broke the kiss with a chuckle. He whirled around toward his warhorse, miraculously stomping on the grass a few hands away. His smile melted something in her as he walked over and rubbed Cosmo down, whispering something Kissa couldn't hear.

Giving Taji a moment, she walked over to the gate. Her eyes drifted upward toward where the prophetic moon blazed. The orb made her feel connected, hinting at an impending beginning she couldn't discern. But her high came crashing down as she witnessed Sapphire city.

It was not a city at all. All that was visible was debris and driftwood scattered across the water. She mourned for the people's homes and livelihoods, washed away as if they never were.

Aya said the kingdom could rebuild, but what would that look like? Would they have to leave their kingdom and journey elsewhere? The most unfortunate aspect was their inability to leave the kingdom. In a few day's time, the waters would recede, but the destruction of every ship left them with no means of escape.

"Come, we need to help your mother get your people to higher ground." Taji's voice wrapped around her like a warm blanket, settling her thoughts.

They crossed the courtyard, being careful of the fissures in the grass. The House of Life's dome had cracks along its side, but it held up to the quakes. Kissa's heart tightened at the thought that her mother had no help. She wasn't sure what difference she and Taji would make at this point. She hoped her father was well on his way.

When she entered the front entrance, her worries melted away. The hospital was nothing short of commotion, a sense of urgency that wasn't present during her first visit. Patients lay in stretchers throughout the atrium and lined up on the far wall, ready for evacuation. Healers were running back and forth collecting items to another area with tables filled with supplies. Others were carrying patients and placing them on stretchers.

Unexpectedly, Kissa saw a familiar face as a healer turned towards her at the table. "Lani?"

Lani met her eyes. Exhaustion clung to her. The normally pristine girl's hair was frizzy. She gave a curt nod and continued her work of organizing supplies.

"It seems despite her schemes, she has a good heart." A voice close to her ear startled her.

She turned and cried in relief. "Benji!"

Before she could say anything more, he swept her into an embrace. Her heart warmed to see her friend and the unexpected hug filled something in her heart. Her eyes widened to see Layla at his side. When Benji put her down, she reached for Layla's hand, but the Dream Walker wasn't having any of that as she embraced her, too.

"You are soaked!" Layla lilted in her ear.

Hearing her charismatic voice made her smile. "Yes, long story." She said, catching the Prince's eye as he took everything in. The look he sent her caused her skin to tingle.

"It is the Prince!" a healer shouted.

"He is here to save us!" another exclaimed.

Suddenly voices shouted out, left and right. Questions about what happened and where to go.

Taji cleared his throat, raising his hands in supplication. "Please, I am here to help. I do not know what caused the shifting of the mountain or the storm, but it is not safe here. We need to get to Serenity."

The commotion quickly resumed, but in a more panicked state. Kissa frantically looked for her mother among the crowd, but couldn't find her. "Have you seen my mother?"

"She is in the healer's dorms, grabbing what we need?" Benji said. "Your father warned us, so we came immediately."

"Where is your father?" Kissa asked.

Benji's eyes turned dark. "My father asked for warriors to assist us, but the king has closed the gates. Because of the newly forged alliance, the king extended haven to the few who didn't go to Zurania for the Harvest Festival within the capital. But once they were closed, no one could leave or enter." He gestured to the healers busy working. "As you can see, we don't have enough volunteers to evacuate everyone."

Kissa's anger flared. Why wouldn't the king let the few who wanted to help do so? Not that it mattered much, because without the help of the warriors, they would never have enough to gather the sick and take them to Serenity. That also meant that her father would not come as they hoped. Kissa glanced at Taji, whose eyes narrowed to slits. She could feel the tension in him, thick and heavy.

"At least the people in the capital are safe," she said. It was the only positive thing she could think of.

A low rumble was Taji's only response. Then he walked off, mumbling something about helping where he could. Knowing she could do nothing to assuage the prince's mood, Kissa took that moment to find her mother.

"Find something for me to do when I return," she said to Benji.

When she reached upstairs, the halls and rooms were empty. She reached the kitchenette, and almost missed her mother on her haunches, busy filling a sack with food and water. Soot and wrinkles stained the pristine white robe she normally wore and her braided hair unraveled at the ends.

"Mama!" she breathed.

Onya turned and looked up with warm honey eyes. "Oh, my dear girl!"

Kissa helped her stand, but didn't let her go as she wrapped her arms around her. She didn't know how much she needed to see her mother until that moment as she shuddered in her mother's embrace. Though Kissa was much taller than her, she felt small in her mother's arms, like a little girl again.

"Oh, how I've missed you." Onya said as they pulled apart.

Kissa wiped the tears from her eyes and blew out a long breath as more ran down her face. Onya's face creased with concern as she rubbed Kissa's cheek.

"You have much to tell me. Come," her mother said. Then ushered her to her private quarters.

Kissa shook her head. "We have little time, Mama. The water is already breaching the courtyard," she argued.

Onya nodded with a pained look. "Let's get you of these wet clothes, at least."

Kissa didn't see the point. They were going to get wet anyway, but she digressed when she saw her mother's determined eyes.

As they entered, she took in her mother's private room. Though it was small, she recognized her mother's trinkets on the small table near the bed. Books and jars of her healing mixtures and ointments on a tiny shelf under the window. On top, her familiar herbs grew in small planters. Her favorite blanket lay across the small room. It didn't seem like the quake even touched her room at all.

"I received your father's letter, but he could only say so much. Please, tell me everything."

So, Kissa did. As she got undressed, dried herself, and put on the dry tunic and leggings her mother handed her, her words spilled out like water without a stopper. She told her everything. Her mother stood in the same spot, listening intently, not saying a word.

Kissa revealed she had visions and the healing gift, but Onya never blinked twice. When she finished, she felt relieved, really. Now her mother could help her make it all make sense.

With a deliberate gaze, her mother walked behind her and undid the braid in her hair. She grabbed a towel and started drying her damp locs. "Hm. So the handsome prince is your Protector, huh?"

Kissa chuckled. Of all things she laid bare, that was what her mother wanted to talk about. But the jest lightened the mood and Kissa embraced the flutters that always accompanied her thoughts of Taji.

She smirked, turning her head to see her mother's teasing smile. "He is not my Protector." Then, her face became serious. "I do not wish for his duties and responsibilities."

"You have affections for him."

The passionate kiss they shared brought heat to her cheeks. What did she feel for Taji? He was incredibly handsome, for sure. With their kingdom in disarray, it all seemed very complicated. One thing Kissa knew for sure was that she was no princess, nor did she feel capable of one day becoming a queen.

"We are friends. Our circumstances prevent anything more."

Onya turned quiet as she braided her locs back into a plait. Then went to her closet and grabbed a scarf. "And what of your duties, Kissa? What do you plan?"

Kissa shook her head, wary. "I'm here to help you get the sick to Serenity."

"And then? What will you do?" Her mother pushed.

Kissa's sigh felt like a damn breaking down. "I don't know, Mama!" Her tears burned as they ran down her cheek. "People say have faith, but what have the Ancients done to earn it? Taji says the prophecy is about me, but I can't make sense of it. I'm given these gifts, but not told what I'm supposed to do with them. No direction, nothing. Darkness is coming, and our people are dying, and I do not know what to do about any of it!"

Kissa's chest heaved. Her mother had a way of pulling things out of her.

"It seems you are at a crossroads," her mother said. "Zuri came to me in a dream. The Oath that bound me has lifted. It is time."

In stunned silence, Kissa could only nod for her mother to continue, though her heart thundered fiercely against her ribs.

"Prince Taji is correct," she said.

Kissa's brows deepened as she tried to prepare herself mentally. Clutching her necklace, she sat on her mother's small bed. She didn't know how to feel about the confirmation.

"Everything we told you on your birth night remains true. Zuri delivered you to us and you...you are my greatest joy." She fidgeted with the scarf with her hand nervously. "What you don't know is the reason we were chosen."

"Since the old kings, when the prophecy was first whispered, keepers throughout the world have been busy preparing for this moment. A secret network, so to speak, charged by the Ancients to guide and see over the gifted. We are called the Custodians." Her mother's voice was just over a whisper.

"Ana the Seeker, the first Custodian, was the First Mother's granddaughter. She knew the gifted were vital and created the secret society. When the war of the Great Divide started, many thought it was time, but generations came and went and none were gifted."

Kissa's mind spun realizing the Custodian's existence from the start of mankind, sharing knowledge and seeking those with special abilities.

"It is deeper and more complex than just one human kingdom. Each nation has their keepers and a gifted, including Sagia." Her mother let that fact settle on Kissa's shoulders.

The Ancient of Life tasked her with finding the gifted, but it seemed they were all over the world. The thought of how she would find them all added to the overwhelming feeling she was struggling with.

Her mother's soft honey eyes turned fierce. "The Ancients are at war. Those who follow the Ancient of Life, and those who follow the Ancient of Wisdom. The contention between them all has been in motion far longer than even our world's existence."

"What does this have to do with humans? We have nothing to do with this war," Kissa said.

"We are part of the war by just merely existing. The Ancient of Wisdom wants to destroy all that the Ancient of Life created. All life," her mother's eyes turned glassy. "We don't even understand the reason, but if we don't fight for our world, we are all doomed."

Kissa didn't like any of this one bit. Not only did the war start with the Ancients, but they dragged humans into it like pawns in a sadistic game. She and the other gifted had no choice but to fight. Kissa was tired of speaking of the self-seeking Ancients.

"So, I assume you and father are Custodians?" she asked.

"We could allow no one to know. We could not even tell you." She shook her head. "Your dear father has great responsibilities, but one duty that surpassed anything else was to protect you at all costs. Nobody could know of you. We didn't even trust other Custodians with this knowledge, in case someone infiltrated our network."

It all felt surreal. Secret networks, keepers of the gifted. Ancients at war.

"Who else? Mira?" Her mother nodded, confirming her thoughts.

"Are my blood parents Custodians?" Kissa asked. A bead of hope rose in her heart.

Her mother sadly shook her head, as though she knew she had dashed any hope she had.

Frustration shot through Kissa. She hadn't had time to figure that aspect of her life out yet. Or any aspect, for that matter. So much had happened since her birthnight. It felt like a distant dream.

Her mother walked up to her and Kissa looked down at where her fingers clasped her keepsake. "Your blood mother gave you this." Her pensive look hinted at a secret. "She is the one who bound your gifts." Her honey eyes looked dead in Kissa's. "Zuri told me when she brought you to us."

Kissa blinked several times as she clenched her new dry tunic to keep her hand from trembling. "What?"

Zuri delivered her to her parents? She bound them with the oath? Kissa's head swam. Why would a goddess deliver her? The Ancient of Life was the one who bound her. She told Kissa herself. Either her mother was mistaken or...

Kissa stood abruptly, shaking her head. "No! There is absolutely, positively, no way that is possible!"

Her mother gave her a look, a mix of concern and expectation, as if she was silently urging her to connect the dots.

Kissa's breath escaped her lips in a shaky, stuttered rhythm, matching the turbulent storm of emotions that crashed through her like a furious squall. "The Ancient of Life is my mother?"

34

REVEALED

Kissa's heart was pounding in her ears and she felt like she couldn't breathe. The air felt suffocating, as if a heavy weight pressed against her chest, making it difficult to draw a breath. "Mama, I have to get out of here. I need to think."

Onya's lips grew thin as her eyes stormed. Her mother was still bound, Kissa realized. She wasn't supposed to tell her even the little that she did. Kissa wasn't even sure she wanted to know. Her mother approached her with the scarf and went to lift it over her locs, when Kissa shook her head.

"No, Mama. I understand that all this time, you and father needed to protect me. But...I'm done hiding myself." She said in finality as she stood and walked over and grabbed her cloak.

She turned toward her mother, ready for a rebuttal, but it never came. Onya's eyes held a sheen of reverence within them. "I understand."

Kissa clasped her cloak, then pulled her hood on, when a subtle vibration suddenly unsettled her. "Do you feel that?"

They both turned to her mother's rattling trinkets on the table. Dread pulled at her gut as the tremors grew in intensity, causing her mother's pots of herbs to fall from their places on the top shelf, breaking into pieces. A deep groan tore through the hospital, and her mother's only window shattered, sending shards of glass through the air, followed by the fierce wind. As she covered her face from the piercing glass, she felt the mass of fear right before screaming and shouting erupted outside the room. A deep crack emerged across the ceiling, and the rain seeped in.

Her mother shouted over the wind. "We need to go!"

In the distance, familiar toll bells sounded. Four in a row—a warning. Confused, Kissa followed her mother out to the corridor.

They gripped the rails to keep from falling as they headed down the stairs. The main room of the hospital was utter chaos. Healers and patients were running outside, while others were trying to keep everyone calm. Kissa had to close off her senses to keep focused.

"Everyone needs to exit the hospital toward the forest!" Taji was shouting orders and directing everyone toward the back exit. When their eyes connected, she noticed the intense anxiety concealed beneath his calm exterior.

Those who could move on their own needed no additional prompting, quickly making their way out of the door. Alongside healers, Kissa noticed Benji, Lani, and Layla rolling cots out. She stayed in step with her mother as they guided the sick out. Worry clawed at her. Benji was right. They didn't have enough people to get everyone to higher ground.

Then, the vigorous tremors stopped.

Kissa scanned around, cataloguing the fear in everyone's face. Another eerie silence enveloped the space. Nobody moved for fear of bringing back the tremors. Then, the sudden sound of the front doors whipping open and slamming against the wall caused everyone to jump out of their skin.

Commander Maru's sudden appearance took her back. Behind him, Leviathan warriors filed after him, immediately moving through the hospital, picking up supplies. Relief replaced her shock as the warriors listened intently to the healer's directives.

Prince Taji walked up to the Leviathan Commander. "It is with great relief to see you and your crew, Commander."

"Your Grace," Maru said with a shallow bow. There was a slight tension between them, as if there were things to be said, but now was not the time.

"Your Grace," a young man bowed dramatically, earning four confused stares with his wide smile.

Taji nodded in reply while Maru rolled his eyes with impatience. If it were not for the disheveled curls in the young man's hair and his green dyed tunic, Kissa would have thought the young man and the Commander were the same. Brothers? Maybe.

"This is Sabu, my Second," Maru said irritatedly.

"And his brother. Don't let him fool you. I am his fave," Sabu snickered, then winked at Kissa in the same breath. "Hello, beautiful."

Kissa swallowed down the laughter that wanted to bubble forth. Even though she responded to the flirtatious greeting with a dismissive nod, she felt the sudden tension in the Prince. She scowled at the inappropriate flutter it caused.

"High Healer, Onya Ashtar. It is a pleasure," Maru said.

"Commander. Did you all come from the capital?" Onya asked with hopeful eyes.

Sabu turned and gestured toward the window. "No, we sailed right up to the pearly gates."

Sure enough, Kissa looked out the window to see a beautiful ship waving the Leviathan flag and a figurehead of a voluptuous sea goddess berthed outside the gates.

A tall woman that looked as if she would gut someone faster than they could blink strode through the courtyard. When she entered, she took her place next to the Commander. She wore all black leathers, like the rest that melded over her curvy body. Her locs were in a neatly wrapped bun. Two daggers rested on each side of her hips. Her dark brown eyes were fierce as she took everyone in.

"Commander, Tomas and Jorge are bringing him in." She reported.

Maru's countenance slipped as he looked at Taji with a weighted expression. Kissa looked back through the window and could see two warriors carrying a body between them, an urgency to their gait.

"Who is it?" Onya asked.

As she said it, the warriors burst in, laying the man on an empty cot. The man looked familiar. He suffered burn marks across his body and half his face blistered red. His uniform appeared ripped and burned. Only high officials wore uniforms.

Kissa's fire rose within her, surging to her fingertips, urging her to heal the man. She quickly clenched them closed for fear that her light would glow and expose her.

"Uncle," Taji's anguished voice tore her heart in two, as he kneeled beside the injured man. "What happened to him?"

Commander Maru dipped his head as he said, "Two nights ago, we noticed at least five ships missing from the Den. The few warriors I had stationed here never saw a fleet exit the harbor. I found it suspicious, so our crew scouted the perimeter and a little further out. We found nothing west of here. However, on our return, our hawk spotted broken parts of a ship floating on the waters to the east, near the Den. That is where we found High Commander Eshu." A darkness crossed Maru's face as his voice turned heated. "The Den has been destroyed!"

Taji's eyes widened. "Our warships?"

"Buried beneath the rock, if not all demolished from the impact," Commander Maru growled. "It must have triggered the quake and surge."

Kissa saw nothing but devastation in the Prince's eyes. "East of the Den?"

"Hell's Conception. Someone ordered the fleet to traverse those waters at least three nights ago. For what, I do not know." Maru seethed as he said it.

Kissa could practically feel the devastation rolling off of Taji. He closed his eyes for a moment as he clenched his fists. "What of the others?" He said.

"There was no sign of our brethren. Your uncle was the only survivor. I could not risk my crew to scavenge those bloody waters," the Commander said resolutely.

The Prince nodded an agreement. "You did the right thing." Then his attention flashed to Kissa. "Can you heal my uncle? What do you need from me?"

Before she answered, her mother's abrupt voice cut in. "I will treat him, but I'm afraid he is in critical condition." She gave Kissa a knowing look before maneuvering next to the High Commander. Then pulled her salves, wrap and a mixture in a small glass from her healer satchel.

Her mother was trying to protect her. Keep her from exposing her gifts. Yet, one look at the High Commander told her he would not heal with natural treatment. The look Taji gave her said he knew the same, but he said nothing. Allowing her to choose for herself, even at the detriment of his own flesh and blood.

Hiding her origins and abilities had become exhausting for Kissa. What was the point of having the gift of healing if she did nothing? They were at war, internally and with divine beings, and Kissa was so so tired of hiding. If there was even a chance, she would save him.

"No, Mama, I will do it!" She approached the cot next to her mother.

"Kissa!" her mother hissed as she gazed at the surrounding warriors.

But she didn't look at them, or her mother. Her attention stayed on the one who believed in her from the beginning. The broken-hearted prince who believed she had the strength to heal his dying mother, and now a suffering kingdom. The adoration in Taji's ocean blue eyes dissolved every fear, every second guess of herself.

Knowing with certainty that the Protector would keep her safe, Kissa undid the clasps of her cloak, and took it off, not wanting it to hinder her. Ignoring the sharp gasps that sounded around her, she evaluated Eshu. Her fingertips glowed as she scanned him, eliciting more gasps. Fortunately, no sounds of unsheathed weapons or clangs of metal reached her ears.

As his internal body revealed itself, she saw the dark smoke trapped within. His lungs were giving up as they struggled to extract the smoke and pump clean air in. Kissa felt the familiar feeling of her Essence leaving her core. She did not go with her light this time, trusting her magic to remove the toxic smoke from his lungs. She felt her fire's contentment in fulfilling its purpose.

Once the High Commander's lungs were clear, she addressed the flash burns, which caused blisters and peeled off his skin. She was thankful that he was unconscious and didn't suffer through agony. But to receive such a burn, it could not have been a normal fire. It was as if Eshu did not see it coming. The pattern of the burns spoke of possibly some type of liquid fire or explosion. Concern rode Kissa.

What happened to you? She thought as her mind blazed with all the possibilities.

She breathed in as she allowed her healing gift to envelop him, as it did the queen, bathing him in soft light. She watched his blisters and burns smooth over, leaving hail skin in its path. Every sound around Kissa grew silent as she concentrated on her work, not daring to look up.

After finishing, she exhaled a long breath as she clenched her hand tightly. Her light winked out. Not ready to face the people, no doubt looking at her with loathing, her eyes stayed on Eshu. His breaths were steady now.

"I've done all that I can," she finally whispered, breaking the absolute silence.

Taji reached over and lifted her chin, so that she could stare into his eyes. They shined with appreciation and something else she couldn't make out, and it almost made her knees buckle.

"You are remarkable, Kissa Ashtar." His touch and his words sent a wave of warmth through her. A collective gasp sounded at the mention of her father's surname.

"It was you!"

The passion of the words forced Kissa to look for its source. Her eyes widened at the crowd before her. Warriors, healers, and even some of the able-bodied sick. Benji stood behind Taji with his arm on his shoulder, smiling. Beside him was Layla, and Kissa swore she watched her. One green eye, the other amber. Even Lani stared at her with a look Kissa never thought she would ever see from the girl—reverence.

Her mother grabbed her hand and squeezed it in silent support. However, Kissa's attention settled on Commander Maru, brows now furrowed in a deep V. The source of the outburst. Her heart pounded, clashing against her ribs. She was prepared to address any accusations the Commander made against her.

Then he said, "It was you that healed our queen."

She stopped breathing. Taji had been protecting that knowledge for fear of the King finding and capturing her. But Kissa finally emerged from her hiding place, her presence and gifts now revealed. With a newfound sense of freedom, she felt a weight lifted off her shoulders, as if she had released a burden into the ether, never to be found again.

Kissa was done hiding.

"Yes, I healed Queen Safiyah," she acknowledged with a firm voice, earning clutched fists to the hearts of every warrior before her. Including Commander Maru.

However, it was the woman next to him who spoke next. Her fierce, dark eyes captured Kissa's with curiosity. "You are the daughter of Commander Ashtar and High Healer, Onya."

A statement, but Kissa nodded anyway. A squeeze to her hand made her look down at her mother. Tears streamed down her now flushed cheeks. They were tears of joy, Kissa realized.

"Every Osmondian here owes you our gratitude," the woman said.

Kissa shook her head. "You owe me nothing." She cataloged every one of the Leviathans holding her gaze, committing them to memory.

A raspy cough cut through the tension in the air. Everyone flicked their attention to the cot. Kissa's heart lurched. The High Commander's eyes were open, staring at the Prince with tormented eyes. He coughed once more, expelling the remaining smoke from his throat.

Maru quickly kneeled down, giving him water from his waterskin. Eshu sipped slowly in his weakened state. After he caught his breath, he said, "The k-king is mad. He ordered us to look for a sword on the islands of the dead. S-Something evil is guarding it." He clenched the prince's sleeve of his cloak, lifting his head from the cot. "Stop him, nephew!" Then he lay his head back on the cot with a grunt. His eyes glazed with a heart clinching look. "They are all dead!" A tear treaded down the side of his face.

Kissa's eyes burned from the turmoil within him—witnessing the death of hundreds of his warriors dying needlessly. The cowardly king sent them to their deaths. Her fire smothered her sorrow with a vengeful burn and her eyes locked on the Prince.

He burned with equal intensity, holding her in his fierce blue depths. Unbridled fury rolled off him as he roared, "Hear me now! The King will pay for his crimes against the kingdom!"

35

HOPE

KISSA

THEY ENTRUSTED THE MISSION of scouting and clearing the way through Za Forest to Kissa and Commander Maru's first mate, Tomeri. Her hawk eyes would prove valuable against oncoming threats ahead of them. Saddled on Cosmo, Kissa awaited her on a small ridge a few paces within the forest, giving her a clear view of their group readying to mobilize.

As Kissa contemplated the challenges that lay ahead, she couldn't ignore the irony of her blood mother being an Ancient. She questioned whether her deep resentment towards them was merely a subconscious thought or something deeper. Despite knowing this truth, it still didn't explain why her mother had abandoned her for 18 long summers, only choosing to reveal herself now. Kissa tried not to dwell too much on her own hurt feelings surrounding the matter. Her focus needed to remain on her people.

As she watched everyone gather before her, her eyes drifted among each of the patients, the ones lying still on their stretchers, hidden by nylon fabric to keep the rain off them. 47 of them, including High Commander Eshu. Her fire stirred within her, beckoning to be used to free them from the darkness, but the fear of her passing out for three days quelled it. There had to be a better way, something Kissa was missing.

Their plan was quite simple, really. On his return, Commander Maru stationed two Leviathans at Osmond's light to warn of oncoming danger. Sabu set sail with some of their crew on Yemanja. Their task was to survey the perimeters to locate the dark shadow ship from Kissa's vision, and, most importantly, they needed to keep their sole ship intact. If Sabu's crew spotted Moorice's ship, one of them would shoot a flaming arrow into the sky to signal the two stationed warriors at Osmond's light to ring the toll bell.

Five tolls was the signal.

Regarding their group, most of the healers and half of Maru's crew carried the immobile sick on stretchers. While the rest of the warriors surrounded them, ready to switch off when the healers grew tired. Taji would lead them out on foot, while her mother, Lani, Benji and Layla stayed among those carrying the sick, assisting where needed. In the rear, Commander Maru led the group responsible for carrying supplies. Overall, their company comprised a little over two hundred people.

There were so many unknowns, but one burned in her mind more than any other. The location of Naomi. Taji revealed to Maru what he found in the Fathomless Pit. As a Celestial, her last words to the king caused an unsettled feeling over their group. It was overly optimistic to think that the Dark Celestials had departed from the kingdom now that Moorice destroyed the Den of Serpents. The kingdom became dangerously vulnerable all at once, ripe for the picking.

So what are they waiting for?

Her father had not met them on the coast, but to make matters worse, neither had Aya. Since her sister left her and Taji in the forest, Kissa continually checked their bond. A familiar wall of nothing always greeted her, as if Aya was too far away. Or, most likely, she blocked her out. The feeling that something was wrong stirred in her soul.

A toll bell sounded in the distance. *One, two, three, four...*

Not Moorice, but still a warning. Was it another quake? Now fully in tune with her empathy, Kissa felt the incredible sensation of Aarusha's pain, and she ached to repair the damage done. The Ancient Mountain wasn't sentient, but the life within was—imbued with the Essence of the Ancient of Life. Aarusha could not withstand too much more damage.

Kissa's eyes snagged on Tomeri as she and her horse parted through the people and joined her. "There is another surge coming."

Her heart sank. Their plan was to go to Osmond's rest, a halfway point, so the healers could take a break. Would they make it? If they did, would it be high enough? More questions and never enough answers. She flicked her attention back toward the way they were going. Upturned trees and stones obstructed the trail. Already, they needed to find a different path.

When she looked back toward the group, she met Taji's cool blue stare. He nodded. They were ready. She took a moment to find Commander Maru, who was carrying a patient with another warrior. Despite his disgruntled exterior, he cared deeply for his people. That he had a woman high in his ranks solidified her own views of the man. He looked up and gave a curt nod.

"Let us get them to Osmond's Rest before it hits," Kissa said, as she signaled Cosmo into motion.

As they led the people up the slope of the mountain, they crossed paths with fissures and repeatedly went around them, impeding their progression. Droplets of rain continued to break through the canopy of the forest and the icy chill made it feel like a winter night. With more growls and curses than words, they eventually made it to Osmond's Rest.

Tomeri inspected the caves that were set into the ridge that would provide cover from the storm. It was the main reason they chose this location to rest. Kissa gripped Cosmo's reins tight as she wordlessly assessed the plateau. It was astonishing to see that the clearing had suffered minimal damage from the earthquakes. Some upturned ground, but no deep fissures, and the handful of trees around were still standing tall.

She trotted over to the cliffs. The other reason for this location—an unobstructed view of the seas and Osmond's Light. Her breath caught as a sinking feeling bloomed inside her. Lightning lit up at a distance. Dark clouds moved ominously across the sky, poised to unleash havoc. The surge now took up the whole west horizon. It would hit soon.

The wind picked up and suddenly, Kissa felt the signature of Moorice's magic, as intense and ominous as the clouds above. The fire in her chest rose in indigitation. Kissa breathed in, calming the stir of her magic.

Where are you? She thought as she stared at the oncoming estuary.

"The surge is gaining momentum. It will hit before first light." Tomeri said, as she settled next to her.

The entire journey, complete resolve spilled from the warrior, and it was the first time Kissa felt fear from the stoic woman. She knew everyone felt the same. This was a magical storm and they couldn't reason with it logically. Anything was bound to happen.

"Do you think we are high enough?" she asked, as lightning above illuminated flashes of the coastal city under water, causing her chest to tighten.

"We can only hope, but we will not make it to Serenity if we do not rest."

Though the warriors trained for all circumstances, the healers could not carry the sick all the way to Serenity. The feeling of something vital tugged at the far reaches of Kissa's mind. Frustration boiled as it slipped from her grasp. It would come to her eventually, hopefully sooner than later.

The others broke out from the trees, crestfallen by the winds and rain that whipped around them as if lying in wait. The warriors rechecked the caves, then they put up tents and laid out bedrolls and blankets faster than Kissa could blink. Somehow, despite the roaring wind, two fires were already started before the last of them made it to the plateau. And to her surprise, a few came back with game for supper.

She and her mother, along with Benji and Layla, assured the patients were comfortable within the caves and distributed soup to all who could eat. Then the four of them made their way to the edge of the cliff. They held tight to one another, for the wind was not letting up. Taji, along with the Commander Maru and Tomeri, were already there, huddled and speaking in rough tones. When they approached, Kissa felt many emotions among the group—fear and anger were at the forefront.

Taji met her eyes and was the first to speak. "We cannot stay here long. With the fissures along the mountain, the flooding will reach the underground tunnels. That cave there," he pointed at a cave near the end of the ridge, "will bring up water from the surge."

"If we leave now, can we travel through the tunnels?" Kissa asked, as her mind turned, planning.

Commander Maru said, "I do not suggest it. We do not know the full damage from the quakes, and we do not want to be trapped between a collapsed tunnel and water."

"Even if that was not the case, the closest passage near Serenity is the Temple," Taji's eyes turned dark. "We would never make it before the storm hits."

Kissa closed her eyes, letting the information settle within. They could not rest long. Serenity was hours away, maybe even more. The feeling of something at the edges of her mind came to her again, and this time she remembered. She recalled the buzz of magic that coated her skin and hummed its magic every time she left her lands and returned. The ward around her family's land.

Open up, and you may find that there are many, gifted and non-gifted, that share in your Destiny. They will help you turn the tides. Together, you are most powerful.

She opened her eyes and took in everyone standing before her. Taji, Benji, and Layla, specifically—a tie to them in ways that she was still trying to comprehend. Commander Maru and his crew were her allies, every one of them. The way they looked to her for guidance mirrored her trust in them.

"We go to my family's land. It is only a league from here," she finally said.

Everyone, except her mother, shared faces of confusion. Tomeri said, "Your home cannot be big enough for everyone to shelter."

"The land is. There are magical wards surrounding it that will protect the people. This is a magical storm, not natural." Kissa knew without seeing it that her land was unblemished from the quake. Warded against magical beings and magical attacks—except her, it seemed.

Her mother met her eyes with pride. "She is right! The sick can stay inside the cottage. We can put up tents around the land for everyone else."

"And there are enough healers and supplies to carry the sick over after the storm," Benji said.

Understanding flashed in Taji's eyes as he stared at her. Kissa's heart flipped in her chest. "The plan is sound," he said.

Six sets of eyes locked on Commander Maru, awaiting his approval. Despite the impossibility of her suggestion, it didn't take him long. "Let's move, then."

ONCE THEY FINISHED EATING, Taji, Maru, and Onya took charge and directed the rest on where to go. After packing up, they set off. Kissa and Tomeri scouted ahead once again.

The terrain proved treacherous as the rain created land slides and prevented them from using torches or oil lamps in the near dark forest. The orange moonlight breaching the treetops was their only source of light.

Raising her hand in front of her, Kissa thought about the little stars firing from her fingertips, beckoning the magic within her. It manifested faster each time she used her gift. She stared in awe at her light, now visibly stark against the dark backdrop of the forest. It swirled between her fingers, white, crimson and gold. It felt crazy that she laughed in the face of her own mother at the thought of magic's existence. Now, she couldn't imagine being without it.

A gasp sounded next to her as her and Tomeri's horses came closer to avoid a muddy slope. "I thought they forgot about us," Tomeri said.

Puzzled by the random statement, Kissa's brow raised. "They?"

"The Ancients," she said. "It has been a long time since I've seen anything proving their existence."

"You believe they are helping us?" It was hard for Kissa to think that anything of late resembled help when everything felt thrown upon her without warning.

"I know it!" Tomeri's eyes held a confidence Kissa wished she felt. "Will you try to help the others?"

It was all she thought about since she first learned about the sickness, the fire behind her inspiration to go to Serenity. All those dreams seemed so long ago as they faced a storm of magical making and Celestials intent on destroying them. They needed to ensure the people lived so she *could* cure them. One thing did not change since the days of her basking in the sun on her cliffs—Kissa will help her people or die trying.

"It is my hope." She turned to Tomeri. "What did you mean when you said it had been a long time?"

Tomeri gave her a look she could not decipher. "When the Commander and I were just crew members, still fresh recruits, we sailed to Dragon's Cove. It was not the first time we sailed the seas, but it was our first quest under a commander and we needed to transport a prisoner to the Halls of Justice. I was a lookout then, stationed in the hawk's nest. The skies were clear and not a cloud as far as I could see."

Their horses split to go around a boulder in the middle of the path. When they came back together, Tomeri continued. Kissa didn't miss a beat, listening intently.

"On our return, we cast off without a hitch, but out of nowhere, the clouds darkened and the wind picked up. Blindsided and trapped between an approaching monsoon and reefs, of all things. A few of the crew jumped ship, only to be swallowed by the massive waves, never to be seen again. After a while, a resolve settled among all of us on the ship. We were going to die."

Kissa's brows raised. Clearly, something happened since both she and Commander Maru were alive and hail. "Then what happened?" Kissa felt vested in the story.

"A flying creature almost as large as our ship approached. Its wings were dark, almost like a blur or shadow in the sky. I know they are only myth, but I thought perhaps it was a dragon. Instead of fire, it blasted wind from its mouth and swept the storm off the path. From the hawks' nest, I watched the dark clouds push north and the seas calm, as if nothing happened at all."

Kissa's brows furrowed. She thought of Aya, but knew with certainty she wasn't the flying creature in her story. "That is a miracle."

"I saw nothing like it. Though we never knew its name, Maru said it was a Celestial in its familiar form. It happened nearly twenty summers ago, but I remember it like yesterday."

Kissa tossed the information around in her mind. Tomeri did not seem like someone who would make up stories or exaggerate details. She felt the genuineness in her story as she told it. Kissa did not know who the Celestial in question might have been.

She had a hard time believing that Moorice or Naomi saved anyone, considering the two were in the realm when the gateway disappeared. However, Aya said she was a transcendent like her mother Zuri, which meant she most likely appeared in the human realm after the gateway was no more. She wasn't entirely sure what that meant now that she thought about it.

A howl ripped through the forest and her thoughts. Kissa's blood turned to ice as she assessed their surroundings.

Tomeri pulled her twin blades out. "What was that?"

Kissa clenched her fists, and her light dissipated. With her satchel, bow, and arrows already securely on, she dismounted Cosmo swiftly.

"Shadow Wolves. It is best to dismount. The horse will only get scared and throw you off." She patted Cosmo's rear. "Go!" He needed no more prompting as he took off into the forest.

"Shadow Wolves?"

"Do not get bitten and stay away from their black blood," Kissa said sharply, her first arrow already nocked. "It is connected to the sickness."

"We need to alert the others!" Tomeri turned her attention toward their company a few paces down the mountain.

Kissa gripped her arm. "They already know. Benji knows what to do. We stay together and fight our way back to them."

They were so close, Kissa could see the two Ancient Za trees that signified the edge of her land in the distance. Someone was trying to keep them from reaching it. She hoped with everything in her that Benji had his sword this time. Leviathan's accompanied them, but just like Tomeri, most of them carried close range weapons.

With their backs against one another, they crept down the terrain. A faint cracking of a branch reached them to their right. Just as before, a wolf as black as night, swirling at its edges, broke out of the brush, followed by two more. The one in the lead came to at least her waist, and its head was as big as her torso. They stalked eagerly, aggressively with their fangs glistening.

"It's like they're made of smoke," Tomeri said.

"They solidify when they attack. Then you can kill them," Kissa said, as the beasts rushed toward them.

Kissa loosed her arrow, hitting the one in the front straight in the heart, then nocked another arrow as it dissipated. A blur of hands and blades, Tomeri cut down the one aiming for their side. Black blood dripped from her daggers. She wiped them off on the grass and they closed ranks again.

Sizing up the last wolf, Kissa aimed for its heart, but it turned last minute, and she hit its shoulder. The beast yelped, but pressed forward, snapping its jaws. She pivoted out of the way too slowly, and it gnawed and ripped the back of her cloak, just missing the skin near her hip. With the beast too close for Kissa to use her arrow, Tomeri didn't hesitate as she stabbed its side, digging deep. The wolf fell limply, then dissolved into a wisp of shadows like the others.

"That was too close." Tomeri quickly helped her stand.

"More are coming. We need to get to the others."

They took off running down the incline. As they got closer, Taji's war drums gave her strength as she pumped her legs to get to them faster. She heard screaming mixed with the howling and cries of both wolf and man. Kissa counted more than a dozen wolves around them. The warriors at the outset clashed, slashed and gutted the wolves, protecting the sick and healers inside their circle.

Not missing a beat, Tomeri ran into the fray, swiping her blades expertly at the closest wolf. Kissa spotted a mound a little further from the group and climbed it. As she reached the top, she let off three consecutive arrows, hitting each target.

To her relief, Benji had his sword, cutting down the wolf before him like a trained warrior. She searched for Taji and found him making quick work of the ones to the west flank. Her mother kept the healers and sick people low to the ground, with Layla and Lani in tow, while the Leviathans that were transporting the sick were providing additional protection. Kissa shot another arrow at a beast lurking toward Commander Maru's back while he hacked another with his axe. Both shadow wolves dissipated.

She scanned the dark forest and noticed the piercing onyx eyes of another creature a short distance away between a copse of trees. This creature was bigger than the others as it sat on its haunches, watching the battle play out. Like the others, its black fur shifted like shadows, but they extended outwards, shifting and swirling. Suddenly, new wolves emerged from the swirling blackness, causing Kissa's heart to cease its beating.

She needed to reach the alpha wolf. Kissa scrambled for a plan to penetrate the circle of wolves surrounding the beast. Kissa needed a distraction.

She turned and loosed her arrow at a wolf creeping up on her left flank. It retracted to shadow and her arrow whizzed through, missing its mark. Readying another arrow, she instinctively followed its course. They became one as the arrow encased in light. Kissa did not have time to second guess her actions, focusing on the trajectory. As before, the beast returned to its shadow form at the last moment as she and the arrow delve straight inside the wolf's growling mouth. When it struck, she returned within herself and watched as the wolf lit up in crimson flames, then incinerated right before her.

Huh.

A sense of calm settled in her at the knowledge of her new ability, but her stomach sank as she looked down at her quiver holding only a half dozen arrows. Kissa's attention fell back on the lone wolf, watching the scene as shadows grew around it, spreading out to its sides like tendrils. Pure panic shot through Kissa as they solidified into another line of shadow wolves.

"Incoming!" Kissa cried out as the beasts charged straight for her people.

She released a few arrows one after the other, accurately hitting its mark, yet it seemed futile as their numbers remained constant. Screams filled the air as the creatures tore into their formation. They ravaged and dragged the Leviathans along the rough grounds. Her heart pounded alongside Taji's cadence within as she tried to find a way through their line to the leader that continued to create the damn creatures with a thought.

Desperation clawed through her chest as Kissa growled her frustration of helplessness. Guilt wrapped around her throat at the realization that they would not make it. They would all die because of her.

The sound of a horn echoed across the dark forest. Everything seemed to pause as the stomps of boots hit the forest floor. Their vibrations reverberated through her body, sounding like a warning and a blessing. Then a volley of arrows soared over her head, whistling as it hit the distracted wolves in their wake. Kissa turned behind her.

Helmed warriors, fitted for war and armed to the teeth, charged past the mound, slicing down the shadow creatures with their blades below. Kissa noted the emblems of both Leviathan and Scorpion engraved on their armor. Maru's crew, now emboldened by their brethren's aid, tightened their formation around the sick and healers. She heard her mother's firm voice across the skirmish as she commanded the healers.

"We are almost at our destination! We need to move!" Commander Maru's brisk voice echoed.

As one, their group marched up toward her family's lands. The warriors, working together with the healers, continued to protect their circle, finishing the shadow wolves crouching closer.

Stomping hooves caught her ear, and Kissa's head whipped around. Her breath left her when she saw the rider. Assessing the scene with determination, Queen Safiyah sat on top of a beautiful mare. So far from the trembling woman Kissa found mere days ago, her aura beamed magnificently as she wore black leathers, like her warriors, with a battle axe on her hip and a short sword in her hand. The relief that coated Kissa's mind and heart made her eyes burn and a genuine smile cross her face.

Chase stood beside his queen. She could see the relief on his face as they nodded to one another. Queen Safiyah's fierce attention fixated on her. A flash of recognition lit up her face. Kissa's heart sputtered.

The Queen immediately trotted toward her mound and sidled up next to her. "Kissa Ashtar!" Her voice was strong, commanding, with no hint of weakness.

Kissa's breath ceased at the mention of her name. She bowed clumsily at the matriarch. "Queen Safiyah! It is an honor." She was a stumbling mess, but couldn't find words to capture the queen's true glory.

The corners of Queen Safiyah's lips lifted, and it felt like the sun rising on the darkest night, bathing her soul in warmth. Her deep blue eyes shined, reminding Kissa of Taji's, but where the prince's eyes held a sapphire hue, the queen's reminded her of the blue quartz—the deeper depths of the sea.

"The honor is mine. I owe you my life," she said.

"It is I who should thank you for helping me finally realize my purpose," Kissa said. Tears burned the back of her eyes at the truth of her words. From the moment she stepped into the queen's chambers, her whole life changed.

"My Queen!" Taj's husky voice, laced with a million emotions, cut through the heaviness between them. He now sat on top of Cosmo, who must have found his master. His impassive face was a facade against their current situation and their company, but Kissa felt the passion and relief thrumming through him like the very seismic waves barreling their kingdom.

"My son. My beating heart in the flesh," Queen Safiyah said. Her love melded into Kissa's being. With a gentle touch on Taji's cheek, she reminded him of the remaining tasks. "We still have work to do."

Queen Safiyah moved past them toward the front of the company. The prince joined her, but stayed behind her, giving her this moment. As Maru's crew took in their queen before them, their eyes widened and their aura shifted in the air. It tasted like hope.

"*With me!*" Queen Safiyah lifted her axe. The collective roar of the warriors was deafening, shaking the very foundation of the surrounding forest.

Taji stayed at his mother's side, and together they led the now emboldened company to her lands. Kissa felt the relief and determination in the healers and warriors carrying the cots in the center as they huddled tight together. Her mother's voice echoed as she encouraged and assuaged the sick. Kissa couldn't see them covered against the rain, but she hoped that if any of them were awake, they were praying to their god.

They needed Osmond's strength right now.

Kissa set her sights on the lone wolf, observing everything, distracted by

Queen Safiyah's arrival. Deciding to use it to her advantage, she left the mound, creeping through the brush and avoiding the shadow wolves. Slowly she made her way around the battle and situated herself behind a tree a few paces behind the enemy, giving her a clear view as she nocked her arrow.

Relief poured in as Kissa saw her people passing the perimeter of her land's borders in the distance. When she flicked her attention to the leader of the shadow wolves, her heart stopped mid beat. A sense of déjà vu washed over her, and the same tingles from long ago traveled up her spine as she glared into ancient eyes. Her fingers itched to let her arrow loose, as the wolf now had only eyes for her.

As it lept in the air toward her, the beast turned into its shadow form, stretching and forming before her. Kissa let the arrow loose, but it sailed straight through the shadows that seemed to grow taller with each breath. The beast was no longer present as the tendrils around its body formed into fawn skin, and a sleeveless, black leather one piece that melded like liquid on a feminine form. Hair as dark as the night skies above them unfurled and fell down her back. Her shadows swarmed around her ankles like an extension of her, and those deep black eyes felt as if Kissa could fall into their depths along with its darkest intentions. Her lips, wrapped in the reddish shade, turned up at the corners.

If she didn't know any better, she would have thought the Ancient of Chaos herself was before her, but Kissa met this female before and now had a name to the eyes that haunted her nightmares.

Naomi.

36

DAUGHTER OF CHAOS

Kissa

Young Kissa crouches in the damp soil, as she gazes over her freshly planted row of arnica. The earthy scent of the plants fills her nostrils, mixing with the crisp morning air. She followed her mother's instructions, placing them a few paces from the cozy cottage. She smiles with pride.

A surge of all-consuming fear crashes into her like a hammer, causing her to stagger and almost lose her balance. She straightens up, shielding her eyes from the bright sunlight, and spots Aya's silhouette soaring in the sky above.

Desperate to understand what is happening, Kissa reaches out through their bond, her mind seeking a connection with her sister. In an instant, her surroundings shift, and she looks down on their home from a bird-eye view. Her eyes sharpen, taking in every detail. Just beyond the borders of their land, she spots a mysterious figure dressed in black, their midnight hair whipping among the wind.

As if sensing her presence, the woman looks up, revealing a smile that sends shivers down Kissa's spine, dredging up her darkest nightmares. Her eyes, blacker than the deepest abyss, send a tingling sensation crawling up Kissa's back.

Caught in a mesmerizing dance, Kissa's attention draws to a swirling movement around the woman's arms, resembling a sinuous snake. Without warning, the woman snaps her arm outward, too quick for her to comprehend. In an instant, the coiling darkness wraps around Aya's delicate throat.

Kissa's scream merges with Aya's terrified fear, intertwining as they plummet through the air like a stone. The ground rushes closer, and Kissa feels her stomach lurching, as if it's lodged in her throat.

Desperation fills her voice. "Aya, flap your wings!"

Kissa squeezes her eyes shut, bracing for the impact. When she dares to open them again, she finds herself trembling in front of her mother.

"M-M-Mama, someone is in the forest. Aya, Mama. We have to get to Aya!"

"Omani!" her mother cries out as she kneels in front of Kissa and wraps her in her arms. Kissa's father approaches with his unsheathed sword. Her mother's voice quivers as she implores, "Kissa, tell us how you know this."

"Aya saw her, then showed me in my mind."

Curling herself into her mother's chest, Kissa can't shake off the haunting image of the woman's eyes or the memory of their freefall.

Her father gallops away on Dream without uttering another word. Even staying close to her mother cannot banish the lingering nightmare of the woman's presence, the sensation of their descent, and the echoes of Aya's distress. Kissa cries herself to sleep, night after night, until finally, two nights later, her father and Aya return.

⚊⬦⚊

"I am pleased to see you coming into yourself, but your bleeding heart will be your undoing."

The cooing voice pulled Kissa back to the present. She glared at the dark monster that haunted her dreams in the flesh—the reason her gilded cage became so much smaller all those summers ago. Her fire rose at Naomi's sinister smile, and she wanted nothing more than to rip it off her face.

Kissa was well aware of the shadow wolves circling around them. Caging her in. A trap she willingly fell into.

"What do you want, Naomi?"

The Celestial's brow rose at her hiss. "Is that the way you greet the one who helped you embrace your true self?" There was a hint of cruel amusement in her voice.

At Kissa's apparent confusion, Naomi's shadows morphed once again. Her skin grew wrinkled and her body hunched over. Now Kissa stared at the crone in the market that sold her the Chonda ring. The trinket she bargained with her soul.

Kissa narrowed eyes. "Then why the wolves?" She eyed them, inching closer as if to protect their master.

Naomi only laughed as she returned to her otherworldly self, then she waved her hand dismissively. "I wanted to open your eyes, Kissa. To start the domino effect of exposing the lies around you." Then she flicked her dark eyes toward the forest as if her attention landed on something else. "To end a thorn in my ass," she said through gritted teeth.

Kissa was already tired of the theatrics. She pulled her bow taut. "I'll ask you again. What. Do. You. Want?"

However, Naomi continued to glare toward something in the forest and made a sinister sound, a cackle of glee. "Bring him to me!"

Before Kissa could comprehend what was unfolding, three wolves broke off, snarling and leaping at their master's order. Their growls reverberated through the dense forest, but the distinct sound of hooves reached her ears. The instinct to protect surged within her as she dared to steal a glance. Her heart dropped.

On top of Cosmo, Prince Taji plunged his blade into the first shadow wolf's side, silencing its menacing advance. He kicked away another, poised to sever its throat. However, the final wolf gripped Taji's cloak from behind with its fangs, ruthlessly dragging him down to the ground.

Consumed by an instinctual urgency, Kissa unleashed her arrows in rapid succession. She went with them, whistling through the air. With unwavering focus, her first arrow found its mark, piercing the skull of the wolf behind Taji. Before it blazed of crimson, she jumped to the other arrow. Kissa didn't have time to guide this one, but her shot rang true and lodged itself into the beast's throat right as it snapped at Taji's neck.

In a blur, she returned to herself, only to find that she couldn't breathe as Naomi's magic wrapped around her, squeezing tight. Her heart hammered as she heard a deep grunt. Kissa watched the Dark Celestial wrap the same slithering tendrils around Taji, ripping his sword from his hands. Employing her shadows, Naomi hauled him across the uneven ground, bringing him to a stop in front of her, face down.

Where ever your light takes you, I am there.

The prince's words mocked Kissa. He was supposed to be helping their people cross her lands. *Stubborn, stubborn man.*

Now she stared helplessly while Naomi formed a sharp edge at the end of one of her tendrils of shadow. Kissa thrashed against the magic holding her, but the damn tendrils tightened the more she moved, squeezing the air from her lungs. Naomi lifted her makeshift sword and swiped the back of Taji's cloak, exposing his tunic and, more importantly, the rucksack on his back.

As if enjoying every moment, Naomi took her time, opening his sack and finally retrieving the tome. Taji said nothing, though their mouths were not bound. His troubled eyes stared back at her in a silent plea. She felt his fear roll through her like waves. Fear for *her.*

Go, his look said. Kissa scowled at him. She wasn't going anywhere without him. They would escape together and take back the book. She just had to figure out how.

Naomi walked over to her with the book now clutched in her grip. "Come now. He will die of old age, eventually. I am just saving you later grief, Kissa. When we are queens in our own right, ruling worlds, the prince will be nothing but a distant memory."

Naomi clearly hated the son of the man who locked her in the darkest dungeons and used her for over a decade. But any sympathy Kissa might have had for the Celestial disappeared instantly. This broad was crazy, unhinged, and she planned to kill Taji.

Kissa's fire rose, and she stoked it, reveling in the feel of it coursing through her body.

"You are so much more than this!" Naomi gestured toward the prince with her shadows. "Humans are nothing. Pathetic and weak! They care about nothing but themselves. When they are wiped from this world, Haava will be ours. It is time you choose the right side."

The Ancients are at war. Those who follow the Ancient of Life, and those who follow the Ancient of Wisdom...

Kissa's fear wrapped around her at the thought of more of her people dying. She thought of the children chasing their mothers, and the couples dancing and laughing at the festival. Benji taking the pain away from those considered forgotten in the underground cavern and his love for Layla. Maru and his warriors who protected the sick with nothing but grit. She thought of Queen Safiyah, who huddled in the recesses of her own mind, living in hell, holding on for her son, her kingdom.

Humans were anything but weak.

Kissa's fire burned for her people. "You are wrong! It is the Divine that has proved selfish and weak, meddling in the affairs of man! Why do you care about our world, our lives?"

Naomi looked at her with disgust. "Your mother was a fool to leave you with them. They have corrupted your mind. Don't you see? We must set things right. We must restore the gateway." Naomi's onyx eyes glinted. "You, my dear, are the key to reclaiming what is ours! Then, when our king is free, Nibiru will be ours at last!"

A shiver ran down Kissa's body as she thought about the Ancient of Wisdom and his unbridled rage. He sent Moorice and Naomi to the human realm, but whoever destroyed the gateway had left them stranded for centuries. And now, with the Ancient of Wisdom imprisoned, Naomi's aim was to set him free. Though Kissa did not know how, she knew Naomi's "favor" for the Chonda ring had everything to do with that.

Over my dead body.

"You sound bitter to me. Are you feeling upset because the Ancients expelled you and your brother from your heavenly abode?"

Her words seemed to hit a sensitive spot as the Dark Celestial growled something otherworldly, right before she grabbed Kissa by the throat. "Do not speak of that traitor in my presence!"

Huh. The siblings didn't appear to be collaborating at all. Another piece of information Kissa tucked away.

From this close, Naomi's eyes seemed to absorb the surrounding moonlight. It matched her vicious smirk, forming on her perfect red lips. "You remind me of him, *Chimera.* Your quick mind, always calculating, always cunning." She tilted her head. "But unlike you, I feel no guilt for slaying the weak. I will kill every one of the gifted, starting with your darling prince."

Kissa's blood froze over. When Naomi released her throat, she walked toward Taji. Her makeshift blade solidified and glistened in the moonlight and stars. Kissa needed to distract her.

"You will pay for the lives taken with your curse. I will make sure of it!"

Naomi's eyes glinted as she cackled at Kissa's words, but she stopped her progression toward Taji, buying her more time. "While I delight in the art of a cruel, slow death, I cannot take credit for the king's pathetic attempt at regicide."

"Liar!" Taji roared. "You killed thousands of my people and tried to kill my mother!"

What is he doing?

She felt the conflict and fear war within him. He was giving her time to escape. *Stubborn man.*

Naomi lifted her blade of shadow. "Did I, now? Are you sure about that princeling? All of those useless books you surround yourself with, and you still know nothing." Naomi now gripped Taji's throat. "Your father kept me in that filthy pit, taking my blood, experimenting on your people! While you sat around, living your comfortable life, blissfully ignorant!"

While Taji wasn't completely unaware of King Lan's deceitful plans, she understood the inner struggle he faced, knowing that his own father murdered his own people and attempted to take the life of his mother. But Kissa didn't. She remembered one more important fact from the Ancient of Life.

It was impossible for the Divine to lie.

Naomi lifted her shadow blade, but Taji only had eyes for her, despite the looming threat to him. The depths of the clearest blue waters stared back at her. Her senses wrapped around him, and they were one in that single breath. She felt his fear like a crashing tidal wave, and Kissa was drowning in it. Fear that he would die and never tell her how he felt about her. Fear that their destiny to save the world together would never be realized. *Together.* In the realm of unspoken words and untrodden paths, their desires danced amidst a symphony of his cadence and her light.

Taji's song swelled inside her as her fire broke free. Her light hummed and the shadows that wrapped tight around Kissa lit up in crimson flame and ash. Now charged with adrenaline and magic, she propelled herself forward, and snatched her bow off the ground, readying it to nock an arrow. But her quiver lay empty.

Time stopped as Naomi's blade sliced across Taji's throat. Uncurbed panic and pain coursed through Kissa as her scream shattered the night air. Her fire blazed through her, unbridled and wild.

You are the light, Daughter! Her mother's voice—her *Divine mother's* voice.

The confirmation settled within Kissa as a fierce growl ripped from her throat, and the air crackled with energy. She harnessed her inner light deep from her well of Essence, channeling it into two arrows that shimmered with a radiant glow. As she released them, they soared through the darkness faster than a take of breath, slicing the air and leaving trails of brilliance in their wake.

Naomi turned abruptly, her eyes wide with fear. She formed a flimsy shield of shadow to block the incoming arrows, but Kissa's light cut clear through them, piercing Naomi's back in quick succession. A guttural cry escaped her lips.

Kissa advanced, determined to end it, but a torrent of shadows swirled around her, shrouding her vision. With barely a thought, she summoned two blades of light from her hands—an extension of her as she slashed and burned down the surrounding darkness separating her from her target.

The vicious growls of the shadow wolves surrounding her fell to the background as her rage drove her through the oncoming snapping shadow of darkness. Kissa watched the realization of the pending doom on Naomi's face as her shadow wolves disintegrated in her surrounding light as if nothing at all.

End Naomi...

End the Curse...

End the Oath...

Naomi snapped her arm out and a tendril of shadow wrapped around her neck, just as she did to Aya all those summers ago. But it was too late. As it squeezed around Kissa's neck, her right blade of light continued its unstoppable trajectory and penetrated itself deep inside the center of the Celestial's chest. Naomi's face morphed into agony as Kissa retracted her blade.

Cracks formed along her fawn skin, and crimson light seeped out of her from the fatal wound. In a flash so bright, Naomi and her shadow wolves vanished. Where she stood moments before, all that remained was a trail of ashes floating in the air, the edges smoldering embers.

Kissa sucked in a needed breath. Her heart raced, and her magic still surged through her veins. She had never taken a life before, and she was uncertain what might happen when a Celestial dies, leaving her uncertain and conflicted.

Taji.

She snapped her attention to his lying form. Her heart pounded. His cadence's absence unsettled her. She kneeled on the ground next to him. The metallic smell of his life blood filled the air as it pulled underneath him. So much blood.

"No, no, no!" Kissa felt his life slipping away.

Her magic urged her to use it as her light wrapped around Taji without even a thought. With her eyes shut tight, she focused her energy on where his life's blood seeped. She yearned for his life not to end this way.

Not like this. As she burned the thought into existence, a vision snatched her from the scene.

Kissa was elsewhere in another time. Taji stood valiantly in his black leathers. Gold gauntlets adorned his hands and a pauldron on his shoulder beamed with an emblem of a mountain with a tree atop it. Raised in his right hand, he held his majestic sword that beckoned her soul. Osiris.

Lightning, the color of his sapphire eyes, shot up from its tip, clawing into the dark sky as it coursed through sword and Protector. He seemed larger than life itself at that moment.

Ngurumo, an ancient male's voice, echoed in her mind.

She was so enthralled, she almost missed the woman standing next to him.

Wearing black leathers and her familiar bow draped over her back, Kissa's sundial and hands flashed with white, gold and crimson light. Her light mingled with the Protector's, dancing around each other to their own song. Together, they bathed the surrounding scene in a wash of light—revealing dead enemies lying at their feet.

A firm hand gripped her chin, bringing her back to the present. She met blazing sapphire blue eyes staring up at her as if she were the sun and moon and everything between. A sob broke from her as a wave of relief washed over her body, causing the light to fade from her hands. Without uttering a single word, Taji wiped away the tears streaming down her face and pulled her close to him.

His scent wrapped around her along with his gratitude that thrummed between them, expressing feelings words would never be strong enough to convey. For a long moment, they stayed that way.

Kissa felt exhausted. In the span of what felt like moments, she used a magnitude of Essence. She pushed up into a sitting position, letting his arms fall to her waist as she skimmed his throat with the tips of her fingers. His neck had fully healed, leaving no scar behind. Taji's hands gripped her hips as his eyes fell closed and a deep growl escaped him. Despite her exhaustion, Kissa's body flushed with heat and desire.

With his eyes still closed, he licked his lips. "We should check on the others."

"We should." She knew when they returned, their duties as prince and healer would take president. Was it selfish to carve just a little time for themselves?

His lips turned up into his familiar smirk, brightening his eyes. Kissa wished to always see him this way. She leaned over and kissed him. Reveling in the softness of his full lips, she felt his arms come around her again, melding their bodies against one another perfectly.

"Sister...he...coming...father..." Aya's urgent voice ripped through her mind with panic.

Kissa shot up from Taji's arms, alarm on her face. "Aya, what is wrong? Who is coming?" Nothing but silence met her on the other end of their bond. "Aya!"

Taji grabbed her shoulders. "What is it?"

"It's Aya. It sounded like she was trying to warn me of something." Kissa tried to reach through the bond again. Still nothing. She looked up and scanned what she could see of the sky, but there was no sign of her sister.

Taji's eyes hardened as the intrusion of the real world shattered their tender moment. Without hesitation, he swiftly retrieved his sword and tome, then marched toward Cosmo, who was casually munching on grass a short distance away beneath a tree.

As Kissa grabbed her empty quiver, her restlessness surrounding Aya and her father returned tenfold. Time was running out.

37

NIGHTMARES

IT FELT STRANGE TO see the Queen of Osmondia standing in her kitchen. Alongside her mother and a few others, they were busy preparing meals for the sizeable crowd consisting of over three hundred warriors, healers, and the convalescent now walking her land. Convalescent was a more fitting term now that Naomi's death magically put an end to the dreadful Sleeping sickness that ravaged their kingdom.

There wasn't one dry eye when the first of the sick woke up, no longer burdened by the cursed black veins that sealed their Fate. Most of them still slept, needing time to recover, but those who gradually awakened were still frail and haunted by the darkness they had endured. A darkness that had no name. Kissa, Layla, Taji, and Benji spent most of the night assisting the healers and providing support to those who awakened. Each of the patients had similar stories to tell, just like the queen, and Kissa's heart shattered a little more with every retelling of their nightmares.

Everyone of them had their own troubles in life that manifested one way or another in their darkness, but one fact stayed consistent in their stories, though. *Shadows.* It was impossible to determine if those who had already died were still trapped or had transitioned to the *After*. An enigma, her mother took on. Between helping those who recovered, she prayed to Zuri, and more than once,

Kissa saw her sitting in the corner reading her books on the Transitioning.

Over their shared meal, Taji and Commander Maru briefed Queen Safiyah about the events following the King's Tournament. Her anger and heartbreak were palpable. Though everyone of them shared her pain, the unnecessary loss of High Commander Eshu's men, and the Den of Serpents devastated the matriarch. Despite all of their attempts to persuade her, she remained unwavering in her decision to leave the safety of Kissa's lands. She needed to inform her people, prevent a civil war, and prepare the warriors for the battles ahead. Even more, she had a treacherous husband to apprehend. The queen departed soon after, with her contingent of warriors, including Chase, High Commander Eshu, and Commander Maru and his crew.

"I think you should go," Kissa said as she and Taji lay in her hammock together on her cliffs.

His fingers trailed over her arm as they watched the twilight sky and sea with heavy eyes. From their viewpoint, the waters seemed calm, though the true damage of Aarusha was yet to be seen. A gentle breeze carried the scent of the sea, but it did little to calm the depth of emotions running through them.

Kissa glanced up at Taji, noticing the furrowed brow and the tension on his face. The weight of his conflicting emotions hung heavy between them. She understood the immense burden he carried, the demands of his duty. Yet, she also knew the depth of the bond that had somehow formed between them. Whatever decision he made, it would be one that he believed was for the greater good.

Taji leaned in and nuzzled into her neck, his lips leaving a path of tingles in their wake that made her toes curl. "What about you, Kissa? Naomi's brother is still out there and if what your mother and sister said is true, this battle has only just begun."

Kissa revealed her discoveries regarding her blood mother and the Custodians, though she half believed it herself. He, Benji, nor Layla seemed surprised in the slightest. Which only managed to further irritate her regarding the entire situation. She wasn't special. She was just...Kissa.

"I will be here, helping my mother and the healers." She turned around to meet his gaze. "I need to know that my father is alive and not locked away in some dungeon, or worse." The commander could hold his own, but ever since Aya's mention of his meeting with the treacherous king, and he hadn't shown up to the coast, Kissa had been worried sick.

Taji tore his gaze away. She watched his jaw clench as he pondered her request. "I will see what I can find out. It will give me time to speak to Maru about helping us retrieve Osiris." His eyes took her in as he lifted her chin. "Then I will return. Promise me you will stay here until then. If something happens to you..."

Kissa leaned in and pressed her lips against Taji's, snatching away his words. War was on the threshold, and anything was possible. If this was their last moment together, she wished to etch the memory of his lips and touch into her mind—not the burdens of promises neither of them could make.

⁕

Kissa gazed at the three moons suspended in the sky. Two of them were waxing moons positioned on opposite sides, creating a cradle for the full moon at the center. Though she had never witnessed them in person, the murals depicted them as radiant and vibrant, shining like the brightest stars, but their brilliance seemed dimmed now and something seemed missing. The backdrop appeared so dark that it resembled the blackest ink spilled across the heavens, as if it had absorbed all the surrounding light, the very Essence of the sister moons.

It was at that moment that Kissa realized what was amiss—there were no stars.

She pulled her attention below the familiar sea cliffs that were not her own. Though it was night now, the realm of Nibiru seemed different somehow...felt different. A sinister feeling tainted the air.

"You feel the work of Sage, and though it has not happened yet, it is one outcome of many."

Kissa followed the voice, to find the Goddess of Creation wearing the same green leathers and flowy skirt, and gripping the same staff as before. In the night, her skin seemed to shimmer even more, making her even more radiant. Her green and gold starlight zipped up, down, and sideways through her golden brown skin.

A star.

Though she told her this before, back then, Kissa couldn't believe any of it was real.

Frustration bubbled up. Some of it caused by the Ancient of Life's cryptic words and the cryptic scene—she did not know what the frustrating goddess was pointing out—but mostly it came from the hurt that buried deep inside Kissa's heart the moment she figured out she was her mother.

"You left me!" The words came out more strangled and angry than she intended.

"I never left you." The Ancient's stoic face seemed acceptant, like she prepared for this very conversation. "I had to keep you safe. It was the only way."

She knew the goddess could perceive the various paths Fate could take based on choices and events. It was likely that she witnessed every outcome of Kissa's life. However, this knowledge did little to alleviate the pain of discovering that not only was she unable to lead a normal life, but her true origins had been stripped away, too.

Her choice.

"What is your name?" All the Ancients had names: Osmond, Desire, Raven, Justice, Miro, Zuri, and Sage. Though none of her world worshipped the Ancient of Life as the others, Kissa wanted to at least know her own mother's name.

"Essa." Such a simple name. Yet, as she repeated it back and forth in her head, a powerful and deep feeling evoked in Kissa. "It is the Divine word for Essential Star," the Ancient said.

Did that mean she was the very first star? The vastness of the thought made Kissa feel quite insignificant. It would mean her mother was the reason all things existed. Did she even have a beginning? Was she even capable of loving Kissa the way she believed she should?

Pushing the sensitive topic aside, Kissa said, "Okay, Essa. Tell me why should I care about the world of the Ancients who caused everything in the first place? This is your problem to fix, not mine, nor the gifted."

The way her mother's eyes dropped gave away the sadness the goddess otherwise hid. The grief in them told Kissa there was so much she still didn't understand. "Your frustrations are warranted, but there is something you need to see."

Essa's hand reached up to cup Kissa's cheek, and despite the warring feelings inside her, she allowed it.

Suddenly, she was no longer standing at the cliffs but... flying. Fear ripped across Kissa's thundering chest as she soared across the dark purple seas. She only flew once before through Aya's eyes and swore to never do it again. But as she sailed over the realm of the god's changing landscape, a sense of euphoria filled her as she let go of her fear and embraced the moment. It felt as natural as running through her forest, and a smile lit up her face.

Kissa journeyed across towering mountains that dwarfed Aarusha in comparison. The peaks seemed to reach the sister moons themselves. The red sand desert from her vision replicated a chilling sea of crimson blood, sending a shiver down her spine. Eventually, she stumbled upon another range of peaks covered in ice. Below, a valley gracefully curved between the bases of two of the mountains.

It was here that countless beings stood in formation. As far as the eyes could see, black and red armor filled the valley. Their helms adorned a distinct black dragon emblem. Continuing to analyze the scene unfolding before her, she realized that there were two distinct groups, separated by a vast expanse of land. A battleground.

On the other side, warriors wore green and gold armor, proudly displaying the emblem of a majestic mountain and a tree. A mixture of anxiety, fear, and unwavering determination wrapped around Kissa's senses. Behind them, something strange floated in the air.

At first, it appeared like a shimmering mirror of light in the distance, but it took on a defined shape as she drew nearer. Constructed from stone, what she thought was a mirror was a perfectly framed depiction of a sun-drenched sky and a lush green forest—a landscape that Kissa would recognize anywhere. A heavy weight settled in her chest as she gazed upon her home.

Suddenly, she stood back at the cliffs. The Ancient of Life's hand still palmed Kissa's cheek. A tear fell from her eyes as she looked up at the inky black sky, piecing together the larger picture.

Those warriors were the very stars that were absent from the heavens above. They were the Children of the Ancients, the Keepers of the Gateway—Celestials. And the threat to her world just multiplied.

"You needed to see what the outcome of doing nothing is. You are not alone, and when the time comes, I will stand beside you, Chimera. We all will," Essa said. The fire in her eyes burned with an intensity that made the fire in Kissa's chest seem like embers in comparison.

"What does it mean? Chimera?" She recalled Naomi had called her that once, but Kissa was too busy trying not to die to ask about it.

Essa's eyes gleamed with unshed tears. "It is your true name. It is what I named you when you were born."

Kissa's brows lifted in surprise. She was certain it meant something in the Divine language. The sound of it caused her Essence to tingle in recognition.

"It means limitless... It means you are everything and more, Daughter."

———◆———

KISSA BLINKED SEVERAL TIMES as her eyes adjusted to her dark surroundings. *Limitless.* The word felt branded on her very heart. She lifted her head and realized she had slept through the entire day. Darkness shrouded the tent—her new room as the sick recovered.

A commotion outside her tent sent a tingling sensation down her spine. A warning. She quickly grabbed her boots, cloak, and bow. As her mind finally cleared from the vision, she thought she could hear the distinct sound of the toll bell. Her heart seemed to hammer along with it. *One... Two... Three... Four... Five...*

Sabu must have spotted Moorice. Hastily picking up her refilled quiver and satchel, Kissa dashed out of the tent.

"Ah. There she is!"

The voice, laced with honey, followed with a chuckle that promised pain. Instinctively, she threw her hands out, fingers splayed wide as her light lit up the scene before her. Kissa's face paled as her magic revealed the last person she thought to see.

King Harold Lan forwent his usual royal robes for black leather with gold armor, like he was prepared for battle. Casually resting his palm on the pommel of his one and half hand sword, he leaned on it with the tip of the blade balancing in the dirt. A gold helm replaced his crown and behind him, twelve Elite stood in all black, blending into the dark forest around them.

Despite the chill in the air, sweat gathered at the base of Kissa's spine, as she tracked another Elite coming from her tent, handing something to the king. Dread sank in the pit of her stomach. The king slowly smiled as he opened the familiar leather tome and the golden inscription on the cover shimmered.

She and Taji had agreed to keep Osiris' book with her, protected by the wards, to prevent Moorice from stealing it, like his depraved sister. It had seemed like a wise decision at that moment. However, what they had failed to think about was that the wards offered no defense against human kings.

But it wasn't the sight of the book that threatened to undo her. In a cruel twist of Fate, a black ring bearing the mark of a dragon on its face stood out against the moonlit sky. The inset rubies sat precariously on the king's pinky finger, mocking her.

The Chonda ring.

38

VEILED INTENTIONS

Taji

TAJI TOOK GREAT PRIDE in his mother's swift action, as she wasted no time in opening the gates and warmly welcoming the displaced residents of Sapphire City into the citadel. Maru, his wife Corah, and his crew stepped forward to lend a hand in helping those with no home find stability. Plans were already in motion to construct temporary dwellings until the waters receded and they could assess the possibility of rebuilding.

Taji's mother commanded over a hundred warriors to assist the Harmons in aiding the recovering individuals in the underground cavern, transporting them to Kissa's lands where they could finally receive the long overdue healing they deserved. With Serenity nearly empty, most of the students and the Shadora Council away in Zurania, Elder Harmon welcomed those displaced into the school.

Despite enduring the earthquakes, Zuberi had remained mostly intact. The infinite steps that wound through the heart of the city had cracked in some places, but were still passable. The shops and homes that spilled over the mountainside had thankfully only suffered superficial damage, and Horus Citadel stood tall as a beacon of hope for Taji's people.

Nevertheless, a heavy air of tension and uncertainty hung over the kingdom, casting a dark shadow on their future. It felt like the charged air right before a storm. They were trapped like sitting ducks, with no means of escape. Their once thriving kingdom now lay broken. But Osmondians were a resilient people who had overcome challenges before. Just as they had done after the War of the Great Divide, Taji knew they would triumph again.

Everywhere Taji went, he heard whispers on the lips of the people. *"Where is the girl who saved our queen and freed us from the sickness?"* they murmured. *"She's a Sagian princess, hidden among us...she is the one from the prophecy."*

Taji's heart ached each time he heard mention of the extraordinary girl who had stolen his heart. They had no clue how close they were to the truth. Even Kissa herself was not ready to embrace her true identity.

She was a Celestial, a divine being. Her mother was the Creator of all living beings, including the Ancients themselves. The Mother of Life. Taji knew Kissa had not even uncovered her full range of Essence and the powers she would soon wield.

He was not worthy of her affections.

What future could he give her? He was a prince of a broken kingdom and he hadn't even fulfilled his destiny of retrieving Osiris. Taji felt torn between his rational mind and his passionate heart. Logically, he knew that their connection could never be more than a yearning. From the moment Taji laid eyes on her striking, otherworldly eyes, he knew she couldn't be from this world.

But that fact didn't stop him from thinking of her, wanting her.

One thing Taji knew for certain was that ever since parting ways with Kissa, he couldn't shake off a persistent uneasiness that settled in his gut. It was more than just the blossoming romantic feelings between them, as if they had always been together. Ancients knew he desired her like the air he breathed, but this feeling was different. It went beyond them.

The disappearance of his father and the Elite, who seemed to evade accountability for their treasonous acts, added to his concerns. Even more troubling was the absence of Commander Ashtar, whom none of the warriors had seen since before the storm. Taji and Chase tirelessly searched the dungeons, his study, and the barracks, but their efforts yielded nothing. Both men were missing, and the shadow looming over the prince gave him a sickening feeling that there was a scheme unfolding right under their noses.

And then there was Moorice and his mysterious whereabouts. Taji did not know which made him the most anxious, an unhinged king with murderous assassins on the loose or a powerful divine with veiled intentions. Moorice's mission was to cripple their kingdom, in which he did successfully, but so far, there were no other sightings of Sagian ships or magical destruction. So what did the dark Celestial want?

Now, Taji kneeled before his mother, awaiting her decision for both enemies. Standing beside her like a steadfast anchor was his uncle, now fully recovered—another miracle. Families, warriors both young and old, packed the throne room, squeezed together, listening intently as their queen determined their steps ahead.

"The traitor formed the very fraction that will end him!"

The burning hiss from High Commander Eshu rattled Taji's bones, reverberating through the throne room and reaching the ears of everyone present. Known for his public composure and control, his uncle wore a visible anger on his face, revealing the lingering trauma from witnessing his warriors perish in such a brutal manner. Taji knew that look. He wanted revenge.

"Haava needs its Protector, now." His mother said calmly, as her indigo eyes, as deep as the ocean itself, stared into his own. "You will bring turned traitor Harold Lan and those with him to justice."

This audience was for the people's benefit, so they understood what was happening. A technicality. Taji and Queen Safiyah already discussed his mission in private. He told his mother of his secret quest to retrieve Osiris, and she gave her blessing. However, as the Protector of the Realm, it was his duty to lead in the search for the king.

Taji no longer had love for the man. He would never call the murderous wretch father again. Now he was the enemy. Wherever he was, either Commander Ashtar was hot on his trail, or worse, captured. He didn't want to think of the latter, but he couldn't overlook it. Omani was a force to be reckoned with, the most skillful swordsman Taji had ever known, but the Elite were a force trained specifically in cutthroat skills of espionage and murder. They were still on Aarusha somewhere and he needed to find them now.

After his mother's proclamation, Taji handpicked one hundred warriors, Scorpion and Leviathan, and most importantly, loyal to the realm. With the help of his uncle, Chase, and Commander Maru, he chose the best of the best. This force would no longer be warriors of Osmondia, but guardians of the entire realm, sworn to protect those who could not defend themselves and exact justice.

Taji named them "Med'Jin—Rangers of the Realm," nomads no longer belonging to one kingdom, but to the people of Haava.

Chase was the first to join—his rider. When Commander Maru and those of his crew, with him, stepped forward, Taji felt humbled. The captain of Yemanja may have been his rival during the King's Tournament, but within a span of a few days they fought and saved lives together, forming something Taji was not sure what to call it just yet. But if nothing else, Maru and his crew were his and Kissa's allies.

"You have shown me your true intentions, young prince."

The seasoned commander's statement said so much in those few words. He wondered if during the tournament, Maru thought Taji was like his father, heartless and self-consumed. It made sense now why he tried to bash the prince's head to pieces.

"We may have missions that take us away for long periods of time, Maru," Taji said. Leaving the fact that he had a young daughter to think of unspoken.

Maru's eyes narrowed. "It is in our blood, our god-given duty to serve the realm."

Before Taji could respond, Tomeri stepped up. Her fierce eyes saying more than words. "Together, we ensure a brighter future for *every* family and child."

Her words resonated something within Taji. The Ancient of Life told Kissa that allies would be gifted and non gifted. As he lifted his eyes to take in the warriors before him, every one of their names, families, and reasons branded into his mind, he felt resolve settle over him. These men and women were part of the non-gifted that would turn the tides in the times to come. He felt it in his bones.

"I, along with my entire crew—are honored to fight alongside you," Maru said, as one by one they pledged themselves to the cause of protecting their future from whatever dark force wanted to rip it away from them.

Taji's mouth clamped in speechlessness when Benji came forward, displaying his sword on his back for all to see. He wasn't in the least surprised that he was choosing to be a Ranger. He lived to serve others. It was his destiny to use his sword and healing gift for the better of the world. *Shaman.*

However, they had not spoken about the tension between them. Benji was angry that Taji put Kissa in danger by asking her to heal his mother, calling him reckless. Now that he knew her larger role in bringing them together and saving the world, his friend was right. So Taji allowed his friend his anger, but seeing him standing before him felt a lot like unspoken forgiveness, and he didn't know until that moment how much he really needed it.

With a spark in his golden eyes, Benji gave a nonchalant shrug. "Someone needs to keep you in line."

Though Taji's face was stoic, a mask he learned to wield all his life, his heart swelled at the thought of his oldest friend by his side. His lips lifted in a smile, and pride shined in his eyes as the healer swore himself to the cause. It felt right. He thanked Osmond for the gift of having a loyal force at his back.

Now it was time to flush out a traitor and divine enemy.

He divided the Med'Jin, with a fraction assigned to scout for any sign of Moorice, led by Maru and Tomeri above ground. The other half, led by him, had the important task of bringing the king to justice, venturing through the underground tunnels. With Isis ready, and Benji and Chase at his side, Taji moved in silence, relying on hand signals as they meticulously searched every hidden passage from the catacombs beneath the library to the Fathomless Pit. As their search continued to come up fruitless, the weight of Aya's words pressed on Taji's mind with every breath he took, adding to the fact that time was not on their side.

Do not leave Kissa.

It felt almost impossible to fight against the urge to divert back to her and ensure her safety, but he had given his word to Kissa and it was his duty to apprehend the traitor. He reasoned that locking the king up would protect her from his clutches to use her, or worse.

The group prepared to descend into the tunnel that led to the First Temple and rendezvous with the other half of their group above ground when a whisper resonated in Taji's mind, crystal clear.

Osmond's Rest.

Osiris. He hadn't heard from the ancient voice since before he almost died at the hands of Naomi. It was Osiris' voice that alerted him to Kissa sneaking off during the battle with the shadow wolves to fight Naomi on her own...

Ice climbed up his spine as fear flooded his veins. Something happened to Kissa.

Forcing calm, Taji raised his fist, and everyone paused. Benji and Chase waited for instruction, used to his *gut feelings*. He still had not told his brothers about Osiris, but he didn't need to. That was the way of their bond.

"Osmond's Rest," Taji said. "That is where they are."

Benji looked at Taji with a calculating gaze. "The coward is trying to escape."

"They?" Chase asked as his hand tightened around the hilt of his knife.

Taji didn't know how he knew, only that it made sense why everything seemed so quiet. The king was buying his time for the perfect moment. "He has Kissa."

They didn't have time to alert Maru and Tomeri. As he changed course, Chase and Benji silently followed, squashing the other ranger's inquiries. He went over their plan a million times in the moments it took to reach the exit, a cave that spilled out onto Osmond's Rest. Taji steeled himself for what they would encounter.

He took one last look at Chase and Benji, who had the same look of determination. Weapons ready with a fire in their eyes. Then Taji swept his attention over the rangers behind him, eagerness filling each of their faces as resolve settled over their group. Some would not make it, but dying in battle was an honorable death for any warrior.

They were ready.

39

THE KING

KISSA

PATIENTLY, KING LAN FLIPPED through the pages of the ancient tome with a triumphant gleam in his eyes. As he did, Kissa thought of all the ways she could put an arrow in his head. Of all the enemies threatening her world, King Lan was the one she loathed the most. He killed thousands of his own people and tried to murder his own wife, all for his greed for power. He was a coward and a waste of the very air he breathed.

The masked Elite circled around her, watching her every movement. Though every fiber of her being screamed to do *something*, Kissa did not break her eyes from the cunning man before her, who now had the power to bring down the world with just a thought. She wondered if he knew the power he held. The smirk on his haughty face told her he did. The real question was, what would he do with it?

One of the Elite inched too close and Kissa's light blazed, ready to burn them all to the After.

"I wouldn't do that if I were you, Kissa *Ashtar*." The sound of her last name on the king's lips froze her fingers.

A grunt and a rustling sound caught her attention from behind him. A few Elite dragged two bound individuals with them. In an instant, her light sputtered out. Forced to kneel against their will with two swords against their chests, was her mother and father.

Neither of them displayed fear in their expressions. Only firm determination stared back at her. It was a contrast to the icy terror threatening to strangle her at the moment. Each breath felt strained and weighted. Kissa feared the king's intentions as he held her parents' lives in his hands.

"What do you want?"

The king smiled like they were chatting over tea. "I have everything I want, thanks to you. I've obtained three of the most powerful weapons in all the realms, and rid myself of a loose end, so to speak. You see, after my wife's *miraculous* healing, I found something very interesting in her chambers. Life changing, really."

Suddenly, Kissa felt a surge of ancient power envelop her, its presence resonating with a familiar, low hum that reverberated through the air. Their surroundings slowed, then blurred into unrecognizable shapes and shadows as it seemed to spin around them. As they stood frozen, the king's eyes never left hers while her family's land disappeared, along with everything else.

Shocking fear closed in on her as everything settled. Kissa recognized the multiple caves set into the ridge ahead, Osmond's Rest. But everything else… Nothing but water as far as the eye could see surrounded them and the moonless sky spread above them. The last surge's relentless power made the water rise exponentially. It almost reached the towering tip of Osmond's Light and submerged half of the kingdom underwater. Kissa's heart ached unbearably at the thought of the destruction inflicted upon Aarusha.

To make matters worse, at the edge of the cliff—now looking more like a partial shore instead—her parents were kneeling with swords at their neck. Her father still wore his bravery, but her mother's eyes were now lined with silver as her amber eyes stared at Kissa.

Seeing her distress, the king narrowed his eyes. "They are alive, for now. That is more than they deserve. Fate has a way of making things right, don't you think? Soon, they will die a treasonous death."

The weight of his words hung heavy in the air. Deep pain overshadowed the fact that the lunatic was still in possession of the tome and ring. Kissa would not accept this as her parent's Fate. The kingdom needed them. *She* needed them.

However, before she could say a word, the otherworldly hum returned. She frantically looked around to see where the king was transporting them to now. However, a gathering of fog formed over the waters a little way out, past Osmond's Light, rolling ominously. Then, just like that, a massive warship appeared. It was at least two hundred hands, and close enough that Kissa spotted white sails with the leviathan insignia snapping in the wind. Its presence sent chills down Kissa's spine as each row of oars dipped into the churning sea.

"It is called a trireme. The first and only of its kind on this side of the world now," the king said with a smile.

With his sudden display of power, his message was obvious. There was no way for them to stop him now. Nor keep him from attempting to retrieve Osiris. Kissa couldn't help the feeling that the destruction of the Den of Serpents played into his hands and he was involved somehow. He made sure both fractions of warriors were stuck in the capital during the attack. This seemed meticulously planned, and he only had the Chonda ring for three or four days. Who was working with him?

As the ship drew nearer, she could make out the glint of polished metal on the deck and intricate carvings depicting golden serpents on its hull. She licked her lips, trying to calm her racing heart.

She whipped around. "Is this your third weapon?" She need to distract him while she planned a way to get to her mother and father.

King Lan laughed as if she said a joke. He approached close enough for her to spear him right into his cruel heart. He lifted his hand, watching her intently. His smile grew wider when her eyes zeroed in on the Chonda ring. "There is a weapon I wish for that surpasses all others." At her confused expression, his hand caressed her cheek as he said, "Come with me willingly, Kissa, and I will lay all your desires at your feet as we rule the world together."

She reeled back from his hand and his words. Putting space between them, she moved closer to her mother and father. "What?" His request sent a ripple of shock through her. He desired to use her, but instead of shackles, he wanted her to join him in his treacherous quest for power and dominance... *and his bed?*

With a steely gaze, she looked directly into King Lan's eyes. "I will go nowhere with you! I will never betray everything I believe in for your diluted promises of power."

King Lan's smile faltered. He truly expected that he could easily sway her, that she would succumb to his flattery and grandiose promises. But Kissa held a power far greater than any weapon or ring. The power to stand up for what she believed in, to fight against injustice, and to protect those who couldn't protect themselves.

His lip curled in disdain. He opened his mouth, but shouts filled the air, blending with the clashing of metal against metal. She looked toward the caves and her heart leaped as Taji, Chase, and Benji exited the cave at the far end of the ridge. They must have used the underground tunnels.

Kissa could see the unbridled anger in Taji's eyes, washing over like waves, as he cut down the first Elite who stepped forward. Osiris' cadence seeped into her spirit as their eyes locked. He came for her.

The Protector looked just as fierce as the vision with Osiris, as he moved like liquid, ducking underneath the next blade and stabbing the next masked enemy in the heart. Benji and Chase flanked him, watching his back as if they had done this very thing a million times. What really shocked her was the warriors behind them, spilling in from the cave and surrounding the Elite. An arrow flew into the chest of an enemy from deeper in the forest, and Kissa's eyes snapped up to find even more warriors.

For the first time since she woke up, hope flared within her.

King Lan unsheathed his sword, standing in front of her as the clash of steel echoed around them. His back was toward her as he bellowed, "Grab your prince! Kill the rest!"

Kissa wasn't about to stand around idle. As much as she wanted to send her light and end the king once and for all, something told her it would risk the lives of her mother and father. Instead, she turned to them, still kneeling near the edge of the water. The commander was already fighting off his captor, slamming the back of his head into their masked face.

With her bow at the ready, Kissa's light surged, and she quickly shot two light arrows into the chest of the Elite, turning him to ash. Her father didn't miss a beat as he now turned and wrapped his bound arms around the other captor's neck that guarded her mother. The Elite dropped the sword from her mother's neck, but they rolled across the ground, tussling, and Kissa found it difficult to get a clear shot.

As she rushed toward them, her heart seized in her chest. The Elite pulled out a knife from his boot and stabbed the commander in his side.

"Father!" she shouted.

She heard her father grunt as the Elite shook him off. Now, with a clear shot, Kissa swiftly sent two arrows his way, but he moved with an unnatural speed, rolling underneath them. Scared that he would try to finish her father, she fired two more. The Elite leaped forward with his knife in hand and Kissa watched in absolute horror as he stabbed her mother right through her chest above her heart.

Kissa screamed, as both arrows hit his neck, instantly incinerating him. Her mother fell forward, but with her wrists tied, she landed on her forearms. Her Jata locs, obscuring everything. She heard her father's wails while swords clashed all around her, but she felt held in time as her mother lifted her head and her amber eyes locked on hers. Kissa found only resolve in her mother's face as her mouth formed four words.

I love you, Firebird.

No! Kissa wasn't about to accept her mother's parting words. Tears gathered in her eyes as she lurched forward to heal her mother before it was too late. She heard her name, and before she could make it two steps, something hard slammed into the back of her head. The impact caused her knees to buckle, and the ground rushed up to meet her.

Amidst the haze of pain, she heard the king's voice. "Amon, take her to the ship!"

She tried to lift her head, but the sharp pain radiated down her neck now, darkening her vision. Kissa reached up and touched the wound, and winced as her fingers felt a deep gash. Blood coated her fingers. The king must have hit her with the pommel of his sword.

Roughly, someone grabbed her shoulders, and another grabbed her ankles. Kissa kicked and punched as they turned her on her back and hauled her up. She screamed as her boot slammed into one of their masked faces. Kissa heard the crunch on impact, but he didn't let go of her legs.

"Put me down!" Kissa wriggled and thrashed, determination to heal her mother fueling every move. She couldn't focus enough to use her light, so she clawed at their arms, fighting like a caged animal.

Suddenly, a powerful whoosh sounded, stilling the night, as a gust of violent wind knocked her and both the Elite that held her flat on the ground. It punched the breath out of her and the pain in her head flared with a vengeance. Black spots crowded her vision and bile crept up her throat. Shouts of terror ripped through the air as she stared at the bright stars above her. Oddly, Kissa found them comforting, as the pain settled into an agonizing thrum and chaos reigned all around her.

"Mama!" she cried out. She needed to get to her mom and heal her. It was all she could do to fight against the oppressive darkness, desperately clinging to her fading consciousness.

The whoosh sounded again, along with another gale of wind followed by a snap that sounded a lot like thunder. She heard her name being shouted, but it sounded so so far away. A dark silhouette loomed above them, casting a veil over the twinkling stars as if draping them in a velvety blanket.

That didn't seem right.

Kissa tried to get up, but couldn't move. She strained her senses, trying to comprehend what she was seeing. It hurt to furrow her brows as she tried to squint up at the night sky. But she didn't need to, because the creature grew more distinct as it drew closer.

The king must have hit her harder than she thought, because she was seeing things.

A colossal creature with wings as black as night unfolded before her. It seemed to defy logic as another rush of wind swept over them, plastering her to the ground. This time the edges of its wings blurred like... *shadows*. As another gust brushed against her, she shivered. The creature's powerful Essence engulfed her, evoking an unsettling familiarity—*captivating and vengeful.*

It was the last thing Kissa felt before the world around her plunged into darkness.

40

DIRE CONSEQUENCES

TAJI

THE PROTECTOR AND TWELVE of his Med'Jin silently crept through the shadows, observing the scene from within the last cave nestled in the ridge of Osmond's Rest. Chase and Benji settled beside him, their eyes scanning the surroundings. He instructed the others to position themselves above ground, surrounding the king and Elite from all sides except the one where the sea met the cliffs.

Astonishingly, the cliffs now harbored a warship.

Taji was intimately familiar with that ship. It was the *Apophis*, his mother's vessel - older and smaller than any other trireme. Gold serpents adorned its sides, appearing as though they were wrapping around the hull, riding the waves. The white sails, symbolizing royalty, fluttered in the wind. However, it was too far to identify any of the crew members on board.

Benji was correct. Harold Lan was attempting to flee. Anger surged within Taji upon seeing the Book of Osiris tightly clutched in the king's hand. He stood boldly in Kissa's presence, as if he had every right to be there, insolently touching her with his other filthy hand. It didn't require an astronomer to comprehend the king's intentions. He desired everything that meant the most to Taji.

His father had always been envious of him—envious of his close bond with his mother, Omani, and his people. Since childhood, the prince had suspected that the king envied his position in line for the throne. Now, he coveted Osiris and Kissa.

Over his dead body.

Every fiber of his being longed to strike the king down for daring to invade Kissa's personal space. But the twenty Elite guards would swiftly intercept him, and that was not part of the plan. Now that he knew where his commander was—tied up next to his wife, and no doubt being used against Kissa—he had to exercise caution. He was confident that the king would not harm her, but he couldn't say the same for the Commander and High Healer, Onya.

Taji wondered why Kissa hadn't eliminated them all already. Her bow skills surpassed anything he had ever seen, and with her light, she could take them down in one blink. What did the king possess that made her hold back?

A bird's caw echoed, signaling that his fellow warriors were in position. As they stood united, he heard Kissa's shout, a perfect distraction.

"I will not go anywhere with you! I will never betray everything I believe in for your empty promises of power."

Pride swelled within him at her words as he silently gave the command. He, Chase, and Benji led the way, surging into the clearing. Two Elite soldiers stood guard just a few feet away from the cave. Chase swiftly slit one's throat, while Taji plunged his dagger into the other's back, piercing his heart. One of the king's men yelled a warning, but Taji was already on his way to Kissa. Benji and Chase flanked him as they fought their way through.

When Kissa's eyes met his, he felt momentarily lost in them. He should have never left her. Now, any wrong move could tear her away from him.

The murderous king unsheathed his sword and stood in front of Kissa, blocking their connection. His traitorous eyes tracked Taji's movements with a smirk on his lips. "Grab your prince! Kill the rest!"

Beside him, Chase growled, urging him not to let the man escape. "We'll watch your back," he assured him.

The Protector moved swiftly, his every movement a blur as he closed in on the man who had given him life. The king raised his sword. He was the former general of the Scorpions, renowned for his strategic brilliance and unmatched combat skills. Thankfully, Taji had inherited those talents as well.

As he approached the king, conflicting emotions raced through his mind. On one hand, he despised the man who had attempted to kill his mother and caused the deaths of countless people. Yet, he couldn't deny the blood that connected them. Besides his mother's eyes, Taji resembled a younger version of his father. For so long, he had yearned for the love of a father who selfishly only cared for himself. But now, as they stood face to face, Taji pushed those emotions aside. There was only one goal—to defeat the man who had inflicted so much pain upon his mother and his kingdom.

Taji's sword clashed against the king's, the sound echoing the decades of training and discipline his father had. However, the prince's movements were fluid and calculated, matching the king's every blunt strike. With a sudden surge of speed, Taji aimed his sword at the gauntlet on the king's arm, stabbing him and disarming the traitor, causing his sword to fly to the ground.

King Lan stumbled back, his face filled with disbelief. "You would kill your father?" He asked. "Then you are more like me than you care to admit!"

"I will never be like you!" Taji seethed.

A smile crossed the king's face, and it was in that moment that Taji realized his words were a distraction. With a frustrated growl, he rushed forward. However, before the tip of Isis could get anywhere near him, the king and his fallen sword disappeared right before his eyes.

Taji froze in disbelief. The smile on his father's face lingered in the air, haunting his confused thoughts. Regaining his composure, he scanned the surroundings, desperately searching for any trace of him. Bodies, both Rangers and Elite, lay motionless on the ground all around him. Across the plateau, Chase and Benji were fighting to get to Onya, who was now on her knees and bound hands, leaning forward as if in pain. She clutched her heart and blood spilled over her fingers. Far too much blood.

Commander Ashtar was crawling toward her with his own injury, shouting something Taji couldn't make out, and Kissa seemed frozen in time as she stared at her mother. It was then that the king reappeared behind her, sword raised.

Taji leaped over the still bodies to get to her. "Kissa!"

A small voice inside him warned he would not reach her in time. Taji watched in almost slow motion as the king he once called father brought down his sword and slammed the pummel against the back of Kissa's head. His body cringed at the impact as she collapsed face down on the ground.

"Amon, take her to the ship!" The traitor said. Then he disappeared again just as an arrow from up top nearly struck his head.

Taji saw red, the color of Kissa's blood leaking from her wound, as anger blazed through him and consumed him completely. How was he able to perform such magic? He was no wizard.

As he ran forward, Amon grabbed Kissa's feet as another Elite grabbed her arms and flipped her over. Kissa kicked the leader of the Elite dead in his face as she squirmed and clawed her way from their grasp. Relief flooded his chest that she was still conscious. Just as Taji was close enough to thrust his sword into the masked enemy that held her hands, a ringing sounded in his ears.

No, a toll bell. *Moorice...*

A wind so fierce, it ripped the wind right out of his chest, knocked him flat on the ground. Taji tried to push against the disarming whirlwind to locate Kissa. He could only turn his head, but he saw her flat on her back, along with everyone else. Was a storm coming?

An enormous shadow suddenly enveloped everything around them, throwing them into unexpected darkness. The wind finally broke enough for him to lift his head as screams broke out all around him—his only warning.

Taji looked up, and everything else fell away. The night sky was all black, like a soot-like stain the color of dark ash, but the edges blurred and moved. Utter fear gripped his heart as the blackness moved and formed into a creature larger than his mother's ship. It flew toward them at an impossible speed.

He gripped the hilt of his sword like his life depended on it. Not that it would do him any good. The creature's wings flapped in the night sky and the edges moved like feathers of smoke as another burst of wind, as strong as a tornado, knocked them all back flat to the ground.

Taji turned to Kissa. She wasn't moving. The cadence that thrummed within him screamed to move and get to her, but his mundane body could not shift underneath the power holding them all down. For the first time, Taji felt powerless as he stared at the girl he was meant to protect.

As he tried in vain to get up, a hand gripped his shoulder. Taji looked over to see Chase. Relief that his friend was alive couldn't overcome the realizing feeling that this creature could obliterate them all.

Chase's eyes widened, mixed with fear and awe. "It's a dragon."

A dragon? Those were myths. But as it drew so close that he saw its tail whip another gust of wind over them, Taji knew he was right. Though the edges of the dragon seemed to blur, scales covered the beast's underbelly and its back legs as they extended with claws as long as his arms. Screams echoed all around. Everything was happening so fast.

He slammed Isis' tip in the dirt beside him, and with all his might, he wrenched himself to stand. Chase made it to his knees beside him. Frustration filled him when another gust of wind slapped them and undid their headway.

Barely lifting his head, Chase tapped him and pointed to his mother's ship. "Look!"

Apophis swayed erratically in the turbulent waters as the gale battered it—a testament to how strong the winds were. On the rail, seemingly unaffected by the williwaw and dragon threatening to demolish them all, was his father. But that was not what had fire coursing through his veins. Standing next to him was the snake—*Rubin Fadel.*

Taji and Benji had been spying on the High Councilor, a gut feeling that he had his hands in the spread of the Sleeping sickness. Benji overheard him speaking to someone in the hush of the night. But when he and Chase followed the trail, the king was the one who showed up in the Fathomless Pit, throwing his suspicions in a disarray. Now, knowing his father was a murderous traitor to the kingdom, Taji knew for a fact they were working together. But other than the hate he clearly had of Osmondians, what did the High Councilor gain in all this?

They seemed to argue about something, but in the midst of a massive dragon descending on them all, they were of little importance. Kissa was only a dozen hands away. He needed to get to her. Screams whipped up around him again.

With everything happening so suddenly, it was hard to focus.

The beast hovered right above them, flapping its massive wings. It opened its mouth, showing razor-sharp teeth that would tear them all to pieces. Then the dragon's long claws wrapped around Kissa's unconscious body, picking her up like a lifeless doll.

"No!" The wind ripped Taji's words away before they even left his throat.

He felt utterly useless as the dragon turned to fly away. With the wind died down some, Taji seized the opportunity to stand. In a desperate move, he hoisted Isis above his head, launching her into the air like a spear. She soared through the sky, propelled by his strength, no doubt from Osiris. As it descended, his aim proved true as it pierced the dragon's hide.

An otherworldly roar rocked the world around them as the dragon's head whipped around, its tail knocking Isis into the water. Time seemed to stand still as the dragon's eyes locked onto Taji's, searing the prince to memory. Its eyes mirrored Naomi's darkness, with a flicker of something bright deep within, though Taji couldn't quite discern what it was. Moorice.

The dragon's nostrils flared with fury. Bracing himself for his imminent end, Taji stood firm, but to his surprise, the majestic creature pivoted and, with a powerful beat of its ethereal wings, soared up into the sky.

Another sudden gust of wind sent them all crashing back to the ground. He could hear Commander Ashtar shouting something. Taji turned his head to see Onya's limp body in Fadel's arms. Then they vanished. Taji's gaze darted towards his mother's ship, only to find it had disappeared as well.

Impossible!

As Taji stood, he let out a fierce growl that pierced the air with his misery. As the dragon's Celestial magic disarmed both them all, the snake and the traitor stole Onya Ashtar right before their eyes. Now, Kissa and her mother were nowhere to be found, along with the book of Osiris and the last remaining trireme. The overwhelming feeling of failure burdened Taji's soul, making him want to yank out his locs as he hunched over, tightly gripping them in his hands.

Aya told him not to leave Kissa, warning him of dire consequences. Maybe he could have stopped his father from taking Kissa in the first place if he had never left. But Taji knew in his bones that Moorice would have come for her, anyway. How were they to defeat a Celestial that turns into a dragon?

Courage...Strength....

Osiris' soothing whispers filled in the cracks of his broken spirit. He didn't deserve it. He failed as a Prince, Protector, and Keeper. Taji did not know where or how to look for Kissa, though that fact would not stop him from trying. Before he could contemplate how, bootsteps sounded behind him, reminding him he was not alone.

He whipped around to find his commander, held up by Chase and Benji. Taji cursed internally. So caught up in his own woes, he didn't even check on his commander and brothers. Tomeri and Maru stood beside them, their expressions just as solemn as his. The surviving Med'Jin gathered around them, all looking worse for wear. Commander Ashtar had lost some color and was bleeding from his side, but that pain paled compared to the internal agony of losing his wife and daughter in one fell swoop.

"All of you fought bravely. There were too many unknown variables, and it seemed Fate was not on our side this night." Then Taji looked into his commander's desolate eyes. "I failed her. I failed them both."

Taji was prepared for Omani's anger. He knew he shouldn't have left Kissa behind. As the leader of the Rangers, this was his responsibility to bear. Every life lost among their brethren and those taken from them was his personal failure. They couldn't save anyone, let alone stop the king or a massive dragon with no magic of their own. He knew he needed to find Osiris first. But how could he ask them to venture through Hell's Conception into even more danger?

Despite memorizing the map in the tome, he never ventured to the Isles of Death, so he could not be certain where Osiris was exactly. Adding to the fact that the traitor and his Elite would be there, if not already. They were basically going in blind and anything could be lying in wait for them.

"I am with you, Protector!" a familiar female voice declared, breaking the brooding silence. Taji glanced up, his gaze extending beyond the warriors, and caught sight of a petite, brown-haired girl perched atop a spirited filly at the ridge. He couldn't fathom how she had managed to navigate her way from

Kissa's lands without an escort. Uncertain of how to respond to her unexpected words, he looked over at Benji's shocked expression.

"Layla, it's too-"

"I have seen the sword in my dreams. I know where it is." Her eyes, both a different color, seemed to penetrate straight into the depths of Taji's innermost fears. "We will soon join forces with Kissa, but first we must find Osiris."

Join forces? She spoke as if Kissa wasn't in any danger. But she was right. They needed Osiris first. As the shock and tension in his chest eased, Taji processed what she said. Layla, often overlooked, was gifted. She was called a Dream Walker, a reminder that she, too, possessed extraordinary abilities and had a crucial role to play in the impending battles.

She dreamed of Osiris.

Layla turned her gaze towards Benji and spoke with conviction. "It is my destiny, Shaman. I have foreseen it. Our fates intertwine. King Lan wields dark magic, granting him sorcery. So, we must retrieve Osiris first. Only then can we save Aya and Onya."

Shock and gasps spread through the crowd. Commander Ashtar forcefully pulled his arms away from Chase and Benji, turning towards the Dream Walker. His voice trembled as he asked, "Onya lives?"

Layla's smile was juxtaposing among the shocked and dejected warriors around her. "Yes, Commander."

A storm seemed to rage in the commander's eyes, so intense that Taji could almost feel it. "He will pay with his life for taking my wife and daughter!" Taji silently vowed to let him.

Then his voice rang out, filled with determination. "In the Isles of Death is a majestic sword hidden by Osmond himself. The treacherous man, formerly known as our king, is on his way to find it. If he does, we will lose this war before it has even started. Our world and those we love in it are in grave danger, brothers! We must find Osiris first!"

Taji's gaze swept across the faces of his comrades, noting the fear that lurked in some of their eyes upon hearing the mention of the Isles of Death. "I will fault none of you if you do not wish to go." His attention landed on Maru, but the Protector found something surprisingly different in his expression.

Maru stepped forward and kneeled on one knee, pounding his fist to his chest. "Protector, we pledged our lives to safeguard the people of this world. We stand by you until the very end."

The unified voices of the Rangers rang out around them. "Until the end!"

Maru stood and clasped Taji's shoulder, gesturing towards the shore. He turned to find Yemanja sailing toward them, Sabu at the helm. Her black Leviathan swathed sails whipped in the breeze as the sun approached the new day, casting its first light rays on her. As he stood next to the Rangers of the Realm and those of the gifted, the ethereal sight of the ship made Taji realize he did something right.

Now it was time to turn the tides in their favor.

41

UNCHARTED WATERS

THE DISTINCT GROANING OF wood and a gentle sway were the first things Kissa sensed. Everything hurt. Even her eyelids as she pried her eyes open. Everything around her was hazy, like a mist settled over her eyes. Fear gripped her as she realized she did not know where she was. The air was heavy with a briny, musty scent.

When she reached for her fire, she discovered only an ember in her chest. Slowly, like fragments of a shattered mirror, her memories started trickling back in, the images swirling in her mind. *The quakes and the surge...Naomi and the wolves, the king, the ring, and the tome... her mother...*

A wail ripped from Kissa's throat.

Mama...

She sat up at once, but fell back down on the cot as a tidal of dizziness washed over her. The last memory gripped her thundering heart tight with sadness so deep she could only curl into herself and let her tears fall as she drifted back into darkness.

THIS TIME, WHEN KISSA awakened, she felt no pain. She reached up to feel for her wound and found nothing. The gash had healed. The absence of the wound only made her feel even more unsettled. She reached for her fire and found it replenished, ready to be used.

How long have I been sleeping?

Immediately, she reached through her bond with Aya, but only a faint static greeted her. Turning her head, she noticed the cramped dimensions of the small room. A bare desk sat across from her against the wall under a small circular window, casting rays of sunlight. A door sat on the other side.

When Kissa sat up this time, she kept steady as her feet touched the smooth wooden floor. Relief filled her as she spotted her bow against the wall in the corner, along with her satchel. Looking down, she discovered a comfortable night shirt paired with matching pants. The material felt light and flowy on her skin, but the thought of someone dressing her terrified her.

Her sundial was tucked underneath the shirt, and she clasped it, settling her nerves as she stood and walked over to the window. It was daylight, and the vast expanse of the open sea stretched out before her, the sun casting a warm golden glow on the water's surface. She was on a ship. Her heart sped up as she recalled the king's attempt to abduct her.

Turning toward the door, she scraped up her courage for whatever lay outside the room. She grabbed her bow and satchel, but oddly, she could not find her boots. Feeling a mix of fear and determination, she summoned her light and opened the door. She found herself in an empty, dimly lit corridor. The musty smell was heavier now, and the sound of creaking echoed through the narrow space.

She cautiously stepped forward. The occasional flickering lantern cast eerie shadows that danced along the passageway. However, her eyes caught on a staircase to the right that led to what she assumed was the deck, if the bright light at the top was anything to go by.

Kissa left the cramped corridor, and when she reached the top, confusion washed over her. She expected to see a large crew of sea farers scrambling around, but she found nothing of the sort. The massive deck lay empty. She furrowed her brows, trying to make sense of the situation. Had the crew vanished? Or perhaps they were below deck?

As Kissa stood alone on the deserted deck, a chill ran down her spine. The silence was eerie, broken only by the sound of the wind rustling through the massive black sails above. She noticed the ship's wood was obsidian too, unlike the polished Za wood she saw on the king's warship. She tried to tell herself that this was a good thing.

As the soles of her feet slapped the wood beneath her, she took in a long breath, trying to make sense of her surroundings. Kissa walked over to the rail. The ship was still making way, seeming to cut through the waves of its own accord. Now that she had a better view, she noticed a gathering of mist further out at sea. It reminded her of when the king conjured the warship out of thin air, but this mist was the length of a mountain range, at least five times larger than Aarusha in the distance. The longer she stared at it, Kissa thought she caught the glimmer of something shrouded by the mist.

Quick boot steps sounded behind her and her heart sped up. As she whipped around, she threw up her brightly lit hands, ready to incinerate the culprit. The heaving owner of the boots wore dark red robes with a golden cincture around his thin waist, but that was not what shocked her. He was taller than Kissa, and though his robe's hood covered his head, dusty rose curls fell down his freckled face. He was *Sagian*.

If Kissa imagined what a wizard might look like, he fit the bill. He seemed a decade or so older than her and his eyes were a pale green, hooded by sharp eyebrows that gave him a stern, sullen look.

"My Lady!" He dipped into a bow, with his hands outstretched as if in surrender. "My name is Soris. I came to check on you to find you were gone. How are you feeling?"

Kissa did a slow blink. For a long moment, she stared at his red curls. This man was Sagian, and he bowed to her like *she* was important. Though it wasn't engrained in her to feel he was the enemy, like Osmondians did, a cautious feeling swept over her. How did she end up on a Sagian ship?

Kissa glanced behind him around the empty deck, as though she might see something that would clarify what was happening. "Um..." Now that she thought about it, despite her broken heart, she physically felt great. "How long have I been sleeping?"

"A little over seventeen days."

Kissa croaked. *"Seventeen days?"* The panic quickly returned.

"My Lady, you suffered a severe head injury. Your Essence sustained you, but ultimately, your body was exhausted," he said. His green eyes watched her as if she were an enigma that fascinated him. He spoke about Essence like it wasn't treasonous to utter it.

Seventeen days.

So much could have happened. Did her mother survive? Had Moorice obliterated her kingdom? *Taji....*Kissa's heart ached as his beautiful blue eyes surfaced in her mind. She would give anything to know her loved ones were okay, but it was a strong possibility that as she slept for half a moon cycle, all her loved ones perished, and she no longer had a home to go back to.

Kissa clenched her jaw. She couldn't think that way. Not across the seas, on an enemy ship destined for who knows where. It didn't matter that he bowed to her or called her "Lady." She needed to keep her wits about her, and would not reveal her weaknesses.

"Whose ship is this? Where are you taking me?"

The man's sharp brows rose to his hairline at her sharp tone. "We are currently aboard the *Penumbra*, the ship of the Wind General. We are sailing toward our homeland." Then he gestured behind her.

Our homeland?

Kissa forced herself to breathe in deeply as she turned her head back toward the mountainous fog that seemed to expand across the horizon now. She was deeply confused. Neither answer really *answered* her, though the name Wind General sounded familiar. Where had she heard that name before?

She looked down at her lit up hands. Threatening him with her Essence wouldn't get her far, especially not a wizard who most likely had more experience than her. Reluctantly, she reeled in her light. "And where is this... wind general?"

Soris' brows furrowed tightly. "I think—"

Bring her, Soris...

The voice, like a sudden clap of thunder carried on the wind, jolted both of them. The voice seemed to come from everywhere and nowhere at the same time. Kissa looked around, but nobody else joined them on the deck.

Soris cringed as he mumbled something under his breath. Then his face smoothed out. "Very well, come with me, Lady Ashtar."

Kissa planted her feet. She opened her mouth to say, *'Lady Ashtar is my mother,'* but the thought caused her eyes to burn, and the words to dry up in her throat. Instead, she nodded for him to lead.

As Soris led Kissa along the port side of the obsidian deck, something strange moved at the front of the ship, a mysterious presence that sent tingles down her spine. She looked over at Soris, but he moved as if nothing was amiss and a ghostly ship moving on its own accord was an everyday occurrence.

Deciding to learn more about her captors, Kissa cleared her throat and said, "I read about a researcher named Soris that had been arrested traversing in Hell's Conception."

His thin lips pulled down in a frown. "We weren't even in Hell's Conception. We had just left Dragon's cove. They were trying to steal my research."

Kissa gaped at him. So many questions bubbled up that she couldn't sort them out. He was *Soris the Wise.* The grimness of his expression told her it was a sensitive topic. King Lan executed each of his crew, and if it weren't for Chancelor Moswen, he would be dead, too. Kissa tucked that information away.

Silence hung heavy between them, but it wasn't for long. As they reached the front of the ship, her eyes caught on a man at the bow. He stood alone, completely engrossed in the vast sea stretched out before him. His hands swayed from side to side and up and down, as if they were dancing to a silent melody. Kissa could almost hear it, intertwining with the rhythmic churn of the sea. He was a towering man, taller than any warrior from Osmondia, with broad shoulders covered in a dark cloak that billowed and swirled around him in gusts of wind, blurring at the edges.

Shadows.

Kissa's heart sped up. Without seeing his face, she knew the thunderous voice came from this man. *The Wind General.*

Soris stopped long before the bow, most likely not to get swept away in the whirlwind. He dipped his head. "Lady Ashtar, I will ensure the cook prepares your meal and I will have someone bring it to your cabin upon your return. My cabin is across from yours. Please feel free to knock if you need anything else." Then he moved past her toward the lower deck.

So there were others.

Kissa wasn't sure how she felt about being left alone with the Wind General, especially since she had no idea how she ended up on his ship or where he was taking her. Though she wore no shackles, she got the inkling feeling that she could not leave on her own accord. It didn't matter. They were in the middle of the sea, most likely thousands of miles from Osmondia now.

The General said nothing, nor did he acknowledge her presence, as if he waited for her to make the first move. Contemplating, Kissa chose that moment to send out her senses and get a read on the mysterious man. As her magic reached him, she gasped. Her senses smacked right into a powerful wall of his magic, a smoldering fortress of shadow and wind. She shuttered at the impact.

Kissa didn't even know such a thing was possible. Curiously, she went with her senses, just as she did with her light, and took in the impenetrable wall. It was a web of some sort made up of glowing threads, very similar to the one that connected her to Benji. Kissa couldn't fathom the power needed to conjure such a ward, and she wondered how he created it.

Amazing, she thought as she analyzed it, fighting against the urge to touch it again.

Suddenly, a portion seemed to slide away. Kissa lifted a brow. She wasn't sure if she wanted to know what lay beyond. With wards like that, the Wind General clearly did not want just anyone stumbling upon his inner sentiments. However, the opening felt like a silent invitation. Her curiosity would one day be the death of her, because with that thought, Kissa ventured inside.

She immediately regretted it as she free fell into what felt like an unending abyss, swallowed by a dark ocean so deep, it seemed bottomless. It was such a contrast to the bright daylight, and Kissa quickly felt disoriented.

Darkness was everywhere, and it felt as cold as burning ice. Bitterness, loathing, betrayal and deep, deep anger wrapped around her, and Kissa didn't know which way was up or down. Genuine fear gripped her at the thought of being trapped in such a place. Kissa only recently started learning her gifts, and it would be so easy for the general to smother her very existence. Noone would be the wiser.

Kissa panicked at the thought. She tried to focus and return, but she had an awful feeling that she was at the mercy of the general. She would leave if he allowed her. As if in answer, a visible thread materialized in front of her, a life-saving anchor connecting her to her physical self. Kissa shuttered in relief, before following it out.

However, before leaving the abyss entirely, she chanced a look back at the maze of darkness that made up the general, and caught a flicker of something underneath the deep sea of resentment. It was the barest light, like the tiniest diamond in a swath of coal.

Hope.

As Kissa came to, she found she was no longer standing. She was sitting on the deck with her back leaning against a mast. The General was was crouched above her with furrowed brows. His skin the color of rich, dark honey, framed by hair, a fiery shade of ginger, was unmistakable. His cloak of shadows and wind seemed at ease now, but his eyes... his eyes whirled and stormed like the dark abyss she just escaped and at the very center of the tempest were the stars of the Cosmos.

"*Moorice,*" Kissa breathed.

His thick brows furrowed even deeper as he studied her. "You remember me."

His voice no longer thundered, but the deep baritone of it still made her bones rattle. Kissa recalled the vision set over two centuries before she was even born. She witnessed Moorice's father, the Ancient of Wisdom, manipulate him into visiting Haava and teaching the Sagians magic that later helped them win the war against Osmondia. Kissa remembered the moment his otherworldly eyes locked with hers and the fear that took hold of her.

She shook her head in disbelief. "How?" It was all she could muster.

Instead of answering, he stood and turned toward the mountainous fog ahead of them. Kissa's heart skipped. They were preparing to sail straight into it. How long had she been floundering around inside his darkness? She stood, taking in their surroundings. It was no longer daylight. The sun was retreating to the west. A shiver broke across her shoulders.

Moorice moved his hands just so, and the thick mist rolled back in waves, revealing two massive dragons made of solid gold standing upright, facing each other. Kissa's jaw dropped.

Taller than even the towers of Horus Citadel, their wings spread out above them, and the talons at the tips of their wings touched to form an arch in the middle. Their vicious jaws were open, revealing vicious teeth as long as her. They both held ruby eyes that seemed to stare right into Kissa's soul as the *Penumbra* sailed underneath them. The air was sultry and arid, and a peculiar energy mingled in it. It felt alive, pulsating with an otherworldly aura, calling to her Essence.

The fog continued to peel back, revealing sandstone bridges with tiered arches within. The mist obscured most of whatever city lay beyond, but she caught glimpses of smooth stone buildings with terracotta roofs on the other side of the arches. She was far from Osmondia, and she didn't need Moorice to tell her where they were. She *felt* it.

As if sensing her apprehension, a wide, predatory smile spread across Moorice's face, exposing teeth as pristine and white as pearls. "Welcome to Sagia, little sister."

EPILOGUE

The Chasm

A SEEMINGLY ENDLESS VOID, engulfed by the pervasive darkness, stretched out before him. Absolute silence filled the air, leaving only the echo of his thoughts raging in his mind. Though the Chasm appeared measureless, it did not compare to the span of unbridled anger that simmered in his spirit. The arctic ice beneath his feet felt like an inferno compared to the empty coldness inside him now.

Betrayed by the one he would have sacrificed everything for, and stripped of his magic. They discarded him like remains, as if he had never created the suns and the moons that gave every breathing creature life. Like it wasn't he who created the balance of the Cosmos and beyond. Like he was... nothing.

The blazing ruby eyes on his ring blazed in the nothingness, revealing the deepened lines around his emerald eyes as the Saaxir's lips lifted into a smile. They did not strip him of *all* his magic.

A deafening roar sliced through the silent Chasm, echoing like a thunderclap. The very foundations of his prison trembled as if shaken to its core. It was only a matter of time and patience now. Something he had plenty of.

For he was the original wizard, and soon, all living beings will discover the consequences of betraying the most cunning Ancient the realms have ever known.

COMING SOON

Tempest Amidst the Flames
Book Two in The Chronicle of the Keepers Series
Want to be the first to hear about updates and new releases in the Chronicle of
the Keepers series?
Visit www.journey2altruism.com

SNEAK PEEK

Chapter One

Conundrum

Essa

Essa shot up in her hammock. Panting, she clutched her chest. Her heart thrummed beneath her hand as a sense of unease crept through her body, growing into a deep-rooted fear that she had never experienced before.

Visions, one of her many gifts, had never disturbed her like this one did. The aftertaste of the dream left a grim future imprinted on her mind. A horrid stain she couldn't wipe clean. She closed her eyes, trying to shake off the remnants of the dream.

Why would he do this?

He was always one step ahead, foiling Essa's every effort. She had caught glimpses of this horrible outcome before, among many others. Now it felt crystal clear, as if no amount of strategizing could prevent this cataclysmic Fate.

Righteous anger surged through her, and she allowed herself to feel it. Her light blazed as her Essence swelled within her. Just before her turbulent thoughts could spiral out of control, a soft cry startled her. Like cool trickles of water extinguishing a raging fire, Essa gasped as she felt the power of pure love and longing emanating from the small bundle of blankets next to her.

Her little one, only a few days old, already displayed remarkable capabilities in the gift of empathy. A hint of pride quelled some of the burning anger within her.

"Shh, shh, shh, go back to sleep, my love."

She pulled back the blanket to gaze at her child. Brilliant, innocent eyes met her own, like a reflection in a mirror. Essa pushed aside her remaining anger. She sensed her baby's hunger cues and latched the baby onto her breast.

She swayed back and forth, humming a melody that calmed them both. The peaceful action cleared her mind, and as she held her child in her arms, she finally found her resolve.

In response, a vibrant and pure energy filled the surrounding space. Essa's closest confident, and the one she called sister in all things, appeared.

"My Queen. I felt your unease in our bond. Is it time?" Zuri asked in their minds to avoid being heard.

The Ancient of Grace shifted into her human form. Her buttery yellow dress with gold accents flowed down her slender curves like water, complimenting her flawless copper skin. Her intense, molten amber eyes told Essa more than any words could convey.

"It is."

From the moment Essa fell pregnant, she and her two closest allies strategized this plan. Still, her heart faltered as she placed her now sleeping baby in the woven basket.

Zuri reached out and touched her hand, their bond radiating warmth and love. "You are not alone. We are with you."

Essa could only nod in gratitude. With great care, she wove a series of protective spells to conceal their Essence. Despite the turmoil in her heart, Essa couldn't help but see all her own goodness, hopes, and dreams wrapped up in her daughter.

A single tear escaped, landing on her tiny hand. She wiped it with her thumb, whispering words of love. "I am always with you, even when you cannot see me." Then, she bound her child's Essence so only she could unravel it at an appointed time.

Essa grabbed her staff and stepped out into the crisp night air, and led them to the edge of her sea cliffs. Though they were mere steps away, the walk felt like eternity, weighed down by the fear of what could go wrong. Yet, the urgency of her task made everything feel rushed.

She glanced up at the sister moons seated high in the heavens, surrounded by a sea of bright stars keeping watch. Seeing the Celestials untouched and bold gave her the final incentive she needed. She waved her staff through the air, causing the golden starlight in the orb at the top to illuminate. The swirling motion stirred up the winds and waves as they crashed against the mountain they were standing on. A rift appeared, growing more prominent as it took on an iridescent sheen.

A cerulean blue sky and lush green forest welcomed them on the other side of the rift, a stark contrast to the dark night sky of their world. Tears streamed down her cheeks as Essa kissed her little one on the forehead. Before she changed her mind, she handed the precious cargo to her sister.

Zuri transformed into a stunning bird with feathers as black as night. Her wings, adorned with fluorescent indigo and sapphire blue tips, spread out as she clutched the basket with her enormous talons. In a swift motion, she darted through the rippled opening and vanished into the realm beyond.

As Essa watched them, a familiar masculine energy enveloped her senses. Her second-in-command, but her first in so many other ways. She flicked her attention to the Divine Warrior, who appeared next to her as white and gold starlight. Then, in a flash of white light, he took his physical form.

He stood in his white and gold armor, with his long Jata locs twisted up in a warrior's bun. His ancient gold sword hummed its magic, caressing Essa's skin with its tune.

With a grim face, Osmond unsheathed the ancient weapon and whispered a few words across the blade. Its cyanic runes flared as lightning currents coursed through the ancient weapon. The Divine Warrior spun the blade before him, then he whispered something else. On his command, the sword speared through the rift into the other realm.

Now, with that part of the plan complete, Essa turned her focus back to her sister and baby. She sent her Essence through the torn fabric of space and time and caught up to her sister, who landed at a little cottage surrounded by massive Za trees. Zuri, now transformed into a human, greeted a burly man donned in leather armor.

The man bowed, and though he appeared stern on the outside, Essa sensed the man's warmth, wisdom, and protectiveness. As they spoke, a petite woman appeared from the back of the house. She stirred Essa's curiosity.

The woman's countenance was softer, and her compassion emanated from her, lustrous and pure. The small woman prostrated herself before Zuri, then when told to rise, she went straight to the basket. She swooped her long black locs to one shoulder as she peered in. Her eyes lit up and Essa felt the woman's heart swell as if it were her own. She reached in and brushed her knuckle against the baby's cheek.

Desperate to know more, Essa went inside the cottage. The aura of love inside the home enveloped her in a snug and toasty embrace. Surprised in a good way, she basked in its pureness, allowing it to fill in the breaks of her heart.

Eventually, Essa went through each room, reassuring herself of her decision. She stopped at one in particular. A sense of simplicity filled the room. Her eyes gazed at a small window showcasing the stunning forest. The sun's rays beamed on a wooden cradle in the middle of the room, and a soft, cream-colored handmade quilt draped over it. Essa felt the hope emitting from both the cradle and the quilt.

She walked over and picked up the quilt, drawn to it. Its threaded weave, made some time ago, leaked hints of sadness. It carried a deep desperation that only a woman could feel—the longing to be a mother.

As Essa thought this over, an unbidden vision appeared. She turned, taking it in.

By the looks of the room, it was a not-too-distant time in the future. A larger bed stood in the room, and toys scattered around the floor. Essa smiled at the scribbles on the walls. The burly man sat in a wooden chair with a book, with a look of a proud father. The petite woman lay in the bed next to her daughter, now a toddler. A tired smile graced the woman's lips.

The corners of Essa's own mouth turned up, and for the first time since she woke up, she felt hopeful.

"It is done!"

Zuri's voice brought her to the present. The glimpse of the future faded away. Essa found herself in the simple room with the wooden cradle and desperate quilt again.

Urgency crowded her thoughts again. She needed to leave since the portal could not stay open long, and her enemy was ever watchful. She took one more look at the chosen parents fussing over her baby, confident in her sister's choice.

Then, she weaved protection over their home and land, giving her blessing.

Upon her return to the sea cliffs, Essa found her face wet with the onslaught of tears. Her hands trembled as she closed the portal behind them, ensuring no other sensed their signature. Zuri approached her and silently touched her head to Essa's. Her sister's energy of love and light wrapped around her broken heart.

Zuri felt she had made the right decision. Yet, Essa felt as if she had left her entire heart in the other realm. How did someone recover from that? She knew then that she never would.

When they broke apart, her sister transformed and flew off, creating a beautiful silhouette in the glow of the three moons and Celestials. Essa normally raced into the heavens with her, but as it stood, her heart felt too heavy with grief. She turned toward her fortress. However, the Devine Warrior blocked her path, startling her.

He was an intimidating figure, even without his majestic sword. His sharp brows furrowed, and his mouth turned down at the corners. His deep sapphire eyes, filled with pain, searched hers.

Essa placed her hand on his chest, feeling his fevered drums pound to his heartache. "She chose well. Now we wait," she said. She hated to see him so broken, but it was all she could give him.

As if understanding her well was empty, the tension eased from his body and his drums slowed their cadence. Then, without a word, he took her hand and led her back inside her fortress. The Divine Warrior's stoney face softened as he lay inside her hammock and pulled Essa back into him.

"I'm here for you tonight," he whispered.

Now, overwhelmed by the path she set in motion and knowing she had done all she could, Essa laid into his chest and let her tears fall freely.

A Note from Syreeta

If you enjoyed *Light Amidst the Shadows*, I would love if you could share it with your bookish and bookstagram friends. It would be wonderful if they could meet Kissa and Taji and escape into the world of Haava, too. Reviews play a crucial role in making this book more visible. Please consider leaving a review for *Light Amidst the Shadows* on the platform where you purchased it, your newsletter, BookBub, social media, or Goodreads. Thank you so much for your support!

I am honored that you took a chance on me and my debut novel, *Light Amidst the Shadows.* Without you, Kissa and Taji's story would never come to life <3

Visit www.journey2altruism.com for the latest updates.

Acknowledgements

Gratitude fills my heart for the unwavering support I received from my family and friends. When I embarked on this journey, the path ahead was uncertain, but with those around me, I finally made it.

Milton Benjamin—the love of my life and biggest source of encouragement. I am so grateful for your confidence in me. You ensured I had all that I needed to pursue my dream, and none of this would have been possible without you.

Monai and Naomi, my ultimate sounding boards and brainstorming companions, thank you for reading (and re-reading) my drafts and sharing your honest thoughts. Naomi, your fresh perspective and invaluable input on the cover design were invaluable.

LeKisha Sweeney, my dear friend of over two decades, thank you for listening to my ideas from the very inception of this book. Your support has remained steadfast through countless discussions and millions of ideas.

To my family, thank you for always being there for me, whether it was to offer insightful feedback or to shower me with words of encouragement. I am forever grateful.

And to all the readers, thank you for joining me on this journey. I sincerely hope you will continue to accompany me as the series unfolds. Anticipation fills me as I look forward to sharing the developing lives of Kissa and Taji, their relationships, and the awakening of new powers.

ABOUT THE AUTHOR

SYREETA BENJAMIN IS AN AUTHOR AND VISUAL ARTIST/DESIGNER LIVING IN TEXAS. FUELED BY HER LIFELONG LOVE FOR STORYTELLING, SHE OBTAINED HER MASTERS IN CREATIVE WRITING AND WROTE HER FIRST DEBUT FANTASY FICTION NOVEL, *LIGHT AMIDST THE SHADOWS.*

SHE FINDS JOY IN THE LAUGHTER AND LOVE SHARED WITH HER HUSBAND, THREE CHILDREN, AND TWO ADORABLE GRANDMUFFINS. ASIDE FROM BEING IMMERSED IN THE PAGES OF HER SECOND BOOK, SHE ESCAPES INTO THE WORLDS OF FELLOW AUTHORS, WHERE SHE CAN EXPLORE ENDLESS POSSIBILITIES AND IMAGINE WHAT COULD BE.